By Ben Crump

Worse than a Lie

Open Season: Legalized Genocide of Colored People

WORSE THAN A LIE

WORSE THAN A LIE

A BEAU LEE COOPER NOVEL

BEN CRUMP

BANTAM
NEW YORK

Bantam Books
An imprint of Random House
A division of Penguin Random House LLC
1745 Broadway, New York, NY 10019
randomhousebooks.com
penguinrandomhouse.com

Copyright © 2026 by Benjamin Lloyd Crump

Penguin Random House values and supports copyright. Copyright fuels creativity, encourages diverse voices, promotes free speech, and creates a vibrant culture. Thank you for buying an authorized edition of this book and for complying with copyright laws by not reproducing, scanning, or distributing any part of it in any form without permission. You are supporting writers and allowing Penguin Random House to continue to publish books for every reader. Please note that no part of this book may be used or reproduced in any manner for the purpose of training artificial intelligence technologies or systems.

BANTAM & B colophon is a registered trademark of
Penguin Random House LLC.

Lyrics on page 10 are from "One Nation Under a Groove" by Funkadelic (1978).
Used by permission.

Hardcover ISBN 978-0-593-87570-4
Ebook ISBN 978-0-593-87571-1

Printed and bound by CPI Group (UK) Ltd, Croydon, CR0 4YY

BOOK TEAM: Managing editor: Saige Francis • Production manager: Jenn Backe • Copy editor: Caroline Clouse • Proofreaders: Pam Rehm, Nicole Ramirez

Book design by Susan Turner

The authorized representative in the EU for product safety and compliance is Penguin Random House Ireland, Morrison Chambers, 32 Nassau Street, Dublin D02 YH68, Ireland. https://eu-contact.penguin.ie

*To my beautiful family and my passionate team,
remember the undertaking to expose the truth is not for the faint of heart*

WORSE THAN A LIE

PROLOGUE

September 1978
Houston, Texas

IT WAS FRIDAY, JUST BEFORE SUNSET, AND MOST OF THE NEIGHBORHOOD kids were playing outside. But not Beau Lee Cooper—he had no time for play. His doting, no-nonsense mother, Ella Mae, liked to say he was born serious, moving through life with a preternatural sense of responsibility, as if on an urgent mission with little time to waste.

He sat in his bedroom at a small desk stacked with books, reading by the fading light that shone through the handmade window curtains. It was where his mother and siblings could usually find him. Next to the books was an issue of *Jet* magazine with Thurgood Marshall on the cover, dated August 24, 1967—six days before Marshall was confirmed by the U.S. Senate in an overwhelming vote of 69–11, becoming the first Black Supreme Court justice. Beau Lee had taken it from the collection of magazines that his mother kept in stacks on a shelf in the living room. She had issues dating back decades and saw them as cultural encyclopedias—compendiums in which Black people were revered and celebrated.

Beau Lee first read the Thurgood Marshall issue of *Jet* when he was six. That's when he became interested in legal matters—major cases and rulings that shaped the quality of life for all Americans. Justice Marshall was his hero and inspiration, and he coveted the magazine like it was a prized possession.

His brothers, Harris and Glendon, didn't share Beau Lee's interests. They preferred playing sports and had spent the entire afternoon with their friends at Emancipation Park. Soon, the streetlights would come on, and Ella Mae would call them in for dinner. Beau Lee's sisters, Jessie and Janice, had returned home hours ago. They knew to be back before the sun dipped low to the horizon so they could help their mother prepare dinner.

Beau Lee listened to catfish frying in a cast-iron skillet. The smell permeated the house.

"Beau Lee!" Ella Mae called from the kitchen.

"Yes, Mama?"

"What are you doing up there?"

"Just reading," he said.

Moments later, she peered through his bedroom doorway. "What's that you're reading?"

He turned toward her, holding the book up so she could see: "*To Kill a Mockingbird*."

"Uh-oh," she said, tilting her head. "You know how that book gets you worked up."

Ella Mae was not surprised that her baby had taken to books the way he had. If he was reading the Harper Lee classic, it usually meant he was upset about something. "Haven't you read that book at least twenty times?"

"Thirty," he said, "and at this rate, I'll read it thirty more times by the end of the year."

The front door slammed. Harris and Glendon barreled into the house and headed straight for the kitchen. They were frantic and huffing as if they'd been sprinting.

They found Ella Mae upstairs in the hallway. Harris stood wiping the sweat from his brow while Glendon braced his back against the wall, trying to catch his breath.

"What's gotten into you two?" Ella Mae asked. "Coming into the kitchen like you don't have home training. You know you can't be slamming that door like that."

Ella Mae studied the boys hard. There was a look in their eyes— a fear she'd seen on the faces of young Black boys and men her entire life.

"What is it?" she asked. "What's happened?"

"It's Mr. Porter," Harris said with downcast eyes. "Police are outside looking for him."

"You talking about Tony Porter?" Ella Mae asked.

Harris nodded. "They said sometime last night he made off with some goods from Mr. Leeds's store without paying."

Ella Mae's arms flew up in disbelief. "They're saying he stole something? That man wouldn't take fruit off a tree."

Beau Lee's sisters came out of their room and joined them in the hallway.

Ella Mae sniffed the air and quickly rushed back into the kitchen. "Doggone it, my fish is about to burn."

The children followed their mother downstairs and into the kitchen, where she tended to the fish, carefully flipping it over and submerging it in the hot grease.

"Everybody knows he was watching *Hawaii Five-O* like he always is, at the same time every Tuesday night," Glendon said. "They know because he has it playing at full volume."

"Can't believe the police are rousting a sixty-year-old man over some foolishness," Ella Mae said. "What's he got to steal for?"

"Even Mr. Leeds said he wasn't anywhere near the store," he said, sounding both physically and mentally exhausted.

"I heard the pastor at St. Episcopal went down to the station and tried to talk to the police, but the police didn't care," Glendon said.

"Police don't care about all that," Ella Mae said, casting her eyes away. "They need receipts and white folks to vouch that Mr. Porter is innocent."

"Mr. Leeds himself said it was all one big misunderstanding and was begging them cops to leave it alone," Harris continued desperately, "but they shined him on, and he's a white man . . . Said that Mr. Porter refused to come out the house and talk to them. So they went and got a warrant. Now they did all that, ain't nothing a white man can say to change their minds."

"That poor man is probably scared to death," Ella Mae said. "So, where is Mr. Porter now?"

"Nobody's seen him," Harris said. "He's run off or is hiding out somewhere."

"If those police catch him, it won't be an arrest or trial," Glendon said. "They'll handle him right then and there. Make an example of him just for making them work so hard."

There was a heavy knock at the door. Beau Lee nearly jumped out of his skin and bit his tongue as he was about to speak. The knock repeated harder and louder, and the kitchen fell silent.

"Y'all keep quiet," Ella Mae said. "G'won upstairs, and don't come down until I call for you."

"But Mama," Beau Lee protested, "who's going to look after you?"

"Do as I say, Beau Lee. Now, get on."

Beau Lee had never heard such a tone from his mother's mouth. She had been stern with him plenty of times, but this was something different—it was grave and immediate, and he knew not to question her orders further.

The family tiptoed from the kitchen with Ella Mae in tow. Beau Lee and his brothers climbed the stairs as the knocking persisted, followed by a man's voice shouting, "Open up!" Beau Lee could tell it belonged to a white man with the kind of authority he'd been taught to fear.

The children congregated at the top of the stairs, keeping within earshot of their mother as she slowly opened the front door. It creaked on account of the rusty hinge, and his mama faced down a white man in a police uniform. Beau Lee and his siblings had been taught to avoid police at all costs, and here one was at their door—a truly unwelcome sight.

"Evening," the officer said. "You the owner of this house?"

"Yes, sir?" Ella Mae said. "Something wrong?"

"Well, that remains to be seen. We're canvassing the neighborhood looking for a suspect. His name is Nathaniel Porter. Are you and your family familiar with him?"

"Can't say I am, Officer. Might've heard the name in passing but never met him."

"That right?" The officer didn't sound convinced. "Figured all you colored folks knew each other around here."

"It's a good-sized neighborhood. Lots of coming and going," Ella Mae said.

"Uh-huh." He cleared the grit from his throat, and his voice sounded harsher. "If he comes around, you be sure to call the station. Understood?"

"Yes, sir."

"And if I find out you've had any dealings with this Porter fellah, I might have to haul you in for aiding and abetting. Do you understand what that means?"

"Yes, sir."

"Then we're settled here," the officer said. "You have yourself a good night."

Mama didn't shut the door right away. She waited a moment, looking out as the man stepped off the porch and continued his rounds. Then, she closed the door slowly, locking the deadbolt and latching the chain.

Beau Lee and his siblings came downstairs and rallied around their mother. She was visibly shaken, and Beau Lee wondered how many times his mother had stood face-to-face with a police officer. It didn't matter if it'd been a dozen times. He knew it never got easier looking a cop in the eye, especially when they were keen on finding someone they were sure had committed a crime.

"Everything's all right," she said, having lost the trepidation in her voice. "Get washed up for dinner."

"Yes, ma'am," they said in unison. Given what their mother had just endured, no one had the gall to protest, and in a single file, they went upstairs to prepare for what would likely be a lively conversation at the dinner table.

Beau Lee broke from the line and returned to his mother's side. He hugged her tightly. "I'm sorry, Mama."

"What are you sorry for? You didn't do a thing."

"I'm sorry for all of us," he said. "I hate that we have to go through this kind of stuff, and I'm sorry you couldn't tell the truth about Mr. Porter. When I grow up, I want to live in a world where Black people can tell the truth without being afraid for their lives. I promise you, Mama, I'm going to make it where people like Mr. Porter can get justice."

"And how do you intend to do that?"

"I'm going to be a lawyer when I grow up," Beau Lee said. "I have to be—there's nothing I want more."

"Sweetheart, you say that to me at least once a week—this is not news."

"It's because I want you to know I mean it," he said. "Especially now."

She reached down and stroked his head lovingly. "Becoming a lawyer costs money, and going to college ain't free. But I'm gonna do everything in my power to make sure it happens. I'll take on more work."

"I'mma keep getting straight A's in school so I can get scholarships," Beau Lee said. "That way, y'all don't have to worry about paying for me to go."

"I just want you to get some time to be young, Beau Lee. Maybe you could try spending more time outside with your brothers."

"No time for all that."

"Kids need to be kids," she said. "Life will grow y'all up fast enough."

"I'm going to get our family out of here one day," he said after a moment. "Get you a big house, and you'll never have to work another day in your life. You do everything for us, Mama, and I'm going to do the rest. And the best part is, I'll be able to help people like Mr. Porter . . . and all our people, all over the world."

"Beau Lee, I—" Ella Mae wasn't sure what to say, but she'd come to take her son at his word. He was more than a mere child; he'd been imbued with a righteousness that amazed and frightened her. She'd learned that the world was unkind to righteous Black boys and often sought to destroy them before they could become men. She desperately wanted all her children to grow up and one day achieve every goal they set their minds on, especially Beau Lee, who had virtue and unwavering pride in himself despite the world telling him otherwise.

AFTER DINNER, ELLA MAE STOOD outside Beau Lee's bedroom with the door open. "I know that's not what I think it is," she said.

Beau Lee looked sheepish. "I got a little hungry," he said.

"After three pieces of catfish?" Ella Mae walked over to the desk and saw that Beau Lee had eaten half of a cheese Danish with white icing crisscrossed over the top. She picked it up. "You and these things. You're not eating this because you're hungry," she said. "It's that hankering you've got for sugar."

"But they're good, Mama. I can't quit 'em."

"I'mma quit 'em for you. I don't need you eating pastries after you've had dinner. Don't you know you'll get cavities, and the dentist ain't cheap?"

She picked up the rest of the pastry. Beau Lee watched it leave in her hand and wished he'd taken more bites.

"Mama?"

Ella Mae stopped in the doorway.

"Yes, Beau Lee."

"I'm serious about what I said earlier. People need someone who'll fight for them so they can be heard."

Ella Mae looked at her son with quiet pride. Beau Lee was a smart boy, a happy boy, even. He was both a realist and an optimist, and hers was an important role. If Thurgood Marshall was his North Star, she'd be his shepherd, helping him stay the course.

"Night, baby. Don't stay up too late."

Beau Lee turned on the beige transistor radio on his desk. The brand-new song by Funkadelic, "One Nation Under a Groove," was playing. It came pouring through the speakers. He loved George Clinton and Parliament-Funkadelic. The music wasn't just funky; it was cosmic, and it spoke to the kind of world Beau Lee imagined, one where everybody was equal, not just on the dance floor but in society.

He closed his eyes and, head bobbing, mouthed the lyrics. He cranked his arms, jutted his hips forward, and bent his knees. He started playing air guitar. Shredding. Tearing it up.

"One nation under a groove
Gettin' down just for the funk of it
One nation and we're on the move
Nothin' can stop us now."

Ella Mae watched from the doorway. Her lips curled into a wide-mouth smile. Despite the ugliness of the day, her son had found a carefree moment, and she was blessed to witness his rare expression of Black boy joy.

1

November 4, 2008

THE GUNDERSON SECURITY PATROL CRUISER WAS DOING FIFTEEN MILES per hour as it rounded the corner of the shopping plaza in Avondale in the northwest side of Chicago. It was driven by Chicago native Hollis Montrose, who tapped the brakes, slowing to a crawl, and idled behind a Macy's department store.

Over the radio, President-elect Barack Obama was making his victory speech from less than ten miles away in Grant Park. Everything about the moment was unprecedented.

When Obama finished his speech, Hollis couldn't tell if he was hearing the roaring cheers of approval and applause over the radio or echoing from downtown. Either way he let the sound fill the car.

Now fifty-three, Hollis had left boyhood long behind, but he still listened to the president-elect's speech with the same glee he'd felt as a child when watching Dr. Martin Luther King, Jr., deliver one on television. He turned up the volume as he continued to survey the parking lot of the Danbury Plaza in his cruiser, a white Dodge Charger.

Working security was Hollis's second job, three nights a week and no weekends, because weekends were for family. By day, he was a police officer for Metra, the rail system that served the Chicago area and northeastern Illinois. It was nothing like being a street cop, a job Hollis had held with the Chicago Police Department for over a decade. Instead, he patrolled the subway and train stations and hopped on and off train cars. Hollis intended it to be his last position before retiring. He continued to patrol the Danbury Plaza parking lot listening to the speech with pride—he was proud to be a cop. Even with all he'd been through on account of wearing the badge, he was able to care for his family, he had a pension, and soon, he'd enjoy the fruits of his efforts as a grandfather intent on spoiling his grandkids. With the money he made working for Gunderson, he'd be able to renovate one of the bedrooms in his home and turn it into a playroom. He had another grandchild on the way and the room would get plenty of use over the years.

Pop! Pop! Pop!

He lowered the volume—it was gunshots, he was certain of it. It was the unofficial way Chicagoland liked to celebrate, and shots were ringing out all over the city. The sound echoed in the distance, but Hollis was still worried. He put pressure on the gas pedal and the car crept back around to the front of the plaza.

On a night like this, there was a strong likelihood of looting and vandalism, but the parking lot was quiet—empty—with no suspicious activity or loiterers.

His cellphone rang in the center console. He glanced down and saw the caller ID. The words "My Rock" lit up the screen.

He answered on speaker.

Raquel Montrose, whom Hollis and her family and friends affectionately called "Rocky," was already mid-sentence and talking at top speed. "I would've called you sooner, baby, but I know you're making your rounds. I said to myself, I know he's listening to the speech . . . You are listening to the speech, aren't you, Hollis? Isn't it the greatest thing you ever heard?"

Her joy was palpable through the phone.

"Oh, I'm listening to it, Rocky," he said. "This whole night is shaping up to be pretty incredible."

"Everybody is outside over here," she said. "I'm sitting on the porch."

The sounds of people cheering poured through the phone. Someone was singing "Amazing Grace" how they'd lead their church choir on Sundays. It was beautiful, and soon other voices joined in.

Pop! Pop! Pop! More shots, only this time it sounded like they came over the phone line.

"Rocky, baby. Go back inside right now. It's too dangerous to sit out there."

"Oh Lord," she said. "I'll never understand people shooting when they're happy."

"Don't know either, but it's a quick way to turn joy into tragedy," Hollis said. "You back inside yet?"

"Yeah, baby, I'm in. Going to take a seat on the couch."

"Good."

"You coming home soon?"

"Working on it."

"I gotta say, Secret Service is going to have their hands full. It's got to be the hardest detail in history, wouldn't you say?"

"It'll be tough," Hollis said. "He'll need the best people around him."

"You know, I was thinking maybe you could apply for his security team."

Hollis laughed.

"What? I'm serious," Rocky said. "Think of all the things you've done in your career. You'd be great at it."

"Are you just angling to find a way to meet him?"

She giggled. "I'm just saying you'd be an asset."

"I don't know . . . the Secret Service is a young man's game."

"Just think about it. How about I go online and see what jobs are posted."

"All right, baby. It's not like I can tell you not to anyway, especially once you get your mind fixed on something." He looked at the time; it was 11:44 P.M. "I love you, and I'll see you in a little bit. Remember, I have to make a stop in Woodlawn to pick up that sanding equipment from Finn so I can start working on the playroom."

"Can't that wait until morning?"

"He said he'd be up, and this is the only time I'll have to get it. Then I'm heading straight home to you, my knockout queen."

Aside from Rocky's sharing the name of the titular character Stallone made so popular, she was indeed Hollis's fighter. She'd always be in his corner, no matter what.

They exchanged "I love yous" and ended the call.

HOLLIS PULLED INTO THE SPACE designated for Gunderson Security vehicles. He exited the car and clicked the remote lock. The car chirped twice as Hollis headed for the glass door, the only entrance to the building. He pulled a set of keys from his pocket and unlocked the door, as it was protocol for the place to be tightly secured, considering Gunderson had a modest cache of handguns, tasers, and pepper spray.

He went into the locker room and took off his quilted black leather jacket and company uniform. He crammed the security shirt into his duffel bag for Rocky to launder. There were three others, fresh and ironed, hanging inside the locker. Hollis kept on the black pants he was wearing, changed his shirt, and put his leather jacket back on. Not all security personnel carried firearms because they weren't willing to risk their lives to protect a retail establishment. As a police officer, Hollis preferred to carry his department-issued 9mm, which remained holstered on his hip. He shut his locker and walked back to the lobby, where he hung his key on an empty hook inside a small security box hidden under the front desk, then locked the box.

"Big night," Joey Henderson said. "Guess America really did the damn thing?"

Joey lived about fifteen minutes from Gunderson Security but always managed to arrive late or just in time. Once, when he had car trouble, Hollis drove to his house, picked him up, and brought him to work. He'd taken on an extra shift just so they could clock out at the same time and Hollis could drive him back home. That was before Joey had saved up enough to buy his truck.

Joey lowered his head so he wouldn't smack it against the doorpost as he entered the lobby. He was a tall, lanky, brown-skinned boy with a curly fade and a diamond stud earring. A red sucker was lodged in his teeth. Hollis thought it looked like a Tootsie Roll Pop. "Gotta give God the glory," Hollis said.

"That's right, Mr. Montrose."

Hollis wasn't sure Joey was much for religion or attending church, but he was always respectful of Hollis's beliefs. "Be blessed and have a good night, Joey."

"You, too, sir."

"And Joey, watch yourself out there. I heard plenty of shooting while on patrol. It sounded like the Fourth of July."

"Hear you loud and clear, sir."

Hollis zipped up his jacket and readied himself for the cold. He gave a departing nod as he left the building and walked to his dark-gray 2004 Ford Expedition, which was parked next to Joey's red Ram truck. As Hollis drove off, he knew he would always remember how he felt the night the first Black president was elected.

2

THE SHARP WIND OFF LAKE MICHIGAN WHIPPED ACROSS HOLLIS'S FACE like needle pricks; it almost felt personal. In the few hours during his shift, the temperature had already dropped significantly. Chicago was brutal in more ways than one, and the bitter cold was a reminder that to survive it, you had to be of sturdy stock. It made him think of Obama's cutting his teeth in Chicago politics. For a Black man to survive in the city's dog-eat-dog political world, he had to be smart, affable, and tactically adept, and Hollis didn't doubt that Obama was all those things and more. He looked forward to the change he was going to bring to the country.

Hollis got inside the SUV, started the engine, and let it warm. After a few minutes, he turned on the defroster and watched as the ice slowly melted from the windshield. The clock on the dash read midnight. . . . It was a new day in America, and despite the late hour, Hollis felt energized.

He turned the heat to full blast, shifted into reverse, and backed out of the parking stall. He thought of Rocky waiting for him at home, and of a piece of German chocolate cake he'd stashed away in the refrigerator that he'd planned to eat in commemoration or consolation, depending on the election results.

Once he picked up that sander from Finn, there would be nothing standing in the way of his celebrating with his wife.

Hollis exited the highway, merged onto South Yale Avenue, and turned left on Sixty-third Street. He drove for another two miles and turned right onto South Woodlawn Avenue.

The street was a lot quieter than he expected, considering he'd been hearing gunshots all night. As if in response to his thoughts, flashing blue lights suddenly appeared in his rearview mirror. There were no sirens. At first he presumed the cruiser would pass him since he hadn't done anything to warrant being stopped, but with no other vehicles on the road, it became clear that the police vehicle was pulling him over. He looked at the dash. It was 12:17 A.M.

Hollis reached into his pocket, where he kept his wallet, so he could be prepared to show the officers his police ID, hoping that would expedite their stop.

"Hands on the wheel!" a voice shouted over the cruiser's loudspeaker.

Hollis quickly put his hands on the wheel, wallet still in his pocket, and stared into the rearview mirror. Two officers, who looked to be white men, were inside the car.

The cops exited their vehicle and approached the Expedition with their guns drawn and pointed. Hollis focused on their faces. One was clearly older. Deep creases had set in around his nose and brow, and his face was locked in a grimace. The younger cop moved like a daisy-fresh rookie—stilted and robotic as if he had graduated the academy mere months before.

Hollis was five blocks from Finn's house, near the intersection of South Woodlawn and East Marquette. He knew the exact streets, because it happened to be right where Joey lived; he'd driven the same route the night he'd picked up and dropped him off at the blue house across the street. Hollis noticed a light on in the window of the second floor. He knew Joey lived with his mother but didn't see a vehicle in the driveway.

Hollis was tired. He hadn't made any illegal turns, he'd used his blinker during lane changes, and he'd exited the freeway at a moderate speed. It was by the book, because that's who Hollis was—as a member of law enforcement, he observed the rule of law just as he'd expect from any other citizen. But with the flashing lights behind him, he made it a point to observe his surroundings. That's when he realized he was on the street in front of Joey's apartment building.

He prepared for the police encounter, stayed calm, and rehearsed what he'd say in his head: *I'm an officer on my way to a friend's house. I'm sure there's been some misunderstanding . . .*

Hollis lowered the driver's side window.

"Put your hands out the window!" the older officer yelled as he approached. His partner came around the passenger side of the Expedition, gun still drawn.

Hollis raised his hands and placed them outside the window.

"I'm a police officer with Metra," he said. "If you permit me, I can show you my badge."

"Yeah, right," the older one said. He yanked the door open and pulled Hollis out of the vehicle, forcing him to the ground. His partner moved around the vehicle and trained his weapon on Hollis.

"Lie flat, with your palms on the ground," the officer said, pressing the heel of his boot into Hollis's back.

"I'm a police officer," Hollis repeated. "I can show you my badge and ID. I didn't do anything."

"Shut your mouth," he said, bearing down on his back as the young protégé watched. "Regardless of that boy being in the White House, you're not in charge here. We are still in charge, and you'll do what we say."

Hollis tried to catch his breath. "Please, officer . . . my wallet is in my back pocket."

"All you should be doing is listening, boy. Understand?" The officer bore his boot down even more into Hollis's shoulder blades. "We clocked you weaving back there. Where are you coming from?"

"But I wasn't weaving." Hollis gasped for air; he started to experience a shortness of breath. "I can get my wallet and show you my police ID. But please, can you get your foot off of me? I can't breathe like this."

"I'll keep my foot here until I feel it's safe to remove it. Got it?"

"I don't want any problems. This is just a misunderstanding. If you give me a chance to explain, I can clear everything up."

"No misunderstanding on our part, boy. Where'd you get this vehicle?"

"I own it. Paperwork is in the glove compartment."

"There've been robberies in this area. Your vehicle fits the description of one that was seen fleeing the targeted location earlier tonight. Same make, model, and color."

"It's a popular model," Hollis said. "Plenty of people drive what I've got."

"And you fit the description of that suspect," the officer said. "Two out of two from where I'm standing."

Hollis coughed hard and gasped for air. The young cop was beginning to look worried but kept his gun aimed at Hollis.

"You've got the wrong person," Hollis said. "I'm just coming from work . . . ."

"If I had a dollar for the number of times I heard that . . . Face it, big boy, it just ain't your night." The officer turned to the rookie and smiled. "Say, partner, how much do you want to bet that if we toss this guy's vehicle we'll find stolen goods? Maybe even narcotics?"

"I'm not a thief, and I don't do drugs," Hollis said. "You've got the wrong person."

"You like dust? That your thing?" he asked Hollis. "Because, if I'm being honest, you do look like the type. So, be straight with me. Did you celebrate tonight by doing a little PCP?"

"I've been a police officer in this city for twenty-five years. I'm just getting off my security guard shift." His back throbbed. "I work for Metra and Gunderson Security, damn it!"

Another cruiser pulled up. Hollis lifted his chin from the pavement and strained to see as two additional officers exited their car and approached the scene—two more white men. One was solidly built, mid-twenties maybe, and short in stature. The other was bloated, his uniform stretched around his gut, and his boots were scuffed. "Well, well," the fat officer said with his partner in tow. "What have we here . . . ?" Both men had their guns drawn.

"Why isn't anyone listening to me?" Hollis asked. "I'm a police officer. Call my supervisor if you want. There's no need for all this . . ."

"You search him yet?" the fat one asked.

"Nope," the cop said, adjusting his boot on Hollis's back.

Hollis turned his head enough to see Joey's apartment. The second-floor light was still on. He thought about screaming out. Maybe if someone was inside, they'd hear him. After all, given the late hour, it was probably the only house on the street that showed any sign that someone was stirring.

Then, he considered the reality that no one was home and someone had left the light on. Since Joey worked late, it was smart to keep a light burning in the house as a deterrent from hot prowlers, would-be burglars, casing the neighborhood.

The backup officers holstered their weapons and began grabbing at Hollis, searching his pockets and along his waistband. Someone grabbed the holstered pistol on Hollis's waist. "Ah, fuck. He's got a gun!" the cop shouted, and his voice broke.

"No, no, it's a service weapon," Hollis said, wheezing. Gravel had dug into his chin so deep it was beginning to bleed.

The primary officer lifted his boot off Hollis's back and kicked him in the ribs. Then he repositioned himself, took aim, and shouted, "Don't fucking move!"

A sharp pain ripped through his torso and Hollis reached up out of reflex to defend the area. He was sure the kick had bruised or broken his ribs.

"He's making a move for the gun!" the officer said.

There was an explosion of gunfire. Bullets entered Hollis's body—his shoulder, arms, lower back, and legs. He felt the hot metal tear through his skin, searing his flesh. *Too many bullets to count . . . too many to survive*, he thought.

His body writhed on the pavement as the four men stood over him, squeezing the triggers of their firearms.

Pop-pop-pop-pop-pop . . .

But Hollis held on, still conscious. For a moment, he saw the night sky through a milky fog. Shooting stars soared above him, and he wondered if he was going home to be with the Lord. He longed for rest, worn to the bone like many Black men enduring in America, but he desired to stay with his loving wife, beautiful children, and grandkids . . . to live out his days alongside them. It wasn't fair—none of it was fair. How could so much be taken from him without provocation? As if his life held no meaning—inconsequential, like that of an insect caught in a gale, whipped and thrashed until splattering on a car's windshield.

Was this his fate?

No, Hollis thought, *this can't be the end.*

He prayed through the pain, prayed it would stop, that the shooting would stop and that he'd live, but the pain and suffering soon hijacked his mind, and between the immense searing in his chest and back, he asked: *Why me, Lord? Why take me now . . . and like this?*

He was bleeding out, quickly fading away. In seconds, he would cease to be. There would be only darkness. He feared the darkness, but as it crept, it coddled him, and the less pain he felt.

He looked toward Joey's house one last time. The light was off—the last glimmer of hope gone.

Then, everything fell silent. He could no longer hear the gunshots and he felt nothing. The world was going dark before his eyes.

The senior officer then yelled, "I'm separating the gun from the suspect and I'm putting him in handcuffs."

Even though Hollis Montrose lay there motionless, face down, his body riddled with bullet holes, the senior officer still sought fit to place him in handcuffs. Then, still holding Hollis's gun, he crouched beside Hollis's limp body, opened Hollis's bloody hand, and forced his pistol into his palm.

3

BEAU LEE ADJUSTED HIS NECKTIE IN HIS BATHROOM MIRROR AND YAWNED. He was in desperate need of coffee. Gigi was sleeping peacefully in bed when he returned to the bedroom and he kissed her soft lips. "Sorry, babe. I hate to wake you, but I've got to head out," he said quietly. "Nellie and Capes are waiting in the limo outside."

Gigi stirred and opened her eyes, turning to him. "No need to be sorry, dear. I always like to see you off."

"Kiss Bianca for me, and tell her Daddy loves her," he said, thinking of their eight-year-old daughter still curled up in her blanket, probably clutching that worn-out bunny she refused to let go of and dreaming about going to Disneyland, especially for the Aladdin ride. She watched that movie a hundred times and still sang along with every song for the length of the movie, the entire two hours and twelve minutes. When she could not get her parents, her grandmother, or Capes to watch the movie with her, she would create an imaginary world with her stuffed animals and have movie watching tea parties with all of her imaginary friends. She was their only child, and Beau Lee relished the way she was navigating the joy and chaos of life in the Cooper family.

"The weatherman said it would be fifteen degrees in Chicago today. You got your heavy trench coat and extra scarves?"

"Sure do, but I almost forgot my Thurgood fedora," said Beau

Lee as he removed the hat from a rack atop their dresser. It was wool, handmade in New Zealand, and had become his trademark look.

"Let me walk you to the door."

"Oh, don't trouble yourself."

Gigi got up anyway. "No, I insist," she said, sliding her feet into a pair of fuzzy slippers.

They walked out of the bedroom and downstairs to the front door. "I definitely got to have my Thurgood fedora and scarf on today as everybody is still going to be in amazement over Obama winning the presidency," Beau Lee said with pride.

"I can't wait to go to school today and talk to the children about what this means for America," Gigi responded excitedly.

"The next four years are definitely going to be some interesting times. On the plane yesterday, I sat next to a man who seemed to have conservative beliefs, and he told me that I need to start looking for a new job."

"What did he mean by that?"

"He said Obama's election proves that racism is over in America, so there won't be no need for civil rights lawyers like me," Beau Lee explained.

"Certainly is wishful thinking," Gigi acknowledged. "But for right now I think you should keep your day job."

Beau Lee laughed and said, "I think you're right. What's your day like, sweetheart?"

"After I get Bianca dressed, I'll meet with the State Curriculum Committee officials to preview the requirements for our student testing next month."

"I wish you luck. I know how rigorous the State is in evaluating the scores of our students at the South Side schools."

Beau Lee's luggage was already parked downstairs. He extended the handle of his roller bag and unlocked the front door.

"Eleven years," Gigi said. "That's how long I've been a principal at that school, and every year they switch up the rules on us. So, nothing that they'll do today will shock me."

Beau Lee gave her a firm squeeze and kissed her again.

Gigi graced her husband's cheek, feeling his freshly shaven skin. "Be safe, you hear?" she said before he walked out the door to the black SUV idling in the driveway.

Nellie, a Black man with a caramel complexion who was about the same age as Beau Lee, rolled the window down. "Good morning, Gigi!" he shouted as she stood in the doorway in her flannel robe.

"Good morning, Nelson," she yelled, waving her hand. "You all have a safe trip, you hear?"

"Yes, ma'am. We'll make sure to get Beau Lee back home in one piece."

"By the way, how long will you be gone?"

"If all goes well, we'll be home tomorrow morning," Beau Lee shouted as he got in. He gave one last wave and blew his wife a kiss before settling beside Nellie, with Capes seated in the third row.

"Good morning, Frat! Did you get enough rest last night?" asked Nellie, oddly chipper.

Nellie and Beau Lee had met as undergraduate students at Texas Southern University and were also fraternity brothers. They called each other "Frat" as a show of mutual love and respect. That deep kinship inspired them to become business partners; they'd formed their law firm ten years ago.

"I'm a little sleep-deprived, but what else is new?" Beau Lee said. "I'll get some shut-eye on the plane." He turned and faced Capes. His head was resting against the window, and his eyes were closed. He was wearing his Harley-Davidson leather jacket, and his scarf and gloves were sitting on his lap. "Capes, are you with us today?"

"I'm always with you, boss," Capes said without opening his eyes.

"You did pack a suit for this trip, right?"

"In my luggage. You know I can't travel comfortably in monkey suits. I'll put the thing on when we land in Chicago."

Beau Lee looked at Nellie and asked, "Mr. Managing Partner, are you okay with this? Time is of the essence when we land."

Nellie, who was typing on his laptop, glanced over at Capes and said, "I've already told Capes that if he delays us at all, there will be hell to pay."

"By the time I'm finished putting on my suit, you all will still be waiting on your fancy luggage from baggage claim," Capes said, refusing to open his eyes.

Before Capes was an employee, he was one of Beau Lee's most loyal clients when he was still doing criminal defense work. Capes often argued that if it wasn't for clients like him, Beau Lee would not have had the opportunity to display his skills in the courtroom and become the great trial lawyer people know him to be today. Three times Capes had been charged with conspiracy to distribute, and three times Beau Lee walked him out of the courtroom with a not-guilty verdict from the jury. It wasn't until Beau Lee transitioned from criminal to civil cases that Capes's luck ran out. He was convicted and sentenced to five years in prison. That time inside the joint gave him the opportunity to reflect on the conversations he'd had with Beau Lee about how intelligent he was and that there was another path for him. After he was released and unable to find suitable employment, he and Beau Lee made a pact that if he walked the straight and narrow and gave up the street life, he could still use his street smarts to be the best legal investigator in the city.

"I'm not worried about Capes doing what he's supposed to do today," Nellie said, looking squarely at Beau Lee. "I'm more worried about you, partner."

They were heading into their pretrial settlement conference and Nellie was feeling pre-action jitters. He's usually the one who had his screwed on tightest to keep the ship running between Capes's laid-back attitude and Beau Lee's lofty ambitions.

"Why's that?" Beau Lee asked.

"'Cause it's a quick settlement opportunity. If we try to be reasonable for our clients and not turn this into a class action lawsuit like you keep hinting at, things should go smoothly. You know the firm could use the money, especially with our expansion plans. A class action suit takes time and it could be months or years before we'd see a dime."

"It's a chess game," reasoned Beau Lee. "You have to trust whatever moves I make, partner."

"Four years of litigation is asking a lot."

"I respect where you're coming from, Frat, and I'm going to sleep on it . . . preferably on the plane."

Nellie grumbled, somewhat unsatisfied, and returned to his laptop.

4

THE DRIVER HIRED TO CHAUFFEUR THEM FROM THE AIRPORT TO THE office of attorney Princess Alvarez, who was representing the Guaranty National Bank, was waiting for them with a sign near the luggage carousel when they arrived.

"Here's our guy," Beau Lee said as they headed his way.

"Greetings, sir," the driver said. "I'll take those." He took hold of Beau Lee's and Nellie's rolling bags. Capes politely rejected his offer to carry his garment bag, as he was managing fine with it over his shoulder. "Welcome to Chicago," the driver said. "I'm parked this way."

They followed him outside and were hit with the chilly Northern air.

BEAU LEE PUT ON THE earmuffs that Gigi had insisted he take. "I know they said it was going to be cold, but this is no joke," he said.

"You're preaching to the choir, boss," Capes said, rubbing his hands together to keep warm.

They quickly climbed into another black SUV, this one was heated. The driver put their luggage in the rear, closed the hatch, and got into the driver's seat.

Capes called to the driver, "How far to the destination?"

"Depending on traffic, I should have you there within thirty minutes."

"Good," Beau Lee said. "Nellie, that gives us enough time to review the police reports again on our three women. After the opening session, Capes, I'll need you to follow up with your contact in the police clerk's office. See if you can get your hands on the documents mentioned in the report. It could be just what we need to blow this case wide open."

Nellie was quick to interject, "Beau, I'm not following you. What could be more explosive than the videos we already have of them being arrested at the bank?"

"I don't know if those documents exist, but I got a hunch, and I want Capes to follow up on it. Work your magic, Capes."

"I got you covered, boss."

WHEN THEY ARRIVED IN THE city, it was frigid, far beyond what they had imagined. Beau Lee, Nellie, and Capes were taking the elevator in an office building in Hyde Park to meet the defense attorney, and Capes was still trying to keep warm despite the heat from the car ride. When the elevator doors opened, they stepped out onto the fourth floor and faced two double doors leading to the lobby of a beautifully decorated law office that didn't skimp on elegance.

Nellie scoffed and said, "With all the mahogany and gold embroidery throughout this office, Guaranty National Bank is certainly paying Princess Alvarez a healthy rate."

"Oh, she's getting bank for sure," Capes said, admiring the marble floor with hints of gold flakes.

As they approached the receptionist's desk, a young woman in a cream blouse greeted them. "Good morning, gentlemen. May I help you?"

"We're with the Beau Lee Cooper Law Firm," Nellie said. "We're here for the settlement conference with Attorney Alvarez and Guaranty National Bank."

"Certainly," the receptionist said, "right this way." She escorted them down the hallway into a boardroom that seemed fitting for a president or the CEO of a Fortune 500.

"There's water on the table, and I could get you coffee if you'd like."

"We're fine, thank you," Nellie said.

"Let me know if you change your mind. I'll be right out front, but you can use the intercom there . . ." She pointed to a device on the wall. "You just push that button, and I'll answer."

"Well, I'll say," Capes said flippantly. "All it takes is a push of a button."

"Otherwise, Attorney Alvarez will be right with you," she said, and left the room.

The men took a seat at the long wooden table. Capes leaned back in the high-back leather chair. "Can you please try not to look so brand-new," Nellie said. "It's just a chair."

"Well, it might be just a chair to you," Capes said, "but it's the nicest one I've ever sat in. You know, we should ask her where she purchased them."

"No point," Beau Lee said. "It'd take three months of your salary for us to afford one."

Capes gasped. "Not happening. It doesn't even have a built-in massager."

A Latinx woman in a navy business suit entered. She was petite, and her makeup was soft, but her presence was commanding. Beau Lee thought she was in her mid-thirties or younger; she was trailed by two older white men in business suits. "Attorney Beau Lee Cooper," she said, extending her hand, "I'm Attorney Princess Alvarez, outside counsel for Guaranty National Bank."

Beau Lee shook her hand. "Pleasure to finally meet you in person."

"And these gentlemen are Mr. Cluse, the General Counsel, and Mr. Wachowski, the Midwest regional director from Guaranty National Bank's main office." Cluse and Wachowski firmly shook Beau Lee's hand.

"Great to meet you all," Beau Lee said. "Let me introduce you to my team. My partner, Attorney Nelson Rivers, and my chief investigator, Brent Capers."

"Hello, gentlemen," Attorney Alvarez said. "How about we all take a seat so we can get started." She opened her leatherbound notebook. "Mr. Cooper, we received the demand letter, and the bank has enough respect for you and your clients to try to resolve this matter without engaging in protracted litigation. However, there seems to be great disagreement on the value of the claims. But of course we're here to listen to your explanation as to why you think they're worth so much."

"Well, we feel that we've made a reasonable demand and encourage you to counteroffer."

"Okay, then . . ." Attorney Alvarez started, taking a deep breath.

"But please keep in mind, the most damning fact in this case is that the Guaranty National Bank checks that were said to have been fraudulent were actually authentic checks issued in Atlanta, Georgia," Beau Lee said. "There was never any fraud to begin with."

"Yes, we understand that, and your claims may have some validity, but we are not without defenses to those claims."

"Some validity?" Beau Lee looked to Cluse and Wachowski and said, "Gentlemen, no jury will be convinced that the bank shouldn't be held accountable for the arrests and false imprisonment of these three Black women who were innocently banking in your branch. We think these are very meritorious claims and that our ten-million-dollar demand is fair and reasonable, especially considering all the extenuating circumstances."

"As I said, we're not disputing that you have some valid claims," Attorney Alvarez said. "However, Guaranty National has major defenses in that the teller violated bank policies. Before calling law enforcement, tellers are trained to first call the company that issued the check for verification. If they're unable to verify it with the issuing company, then they're supposed to call the Guaranty National Bank regional call center manager. Of which she did neither. Therefore, we think it's not completely out of the realm of possibility that the bank could win a motion to dismiss on summary judgment."

"I agree, Attorney Alvarez, that there is nothing outside of the realm of possibility in a court of law when you're fighting on behalf of marginalized minorities in America"—he gave her a look—"but the problem for Guaranty isn't what will transpire in a court of law, but what will transpire in the court of public opinion when we file our lawsuit and the videos are released."

Capes perked up upon hearing the mention of the video. He gestured to get Beau Lee's attention. "Excuse me, Attorney Cooper. I'll need to excuse myself to run the errand we discussed."

"Certainly, Mr. Capes," Beau Lee said. "Pardon the interruption, Attorney Alvarez. I believe you were about to respond?"

"Attorney Cooper, we indicated when we set this settlement conference that we were attempting to resolve these claims amicably without a lawsuit being filed. But your demand for such a grand sum is preposterous."

"It's far from it."

"We conducted a focus group, and the highest verdict returned in the mock trials for each of your clients was two hundred thousand dollars. I'd add that we discovered that two of your clients had previous arrests. So how does this differ from their past arrests? How is this more traumatic, given their criminal histories?"

Nellie was slow to counter. He cleared his throat and began: "Attorney Alvarez, we're aware of those arrests. Ms. Camille Abernathy was arrested as a juvenile, stemming from a high school function with a dozen other youths, and all the charges were dismissed. As for Ms. Juanita Crumity, she was cited after her car was rear-ended when she failed to furnish proof of insurance. It had lapsed two months prior, and she'd been unable to pay it. It's important to note that she was given a notice to appear and was not taken into custody."

Feeling compelled, Beau Lee chimed in: "Attorney Alvarez and gentlemen, my mission is to raise the value of Black lives. So, before we go any further, maybe you all should meet privately and determine what your counteroffer is. And then we'll respond, presuming we can make progress versus this continual back and forth. We're happy to step out and give you all some privacy."

"Why, Attorney Cooper, you're our guest," Attorney Alvarez said. "Please stay, and we'll confer in my office." She got up from the table with her clients and exited the boardroom.

5

AN HOUR PASSED, AND BEAU LEE AND NELLIE FINISHED AN ENTIRE CARAFE of coffee. The receptionist knocked at the door and entered holding a folded piece of paper. "Attorney Cooper," she said, "Attorney Alvarez asked me to submit this written offer to you. She instructed that you contact me when you have a response. She also asked that I provide you with these lunch menus. Feel free to order whatever you'd like."

"Thank you," Beau Lee said, taking the note and menus. When the receptionist left the room, he unfolded the paper and began reading aloud:

> *In response to the plaintiff's $10 million dollar demand for your three (3) claimants, the Guaranty National Bank neither admits nor denies any liability but elects, for business reasons, to offer the three claimants $1 million globally, as full and final settlement of any and all claims.*

"Well, that's better than what I thought their first offer would be," Nellie said.

"Yeah, it's not a bad start," Beau Lee said.

"What number do you want to send back, partner?"

"This is the first round. I don't want to give too much ground in this early stage. I figure we won't get anything close to settling until at least four or five rounds."

"I agree," said Nellie. "So again, what number do we want to send back?"

"I'm only inclined to move down a hundred thousand from our original demand."

Nellie was astonished. "Beau Lee, that may offend them. We can even match their one-million-dollar move by lowering our demand to nine million. That would still give us a midpoint of five, which is two above what we'd agree to take to settle the case."

"I hear you, but for right now, just follow my lead. We're going to deduct a hundred thousand and see how the pot stirs."

"All right, partner," Nellie said, shaking his head. "I hope we don't blow it. This is the difference between us and our clients walking out with money today versus the firm having to come up with tens of thousands to pay for protracted litigation over the next four years."

"Trust me, Nellie, they're not going anywhere. Now, how about we order us some lunch?"

TWO MORE HOURS HAD PASSED by the time Attorney Alvarez, Mr. Cluse, and Mr. Wachowski rejoined Beau Lee and Nellie in the boardroom.

Princess Alvarez seemed to be losing patience with the need to remain hospitable. "So, Mr. Cooper. Where do you stand?"

"Attorney Alvarez, I don't mean to be disagreeable in the least. But I did come here to try to resolve these claims for their full value and not to give Guaranty National Bank a blue-light special for the inhumane and horrific false arrests and wrongful imprisonment of three innocent Black women."

"Attorney Cooper, as a Puerto Rican woman, it is never lost on me the level of discrimination that women of color have to face every day in America," she declared. "But you know very well that if this matter goes to trial, there is no way a jury will award your clients each over nine hundred thousand for a mere five hours in the county jail. Let's be real. These women only make eight dollars an hour. This million-dollar offer divided between them is a fair settlement. I suggest you discuss it with your clients before you so callously reject it."

Beau Lee didn't flinch. Where another attorney might have raised his voice or bristled at the dismissive wave of her hand, he simply straightened his papers and spoke with measured calm. "We have discussed today's settlement conference and have full authority from our clients to act on their behalf. My questions to you and your clients are: Have you discussed with your board of directors the implications once we have the press conference and show the world the video of how you treat your Black customers—with prejudice and false accusations? And, how many other Black and brown people across America are going to call my office with similar claims once it gets all over the news?"

It wasn't the sharpness of his tone that carried weight, it was the steadiness. Beau Lee's composure held the room, showing strength not in anger but in discipline. He let the silence afterward linger just long enough for everyone to recognize that his confidence came from certainty, not bluster.

She shook her head in disgust.

"I suspect none of you have ever been arrested and put in jail ever in your lives," Beau Lee said rhetorically. "Well, neither have I, but I've known plenty who have, and the impact that it has on their lives is something you'd never understand. You say that being falsely arrested and booked in the county jail for five hours isn't a big deal, but how would you know? What do you know about being behind bars and having your freedom taken?"

There was a knock at the door, and the receptionist entered with Capes, who was holding a portable DVD player. "Attorney Cooper," she said, "Mr. Capes is back."

"Gentlemen, how about we chat outside," Capes said, signaling to Beau Lee and Nellie.

"My sincerest apologies," Beau Lee said. "Will you excuse us?"

"Take your time," Attorney Alvarez said, showing no signs of being frazzled. "We'll be right here when you return."

They walked outside. "Boss, you ain't gon' believe what I'm about to show you." Capes was practically beaming.

"You were able to get surveillance from the police car," Beau Lee said enthusiastically.

"Better than that, I also got the jail surveillance video," he divulged.

"That's why you my main, Capes," Beau said as they dapped each other with their fist.

"It's just gon' cost me a dinner date tonight with the clerk who worked at the police records department," Capes said as his face lit up.

"The firm will gladly cover the dinner, Mr. Capes," said Beau Lee.

WHEN BEAU LEE, NELLIE, AND Capes reentered the boardroom, they had a different air—particularly Beau Lee, who seemed even more confident than before.

"As I was saying before we stepped out," Beau Lee said, "I can't begin to explain to you the trauma associated with being arrested, booked, and imprisoned for five hours based on a false and racist allegation, but Mr. Capes here, who is not ashamed of his past, knows the impact of the experience . . . of being processed through the *system*. Do you care to enlighten them, Mr. Capes?"

"It'd be my pleasure," Capes said. "I just took a trip to the police clerk's office and discovered new information that made clear just how traumatic this incident was for our clients. Case in point: After our clients were booked, fingerprinted, photographed, and put into the general population at the Cook County Jail, they were required to submit to a hepatitis vaccination. You see, Hep C spreads like wildfire in jails and prisons. When our client Ms. Juanita Crumity was told by the jailers that she had to get the hepatitis shot, she suffered a panic attack. She had trouble breathing, couldn't stand up straight, and her vision got blurry . . . according to the documented account. In other words, she had an acute physical response brought on by trauma. It was only made more traumatic when jail staff threatened to restrain her if she didn't voluntarily receive the vaccine, which she ultimately agreed to."

"I was unaware," Attorney Alvarez said. "But I still don't see how this warrants the compensation you're asking."

"That's only part of it," Beau Lee said. "Unlike the bank surveillance videos that had no audio, Mr. Capes has shown me police body camera footage accompanied by the audio recording of Ms. Crumity's heartbreaking reaction as the jail's medical staff forced the needle into her arm. This ordeal was psychologically traumatizing. She hollered and fought while in handcuffs. Do you see how these images could be damaging? It's not just about our clients' humiliation and false imprisonment. This is about all the executives at Guaranty National Bank, whose employment will be in jeopardy because you all refused to settle this fairly and forced me to go show the world these videos."

Cluse and Wachowski looked worried as they mumbled among themselves.

Beau Lee continued. "Perhaps you should watch the videotape of Ms. Crumity at Central Booking for yourself, then provide your counteroffer."

"I'd need time to confer with my clients."

"Time is something we are running out of, Attorney Alvarez. It's now after three P.M., and we're getting close to the end of the day. I can't say how much longer our clients will entertain these pretrial settlement negotiations, but I know that if I go back to them without a settlement on the table, they may instruct me to file our lawsuit."

"Sounds like a veiled threat."

"Just a reality . . . which can sometimes be harsh."

The room was silent as he handed her the DVD.

* * *

THIRTY MINUTES LATER, ATTORNEY ALVAREZ entered the room with Cluse and Wachowski. The men looked browbeaten.

Alvarez spoke sharply, having lost her cordialness. "We reviewed the body cam footage," she said. "And we recognize the horrific ordeal your clients went through. However, we still find your monetary demand astronomical."

"Then let me provide more context," Beau Lee said. "You see, Ms. Abernathy is about five feet three inches, and since we've concluded that none of us have ever been arrested, we don't know what it's like to be placed in handcuffs and thrown in the back of a police cruiser. So, let me give you an idea. You're thrown into the back seat of a police cruiser that uses shoulder harnesses that fasten across the body and are designed for a man of average height and build. No matter the size of the detainee, the shoulder harness is not adjustable. Therefore, when Ms. Abernathy was put into the back seat of the police cruiser in handcuffs, the shoulder strap that normally would come across the chest of an average-sized man came across her neck, right under her chin . . ."

Beau Lee pointed to his windpipe and continued. "You see, this is where the strap would have crossed over Ms. Abernathy's windpipe, as exhibited in the video, restricting her airway. Which is why she was squirming but managed to yell, 'I can't breathe!' which is why we won't accept a penny less than our demand."

Cluse and Wachowski quietly conferred to each other. Then, Cluse leaned over and whispered into Attorney Alvarez's ear. Her eyes were downcast as she listened.

"Attorney Cooper, you've proved your point. My clients have agreed to your terms and look forward to putting this ordeal to rest." She stood and extended her hand for Beau Lee to shake.

"I'm never sure what to say in these instances, but I appreciate your openness to negotiating and am glad we could conclude with a satisfactory outcome for all parties."

"Well, that's open to interpretation, but yes, I'm glad we reached an agreement. Take care, Attorney Cooper. My receptionist will see you out."

She walked out of the room with her head held high while Cluse and Wachowski looked like they'd lost their life savings at the roulette table. Beau Lee always marveled at how the people who represented big banks and corporations acted as if losing a lawsuit meant the money came out of their personal bank accounts. They took the loss so personally, but for Beau Lee, it was the only way for them to understand that Black life held value, and it was not to be trampled over by prejudice and racism.

6

BEAU LEE LED NELLIE AND CAPES THROUGH THE LOBBY. EACH MAN HAD A big smile and a jaunty, rhythmic walk that proclaimed their victory. This case will be Beau Lee's second largest settlement behind the eight-million-dollar lead-paint poisoning case settlement where Beau Lee exposed that Texas state didn't remove the lead paint in the Black school districts like they did in the other school districts. That settlement allowed him and Nellie to form a partnership where they could hire additional employees and buy their own office building in downtown Houston. Beau Lee and Nellie understood this moment because settlements like this are few and far between.

"Beau Lee Cooper, as I live and breathe!" a voice called from behind.

Beau Lee stopped, turned around, and saw the man he'd come to know as Brother Harpo standing with an older Black woman adorned in a wool sweater, and a younger Black woman who was well into her pregnancy and cradling her bump.

"Brother? Is that you?" Beau Lee asked. "If it isn't the best non-lawyer-lawyer community activist I know!"

"And don't you forget it!" Harpo said as they met mid-hallway for an embrace.

Brother Al-Shaheed Harpo was a tall Black man with gray dreadlocks dressed in an elegant brown houndstooth suit, Italian loafers, and a wool scarf, and he was walking as if he were gliding on air. Even under the dim lights of the hallway, his russet wing tips shimmered.

Beau Lee hadn't seen him in over a year. Not since they had worked together to aid people from his hometown who were victims of "Cancer Alley," the epicenter of Louisiana's fossil fuel and petrochemical industry. Like Capes, he was a returning citizen who served ten years in the joint. When all of society had given up on him being a law-abiding member of society, Beau Lee recognized his heart for trying to better himself and the communities that he once pillaged when he was a street gang leader in his younger days. While he was on the inside, he committed himself to self-improvement by reading books, filing legal appeals, and watching the Oprah Winfrey television show every day. The most trouble he found would be when he got into physical altercations with other inmates about turning the TV on at 4:00 P.M. to watch *Oprah*. That's how he earned his nickname Harpo, which was Oprah spelled backward and the name of her production company.

"What are you doing in Chicago?" Beau Lee asked.

"When I got out I went home to be with my family after Hurricane Katrina. After I got them situated, I came to Chicago to be close to my daughter who graduates from high school next year," Harpo said.

"That's a real good thing, my brother," Beau Lee affirms. "Harpo, you remember my managing partner, Nelson Rivers, and my investigator, Capes."

"Yes, yes, greetings, brothers," Harpo said. "It's a pleasure to see you all again."

They all shook hands.

Harpo's demeanor changed from gleeful to somber as he nudged the women forward. "This is Mrs. Raquel Montrose and her daughter, Jamillah," he said. "Her husband, Jamillah's father, Hollis, is at

Mount Sinai Hospital in critical condition. I'm sure you've seen the news of his arrest, which resulted in him being shot ten times in the back by CPD."

"I'm familiar," Beau Lee said. "Caught a bit about it on TV this morning."

To Mrs. Montrose, he said, "I offer my sincerest prayers and condolences to you and your husband."

"Beau Lee, it must be kismet to run into you like this . . ."

"Why's that?"

"We're here to meet with Attorney Alvarez about this tragedy, but if I may be so bold, we desperately need you on the case."

"Isn't Attorney Alvarez already representing your family, Mrs. Montrose?"

"Attorney Alvarez goes to our church," Raquel said. "She represented Hollis in a discrimination suit against the CPD, and now that they've gone and shot my husband, I'm feeling like we need people like you . . . people with a specialty of fighting these types of injustices."

"Well, I'm sure that Attorney Alvarez will be able to provide exceptional legal services. Having witnessed her in action, she is a *very* good lawyer."

Jamillah spoke up for the first time, removing one hand from her bump to take hold of Beau Lee's arm. "Please, Mr. Cooper," she said, imploring him. "We need you to reconsider. My father . . . our family . . . we need *you* on this case."

"You've got a way of bringing national attention to matters like this, Beau Lee," Brother Harpo said. "And without the media spotlight, this case could be swept under the rug."

Mrs. Montrose was a spitfire, Beau Lee could tell, and her very justified anger was beginning to show. "We just can't let them get away with this," she said. "They tried to murder him."

Beau Lee could feel the lump forming in his throat. He knew her pain and heartbreak all too well. "I can give you my direct number," he offered. "Discuss your matter with Attorney Alvarez. If you don't feel satisfied, then you call me."

Alvarez walked into the lobby just as Beau Lee was handing Mrs. Montrose his card.

"Attorney Cooper, you're still here? How surprising."

"We were just leaving."

"Were you? Because it looks like you're in the process of talking to my clients and exchanging business cards."

"It's not what it looks like, Ms. Alvarez—"

She quickly corrected him. "Attorney Alvarez."

"My apologies."

"First you fleeced my clients into overpaying for what I still believe was a completely defensible case for the bank. And now you're in the lobby of *my* office trying to solicit *my* clients. Tell me why I shouldn't report you to the state bar?"

"I am not trying to steal your clients. In fact, I assured them you would do a very good job of representing them," Beau Lee affirmed.

"Please leave, Mr. Cooper. Now."

"Thank you again for your hospitality," he said, then looked at Mrs. Montrose. "I will continue to pray for you and your family. Brother Harpo, it's always good to see you. Capes, do you have our coats?"

"I have them right here, boss." Capes handed them to Beau Lee and Nellie.

"We wish you all a good evening," Beau Lee said as the men made their egress.

7

"OF ALL THE TIMES . . ." CAPTAIN BRADY O'KEEFE SAID, RUBBING HIS HEAD where much of his hair had receded. He slammed his office door shut and looked menacingly at officers Jackson "Jack" Dunham and Chaz Rossi. "What the hell were you two thinking, not running the plate?"

"We're sorry, Sarge, but what were the chances he was Metra?" Jack asked. "Especially on that side of town and at that hour."

"A fishing expedition . . . that's what you two decided to embark on," Brady said. "Of all the nights to play it loose, you picked the night Obama gets elected. I don't know what you were thinking."

"The guy and his SUV fit the description."

"It's standard practice," Brady said emphatically. "Not optional. The first thing you do is run the goddamn plates!"

"We were sure we'd find something," Chaz said. "And the guy swerved a few times like he was itching to make a break for it. We had to move on him quick."

"You're putting that in your report as the rationale for the traffic stop?" Brady asked. "Because they're going to scrutinize the hell out of whatever you write before the ink dries, so you'd better have your fucking story straight."

"We're still working on our reports," Jack said. "But Chaz is right.

We observed him driving erratically, and the vehicle matched the description of one seen leaving those warehouse robberies from a few nights ago . . ."

"Jesus, you're still working on the report?" Brady put his hands on his hips like a disappointed father. "And you think saying he was driving a little reckless is going to fly when all you've got is a couple of swerves?"

"What does it matter anyway? He had a gun and took a shot at us," Chaz said.

"It matters, you idiot. In this climate it all matters. You need a justified reason for making that traffic stop that put a cop in the hospital."

"Look, we did our jobs," Chaz said. "It was a clean shooting. Forensics will show that."

"It doesn't matter what you think you did right. When the marches commence, it'll be your faces on the evening news, and they'll be calling for your heads. For all you know, the guy's got a spotless record. He could be the saint of all cops. Decades on the force without a single complaint or blemish. People might line up around the block to speak on his behalf."

"Never met a Chicago cop without at least something he's not proud of on his record," Jack said smugly.

"First time for everything, smart-ass." Brady balled his fist tight, looking at the men before him. "Who the hell do you yahoos have to speak for you? Have you seen your records?"

"We got you, Brady," Chaz said a little too confidently.

"No—no, you don't have me. What you have is a department that will fuck you so fast it'll make you shit your pants, and if anything comes out about this ID business—"

"Brady, it's like I told you, he didn't have it on him," Jack said. "No license. No police identification. All he had was his piece. That's the information we acted on. Any decent cop in our shoes would've done the same."

Brady took a seat at his desk, which had seen better days. Aside from the scuffs and knicks, the wood was beginning to fade, much like he feared his career was. "You two had better fix this. Get me?"

"Don't worry," Jack said. "It'll play out how we say."

"I'm just thinking out loud here," Chaz began. "But say the vehicle didn't have a plate, or we couldn't read it?"

"Chaz, what the hell are you saying?" Jack asked. "Just keep quiet."

"I'm saying, what if we couldn't see it, which was why we couldn't run it," Chaz continued. "If the plate was missing or defaced, we're in the clear. It justifies the stop . . . Right?"

Brady slammed his fist against the desk and stood, sending the chair spinning into orbit and smashing against a filing cabinet. "I don't want to hear any of this shit. As a matter of fact, I don't care what you do because, as of this moment, you're both on leave until the shooting team concludes their investigation."

"We're sorry, Brady."

"And stop calling me Brady. We ain't on a first-name basis anymore. I have the right mind to take this up the chain. You went and shot the wrong asshole, and now you two's ship is sinking, but I ain't going down with you. No one's going to take my pension, goddamn it."

"But sir . . ." Chaz looked as if he wanted to beg. He was a witless rookie in every sense of the word.

"From here on out, you two are on desk duty," Brady said. "You're ordered to finish your reports and wait for Internal Affairs at your desks. I'd suggest calling your union reps. Give me your pistols."

They unholstered their firearms and set them down in front of Brady, who placed them in a metal cabinet and locked it.

"Now get the hell out of my office." Brady recovered his chair and wheeled it back to the desk.

Jack exited the office with Chaz following behind. The precinct was busy as usual. Other officers' eyes were on them, judging them, he thought. No one knew the particulars of the incident, but enough details had made the rounds that four cops had shot someone, and the person was possibly a Metra cop. Speculations were swirling that Hollis had been with CPD earlier in his decades-long career. Jack figured that once Hollis's law enforcement background was corroborated, it'd be all over the news—a running loop on every major local and cable network—and soon, reporters would be camped out on his front lawn. The moment a cop's face became part of the city's collective memory, it would be impossible for that cop to work. He wouldn't be able to patrol or investigate any crime. No one talked to cops whose faces had been seen all over the news, especially if they were accused of a dirty shooting.

"Fuck," Chaz said, sitting at his desk. "What the hell are we supposed to do? Just wait around for those jack-offs from IA to come and officially suspend us?"

"What you said back there about the license plate . . ."

"Yeah?"

"You think it could work?" Jack asked.

"I mean, it's worth a shot."

"It might be the angle we need to prove we acted the same as any other cop would in our position—a dark street, suspicious vehicle, a driver with no ID, and a plate we can't read."

"Mitigating factors."

"We need to get to impound."

"What about Internal Affairs?" Chaz asked.

"Like you said, it's not like we can wait around all night. They can fucking reschedule."

"Well, shit," he said. "What are we waiting for?"

8

WHEN JACK AND CHAZ ARRIVED AT THE IMPOUND LOT, JACK FLASHED HIS police ID to the gate attendant and entered without issue. They parked far away from other patrol cars, some unmarked. It was best to limit being seen by too many officers and personnel, which meant getting in and out as fast as possible.

"Any ideas?" Chaz asked. "Or do we just wing it?"

"Winging it is what got us in this mess in the first place," Jack said. "We should've run the damn plates."

"No use whining about it now. It's done, but we've got a way to fix it."

Chaz had the type of overconfidence that Jack typically despised, especially in a rookie, but also envied. If he'd had Chaz's confidence in high school, he might've asked a girl to prom, tried out for the baseball team, or run for class president. Who knows, maybe Jack wouldn't have become a cop. Instead, he might've worked in finance, wearing three-piece suits and a Rolex, strolling down LaSalle in Ferragamo wing tips. *Who was he kidding?* Being a cop was in his blood, his DNA. He wasn't made to do anything else.

"So . . . ?" Chaz asked.

"I'm thinking . . ."

Getting access to an impounded vehicle required authorization.

Once a vehicle was logged in, an officer needed multiple sign-offs to access it, which was something Jack couldn't fake.

"You know who's on shift?" Chaz asked. "Maybe they'll do us a solid."

"Could be Santiago," Jack said.

"You cool with him?"

"Went out with his ex-girl once or twice."

"He knows that?"

"Doubt it."

"Damn, Jack. Is there anybody's ex-girl you haven't put the squeeze on?"

Jack shrugged. "What can I say? The ladies love them some *Jack D.*"

"Well, if Santiago's on duty, let me do the talking," Chaz said. "He's always been a stand-up guy with me."

The two of them got out of the patrol car and headed toward the small office adjacent to the impound lot. They knocked on the steel door and waited. Jack noticed the security camera angled high above. He put his back to it and looked down at his boots.

The door buzzed. The men entered a narrow hallway and walked to a service window at the end, where an officer stood drinking coffee from a Styrofoam cup.

"My man, Santiago," Chaz said, oddly upbeat.

"What do you want, Chaz?"

"Long time no see. How ya been keeping?"

"Same as usual. Long-ass hours," he said. "I'd say I miss patrol, but I'd be lying, especially on evenings like this. I bet you two are freezing your balls off. What's it . . . thirty degrees outside?"

"Yeah, something like that."

"I heard you guys had some action last night."

"News travels fast."

"Around here, we've got nothing better to do but jaw-jack."

"Don't believe everything you hear," Jack said. "The shooting was clean."

"I hadn't heard otherwise."

"Good."

"So, what's up?" Santiago set his cup aside. The steam collected against the window, leaving behind a wet residue. "I know you didn't come down here to shoot the shit."

"We need to see the vehicle from last night's 11-95," Chaz said. "I left my phone inside."

"Your cellphone?" Santiago looked skeptical and eyeballed Jack. "How'd your rookie leave his phone in a suspect's car?"

"Hey," Chaz said, "I'm not a rookie."

"Could've fooled me."

"Accidents happen," Jack said. "The phone must've slipped out of his pocket when we were tossing the vehicle."

"Yeah, must've," Chaz said.

"Two regular keystone cops. So what do you want me to do about it?"

"What do you think?" Jack asked. "We need access."

"You know that's against policy. If you don't have a warrant, you ain't getting back there."

"We're not asking to take it for a test drive," Chaz said. "We just need a few minutes to find my phone. My old lady is up my ass about it. She can't call and text me twenty times a shift, and it's making her nuts."

"We'll make it worth your while," Jack said. "You still a Bears fan?"

"Till the day I die."

"Box seats. Bears versus Cardinals."

"Box seats? Bullshit!"

"Did I stutter? I can get you two tickets, easy."

"You guarantee I'll be up in the box? Because stadium seats are like sitting on icicles."

"The only thing cold will be the beers," Jack said. "But answer me this: If you Puerto Ricans love warm weather so much, why the hell do you move to all the cold places? I mean Chicago, New York, Jersey?"

"Fuck you, Jack."

"I'm kidding, man. Grow a sense of humor."

"For that, you better throw in free parking at the stadium."

"All right. All right," Jack said, "I'll cover your parking."

Santiago sighed, torn between protocol and box seats. "What's the make and model of the vehicle?"

"A gray late-model Ford Expedition."

"Yeah, we got that," Santiago ran his finger across a spreadsheet. "Aisle six. Spot twenty-four."

"Got it," Chaz said.

"So, when do I get my tickets?"

"I'll swing by at the end of the week," Jack said.

"You assholes better not be bullshitting me."

"Jack's good for it," Chaz said. "You'll get your damn tickets."

Santiago pressed a button under his desk, and the door to the right of the window buzzed. "And make it quick," he said. "I don't need anybody asking what the hell you two are doing out there."

They walked onto the dirt lot. Rows and rows of cars populated a few acres. They turned on their flashlights and began making their way to aisle six. Some vehicles still had yellow stickers on them. Others had pink, which meant they'd been impounded for longer than three months and were slated to be sold at auction.

"I think that's it," Chaz said, shining his light on the Expedition.

"Yeah, that's the one," Jack said. "Let's make this quick." He reached into his pocket and pulled out a Swiss Army knife. He approached the rear of the SUV, flicked out the screwdriver from the red hub, and began removing the plate while Chaz kept a lookout.

Once the plate was off, Jack bent it twice longways in the center, forming a crease and making it difficult to read the red digits. "That should do it," he said, screwing the plate back on.

"Easier than I thought it'd be." Chaz grinned like he'd won something.

"Sure, candy from a baby and all that."

"We better get back to the precinct and finish our reports," Chaz said. "We still have IA to deal with."

"Don't worry about IA," Jack said, putting the knife back in his pocket. "All we need to do is keep our stories straight. They're going to try and pit us against each other, same with the other cops, but know this . . . we're the only ones that can sink us."

"I hear you, Jack, but what if the others aren't on the same page we are and tell something different?"

"We made the traffic stop. What the hell do they know? The first responders own the scene. . . . That's us. What we say happened is what happened. All they did was show up and facilitate the arrest."

"They fired, too."

"They were backup, and they did their jobs. Same as us."

"Right," Chaz said, hanging on Jack's every word. "We own the scene, and we did our fucking jobs."

"Good," Jack said approvingly. "Now, let's get back to the car. It's freezing out here."

They headed in the direction they'd come, walking fast between the frozen cars, moving as if they'd hit the jackpot, and for Jack, he had.

9

BEAU LEE, NELLIE, AND CAPES STOOD IN THE SWANKY HOTEL SUITE THEY'D be staying in during their time in Chicago. It had a view of the city, and the décor didn't stray much from what they'd encountered in the lobby—red wallpaper, gold accents, and argyle curtains with tinsel, also gold. The older hotel had an early-nineteenth-century aesthetic with oiled wood panels, hand-painted cathedral ceilings, candelabras, mosaic-tiled floors, and a profusion of red and gold accents. Out of the many hotels Beau Lee had stayed in over the years, the older ones offered the most charm.

Under other circumstances, he'd tour the historic building, taking pictures and sending them back to Gigi, who had a penchant for old buildings and interior design, but it had been an arduous day.

"Not too bad," Capes said, admiring the room. "Little old-looking but comfortable."

Beau Lee's phone vibrated. "Must be Gigi," he said, pulling out his Blackberry.

"Tell her I said hi," Nellie said. "Capes and I are going to grab some drinks from the vending machine."

"I spoke too soon. It's a Chicago area code," Beau Lee mumbled as Nellie and Capes left the room. "Hello?"

"Attorney Cooper. It's Mrs. Montrose."

"Evening, Mrs. Montrose. Everything all right?"

"I wanted to apologize for today," she said. "It was never my intention to overwhelm you."

"You don't need to apologize."

"I spoke to Princess . . . I mean, Attorney Alvarez. We've all agreed you're the best person to help us."

"*All* of you agreed? Including Attorney Alvarez?"

"Yes, that's if you're still open to representing my husband . . ."

Beau Lee took a moment, weighing the circumstances surrounding the case.

"Mr. Cooper?"

"Yes," he said. "I'll take your husband as a client."

"Praise God," she said. "Thank you."

"But I must caution you, it won't be easy."

"In my experience, nothing ever is," she said. "Except loving Hollis. He's a good man, Mr. Cooper, and he deserves justice."

"I agree."

"So, tell me, Attorney Cooper. Let me know what you need from me to get started?"

"Well, I'll need to do my due diligence of course, but without question, I'm going to file a civil lawsuit against the CPD."

"But they haven't pressed charges against Hollis yet. Would that not be getting ahead of ourselves? Besides, Princess already has a lawsuit against the Chicago Police Department on Hollis's behalf for workplace discrimination and a host of other things."

"This stems from his previous employment?"

"That's right," she said. "Hollis was with CPD for over a decade. Passed up for promotions left and right. He always knew it was a race thing. They treated him poorly from the start and never tried to hide it. Always the optimist, he thought things would get better over time, but they just got worse. When he couldn't take it any longer, he filed a lawsuit, resigned, and, by the grace of God, was hired by Metra."

"And the lawsuit? What became of it?"

"Princess tried her best, but it never gained traction. CPD kept saying they were investigating Hollis's initial complaint, and the lawsuit couldn't go forward until they concluded their internal investigation. Last I checked, the investigation was still ongoing. Hollis hasn't worked for them since Clinton was in office."

"I see," Beau Lee said.

"It's no fault of Princess's. She's a bulldog when it comes to things. Never gives up, you know? I imagine you two have that in common."

"So I've been told," he said. "I'll try to put this delicately, Mrs. Montrose. Your husband is in critical condition after having had an encounter with the police. He may very well be innocent of wrongdoing and did nothing to warrant the stop, but the police will find something to justify their actions. What we have to do, and do it quickly, is file a lawsuit that'll bring this the media attention it deserves and will force the police to charge Hollis."

"You want to back them into a corner?"

"Precisely. Otherwise, each day that goes by allows them to leak information that starts to paint Hollis in a way that suits their case."

"I see . . ." Mrs. Montrose went silent.

Beau Lee paced the room. He walked to the large window and looked out at the sprawling city that glimmered under a full moon. "This city, like many in America, is as beautiful as it is ugly. Your husband encountered its ugliness in great measure, and for that, I'm so sorry. But our greatest weapon to combat the ugliness is to shine the light of truth onto it."

"Yes," she said, "the truth will set Hollis free."

"The truth tends to come with a price tag," he said. "But no matter the cost, I will fight for Hollis and your family."

Capes and Nellie loudly entered the room after grabbing colas and plopped down on the queen-size beds. Beau Lee stepped into the adjoining room, which had another bed with the same amenities: a wet bar, fridge, and TV.

Mrs. Montrose resumed talking: "And you think people will care when they hear about what happened to my Hollis?"

"Mrs. Montrose, these days, Black men being victims of gun violence is a regular occurrence. There's no shortage of apathy out there when it comes to our lives, so we have to make people care."

"And that's what you do?"

"First I make them understand, then I make them feel. Lastly, I remind them that if it happened to Hollis, it could happen to them and anyone they love. I bring the tragedy to their doorstep, to their dinner tables, into their living rooms. They have to live with it day in and day out until they get so fed up that they have no choice but to act."

"Act? How do you mean?"

"The power is in the people. We have to harness that power and direct it at the police and the city, but the first step to doing that is filing a lawsuit against the people responsible for what happened to your husband."

For a couple of seconds, Mrs. Montrose's heavy breathing was the only thing Beau Lee heard on the line. He recognized the magnitude of what she was going through, and the notion of filing a lawsuit at the same time her husband was fighting for his life would likely deplete whatever reserve of strength she had left.

"Okay," she said in a soft voice. "How much?"

"Fifty million."

"My goodness."

"It's a small price to pay considering what Hollis has lost. He'll spend the rest of his life needing medical treatment and care. His loss of income could impact your family for generations. And everything he wanted to do, and the plans he had for the future, were forever altered the moment those guys pulled their triggers. Yes, fifty million is a drop in the bucket for the devastation they've caused your family."

"I understand that, but do you think they'll actually pay?"

"Well, I'll try my damnedest to make sure they do."

"You know . . ." She paused to gather her thoughts. "I wasn't sure about you at first. I'd seen you on the news once or twice but didn't pay much attention to the cases. When Attorney Alvarez and I spoke after we initially met, she deferred to your firm and recommended that you be our lead counsel. She said you were good. Maybe even the best at what you do. Just about called you a genius, and that means a lot coming from her. You know, she was an Oxford Scholar."

"Attorney Alvarez is an exceptional litigator, but I am surprised by her complimentary assessment of me."

"Oh, Princess might come off like she can't stand you, but believe me, she's got nothing but respect for you."

"That puts me at ease a little."

"God's working through you, Beau Lee Cooper. He's surrounded you with good and honest people, so use them."

"Yes, ma'am."

"You'll do right by my husband, about that I have no doubt."

"I'm going to do the only thing I know how to do—fight for those who can't fight for themselves."

"God bless you."

"Yes, Mrs. Montrose, he has and will. Talk soon."

Beau Lee turned to see Nellie and Capes looking at him with disbelief. "Weighty promises you're making before you even know the full story."

"I know enough to know something isn't right with that shooting."

"C'mon, Beau Lee, we can't help everybody," Nellie said. "We're spread thin as it is."

"If not us, then who?"

"We can recommend someone else. What about Elsworth Butterfield in Indiana? Seems like this could be a good fit for him."

"He's got dementia."

Nellie looked shocked. "Oh, I didn't know," he said. "His law firm's still running?"

"Shut down last year."

"Damn."

"I've already agreed to help the Montroses. There's nothing else to discuss."

"So that's it? You're making all the decisions now?"

"I'm telling you, Frat. Our firm is the right one for this case. I can feel it."

"You've always got a feeling, but you shouldn't have agreed to it without talking to me first, Beau Lee. We're in this together, remember?"

"I know. I know. I'm sorry."

"Things are getting sloppy, and I don't like sloppy. This firm doesn't run with one person at the helm. It takes all of us."

"I know and respect that, but I couldn't let that poor woman think there wasn't any hope for her husband."

"Okay, and what about Alvarez? How do you expect to work with her after playing hardball in the mediation?"

"We'll have to find a way," Beau Lee said. "She's a professional, and at the end of the day, I know she just wants to help the family. That's why she filed a civil suit on Hollis's behalf years ago."

"What civil suit?"

"It was for racial discrimination and harassment," Beau Lee said. "It doesn't sound like the city's even entertaining it. Alvarez hasn't gotten far."

"You think it's a possibility Hollis might've been targeted for filing against CPD?"

"Either that or it was a horrible coincidence."

"How long has his suit against the CPD been going?"

"Years," Beau Lee said. "Seems like if they wanted him silenced, they wouldn't have waited so long."

"Look, I get it—I do," Nellie said. "As long as we've been knowing each other, you've never been able to turn a blind eye to the suffering of our people. It's what I've always admired about you. But this case is big—huge, even, and I don't think we can take this on without other things falling by the wayside."

Capes cleared his throat. "And that's my cue . . . I'm going to check out the pool area," he said, quick to excuse himself. "Room key, boss?"

"Since when do you swim?" Nellie asked.

"I don't," he said. "I'm more of a hot tub aficionado."

"Go ahead." Beau Lee handed Capes the key card, and he left.

"I don't think I have any choice but to get involved, Nellie." Beau Lee worked his temples with his fingers. "This one has a hold on me something fierce, so I'm asking that we find a way to make it work."

Nellie sighed. "There's no changing your mind, is there?"

"Afraid not."

"Even if you file another civil suit on Hollis's behalf, the city will only move to dismiss it. One suit is bold, but two is audacious."

"Maybe . . ."

"It could blow up in your face, Beau Lee, and you'd be taking our firm down with you. Pulling something like that could get you disbarred."

"It's a risk I'm willing to take."

"My Lord, you are a stubborn one."

Beau Lee gave a small smile. Nellie knew him best. They'd been through thick and thin and he knew that their dynamic—one where Nellie focused on the business element of running a law firm and Beau Lee took the big swings and handled the litigations and legal strategies—was what had allowed their law firm to thrive for as long as it had. "Guilty as charged."

"All right, then," Nellie said. "We'll have to delay opening the new branch for the time being. I'll do my best to keep things back in Texas afloat and start looking for legal assistants to help with the load."

"Thank you for having my back on this."

Nellie hugged Beau Lee. "I'll always have your back. You know that." He released him and both men coolly reclaimed their personal space. "The real question is, how are you going to break all this to Gigi? She's expecting you to be on that plane when it lands in Houston tomorrow."

"Chocolate and flowers?"

"You'll have to do better than that."

"You're right. . . . I'll think of something."

"And you're meeting with Alvarez sometime soon?"

"I'll make some time tomorrow."

"I guess she wasn't too far off. You are snagging her client."

Beau Lee ignored that. "I'll also need to talk to Hollis's partner, Finn Doyle. I'm hoping he'll be able to shine some light on Hollis's professional life and help me paint a picture of the type of officer he is."

"You've got your work cut out for you, that's for sure."

Beau Lee looked at his watch. "It's getting late, and I need to sleep off that steak." Beau Lee put his arm around Nellie. "I love you, brother," he said. "Couldn't do any of this without you."

"Oh, you'd be a mess without me."

The two men laughed as they often did . . . through pain and in the face of the insurmountable task ahead of them.

10

THE NEXT MORNING, BEAU LEE, NELLIE, AND CAPES ENTERED A QUAINT diner and were immediately overcome by the smell of frying bacon, griddle cakes, and coffee brewing. Beau Lee craved a hot cup of joe. He hadn't slept well, though the hotel's mattress was comfortable enough. His mind had been on Hollis for the entire night, causing him to wake when thoughts concerning the case bombarded him. So many questions . . .

Not sleeping well caused wild fluctuations in his appetite. Around four A.M., he'd gotten up, left the hotel room, and walked to the vending machine at the end of the hall, where he almost gave into temptation by purchasing his favorite: a cheese Danish. But he could hear Gigi's voice in his head reminding him that eating sugar at odd hours would lead him on an unhealthy path. His last high-profile case had led to stress eating. He'd consumed one or two Danishes a day. By the time the case concluded, he'd gained ten pounds and was diagnosed with prediabetes.

The hostess was a tall, red-headed woman in her golden years. She was dressed in modest workwear and thick-soled sneakers. "How many?" she asked.

"Four," Beau Lee said. "We're expecting one more to join us."

"All right," she said, grabbing four menus. "Right this way."

She escorted the men to a table near the window with a view of the street. They sat and began perusing the breakfast options.

"Grits sound good," Capes said. "A couple of slices of toast, and I'm set."

"You sure this Doyle fella's coming?" Nellie asked. "We've never had a cop want to cooperate in an investigation before."

"We've never had a case where a cop was the victim," Beau Lee said.

"And when are you planning to see Alvarez?"

"Right after we talk to Officer Doyle."

"Well, about that," Nellie said, pushing his menu aside. "How long do you think you'll be here in Chicago?"

"As long as it takes."

"He won't be lonely," Capes said. "I'll be watching his back and keeping him company every step of the way."

"I'm going to hold you to that," Nellie said. "This ain't our town, and from what I hear, things work differently around here. Not always on the up and up, if you get my drift."

Capes shrugged. "It's nothing we can't handle."

"What time is your flight back home?" Beau Lee asked.

"Later this afternoon," Nellie said. "Three-thirty."

"Want us to roll with you back to O'Hare?"

"Don't bother. You've got enough to deal with as it is. I'll be fine."

A bubbly, fair-skinned waitress planted herself tableside. "And good morning, gentlemen," she said. "What can I get you all?"

"Coffees for the table," Nellie blurted. "Extra hot."

The waitress wrote on her order pad. "Got it. . . . Do we know what we'd like to eat?"

"Grits was sounding good, but I'll go with the biscuits and gravy," Capes said. "Scrambled eggs and bacon on the side."

"Grits, eggs, and bacon," Beau Lee said. "Extra butter for the grits, please."

"And how about you, handsome?" the waitress asked Nellie with a flirtatious grin.

He groaned. "Plain oatmeal. No butter. No brown sugar, either. Just the berries on the side."

"A healthy choice," she said. "I like a man who watches what he eats."

Nellie's frown quickly faded, replaced by a slick smile.

"That'll be all?" the waitress asked.

"Yes," he said. "Thank you very much."

The waitress winked. "I'll get that going for you." She reached across the table to collect the menus and noticed the extra one. "Oh, are you expecting someone?"

"We are," Beau Lee said. "Not sure when he'll show."

"Well, when he does, I'll circle back around."

"That'd be great."

The waitress returned to the kitchen and a moment later came out with a carafe and three mugs. She set them on the table and began to pour the piping-hot coffee. "Cream and sugar are on the table," she said, "but let me know if you need extras."

"Will do," Beau Lee said. He waited until she was out of earshot and elbowed Nellie's arm.

"What?" Nellie asked.

"I'm just looking at a guy who likes to watch what he eats," Beau Lee said mockingly. "Man, she's feeling you."

"Ah, give me a break."

Beau Lee looked toward the door, anticipating Finn's arrival. "I hope this guy doesn't stand us up."

"Any idea what he looks like?" Capes asked.

"Not a clue, but Mrs. Montrose said he'd have no problem recognizing us."

"What did she mean by that?" Nellie asked.

"Only that he's seen us on TV a few times."

"Yeah, he was probably cursing at the screen. I'm uneasy about this whole thing. Again, we have never had an officer want to cooperate in an investigation before."

"Let's give him a fair shake," Beau Lee said, taking a sip of coffee.

"Mrs. Montrose says he's a loyal friend to Hollis and is real torn up about what happened to him."

"I bet," Capes said.

"Look, let's check all the bias at the door. We don't want cops jumping to conclusions about us, so how about we avoid doing the same?"

"You're right, boss," Capes said. "Everybody starts with a clean slate."

What Beau Lee knew of Finn was that he was a fifteen-year veteran of the Metra police department and had been Hollis's partner for eight of those years. The way Mrs. Montrose described him made him sound like most veteran officers Beau Lee encountered—gruff and worn-out—and he expected Finn to look the same way.

The waitress arrived with a large tray and lowered the plates of steaming food and Nellie's bowl of oatmeal with a side of fresh berries onto the table. The steel-cut oats looked pathetic next to Beau Lee's and Capes's platters of carbs, fluffy eggs, and slices of fatty pork.

"Can I get you gentlemen anything else?" she asked.

"Looks like we've got everything we need," Beau Lee said. "Thank you."

The waitress beamed with satisfaction and returned to the kitchen. Beau Lee sprinkled salt and pepper on his grits and pushed a pad of butter onto the creamy white hominy. It began to melt as he took a bite of bacon and chewed like he hadn't had a meal in days.

A short, stocky man with a bulldog's face entered the restaurant and stood a moment. He stroked his silver mustache as he scanned the booths packed with patrons. His bushy brows were like canopies over his probing blue eyes. He locked onto Beau Lee and approached with heavy steps.

"I think this might be our guy," Beau Lee said. The man carried a manila folder and held himself with the confidence and authority that only came from wearing a badge and carrying a pistol that had enough punch to blow a hole through meat and bone.

Beau Lee wiped his hands on a napkin and slipped out of the booth to greet him. "Detective Finn Doyle, I presume."

"Chicago's own."

"Nice to put a name to the face."

"Likewise, Attorney Cooper." Finn shook Beau Lee's hand. "It's terrible we're meeting under these circumstances. I'm sick over what happened to Hollis. I haven't been able to think about anything else since I got the news."

"The sentiment is shared by his family and so many others," Beau Lee said. "These are my associates, Attorney Nelson Rivers and our firm's investigator, Brent Capers."

"Nice to meet you all," Finn said, offering his hand for quick shakes.

He was gruff but polished—a crisp collared shirt under a peacoat, pressed slacks, and shined loafers—an appearance that didn't deviate much from what Beau Lee had expected.

Finn removed his coat and hung it on a hook fixed to a wall with black-and-white photos of the historic coffee shop throughout the decades. The photos told a story—the shop was a staple in the city where politicians and celebrities had dined over the years. Even Muhammad Ali had broken bread with the Honorable Elijah Muhammad in a booth that looked vaguely similar to the one they were sitting in.

Finn sat down, placed the manila folder on the table, and rolled up his sleeves.

"Never been here before. How's the coffee?" he asked, his thick forearms displaying faded tattoos that Beau Lee struggled to make sense of.

"Not bad. I left a menu for you. Hungry?"

"Oh, I can always eat," he said, pulling what appeared to be a partially redacted police report from the folder. "Rocky—er, Mrs. Montrose said this would help you. It wasn't easy to get, but a guy owed me a favor. Not sure who filed it. Someone blacked out the arresting officer's info with a Sharpie."

"Not uncommon with leaked reports," Beau Lee said. "Can I take a look?"

Finn handed the report to Beau Lee. "Sure, look that over, and I'll see if this place serves up corned-beef hash."

Finn flipped through the menu while Beau Lee read the report. He immediately scanned the summary of events, noting Hollis's failure to identify himself as law enforcement. It was the first sign that the report was likely full of falsehoods. Rocky was adamant that Hollis always notified officers he was police when stopped, and Beau Lee had little doubt that it was true. Next was the suggestion that Hollis had been aggressive toward the officers. The words "threatening" and "combative" popped off the page. But what Black man in his right mind, let alone a cop, would behave that way during a traffic stop or with any police encounter? Lashing out or becoming combative was like rolling the dice during roulette and hoping it landed on red. It was the great unknown—the officer's disposition, their incomplete knowledge of the law, and inclination for bias or profiling could often dictate the outcome.

Beau Lee continued to read, eventually arriving at the most damning sentence: "Suspect drew his firearm, aimed it at arresting officers, and fired two rounds. In response, officers opened fire, striking the suspect numerous times in the back . . ."

Beau Lee felt nauseous, and his chest pounded. He struggled to calm his breathing.

Finn looked up from the menu: "You all right, Mr. Cooper?"

Nellie dropped his spoonful of oatmeal into his bowl. "Beau Lee?"

"Excuse me," Beau Lee said. He sprung from the booth and headed toward the rear of the restaurant. He rushed into the men's bathroom, entered a stall, and vomited his breakfast into the toilet. There were so many police reports he'd read in his line of work. Plenty of them were disturbing, but this one had really gotten to him. He couldn't help but envision what Hollis had gone through—lying on the pavement, suffering and pleading for help. It was an ancestral cry, a lament that spoke to the terror that had been enacted on Black bodies since their arrival in what would become the United States of

America. The unmitigated torment and persecution of Black people was one of the greatest atrocities carried out in history, and Beau Lee wondered, even with a Black president in the White House, if it would ever end.

He stepped out of the stall, rinsed his mouth clean with water, and looked himself over in the mirror. His eyes were tired and sunken. He took a deep breath, adjusted his tie, left the bathroom, and returned to the table. Finn was drinking coffee, and a hearty helping of corned-beef hash was plated in front of him.

"You okay, Counselor?" Finn asked.

Capes asked, "Yeah, boss, you good?"

"I'm okay. Something went down the wrong pipe is all," Beau Lee said. "Now, about this report . . ."

"Welp, that report is a load of bullshit, that's for sure . . . excuse my French," Finn said. He shoved a forkful of hash into his mouth and chewed loudly. "I don't know where to start," he mumbled between chewing. "Whoever wrote it graduated from MSU."

"MSU? I don't follow."

"The School of Make Shit Up."

"How about the initial traffic stop?" Nellie said. "Start there."

With Hollis still in a coma, the team began their hunt for the truth.

"All right. They didn't run Hollis's license plate because they claim it was illegible, but that's not why they stopped him. Apparently, they observed him for half a mile on the highway swerving and crossing lanes without signaling."

"So they thought he was drunk?" Beau Lee asked.

"They suspected intoxication. They weren't sure if it was alcohol or narcotics."

"Did they notify dispatch after pulling him over?"

"Not right away." Finn wiped the grease from his mouth. "It wasn't until Hollis was pulled out of his SUV that a call was made for backup."

"I don't see why they pulled him out," Beau Lee said, still looking over the report. "Doesn't sound like they followed procedure."

"They're citing mitigating circumstances. Since they weren't able to read the license plate, they couldn't run it. And they suspected the vehicle might've been used in the commission of an earlier crime. By all accounts, they approached it as a high-risk traffic stop, which might've been the reason for extracting Hollis from the vehicle."

"All the more reason to call it in once they pulled him over, right?" Capes asked. "If they actually thought it was a high-risk stop . . ."

"Sure, if they were telling the truth, but they're not," Finn said. "Even if Hollis were tired, which could've accounted for the swerving, he would've gotten a cup of joe before leaving Gunderson. He's done it plenty of times. As for the vehicle being suspected for the commission of a crime, I did some digging." Finn took a quick sip of coffee, washing down the hash. "There was a string of warehouse robberies in the area a few weeks ago, but witnesses stated they'd seen a blue minivan leaving the scene, not a gray SUV."

"What about Hollis's firearm? The report says it was discharged?" Beau Lee asked.

"More bullshit," Finn said. "Hollis wouldn't pull his weapon on other cops, and he damn sure wouldn't have fired it. Besides, he was on the ground and had no position of advantage. It goes against training. Pulling that weapon and firing would've been the equivalent of putting the gun to his own head and squeezing the trigger."

"Yeah, sounds sketchy to me," Capes said.

"If Hollis's holster has double retention, which I'm pretty sure it does, it's even harder to draw under distress. I mean, all of 'em weren't just twiddling their thumbs. If they were actively trying to subdue him, they would've noticed the firearm right away."

"Double retention?" Beau Lee asked. "How's that work?"

Finn held his hand up in a U-shape and wiggled his thumb. "See, most tactical holsters don't allow a firearm just to come out smoothly. A person's thumb has to engage a release button, allowing it to be pulled out," he said, demonstrating the movement. "It's what helps prevent an officer from being easily disarmed. Now, from the position they claim Hollis was in, I can't say getting that gun out would be impossible, but it damn sure wouldn't have been easy."

"And the department's going public with this report?" Beau Lee asked.

"Sounds like they might be making a statement this evening."

Beau Lee noticed a group of patrons sitting in a booth at the far end of the restaurant. They had paused eating and were looking toward the TV above the counter. One of the servers was turning up the volume when Finn recognized Hollis's vehicle on the screen.

"Oh hell," Finn said. "It can't be . . ."

Beau Lee squinted. It was hard to make out what was happening in the grainy footage. "What is it?"

"Somebody recorded Hollis's traffic stop."

11

BEAU LEE STOPPED CHEWING. HE FELT THE ADRENALINE START TO RUSH through his body. "That means we've got a witness out there."

"Maybe more than one," Nellie said.

They continued to watch the footage as the officers surrounded Hollis, and then the gunshots could be heard—a series of anxiety-producing pops echoed throughout the restaurant. Patrons gasped and shouted at the TV. The reporter cut in: "As a reminder, please be mindful if you have younger children in the room at this time . . ." The video continued with the officers' removing Hollis's firearm and gathering near the front of a cruiser.

"My God," Finn said, speaking through a clenched jaw.

"The gun wasn't in his hand," Beau Lee said, feeling his rage returning. "Their hands went straight to Hollis's waist."

"How can you tell?" Nellie asked. "Visibility is garbage."

"I just know."

The cops had made a wall around Hollis, obscuring the camera's view, but Beau Lee had a good eye. He was trained in seeing things people tried to hide. It was only a second of footage, maybe two, but he saw the holstered firearm just as an officer's back and rear filled the camera's frame. The footage wouldn't be able to win them the case, but it showed Beau Lee the truth.

The reporter appeared onscreen, rattled—a Black woman wearing a pink blouse with a slight sheen that reflected the bright studio lights. For a moment, her eyes were cast downward in her lap, and she looked like she was unable to continue. Then, gazing directly into the camera, her lip trembling slightly, she said, "We received this footage within the last fourteen hours. It has also been uploaded to the video file-sharing service YouTube. We are in the process of verifying who may have uploaded it and sent our station the file's link. We believe the video footage may show the attempted arrest of Hollis Montrose, who we've verified is a policeman with the Metra Police Department. Mr. Montrose is being hospitalized and is currently in critical condition. We have reached out to the Chicago Police Department for further comment and have not received a response. We will continue seeking answers"—she cleared her throat and sighed—"We now cut to Jet Cardiff, who is outside Mount Sinai Medical Center, where Mr. Montrose is said to be receiving care."

Finn sat down, pushed his food aside, and leaned across the table. "You know what this means, don't you, fellas?"

"We need to talk to whoever made that video," Beau Lee said. "ASAP."

"And did you notice the vantage point? They might've recorded from the second story of a house or building."

"So, the witness is a resident of the neighborhood," Nellie said. "Probably lives in one of the homes across the street."

"This thing is all over the news now," Finn said. "Those cops will be thinking the same as us. They'll want to get their hands on whoever recorded that footage, and they'll start with the neighbors."

Beau Lee looked at the report again. "The arresting officers say that the license plate couldn't be read in what seemed like normal conditions. Did the plate look illegible to you?"

"Hard to say," Finn said. "Not that easy to make out 'cause the video's so grainy."

"There's only two names on this report, but the video showed four shooters."

"Oh, right. I looked into that," Finn said. "The other two responding officers were on their way to 21 District Station."

"For what?"

"From what I could gather, there'd been a retirement party for their old captain. One of those all-nighters," Finn said. "The call came in, and they decided to provide backup."

"Is it unusual for cops to respond to a call outside of their district?"

"Not really," Finn said. "But those two fellas who made the stop, Jack Dunham and Chaz Rossi, got themselves a nasty reputation."

"How nasty?" Capes asked. "'Cause what I just saw in that video made me lose my appetite."

"Lots of citizen complaints from what I hear."

"Any lawsuits?" Beau Lee asked.

"Nothing I found, but you'll see what I mean when you subpoena their records."

"Thanks for this," Beau Lee said, putting the police report back into the folder.

"I'd do anything for Hollis," Finn said. "He's like a brother to me. Wasn't always that way, but I wouldn't change it for nothing."

"We better get going," Beau Lee said, reaching into his pocket. He took out his wallet and began counting bills.

"I've got it," Finn said. "Your money's no good here."

"It's fine, really—"

"No. I'll take care of it, and if you guys need anything, give me a call."

"All right," Beau Lee said. "Thank you."

"Sure thing." Finn waved to the waitress and said politely, "The bill when you get a chance, please." It was a departure from his overall gruff tone, and Beau Lee wondered if Finn had daughters at home. He'd seen plenty of hard-edged men turn to putty around their daughters. Himself included.

"Give me one sec," the waitress said, balancing two large plates of food.

"Take your time." Finn turned abruptly to Beau Lee like a thought had dawned on him, and said, "Where you all off to now, Counselor?"

Beau Lee picked up his hat from the booth and put it on. "We need to talk to Hollis's attorney."

"I thought you *were* his attorney?"

"It's complicated," Nellie said. "But we're getting it sorted out."

"And after that, we're going to see if I can find whoever shot that video before Dunham and Rossi do."

"You guys are a bit like strangers in a strange land," Finn said. "How about I meet you at the scene in an hour or so?"

"You sure you want to get involved?" Capes asked. "You are police, after all. How's that going to look?"

"None of that matters now. Hollis is my friend, and that comes before all else."

"It could be useful having someone with us who knows the city," Beau Lee said. "We'd appreciate any help you can give, Officer Doyle."

"C'mon, boss, is all that necessary?" Capes asked. "I'm good in any hood. We can make our way without five-o. Him being there could make whoever we talk to clam up."

"I'm making the executive decision here," Beau Lee said. "Officer Doyle will meet us in two hours at the scene. That should give us enough time to meet with Alvarez beforehand."

Finn grinned like he'd scratched the winning number on a two-dollar lotto ticket. "I'll be there," he said. "I want you all to know I'm in this for Hollis. I'm going to get justice for my brother, no matter what it takes."

Capes rolled his eyes. "Easy there, cowboy. Our battlefield is the courtroom. Not the streets. We're not interested in any billy club beat-downs. No dangling people off balconies for answers."

"Maybe you've seen *Serpico* one too many times," Finn said. "We aren't all dirty. And you best believe I'm nothing like those animals who shot Hollis."

Capes mumbled under his breath, "Time will tell . . ."

12

CAPES WAITED OUTSIDE THE DOOR WHILE BEAU LEE AND NELLIE TALKED to Alvarez in the executive suite. The only thing that separated her from them was a long customized desk made of black marble. The designer piece of furniture and her chic office proclaimed that she was young, hip, and had achieved notable success.

"So, Beau Lee Cooper . . . are you here to conduct a mea culpa?" she asked, palms pressed flat on her desk.

"And what would I be apologizing for?"

"I don't want to say you poached my client, but yeah, you poached my client."

"I wouldn't say poached."

"What would you call it?"

"Divine intervention."

"You think a great deal of yourself, don't you?"

"I'm nothing more than a man led by conviction," Beau Lee said. "And I intend to get justice for Hollis Montrose—and I believe you want that as well, correct?"

"Of course."

"Then I don't see any need for hostility between us. We both understand what's at stake. There's only room for one war, and that's the one we're going to have to fight against the CPD and the City of Chicago."

A framed diploma from Stanford University Law School touted Alvarez's pedigree, along with numerous commendations from legal boards and the National Bar Association. She was the real deal, as bona fide as the silver-framed photo of her and then-Senator Barack Obama.

"Our firm only wants to serve Mr. Montrose and his family," Nellie said. "There's no place for ego in that."

"*Ego*? You think I'm the one with the ego problem?"

"This isn't productive," Beau Lee said. "We're wasting precious time. Which is something Hollis Montrose may have little of."

Beau Lee's words resonated, and Alvarez bit back whatever she was going to say.

"You're right," she said. "I have a great deal of respect for the Montrose family, and they mean everything to me. If Rocky believes that having you on this case gives us an advantage, then I'm all in."

"Good."

"I'm glad we've gotten all that out of the way," Nellie said. "But you should know where we're coming from, Attorney Alvarez. You should know our world—our *reality*—and we've held the hands of so many in Mrs. Montrose's situation."

"What does that mean, exactly?"

"In our practice, we've had to sit with more grieving wives, mothers, grandmothers, and aunts, and that wailing, that deep bellow of pain and sadness, is something I'll never get used to hearing. I can tell you that we didn't come here to lose, but you should know that the Chicago Police Department will leverage the best prosecutors the state has to offer to ensure those officers never spend a day behind bars."

"I understand that," she said. "So, you intend to file a pro hac vice?"

"Illinois maintains reciprocity with Texas," Beau Lee said, "which means we shouldn't have too many hurdles to jump for me to act as co-counsel for Mr. Montrose."

"I'm well aware of how reciprocity works, Mr. Cooper."

Alvarez crossed her arms and took a beat, glaring at Beau Lee and Nellie. "How long will it take you to file this astronomical lawsuit you promised Rocky?"

"Not sure, but I'll get started on it immediately. In the meantime, I'll need you to fill me in on the details regarding Hollis's discrimination suit against the CPD."

Alvarez took a deep breath. "We can get started today," she said. "Are you both assisting as co-counsel?"

"Actually, my colleague Nelson here will be returning to Texas. He'll offer support remotely. And my investigator, Capes, will remain active here in the city. He'll be digging up whatever he can on what happened the night Hollis was shot."

Alvarez looked puzzled. "Capes? You mean the mouthy guy?"

Nellie laughed. "That'd be him."

The quip at Capes's expense lightened the mood, and Alvarez flashed a partial smile.

"I take it you have a coffeepot?" Beau Lee asked.

"Drip. Espresso. Cappuccino. It'll make them all."

"Good, because it's going to be a long day."

"Beau Lee," Nellie said. "A word outside?"

"Excuse us," Beau Lee said.

"I'm not going anywhere," Alvarez said.

They stepped outside her office into the small lobby where Capes was waiting, texting on his cellphone.

"Looks like you've got things squared away with Alvarez," Nellie said. "I can probably head over to the airport now."

"All right, Frat." The old friends embraced for a moment. It wasn't unusual for Beau Lee to express his love for everyone in his life, often with a hug or hearty handshake.

"My flight leaves in four hours. Plenty of time for me to get some work done while I wait. I'll let you know when I'm back in Texas. As for you two," Nellie said, slipping from Beau Lee's hug and looking at Capes, "both of y'all be careful out there."

"You know I will," Capes said. "But do you really think we can trust Doyle?"

"There's only one way to be sure. Don't let your guard down. Things in this city aren't always what they seem. Mrs. Montrose might've put her trust in Doyle, but we need to be cautious."

"I think you should go meet him without me," Beau Lee said. "It's more productive if we divide and conquer. You and Doyle can investigate, and I'll get going on the lawsuit. Alvarez can fill me in on the status of Hollis's current case against CPD."

Capes's eyes bucked at the idea: "You want me to roll around *this* city with five-o?"

"You can handle it," Nellie said.

"I know I can handle it, but come on. Maybe I can dig into things on my own?"

"Time is of the essence here. Working with Doyle will speed things up. He can open doors you can't."

Capes looked resigned. "I'll do the best I can, boss."

"I know you will. Now, let's get to work."

13

THREE CUPS OF COFFEE LATER AND BEAU LEE STILL HADN'T SMOOTHED things over with Alvarez. She wasn't difficult to read. In fact, there was no mystery at all about how she felt about working with him. She clearly saw him as an interloper, but it didn't stop him from trying to win her over.

"So . . . where are you from?" Beau Lee asked while flipping through a stack of briefs.

"West Side of Chicago," she said. "Born and raised."

He smiled. "That explains a lot."

"No offense to folks who think it's all rough and tumble, but there's so much more to my neighborhood than what the news shows."

"I don't doubt that. I know Chicago's got layers."

"You're absolutely right."

"Why Chicago, though?"

"Besides the fact that it's home? The food, the people, the rhythm of it all. Chicago summers. The block parties. The music blasting from somebody's front porch. It's a culture all its own," she said. "There's no place like it on earth."

"Sounds like the same love I've got for Houston. And how'd you end up back here practicing law?"

"That's a long story . . ."

"How about the summary?"

"I left Chicago for college—got my BA in social science from UCLA, then my master's in social welfare from USC, and my JD from Stanford. I was twenty-five by the time I wrapped all that up. Then I went abroad to Oxford as a Rhodes Scholar and completed a degree in civil law."

"Impressive doesn't quite cover it. You're a powerhouse."

"After school, I clerked for a judge, then did some time at a few high-profile firms in L.A. and New York—corporate law mostly. Cut-throat stuff. Represented companies with more money than sense. You already know how that goes."

"Working for yourself means less tyranny?"

"Are you referring to my banking clients?"

"Not specifically, but if I were to cast this in biblical terms, they'd be Goliath."

"As much as I'd love to only take cases like the Montroses', I'd be paying off student loans until retirement."

"You get no flak from me," he said. "But what made you decide to leave Southern California?"

"I loved L.A.—the weather, the energy, the West Coast vibe. But something in me knew it wasn't where I was meant to plant roots," she said. "I thought about trying D.C., Boston, maybe New York . . . but none of those places felt right, either. They were already oversaturated, crowded with people doing the same kind of work. Chicago just kept tugging at me. It's home. It's where this Puerto Rican abogada belongs. It's where I was meant to be. And even with all its challenges, there's real opportunity here. It was six years ago that I started my own practice here. I've been building ever since. I serve as outside counsel for many corporations. It allows me to make sure my overhead's covered and do some necessary good for the community."

She shifted to grab a stack of manila folders from her briefcase and placed it on the coffee table between them. "Here's everything I have on the CPD. Plenty of corroboration for Hollis's claims, along with a copy of the complaint he filed. The trouble was, I couldn't get anyone to go on record."

"What's the case's status now?"

"It's stalled," she said, putting the pen down. "And, if I'm being honest, things aren't as clear-cut as I originally thought. Hollis made some incendiary statements about the department online. Venting, really, but they were enough to color him 'disgruntled.' All I can say is that the lawsuit made enough of a fuss that a good number of the cops named in it were forced into early retirement. A small consolation given what Hollis experienced."

"A small consolation, indeed."

"So, how much do you think you'll get out of the CPD?" she asked.

"I plan to sue for fifty million."

"Sure, Mrs. Montrose told me that, but how much do you think you'll actually get?"

"Fifty million. Maybe more."

Alvarez nearly choked. "While it wouldn't be the first lawsuit, it would be one of the largest civil suits against the police department in Chicago history."

"Good—it's what they deserve."

Alvarez knew the importance of this fight, but she also knew the history of the Chicago Police Department all too well.

"Beau Lee, you may not be aware, but in the late nineteen-sixties, a group of Black officers formed the Afro-American Patrolman's League (AAPL), led by Edward 'Buzz' Palmer. Those officers had seen enough injustice and began documenting complaints from Black citizens and fellow officers about harassment, brutality, wrongful shootings, theft, intimidation. Over time, they compiled more than three-hundred thirty-one boxes of evidence. Lawsuits were filed. Investigations were launched. The AAPL demanded accountability and pushed for the advancement of Black officers within a system built to keep them in the margins. And you know what happened? The CPD retaliated—they had a machine within the system. Officers who spoke out were reassigned to powerless beats. Passed over for promotions. Blackballed. The message was clear: stay in line or be erased.

Rocky said that Hollis knew this history well. He admired Palmer. He saw himself in the fight the AAPL had waged. But even with all that came before, no case had ever cracked the system open the way Hollis was hoping to. No victory had ever come close."

Alvarez continued. "I mean, you just got here. You don't know how this city works. If you think the powers that be are just going to sit back and let you file some massive lawsuit and make the city's police department out to be a corrupt, racist, or anything else they are organization, then you're going to have a war on your hands."

"I'm prepared," Beau Lee said. "Been fighting injustice since I was a boy. I don't know anything different. The same goes for my firm. We fight for those who are forgotten, marginalized, and silenced. A lawsuit like the one I intend to file will force people to finally pay attention."

Alvarez gave an approving nod. "The invisible becomes seen . . ."

"What's that?"

"Just something my mother used to say. She was what some people called the ideal Catholic. Never missed mass. Quick to offer a scripture for what ailed you. Anytime things got rough, she'd remind me that God might not be seen with the naked eye, but he always makes his presence known—visible."

"Reminds me of mine. At eighty-eight, she makes it to church every Sunday."

"My mom would say that seeing the invisible meant walking in faith. Believing with your whole heart that God can and will move mountains."

"A wise woman."

Alvarez nodded. "We lost her four years ago to a car accident."

"I'm sorry . . ."

"Thank you. She lived a rich and full life. Something I aspire to."

"Prayerfully, my mother is still here and will be for more years to come," he said. "Not sure what I'd do without her."

"I like to think that even though my mom is gone, I honor her with the work I do."

Beau Lee smiled, and for the first time since meeting Alvarez, he felt like they had found some common ground.

"Another cappuccino?" she asked.

"Sure."

"Cinnamon?"

"You read my mind."

14

"RIGHT HERE IS GOOD," CAPES SAID, SIGNALING FOR THE CABDRIVER TO park along the curb a few feet from where Hollis was shot. He immediately noticed a Crown Vic parked across the street; the window was down, and Finn Doyle was behind the wheel.

Capes had never been fond of Crown Vics, the vehicle police departments most often used as patrol cars. Even seeing one parked without police insignia made the hairs on his neck stand at attention. Finn's was unmarked, gray, and tinted, with a cluster of antennae on the hood. It was a typical surveillance vehicle used for undercover operations. Capes had been inside a few throughout his life and knew they were uniformly outfitted with a shotgun mounted between the seats, a first-aid kit in the door panel, a radio, and more than likely a dated computer terminal.

Capes walked over to the driver's side of the sedan.

"Where's the counselor?" Finn asked.

"He's got more pressing matters, so he sent me."

Finn looked Capes over from head to toe, then said snidely, "All right. Hop in."

Capes made his way to the passenger-side door and joined Finn inside.

"Neighborhood doesn't look that bad," Finn said. "Working-class, sure, but it looks like people take care of their properties."

"Were you expecting something else?"

"It's Chicago—corner boys, dopers, hookers—no telling what you'll find on some of these streets."

"Look, I know how the thin blue line cuts," Capes said. "Don't feel like you have to go out of your way. If people know you're helping our firm, it might—"

"*People* . . . *People* . . . You think I give a damn what they think?" Finn turned his nose up in disgust. "You want to know how Hollis and I became friends?"

"Yeah, okay . . ."

"These *people* you speak of had their opinions about us partnering up at Metra. White and Black cops don't really partner up too much."

Capes shook his head. "Yeah, I've heard that."

"Truth is, I wasn't too keen on working with him, but Hollis was a good cop. He'd been a cop a lot longer than me and had been with CPD for years before he left. I figured I could learn from him."

"Was it a good partnership?"

"He's one of the best partners I've ever had," Finn said. "Didn't matter, though . . . a couple of assholes on the force saw how well we jelled and decided they didn't like it. First it started with jokes . . . Ebony and Ivory, Salt and Pepper, Jungle Fever. We let all that roll off our shoulders, but then they tried to ruin Hollis."

"How so?"

"Basically, they wanted to run him out of the department. It was mostly hazing. Taping pictures on his locker . . ."

"Pictures of what?"

"I don't know . . . Africa, I think."

"Africa?"

"Like jungles and gorillas with a tag that said: 'Answer the call of the wild,' and 'The bush is waiting.'"

"That's messed up."

"Goes without saying. I told them to back off. Then, they found out about the lawsuit Hollis filed against CPD, and some of those assholes thought I'd side with them. Cops who sue are usually blackballed, but Hollis worked his ass off to join Metra, and in the end, they couldn't deny him. He scored the highest in the academy and was whip-smart. Metra's been lucky to have him, but these people you talk about, well, they saw Hollis as a turncoat and didn't think he could be trusted."

"Good ol' tribalism."

"Is that what they call it?" Finn asked but didn't wait for an answer. "I saw it as cliquing up, but these guys only wanted to get rid of the one Black man in our unit so things could go back to how they used to be."

"Which was what?"

Finn swallowed hard and said, "Lots of colorful language around the breakroom. People were openly saying whatever the hell they wanted about women, people of color, and those with sexual preferences they didn't like. It was locker room talk all day, every day, because they didn't think anyone gave a damn."

"Did you give a damn?"

"Back then, not enough, to be honest. I'd ignored all the slurs and shit-talking until Hollis showed up."

"What changed?"

"Those guys realized Hollis had already sued one department and decided they didn't want to go through all that. So, they chilled out . . . mostly."

"No, I mean what changed for you?"

"I respected Hollis," Finn said. "I didn't know many Black people growing up. Gone to school with a few, but other than that, I barely interacted with anyone who didn't look like me or have an Irish last name." Finn eyed a car that slowed as it passed. The passenger's head poked out the window. "Would you look at this shit," he said, getting heated, which didn't seem to take much.

The passenger was a blond teen girl wearing a knit cap. She stared at the remnants of Hollis's blood in the street, a large stain that hadn't been washed away, and began taking pictures of the large red circle with her phone.

"What the hell is wrong with these people?" Finn asked. "Damn sickos."

"I ask myself the very same question multiple times a day," Capes said. "Haven't come up with a good answer besides the obvious . . ."

"And what's that?"

"What happened to Hollis carries the same weight as a squirrel getting hit by a car. It's worthy of a brief consideration. How sad for that squirrel. If only it had run faster or picked another street."

"Nah, people don't think that way about Hollis," Finn said. "He's a cop."

"I wish I could agree, but I promise you that people will blame Hollis for what happened to him. It won't matter that he's a cop."

"That's a really cynical outlook you've got there."

"Wish it wasn't that way, but I haven't seen anything different."

"These assholes better move it along." Finn was growing more agitated watching the sightseers. He placed his hand on the car horn. "I'll give them one minute to move on, and then I'm getting out."

"They haven't broken any laws," Capes said. "Ogling a crime scene is all kinds of fucked up, but not illegal."

"I'm sure I could find something."

The passenger finally pulled her head back into the car, and the driver continued down the street.

"I guess it wasn't too hard for people to figure out where the shooting took place," Capes said. "Maybe the video captured a street sign or something easily recognizable?"

"People probably recognized this empty field," Finn said, noting the fenced-in, overgrown lot.

"Why? Did it used to be something important?"

"Nah, it's owned by Halpern Construction, and they've got these bright yellow signs that can't be missed." Finn pointed to the sign fixed to the fence with the company's name. "We've got empty lots all around the city, and Halpern owns most of them. You can't help but notice their signs."

"You want to finish telling me about you and Hollis being BFFs?"

"Long story short, it probably makes me sound shallow, but Hollis was good at his job. Working with him made me a much better cop, and if I'd had to put up with a fraction of the shit he did, I would've quit a long time ago."

"Why do you think Hollis didn't quit Metra like he did CPD?"

"One shift, Hollis spotted a guy in a heavy coat. Mind you, it was late April, unseasonably warm, too. He followed him through the station, then approached. The guy made a run for it, but Hollis was quick. Turns out, the guy he tackled had two hunting knives and a pistol in his waistband. He'd just killed his grandparents and an uncle over on the South Side."

"Shit."

"That day, Hollis caught a killer and made sure that guy didn't take anyone else's life. After that, those officers that gave him shit started showing him the respect he was due."

"And all it took was him doing his job?"

"There's nothing easy about this kind of work, but it's especially difficult for cops like Hollis."

"Like Hollis?"

"You know what I mean," Finn said. "For Black cops. People will always see the badge second."

"That's the damn truth."

"It's good your boss is involved now. You know, I've followed a few of Cooper's cases. Not easy wins."

"Nope—but he's the best, hands down. I've learned invaluable lessons working alongside him."

"How long have you been a PI?"

"A little over a decade now."

"You're licensed in Texas?"

"No," Capes said. "I'm what you'd call unregulated."

"Say more."

"Got in some legal trouble years back. Just being a dumb kid. Caught a felony, which means I'm not eligible for a PI license in Texas."

"What kind of trouble?"

"Nothing . . . it was a long time ago," Capes said. "You think we should get out and start knocking on doors?"

"Yeah, we ain't getting any younger."

15

THE TWO MEN EXITED THE CROWN VIC AND WALKED TOWARD HOLLIS'S bloodstain. It had become a fixture on the concrete. Finn formed a box with his fingers, squinted one eye, and framed the window above them as if he were looking through a camera lens. "Seems like the right vantage point," he said, crouching. "That's got to be our window."

"How should we handle this?" Capes asked. "We don't want to be accused of witness tampering."

"We're just looking to have a conversation," Finn said. "We'll knock and see what comes of it."

Capes followed Finn across the street to a residence and stood at the bottom of the stairs while Finn ignored the doorbell, knocking hard three times with the fat part of his fist.

"Excuse me? Who are you?" a woman's voice asked from the porch next door. She drew the attention of both men.

"Ma'am, we're looking for the people who reside here," Finn said. "We'd like to talk to them."

"You police?"

"Yes, ma'am."

Capes looked on in silence as the woman came off her porch and began shuffling toward them.

"Both of you are police?" she asked, looking hard at Capes.

"Do you know the people who live here?" Finn asked, overlooking her question.

"Been knowing them for decades," she said. "I remember the day they moved in."

"Well, you must be the right person to talk to."

"All that depends, Officer. I don't know who the hell you are."

"I'm Officer Doyle, and this gentleman is Capes."

"What kind of name is Capes?" she asked. "And you still didn't answer my question. You a cop?"

"No, ma'am. Just a concerned citizen. And my name is actually short for Capers . . . that's my last name."

"Uh-huh. Y'all smell like trouble, and we've had enough trouble over here."

"We aren't here in any law enforcement capacity," Finn said. "We're just hoping to talk to your neighbors."

"Well, I'm Mrs. Gaither."

"It's a pleasure, ma'am," Capes said. "Please know we aren't looking to cause any trouble."

"How do I know that?"

"You'll just have to trust us," Finn said.

"You're not from around here, are you?"

Finn looked perturbed. "Beg your pardon?"

"Not you," she said. "I'm talking to Mr. Capes."

"No, ma'am. I grew up in Atlanta."

"Thought so," she said with her hands on her hips. "I heard a little bit of that accent peeking out. You remind me of my ex-husband. He was from Charleston—Low Country. I called it *slow* country."

"Slow can be good."

"Speak for yourself," she said. "I liked the bottle and dancing too much for him. He decided to get up and leave one day. His loss, though."

"Ma'am, we're a little short on time," Finn said. "Can you tell us anything about the folks who live here?"

"Lots I could tell you, but the question is, should I?"

"Mrs. Gaither, we're just trying to help," Capes said. "I promise you that your neighbors aren't in any trouble."

"Mr. Capes, you look like a stand-up man, but this guy here, whatcha say your name was . . . Doyle?"

Finn grumbled and stepped off the porch. "That's right, Finn Doyle," he said.

Mrs. Gaither sniffed and said, "Seems like we've crossed paths before."

"I think you're mistaken," Finn said, becoming more aggravated than Capes had seen him yet. "Are you able to help us or not?"

"See, that's what I'm saying," Mrs. Gaither said. "I'm not sure I like your attitude."

Finn sighed. "Just our luck. We've got a feisty one."

"How about we take some time to chat, Mrs. Gaither? Just you and me," Capes said. "You don't mind, do you, Finn?"

Finn's face was locked in disbelief. "You serious?"

"How about you wait in the car? I'll join you when we're done."

Finn clearly looked slighted but began walking back to the Crown Vic muttering to himself.

Mrs. Gaither waited until Finn was gone, then moved closer to the short chain-link fence that separated the properties. "I know why you're here," she said. "It's about that man those cops shot."

"Did you see what happened that night?"

"I heard a commotion. Sounded like gunshots, but sadly, that's not too uncommon around here."

"And your neighbors? Can you tell me about them?" Capes asked. "Do you know if they saw anything?"

"I can't speak to what they did or didn't see, but the boy, Joey, left town this morning. He seemed to be in a hurry."

"Joey?"

"Joey Henderson," she said. "Lives there with his mother. She's a personal assistant for a banker or CEO . . . something like that. She leaves the boy alone a lot, but he works. Some kind of night job."

"How old is he?"

"Twenties."

"And it's only the two of them living there?"

"Well . . ." she whispered conspiratorially. "Sometimes Joey's lady friend stays overnight for weeks at a time. Not that it's any of my business. I may be old, but I'm no prude. The girl seems sweet enough."

"Do you know her name?"

"Oh, I couldn't be sure. I've only spoken to her once or twice," she said. "Maybe Darla or Darisha."

"You said he was going out of town?"

"That's what he said. He was packing up his truck with luggage and food. Seemed like he was planning to be gone for a while."

"Did he say where he was headed?"

"Philadelphia. Said he had family there. I remember because it was the first time I ever heard him speak of having family in the Northeast, and I myself spent two years at UPenn."

"Is that right?"

"What, I don't look like a college girl to you?"

"Not saying that at all, ma'am."

"Oh, I'm just teasing you," she said with a playful grin. "I studied business for a bit before having to drop out. It's the greatest regret of my life. Sometimes I wonder where I'd be if I had finished my schooling, but I fell in love, and well, you know how that goes. But you didn't come to hear my sad story . . ."

Capes reached for the woman's hand and held it between his palms. "Thank you for speaking with me," he said. "You've been a real help."

She blushed, her cheeks rosy in the unforgiving chill. "Oh, I don't know about all that . . ."

"Just one more question," Capes said, looking back at the Crown Vic, where Finn sat inside sulking. "Has anyone else come by the Hendersons' home?"

"No, you're the first and only."

Capes reached into his coat pocket and pulled out a business card. "Well if they do, can you give me a call?"

Mrs. Gaither took the card and looked it over. "The Beau Lee Cooper Law Firm," she said. "Is he big-time?"

"It's a growing firm, ma'am."

"Well, hell, any lawyer willing to take this kind of case has balls. I hope you all make them cops sorry they ever shot that man."

"We're going to get justice, ma'am."

"I hope you sue them into the next century," she said with more pain than anger in her voice. "Straight into oblivion."

Capes understood how Mrs. Gaither felt. Hollis wasn't her blood relative, but they were still family. It was the collectiveness of the Black experience, something he believed had been transmitted across generations, beginning in ancient Africa, where the notion of the individual didn't exist—there was no "I," only "we," and together we'd rise or fall.

Capes waved goodbye to Mrs. Gaither and began walking back to the car. Finn had lit a cigarette; he held it between two fingers as his arm hung out the window. Capes got into the car. Concerned the smoke would stink up his attire, he asked, "You mind putting that out?"

"So, is this how it's going to be?" Finn asked. "I'm supposed to be your sidekick?"

"Sidekick? Nah, man."

"Then what the hell was that?"

"Mrs. Gaither was uncomfortable with you being there. She wouldn't have told us anything useful."

"*Uncomfortable?* What the hell did I do to make her uncomfortable?"

"I can't say, but you being there wasn't going to get us anywhere," Capes said. "Now, I'm sorry if you got offended. That wasn't my intention, but it's like you said: We have to do whatever it takes to get justice for Hollis. Even if that means letting me drive now and again, and you taking a back seat."

"I can handle that, but don't forget who's the cop in this relationship."

"I'll never forget that," Capes said. "Now, will you please put out the damn cigarette?"

Finn flicked his cigarette into the street and rolled up his window. "Happy?"

"Thank you."

Capes quickly gave Finn the rundown on what Mrs. Gaither said.

"Any idea how we find them in Philly?" Finn asked.

"No clue. But I want to check in with Gunderson Security," Capes said. "Get a sense of how Hollis was behaving before he left work."

"What do you mean?"

"I'm just covering our bases."

"You think Hollis was drunk or something? Then you don't know him at all. I don't care if the Cubs won the World Series. He'd never drink on a shift."

"No," Capes said. "God, no—that's not what I'm saying at all."

"Then what?"

"I'd never cast any accusations on him, but if he was driving erratically, we need to rule some things out."

"Like what?"

"Medical emergency. What if he was experiencing something—stroke or heart attack? That would account for the swerving and maybe any odd behavior during the traffic stop."

"Who said anything about odd behavior? Are you actually considering that the report was written with integrity?"

"We don't know what really happened," Capes said. "That's the point I'm trying to make, and getting more information will only help us better piece things together."

"Seems pretty black and white to me."

"Information changes situations . . ."

"What's that you just said?"

"It's something Beau Lee likes to say. Information is currency. The more we have of it, the better."

Finn couldn't argue with logic. "I guess I've got blinders on," he said. "But you're right. We'll leave no stone unturned. No surprises."

"Glad we're seeing eye to eye."

"We'll start at Gunderson like you suggested," Finn said. "Retrace Hollis's steps and get a feel for what he might've been experiencing before the traffic stop."

"That's the move," Capes said. "The hours leading up to Hollis's police encounter could be critical in this investigation."

"You're not so bad at this," Finn said. "Shame about the felony. You might've made a good cop."

"Nah, black polyester isn't really my look."

Finn laughed louder than the joke warranted, then shifted into drive and accelerated down the street.

16

BEAU LEE HAD EATEN TWO TUNA SANDWICHES AND A BAG OF CHIPS FROM the corner deli where Alvarez frequently ordered lunch deliveries. She had just finished her club salad. He'd made significant headway in reviewing Hollis's current litigation against the Chicago Police Department. Alvarez had done thorough work, exposing a pattern of behavior that was pervasively hostile, and which resulted in Hollis's being denied multiple promotions without explanation, as well as being subjected to varying degrees of racially insensitive remarks. Unnamed witnesses corroborated the behavior. Some had even experienced the torment themselves but refused to go on record out of fear of reprisal.

Alvarez's phone vibrated. She glanced at a text and quickly set the phone back down. "The police are holding a press conference about Hollis's shooting."

"Already?"

She took a remote from her desk drawer and turned on the flat-screen mounted on the wall.

"It's started," Beau Lee said. "Hopefully we didn't miss much."

They watched the entire conference in silence. The department spokesperson didn't offer much; the investigation was ongoing, charges would be forthcoming, and there was the ubiquitous promise of a thorough investigation.

Afterward, Alvarez said, "Doesn't make sense. Why aren't they filing charges? They were so sure Hollis was guilty, enough to shoot him, and now, nothing?"

"In my experience, the police department reviews the evidence and institutes a roundtable tribunal with the superintendent, deputy superintendent, the chief, and city attorneys. They'll consider charges and how to shield the department from legal action, which could mean throwing those officers under the bus. But you're right. I can't see a scenario where they don't charge Hollis with something. It's the only way they'll be able to justify his shooting and arrest."

Beau Lee's phone rang. "Here's Capes now," he said, accepting the call. "Capes, go ahead."

"Hey, boss, got an update for you. Sounds like the witnesses might be headed to Philadelphia."

"Any idea why?"

"Could be a family connection. Doyle seems to think if we hurry we can catch up with them. We could pick you up. Might be best if you're with us."

"Agreed," Beau Lee said. "Give me a call when you're here, and I'll meet you outside."

"We're going to drop by Gunderson Security to check something out. Then we'll be on our way to you."

"All right."

Beau Lee ended the call.

"What's going on?" Alvarez asked.

"Capes might have a lead on the whereabouts of whoever recorded Hollis's shooting. They're on their way to pick me up."

Before he could put the phone back in his pocket, it chimed loudly. Not the default chime either, but the one he specifically selected for Gigi. She had sent three text messages back-to-back. "Excuse me a second. I need to respond to this."

He stepped into the small lobby outside Alvarez's office and wrote:

Hey, my love. Everything all right?

Seconds later, she responded:

Just checking on you.

Even when communicating over radio waves on pocket devices, he could sense his wife's worry. He sent her a reassuring response that everything was fine and that they were making headway, to which she responded with a heart emoji. Subtle but enough—just knowing she was thinking about him and praying for him was always enough.

17

THE SURVEILLANCE ROOM AT GUNDERSON SECURITY WAS SMALL, CRAMPED, and hot. The three computer towers hummed while a large motherboard was plugged with colorful peripherals. The electronics emitted so much heat that two large fans were needed to keep the room at a bearable temperature, yet Capes felt a sticky band of sweat emerge under his shirt collar and found himself thinking fondly of the snapping cold that awaited him outside.

They sat watching Martin, the shift supervisor, scroll through surveillance footage while sipping from a cola can. He seemed unbothered by the heat and droning computers. It was his domain, and Capes wondered how many hours Martin had had to spend there before he became immune to discomfort.

They'd already seen footage of Hollis's arrival at work. Nothing appeared out of the ordinary as he parked his SUV and entered the office at 6:49 P.M., eleven minutes before the start of his shift. However, Capes was more interested in how Hollis ended his shift, specifically if he appeared exhausted or on the cusp of experiencing some type of medical emergency.

"He seems fine to me," Finn said, leaning over the desk of monitors. "I see no signs of distress or serious fatigue."

Martin toggled through more surveillance footage with his mouse, sliding along the video's timeline. "I didn't talk to Hollis much during his shift, but I greeted him on his way to the locker room," he said. "He was in a good mood, with a smile on his face, per usual. You could ask Joey if he noticed anything else. He was the last to talk to him."

"Joey?" Capes asked. "Joey who?"

"Joey Henderson," Martin said, pointing to Joey in the black-and-white footage. "His shift starts when Hollis's ends, so there's some overlap there, mostly because Joey's late. They usually spend a few minutes talking. I think Hollis has been a kind of mentor to him."

Cape's expression was somewhere between shock and surprise. "When was the last time you heard from Joey?"

"Not since his shift ended early this morning. He's got the next few days off," Martin said, spinning around in the office chair to face a befuddled Capes. "Why?"

"Martin, you've been a big help."

"We appreciate you allowing us to view the footage," Finn said. "I know it goes without saying, but it stays between us."

"Well, Hollis isn't just a good employee, he's a wonderful man. If I'm going to break Gunderson policy, it's going to be for a good cause, and I can't think of any better than helping Hollis."

Capes added, "We've got another favor to ask you."

"Shoot."

"Joey Henderson's address . . . Is there any way we can get that?"

Martin paused, scratching the white stubble along his jawline. "That's a big ask. I want to help, but I'm afraid divulging employee information is pushing it, gentlemen."

"Understood," Capes said. "How about I show you an address, and if it's Joey's, all you've got to do is nod?"

"I don't know . . ." Martin said as Capes wrote Joey's home address on the back of a business card. He slid the card across the desk. "Just a nod to confirm. That's all we need."

Martin studied the address for a moment, then nodded.

"Well, I'll be damned." Finn shook his head in disbelief. "In all my years, I can't say I've ever seen this kind of thing happen."

"We might've just caught the biggest break of our lives," Capes said.

"The thing is," Finn started, "if Joey was working here at the time of the traffic stop, there's no way he could've recorded what happened from his home."

"The girlfriend," Capes said. "She had to have been the one recording. Martin, do you mind pulling up the footage of Joey's vehicle entering the parking lot before his shift?"

Martin hovered the cursor over a thumbnail and clicked, expanding a video across the large monitor. Joey's Ram truck was parked next to Hollis's SUV.

"That's Hollis's vehicle," Finn said. "I wish they had a better angle of his license plate. I can't tell if its defaced or not."

"I can try to zoom in," Martin said, clicking until the image of the license plate consumed the screen. "Darn, too pixelated. I've been telling corporate we need better cameras."

"Even so, the plate looks fine to me," Capes said. "Makes you wonder why they couldn't see it."

Finn reached into his pocket and took out a small notepad and pen. He began writing down Joey's license plate, along with the color, make, and model of his truck.

"You gentlemen got what you need?" Martin asked, appearing skittish with all the legal talk.

Capes understood Martin's apprehension. Most people want to avoid being subpoenaed and having to testify in court, and while he had no intention of deposing Martin or calling him to the witness stand, he'd involved him far more than he intended, and it was time for them to leave.

"I'm glad to do the little I can for Hollis," Martin added, wheeling his chair away from the desk. "I know he would've done the same for me, but if it's all right with you, I need to get back to work."

"We understand. Don't mean to hold you up," Finn said, placing the notepad back into his coat pocket. "Again, we appreciate your help."

Martin stood and opened the door for Capes and Finn, who exited into the hallway. Martin led them to the front entrance and passed the breakroom, lockers, and equipment room.

"I'm really hoping Hollis pulls through," Martin said before showing them out. "Some of the employees are talking about holding a candlelight vigil for him at the hospital. You think that'd be all right?"

"I can speak for Hollis's family when I say that it would be a welcomed gesture," Finn said, turning up his coat's collar and stepping outside.

Martin smiled through his somber disposition. "You two take care," he said, closing the door.

The men began walking back to the Crown Vic as snow flurries melted against their faces. All morning, the sky had looked as if it were going to snow, and it was finally making good.

"I better start the search for Joey's vehicle," Finn said, digging in his pocket for the car keys.

"You sure you want to go down this road, Doyle?"

"What'dya mean?"

"Pretty sure if a police officer uses resources for reasons outside of an official investigation, it's a terminable offense."

"Let me worry about all that," Finn said, "and if this weather is any indication, traffic ought to keep Joey and his girlfriend in place for a while."

The snow was starting to come down heavier, collecting on Capes's shoulders and straight-brimmed Atlanta Falcons cap. Finn looked unaffected by the cold; clearly he was acclimated in a way Capes was not.

He considered Finn's suggestion.

"No point in worrying about that now. They're in a gas guzzler and I'm betting they've made at least two pit stops to fill up. If they're bogged down in the weather, we can catch up to them with the lights and sirens," Finn said, unlocking the car doors with his remote.

The men got in the car. Capes took off his hat and brushed off the snowflakes. He worked his brow and squeezed the skin at the bridge of his nose to relieve the pressure building in his head.

"Cold getting to you?" Finn asked. "I'd suggest a heavier coat."

"The cold and the fact I'm trying to figure out how exactly you intend to find Joey and his girlfriend."

"Since 9/11, Metra has shared a surveillance system with all the law enforcement agencies in Illinois. I'll search his license plate, and any camera that might've captured his truck going through a toll or entering the highway will give me the exact time and location. From there, I can pinpoint where he is and where he might be headed."

"Then what?"

"I play nice and get whatever local or state agency to detain them before they cross state lines."

"On what grounds?"

Finn looked at Capes with exasperation. "They're witnesses to Hollis's attempted murder. I'll be sure to let whatever agency tasked with detaining them know to hold the vehicle until we arrive. They won't be taken to the station or anything like that."

"You mean they won't be treated like criminals?"

Finn struggled to get his words out. "I mean, well . . . yeah, I guess that's what I'm saying."

Capes needled Finn with a look of his own. "Do you not see how reckless that is?" He raised his voice. Finn had struck a nerve. "They haven't done anything to justify being stopped, yet you want to put them in a shitty and dangerous situation. Have you not learned anything from what happened to Hollis?"

"What the hell do you mean by that?"

"Police encounters often don't end well for *us*. All it takes is a cop being on edge, feeling threatened or downright trigger-happy, and things can go from bad to worse real quick. You could be lighting the fuse on something you've got no control over."

"I told you I'd do whatever it takes to help Hollis."

"But not like this," Capes said. "We don't need any more police involvement and risk someone else getting hurt."

"Then what do you want to do? Wait until they cross state lines, make it into Pennsylvania, and then what? Search all of Philly for them?"

"If we have to, yes, but what we can't do is put innocent people in harm's way."

Capes had a complicated relationship with the law but hadn't lost faith in it, believing that if applied equally, it was just. He didn't know Doyle well enough to suggest he was corrupt or amoral, but maybe there were lines Doyle was willing to cross, which made Capes wonder how many times in his career he'd strayed from his sworn oath and duty. It didn't matter if his heart was in the right place and he was trying to do whatever he could for Hollis; there was no justification for violating someone's rights.

"Well, let's hope it doesn't come to us having to resort to anything that makes you uncomfortable," Finn said, shoving the key into the ignition and starting the car. "Just know that I respect where you're coming from, but Hollis is my partner. It's a bond most people don't understand, but know this, like I said before, we aren't all like those assholes who shot him. The majority of us wearing badges, working long shifts for shitty pay and more stress than you can imagine, are doing the best we can."

"Maybe that's true, but unfortunately for you, all it takes is cases like what happened to Hollis for people to lose faith. See, Doyle, Black folks aren't clairvoyant. We've got no way of knowing the intentions of the cops who stop us. We can do everything right during a police encounter and still end up shot or dead, all because we looked a cop in the eye, moved too fast, or said the wrong thing. That's our reality. We don't get the luxury of the benefit of the doubt. Cops judge us before running our plates or checking our driver's licenses. We're deemed high-risk the moment they see the color of our skin."

"Yeah, I get what you're saying, but police stats aren't made up. And sure, sometimes they cloud the way we do our jobs. Call it stereotyping or profiling, but that's *our* reality."

Capes knew how conversations like theirs could drag on and result in frustration and animosity. "It's nothing we'll solve sitting in this car," he said, watching the snow collect on the windshield. I respect your point of view, but for Hollis's sake, let's agree to disagree."

"All right," Finn said. "You mind if I ask you one more thing?"

"If you have to . . ."

"Do you think having a Black man in the White House is really going to change things?"

Capes didn't have a good answer; he wasn't sure he had an answer at all. "Do you?" he asked.

"I think it might," Finn said. He sounded hopeful, which surprised Capes. "It definitely can't hurt, but then again, he's just one man."

18

O'MALLEY'S WAS A DIVEY IRISH PUB LOCATED ON THE SOUTH SIDE FRE-quented by off-duty cops and White Sox fans. There was a custom-built wooden bar, gold tiled ceiling, and red padded stools. The bar's most appealing feature was a room near the kitchen typically reserved for private parties like retirements and birthdays. It was where Jack and Chaz held court entertaining bouncy twentysomethings they met on shifts. Chaz called them badge bunnies, but to Jack, they had the power to make him forget every ill thought, especially during those few hours with blow jobs in the bathroom stalls, which made Jack feel like he was sitting on top of the world. But instead of downing whiskey shots and tongue-kissing *betties,* he and Chaz had gathered in the mahogany room with Rory Caruthers and Leonard Johnson, the other officers present during Hollis's traffic stop. They, too, had been placed on administrative leave pending the investigation and worried suspension was next, and that their jobs were on the line.

"That fucking video," Rory said. "It's going to fuck us. I know it!"

"Keep your damn voice down," Jack said, sipping his beer. "The whole bar doesn't need to know."

"How is it you're so calm?" Rory got up from his seat and began to pace. "Did you even see it?"

"It's nothing to worry about."

"How the hell can you say that?"

"Whoever recorded it hasn't come forward, have they?"

"So what?"

"That should tell you something," Jack said. "It means they don't want to be involved, and unwilling witnesses are my favorite kind."

"Then who do you think recorded the video?" Leonard asked. He was a skinny man with a distinctive gap between his front teeth that looked like goalposts.

"It must've been filmed from a house across the street. I say we go and talk to the little wannabe moviemaker and come to an understanding."

"It's already out in the world," Chaz said. "And if whoever shot it was smart, they've skipped town."

"Or lawyered up," Jack said, taking another sip of his beer. "The image quality is shit, anyway. You can barely see our faces."

"Is that what has you so relaxed, Dunham?" Rory asked. "You think because there's no close-ups and that there's no fucking spotlight shining on us, that'll make a difference? It's clearly us."

"Even if that video becomes evidence, all it shows is us doing our jobs. The guy had a gun, remember? That's not in dispute. As long as we keep our stories straight, we won't have any problems."

"And what story is that?"

"Easy, Rory," Chaz said. "Take it down a notch."

"To hell with that. This guy's acting like he's got all the answers. IA's gonna meet with me tomorrow, and I want to hear from our fearless leader exactly what I'm supposed to say."

"It isn't rocket science, rookie. The guy didn't identify himself as a police officer," Jack said. "He pulled the gun and popped off a round. We were under threat and reacted as our training dictated. That's all that matters. That's what you'll tell them, smart-ass. You think you can handle that?"

"You want me to say I saw the guy pull his weapon and fire?" Rory asked. "Because you and I both know that didn't happen. All I heard was you call out that he had a gun, and we lit into the bastard like it was fucking target practice."

"You sound really stupid and reckless right now," Jack said. "What exactly did you write in your report?"

"We haven't submitted our reports," Leonard said. "Our captain told us to hold off. How about you two?"

"We submitted ours," Chaz said. "They're making their way up the chain."

"It sounds like we're all pretty much in limbo," Jack said. "But I swear, Rory, if you—"

"If I what? Write what I actually saw? Tell IA that the guy's hands were empty and I never saw him fire a shot? Maybe I should say how you snatched his wallet, too."

"What the fuck did you say, rookie?"

"Don't think I didn't notice," Rory said. "Where is it, Jack? Did you burn it?"

"I don't know what the hell you're talking about. The guy didn't have a wallet. No ID. No badge. Nothing, and you know that."

"Or maybe in the chaos you were able to get rid of the wallet," Rory said. "But you remember, don't you, Jack?"

Jack slammed his mug on the table, causing the ale to spill. "Get your fucking partner in line, Leonard, or I swear—"

"C'mon, Rory. Listen to Jack," Leonard said. "We stick this out together. Keep our cool, and everything will be fine."

"Maybe you should get your eyes checked, Rory." Chaz rolled up his sleeves, revealing tribal tattoos. Chaz thought they made him look like a hard-ass and that they would get him attention from women.

"You want to be a tough guy, is that it?" Rory stood his ground and began rolling up his own sleeves. Even though Chaz was bigger than he was, Rory had spent years in boxing gyms. He'd even had a few amateur bouts, and he playfully referred to himself as a *low-key knockout artist*, but on this day, he wasn't playing.

"Settle down, fellas," Leonard said. "Be smart about this. Let's not lose our cool. Jack, just tell everybody where the wallet is so it doesn't come back to bite us in the ass. The guy was a law enforcement officer. We know he had a wallet."

Rory said, "I saw you grab it, Jack. So what did you do with it?"

"I'm looking out for all of us. I put it back in the SUV so it matched our story that it wasn't on his person, you young fuck," Jack hissed, trying to keep his voice low.

"Like hell you did," Rory responded.

"Fuck this guy," Chaz said and swung at him.

Rory easily evaded Chaz's haymaker, dodging the punch and delivering an uppercut to his chin. Chaz fell back, slamming into the wall and jarring the table as he went.

"Shit!" Jack said. "You assholes made me spill my beer." The ale rolled across the table and dripped onto the floor. "Get up," he said, snatching Chaz by his collar and yanking him to his feet.

"Lucky fucking shot," Chaz said, palming his bruised chin.

"You clowns can do whatever you want," Rory said. "But you're on your own. Leave me out of it."

"What are you saying, Rory?" Leonard asked. "We're partners, remember?"

Rory snatched his biker jacket and motorcycle helmet from a chair. "Call your union rep, Leo. Otherwise, you'll be fucked like these guys."

"You're a goddamn fool," Chaz said. "This isn't the way it's supposed to be. We stick together. That's what *real* cops do."

Rory headed out of the room, then paused, looking back at his fellow officers with disgust. "Leo and I never should've responded to that call," he said. "You idiots were better off on your own. Now some cop's lying in a hospital fighting for his life, and our jobs are on the line, and for what?"

"You're going to fuck us, I know it," Jack said. "Do you want us to lose our pensions, our families, our livelihoods? Because that's what'll happen if you tell anybody anything different than what we put in those reports."

"Go to hell, Jack." Rory walked out, leaving his accomplices to wallow in worry.

"Can you believe that fucking guy?" Chaz was still rubbing his chin, leaning against the wall. "We can't let him just leave like that. What if he goes to IA?"

"He won't," Leonard said. "Let me talk to him. He's just a little on edge right now. It's understandable."

"You need to get him on board," Jack said, taking hold of Leonard's shoulder. "First responders make the scene, you know that. Whatever we say happened is what happened, until disproven, and if we're smart, that won't happen."

"Yeah, I got it, Jack. I said I'll talk to him." Leonard looked at his watch. "I need to go. My wife's making Stove Top tonight, and she doesn't like it when I'm late."

"Listen up, we don't talk about this case to anyone. Not our wives, girlfriends, or mothers, and be careful of reporters. They're sneaky devils." Jack was eyeing Leonard, intent that he understood every word. "Someone tries to strike up a conversation with you at the bagel shop or deli, keep your fucking mouth shut. Loose lips sink ships, got it?"

"Yeah, yeah. I gotta go." Leonard put on his bubble coat and White Sox hat and headed toward the exit.

"What do you think?" Chaz asked. "Can we trust them?"

"Would you trust a ten-dollar hooker?" Jack asked.

"I need a shot of bourbon. Maybe it'll stop my jaw from clicking."

"Give me a break . . ."

"What? The guy's got a solid uppercut."

"I'm leaving."

"Where to?"

"Don't worry about it. Just nurse your boo-boo. I'll call you tomorrow."

"Okay, Jack. Tomorrow, then."

19

JACK LOOKED UP FROM BETWEEN HEAVEN'S LEGS, GLANCED OVER HER navel, and appreciated the abundance of shiny curls that draped over her shoulders. She was a raven-haired beauty—a stone-cold stunner who seemed too pretty for life in blistery Chicago. Jack always thought she was more suited for Miami or Hollywood, but he was grateful all the same that she didn't live in either of those places.

"Jack, tell me, how was work?" she asked between sensual moans.

"It was okay," he said casually. "Humdrum, really."

"I didn't think that was possible."

"Trust me, baby, it was uneventful. . . . Plus, I'm kind of in the middle of something here."

Heaven forced his head up. "Since when don't you tell me how your day went?"

"I wish there were something worth telling, but I've got nothing."

Jack's cellphone rang. It was the phone he had exclusively for comms with Chaz. "Damn it. I'm sorry, darling," he said, reaching for the phone. "I've got to take this."

Heaven gave a frustrated sigh and buried her face in a pillow.

He answered: "What is it, Chaz?"

"Turn on the news," he said, sounding frantic. "Brass is holding another press conference. They must have something. You think Rory talked?"

"Fuck," Jack said, grabbing the remote, turning on the TV, and flipping channels.

"What is it, baby?" Heaven asked. "What's wrong?" She moved toward the end of the bed, where Jack stood naked on the phone.

He located the news broadcast and turned it up loud. Top brass—high-ranking members of the Chicago Police Department—stood addressing reporters and a large crowd. The police chief and mayor were behind a podium, while other officers in dress blues and topcoats fanned outward along the steps of City Hall.

"As most of you are aware, we have launched a formal investigation into the shooting of Hollis Montrose, an off-duty Metra police officer," the chief said. "The shooting involved four of our officers, all of whom are currently on administrative leave pending the investigation. As of now, no charges have been filed against Mr. Montrose; however, we believe they are imminent. I want to remind the public that investigations of this magnitude take time, and we continue to ask for patience. We now open it up for questions."

The chief acknowledged a reporter in the crowd and the camera panned to a Black woman in a green overcoat. "Carla Whitlock with WGN," she said.

"Yes, Ms. Whitlock."

"We're hearing reports that a gun was found at the scene, possibly belonging to Mr. Montrose, and that it may have been fired. Is that accurate?"

"There was a gun recovered at the scene, and it is believed to have been in Mr. Montrose's possession at the time of the traffic stop."

"Was the gun fired?"

"At this time, we cannot confirm if the gun was fired, but our forensics team will conduct all necessary tests and report those findings."

"What about body cams? Were the police officers wearing them at the time?"

"None of the officers were using body cameras."

"Do you think that if they had, you would have a clearer interpretation of the events from that night?"

"What are you implying?"

"That perhaps the body cameras would've illuminated the more obscured aspects of this case."

"I don't want to waste time with hypotheticals, Ms. Whitlock."

"I understand that sentiment, Chief," she said. "But do you intend to have all officers in the department use body cams in the foreseeable future?"

"Body cameras are a critical resource that help protect officers and the public and bring accountability. They are something we're looking into for all of our districts. So far, we have equipped three of our districts with body cameras as part of a pilot program and anticipate their use will be more widespread in the coming year."

"And one more question, Chief," Carla said, looking at her notes. "We've all seen the video circulating online and on some news outlets. The video appears to depict the traffic stop and subsequent shooting. Have you been able to determine the authenticity of the video and where it originated?"

"No."

"Is that something you're actively looking into?"

"Yes, of course. Where the video originated and what it shows are of utmost interest to our investigation."

"Do you care to elaborate?"

"Not at this time, Ms. Whitlock. But please know this: We are running a thorough investigation."

The crowd stirred. Multiple reporters raised their hands.

"Fuck," Jack said again, turning off the TV and tossing the remote aside. He sat at the edge of the bed with his left leg bouncing.

Heaven scooted behind him, wrapped her legs around his waist, and started rubbing his back. "What's all this about, Jack?"

"People hate us until they need us," he said. "And then want us punished when we do our jobs effectively, but no one's focused on the facts."

"You really think people hate cops?"

"Well, they sure as hell don't love us." Jack was beginning to sober up. He was never in his right mind when he drank, and he'd already said too much. "But never mind all that. Some things will never change . . . at least not in this city."

"Seems like a glib way of seeing your job. If it's so bad, then why do it?"

"I ask myself that every shift," he said. "Not sure I have a good answer."

Heaven looked at the clock. "It's getting late," she said. "I should get back to my place, still have some reading to finish."

The mood was dead. She got out of bed, put on her bra, and fastened it.

"You don't want to hang around a little longer?" he asked.

"I probably shouldn't."

"I need you to know something, and I need you to really listen."

Heaven slipped on her lace panties. "Okay."

"Are you listening?"

She paused and looked him in his eyes. "Yes, Jack, you have my undivided attention."

"Good, because I'm only going to say it once, and I don't care if you want to hear it or not because it's the truth."

"All right . . ."

"I can't get you off my mind," he said. "And I've worked over plenty of reasons why. You're beautiful, you're dynamite in bed, you never bore me, and if I'm being honest, I can't imagine my life without you."

"Look, Jack—"

"Let me finish . . . please?"

She nodded.

"What I'm trying to say is, I love you, Heaven. And it ain't about all the stuff we do in bed, either. It's beyond that for me. I see us on a beach somewhere or living in the countryside making a life for ourselves."

Heaven giggled. "You mean like on a ranch?"

He smiled at her. "I don't know. Maybe? I'm trying to say, I see us together and happy."

"That's really sweet, but I want to know you, Jack. The *real* you."

"You do know me."

She walked over to him and gave him a hug. "I know the little bit you've told me, which isn't much. But if this is love, we can't have any secrets."

Jack's thoughts were scattered. She smelled so good, and he leaned into her. Heaven weakened him and made him unable to see beyond what she wanted.

"Do you understand what I'm saying?" she asked. "I don't want us to hold anything back."

He encircled his arms around her waist. "Yes, I understand."

"I know you've got some things you keep from me, and I'm not saying you need to tell me all of it. I just need to feel like our connection is more than physical, that it's deeper."

He exhaled.

"Okay. There are some things I did . . . some things I let happen. And once I tell you, you'll either run, or you'll understand why I haven't slept through the night in years."

Then, just above a whisper: "You sure you want to know?"

She nodded once, steady.

"Then I'll tell you. But after this, nothing will be the same."

20

HIGHWAY TRAFFIC WAS NEAR A STANDSTILL AS THE CROWN VIC FOLLOWED behind a snowplow. Finn had turned off the lights and sirens, having estimated that using the emergency equipment helped them shave off nearly an hour of travel. Motorists had parted for them as Finn reached speeds of sixty and seventy miles an hour, careful to keep in the lanes that had been plowed and salted.

But once the snow piled to over a foot, he slowed down and took caution, as some vehicles had stalled on the shoulder. Beau Lee sat in the front passenger seat while Capes was in the back, much to his chagrin.

"How much longer?" Beau Lee asked while texting Gigi. "It's looking treacherous out here."

"GPS says ten minutes," Finn said, gassing the car enough to move a few inches before having to brake again. "You texting your wife?"

"How'd you know?"

"Men get a particular look when they text their wives. Have you been married long?"

"Happily for twenty years," Beau Lee said.

"Commendable."

"Can't take all the credit. I'm blessed to have found a good woman who doesn't mind putting up with a man like me."

"Man like you?"

"I'm away more than I'm home. Sometimes, when I'm home, I'm too tired to be much good around the house. And I snore."

Finn laughed. "We got that in common," he said. "I take it you married young?"

"By today's standards, it seems that way." Beau Lee sent the text to Gigi and slipped the phone back into his suit pocket. "We had our rough patches but always made it through."

"Same here," Finn said. "We haven't hit the twenty-year mark, but we've got eighteen years under our belts. There was a time when working put a real strain on things for us. It took me a while to find a good balance."

"What was it about the work that did it?" Beau Lee asked.

"Long hours, mostly, and I can't say I was the most attentive husband."

"How did you two get back on track?"

"Funny," Finn said, "I took Hollis's advice. He told me if I could spend twelve hours a day working, I could spare at least two hours for my wife. Two hours turned into three, then four, and I realized that time is currency. Maybe a case or two took longer for me to close, but what I got in return was a better relationship with my wife."

Capes piped up: "Sounds like Hollis gave you some game. Brother sounds wise."

"Far wiser than me," Finn said. "I've always looked up to him, you know? Like a big brother."

"Yeah, I get that." Capes looked out the window. "Man, look at this snow. Is this normally how much comes down this time of year?"

"Pretty much," Finn said. "You get used to it after a while."

"Nah, man, I don't think I'd ever get used to this."

The plow exited an off-ramp. Finn picked up speed, taking advantage of the freshly salted roadway. "Now we're talking," he said. "We should make up time."

Beau Lee could see a gas station sign in the distance, along with neon fast-food signs and what looked to be a billboard for an all-night diner located at a truck stop.

Finn accelerated, and the car felt as if it was losing traction.

"Easy," Beau Lee said. "Let's make it there in one piece."

"My bad, counselor."

As they neared the off-ramp, Finn turned on the car's emergency equipment, blue lights without sirens, and proceeded through intersections. They pulled into the diner's parking lot, parked, and quickly exited the vehicle. Finn took the lead as he canvassed the parking lot for the vehicle, boldly walking into the restaurant with his familiar scowl as Beau Lee and Capes stayed a few steps behind.

Beau Lee looked to a rear booth, where a young man and woman sat across from each other munching on a basket of onion rings and nuggets. He nudged Finn and pointed: "We should talk to them."

"I'm on it," Finn uttered, and they walked toward the hapless couple. "Excuse me," he said, showing his badge. "Mind if we sit?" He didn't wait for an answer and squeezed in beside the woman in the booth.

"What the hell are you doing, man?" The young man postured with his hands up. "I don't know you."

"Relax," Finn said. "We just want to have a conversation."

Beau Lee looked at the woman. "Room for two more?" he asked, removing his hat.

She looked at him for approval, then nodded.

"As my associate here said, we just want to talk," Beau Lee said, sliding into the booth and calmly placing his hands on the table. "We believe you can help us."

"Joey Henderson, right?" Capes asked, sitting at the end of the booth. "You kind of look like a Joey."

"How do you know my name?" Joey asked. "Who the hell are you guys?"

"You work with Hollis Montrose at Gunderson Security, right?"

"Who's asking?"

"We know you do," Finn said. "Just like we know you filmed that traffic stop and posted it online."

"Man, I don't know anything about that. How'd you find me, anyway?"

"All it took was a call to locate your license plate; surveillance has come a long way. Cameras are everywhere. Especially at tolls, and with the snow coming down like it was, it made sense for you to stop over for a bite until things cleared up."

"You FBI?"

"No," Finn said. "We aren't here in any law enforcement capacity."

"So, who are you, then?"

"Good Samaritans."

"Bullshit."

"You aren't in trouble, Joey," Beau Lee said. "We're hoping you could help us. Hollis Montrose is your friend, isn't he?"

"Yeah, Mr. Montrose is good to me."

"And you want to help him, don't you? That's why you uploaded the video."

"It's not illegal to post a video."

"We're not saying it is," Finn said. "We just need to know what you know."

"All I know is what's on that video. Nothing more than that."

"Look, we want to help Hollis, too. I'm his attorney, Beau Lee Cooper."

Beau Lee made introductions around the table, and when he got to Finn, Joey's eyes lit up.

"Hold up, you're Mr. Montrose's partner?" Joey asked, eyeing Finn like he was a celebrity. "He talks about you all the time."

"Does he now?"

"Yeah, but the way he talked about you, I just thought . . ."

"What?"

"He made you sound . . . you know, cool." Joey waffled. "I guess I just thought—"

"Thought what?"

"Uh, that you were a brother."

"A *brother?*"

"Yeah, man. I thought you were Black."

Finn's laugh was an unexpected bellow. "What, an Irish guy can't be cool?"

Joey smiled. "I guess you got some swagger. I saw the way you came in here, looking like you owned the place."

"Oh, you noticed that?"

"Made me think of that bald actor on *The Shield.*"

Finn looked at the perforated ceiling, picturing the bald white actor decked out in a black tee and matching leather jacket. The name was on the tip of his tongue—"Chiklis," he said. "Michael Chiklis."

Beau Lee's attention was on the woman sitting next to Joey, who looked to be suffering. "Miss, are you okay?"

"This is Darian, my girlfriend," Joey said. "She's got migraines. They tend to get worse when she's stressed."

"Is there anything we can do for you, Darian?" Beau Lee asked. "Something for the pain?"

She was bone tired, with bloodshot eyes. "No, sir. It'll pass."

"You sure?" Capes asked. "You're not looking too good."

"It's the lights. They tend to make things worse."

"We should probably go," Joey said.

Darian took hold of Joey's arm as she struggled to focus under the fluorescent lighting. "Not before you tell them," she said.

"Tell us what?" Finn asked.

Joey cast a quick, nervous glance at Darian, before looking over at Finn. He cleared his throat and shifted in his seat. "Something you guys should know," Joey said. "I didn't shoot the video. Darian did. All I did was upload it."

"Figured as much," Finn said. "Unless you were Superman, there was no way you would've gotten home from Gunderson in time to record Hollis's traffic stop."

"Darian, can you tell us anything else about that night?" Beau Lee asked. "Maybe something you heard the officers say when they stopped him?"

"I'm sorry," she said, massaging her temple. "I can't think straight when I'm like this."

"You don't need to apologize. You sure there's nothing we can get you?"

"She usually keeps her migraine medication handy, but she's all out," Joey said.

"Just aspirin every two hours," Darian said. "It's the only thing that's been working."

"I told her she needs something stronger," Joey said. "We tried getting to a drugstore, but the snow was coming down too hard. The only place we could stop was this diner."

"I think we can help you out," Finn said. "How about we go back to Chicago? We can get you set up someplace and see about getting Darian's medication."

"Why would you do all that?" Darian asked.

"I'll be straight with you. We need your statement about what you saw happen to Mr. Montrose."

"But what about the video . . . ?" Joey sounded bewildered. "The whole world can see what those cops did. Isn't that enough?"

Beau Lee spoke softly: "I'm afraid not," he said. "If we can depose you and get you on record, you might not have to testify in court."

"*Might* not?"

"I can't give you any assurance at this time, but I'll try my best to keep you off the stand."

"I know what happens to people who record the police," Darian said. "They get harassed by cops and end up in jail on bullshit charges."

"That's right," Joey added. "Cops don't forget shit. They'll hound us. That's why we're going to Philly, just until things cool down."

"I get it. Trust me, I do. But this isn't something you can outrun," Finn said. "We need you to think about Hollis—"

"Look, man, Hollis is my friend," Joey said loudly, drawing attention from other diners. "I want to help, but we don't need any more trouble."

Beau Lee recognized the fear in Joey's and Darian's eyes. He'd seen it in his mother's eyes the night she came face-to-face with a police officer. Joey was right. People who had filmed the police found themselves prosecuted for minor offenses, sometimes serving jail and prison time. If the harassment was really bad, they'd leave the city where they grew up—their homes—to escape being under the police's thumb.

"Can I ask you something, Darian?" Beau Lee angled himself in the booth to face her. He looked into her eyes and asked, "What made you record the traffic stop in the first place?"

Darian was quiet as she contemplated his question. She continued to knuckle her temples, then said, "I just felt like something was wrong."

"A feeling?"

"Yes, a feeling . . ." She looked as if she wanted to cry; the trauma was discernible. "I thought they were going to kill him. I was sure of it."

"Can't you just take the video to the FBI or something?" Joey asked. "They can tell if it's authentic, can't they? They've got machines and software for that. Tell them you talked to us. Hell, have them call us, and we'll tell them exactly what we're telling you now."

"That's not how this works," Beau Lee said. "It's a criminal matter. The cops involved could face charges that could potentially put them away for life."

"Good," Joey said, "they deserve it!"

"Yes, but we can't make that happen without your full cooperation."

"Look, you two, we're begging here," Finn said. "Hollis needs our help. We wouldn't be here if there were another way, but there isn't. Please come back to the city. We'll get you a place for the night. We can keep you two safe."

"We got your backs," Capes said. "No harm will come to either of you. I promise you that."

"How the hell are you going to promise something like that?" Joey said. "We're talking about Chicago PD here. We shouldn't need to be kept safe from them. They're supposed to be protecting us."

"You saw what they did to Mr. Montrose," Darian said. "They shouldn't be on the streets. Who knows, they might've already done this to someone else, or who's to say they won't do it again?"

"What are you saying, baby?" Joey asked with a furrowed brow. "You want to go back to the city with them? You want to go on record?"

"I do," she said. "It's the right thing, Joey. Those cops need to answer for what they did. Period."

Finn looked outside. The snow was starting to amass on the Crown Vic. "If we're going to go, we might want to roll now," he said. "Before they shut down the highway."

Darian groaned; she could hardly keep her eyes open. "This headache's getting worse," she said. "Joey's right. I need something stronger."

Beau Lee pulled out his phone and searched for the nearest drugstore. "There's a CVS two miles from here. Joey, do you think you could follow us?"

"Yeah, I can manage that," he said, taking one more bite of an onion ring. "Where are you going to put us up for the night? Because there's no way we can stay at my mom's house, and Darian's place ain't even a consideration."

"We have rooms booked at a hotel," Beau Lee said, getting up from the booth. "I can book you another."

"Yeah, no one will look for you there," Capes said, then whispered to Beau Lee, "what if they're all booked up, boss?"

"Then give up your room, and we'll bunk together in the double queens."

"Ah, man, but you snore too loud!"

"You'll survive."

Beau Lee reached his hand out for Darian to take, and he helped her to her feet.

"Hold on, I've got to pay the bill." Joey skimmed the bill, totaling $34.67. "Haven't seen our server. She probably went on break or something."

Beau Lee pulled two twenties and a five from his wallet and dropped it on the table. "That'll cover it," he said. "Let's go."

"Works for me," Joey said, last out of the booth.

They all walked past the counter. Capes escorted Joey and Darian outside. Beau Lee noticed that no one was at the register. A busser was busy collecting dishes. Beau Lee got the young man's attention and said, "Please let our waitress know we paid. The money's on the table. Tip included."

"Sure, okay, sir," the busser said. He showed little care as he continued to fill a bucket with dirty plates.

Finn looked at Beau Lee perplexed but said nothing. Beau Lee didn't expect him to understand, but he'd gone his entire life under a cloud of suspicion for no other reason than his skin color, and he didn't need anyone thinking they'd skipped out on the bill.

Outside, the group climbed into their vehicles and escaped the blowing snow. They started their engines; wiper blades batted snow from the windshields and exhaust poured from the tailpipes. Finn navigated the vehicle over the slick ice as he eased out of the parking lot. Joey gripped the wheel tightly as he followed closely behind.

The two-car caravan drove toward the CVS, which was located in a shopping center. Beau Lee prayed that neither vehicle would slip or get stuck in the mounting snow. They had a few hours' drive ahead of them. He dialed the hotel's front desk and requested an additional room for Joey and Darian.

"Yes, we have a room available," the front desk receptionist said. "However, it's only a queen. Would that be fine?"

"It'll have to do," he said. "Thank you."

"Not a problem, Mr. Cooper."

21

THE NEXT MORNING, BEAU LEE WOKE AROUND SIX AND GOT DRESSED. HE let Capes sleep in, knowing the long drive had taken a toll, and he needed him well rested. Beau Lee wished he could've slept in as well. He was sleep-deprived, having spent the early-morning hours preparing Joey's and Darian's affidavits for the lawsuit.

He took a taxi to the hospital and arrived shortly after eight. A modest protest for Hollis had amassed on the green mound in front of the hospital where people held signs demanding justice. Doubt about the validity of the shooting was starting to permeate the city. The opinion that the police had shot an innocent man was growing.

Greatly in need of coffee, Beau Lee stood in line at the kiosk in the hospital's lobby. The barista was serving fancy caffeinated drinks and pastries. He took out his phone and dialed Gigi.

"Good morning, my love," he said. "How are you?"

"Good morning yourself. How's my husband faring in Chi-Town?"

"Well, I believe it's around twenty degrees right now, but I'm coping. My body might not be equipped for this level of cold. The Texas in me is struggling, but I'm fixing to get myself a hot drink, so that should warm me up."

"Lord have mercy, that is cold. But, you know, I wasn't only asking about the weather. How are things going with the case?"

"Pulled another all-nighter," he said, muffling a yawn. "Managed to find and depose the witnesses to Hollis's shooting. I believe I've got what I need to file the lawsuit."

"That's good, baby!"

"I'm planning to get it filed by the end of business today. That should get the city's attention."

"I guess that's how you let your presence be known, isn't it?"

"You know me. I tend to make grand entrances."

"Next!" the barista called, already irritated and looking at Beau Lee. "Sir."

"Gotta go. My turn to order. Talk soon, okay?"

"All right," she said. "I love you."

"Love you, too."

Beau Lee ended the call and stepped forward to order.

"What'll you have?" the barista asked, head cocked and eyes rolling. "Just so you know, specialty drinks will take some time, but you can wait over there." She pointed to three customers waiting off to the side, heads down, on their cellphones.

"Drip coffee's fine."

"It's a medium roast. We're out of light roast."

"That'll do."

"Anything else?"

Beau Lee searched the pastry case and his eyes landed on a cheese Danish. After the long night he'd had, he needed a pick-me-up. "Is that a cheese Danish?" he asked, pointing at the long braided pastry with custard-like filling.

"Uh-huh."

"I'll take one."

"Warmed up?"

"Sure."

"It'll be a wait."

"How long?"

"It will take a minute!"

"On second thought, I'm sure it's delicious as it is."

The barista grabbed the pastry with tongs and slid it into a bag. She poured the coffee into a large paper cup, pressed a lid on top, and dropped it into a cardboard sleeve.

She handed him his breakfast without a thank-you and called the next customer in line.

Beau Lee was accustomed to a certain level of geniality that was customary in down-home Texas, but he was learning that was not the case in Chicago.

Beau Lee took the elevator up to the trauma unit and stepped into the lobby, where he was greeted by Rocky and Finn, who also had a coffee and looked far from rested.

"Good morning," Rocky said. "I hear yesterday was eventful."

"Good morning to you both," Beau Lee said. "And yes, it was."

"Well, our family is eternally grateful for all you're doing." Rocky hugged Beau Lee, mindful not to jostle his coffee.

"It's a team effort."

"How'd you sleep?" Finn asked.

"I shut my eyes for a few hours. Not sure I'd call that sleep, though."

"I take it our two witnesses are cooperating?"

"Got them on record. No issues there."

"They seem like good kids," Finn said.

"I still can't get over all this unfolding right outside Joey Henderson's house," Rocky said. "It's like divine intervention."

"Divine intervention?" Finn asked.

"Sure," Rocky said. "I'd like to think it was more than a coincidence."

Finn held a beat, then took on a serious glare.

As the elevator doors opened, Beau Lee tracked Finn's eyes and Finn glared as a man stepped out. He wore a baseball cap and hoodie under his biker jacket. His motorcycle helmet was in his left hand.

Finn's reaction to the man put Beau Lee on high alert.

"You seeing this, Counselor?" Finn asked.

"I am."

The man had a confident walk but also seemed out of place, as if he'd never visited the trauma floor before, and he was making a beeline toward them.

"What is it?" Rocky asked, noticing Beau Lee's change in demeanor. "Something wrong?"

"That man coming toward us, have you ever seen him before?"

Rocky stared hard. "No. I don't recognize him. Do you, Finn?"

"Never seen him before."

Beau Lee made sure his hands were free, and he stepped in front of Rocky. Maybe he'd been a fool not to wake Capes up and have him accompany him. At least, that's what Capes would say, respectfully, of course. Still, Finn was armed and eagle-eyed, having been first to spot the potential danger.

If the man was crazed, it wouldn't be the first time Beau Lee had encountered such an individual. Police-involved shootings had a way of drawing in avid law enforcement supporters with deep ties to right-wing organizations and hate groups. Beau Lee had had run-ins with many of them over the years, especially when trying cases in Texas, Florida, and Alabama. Since the launch of Obama's campaign, he'd noticed a rise in more brazen activity outside courthouses, such as buckets of red paint meant to resemble blood being tossed from moving vehicles onto courthouse steps. Someone entering a hospital with intent to cause harm was at the forefront of his mind.

"Identify yourself," Finn said, his hand near his service weapon. "Don't come any closer!"

The man stopped and looked at Beau Lee and Rocky. "Are you the Montrose family?" he asked.

Finn repeated his command: "I said identify yourself."

"Okay, okay. Take it easy. I'm a cop."

"And . . . ?"

"Name's Rory Caruthers," the man said. "Can we talk?"

22

THE FAMILY MEETING ROOMS ON THE TRAUMA FLOOR WERE ALL OCCUPIED, so Beau Lee found a small empty chapel. Rocky went to sit with Hollis while Beau Lee and Finn listened to Rory Caruthers for fifteen minutes as he recounted the night Hollis was shot. It was difficult for them to hear the details, particularly as Rory described Hollis's cries and pleas for the officers to release him.

"We were only providing backup," Rory said, reiterating his role in the shooting. "Johnson and I didn't have the full picture. Only what was broadcasted over the radio. It seemed like a routine call. Nothing out of the ordinary—but nothing about it was routine."

"Why didn't you go to your superiors with this?" Finn asked.

"I'm a rookie. It would've been my word against two officers—one a veteran, and the other with far more arrests under his belt than me. Who do you think the department would believe? They've already got their minds made up about this case."

"What do you mean?"

"It's only rumored, but when some of the guys heard about Hollis, they celebrated," Rory said. "I don't know much about his time with the CPD, but he must've made plenty of enemies."

"The lawsuit . . ." Finn said. "Those guys are still salty about that."

"Rory, are you saying Hollis might've been targeted because he complained to IA and tried to sue CPD?" Beau Lee asked.

"All I'm saying is, a good number of people in the department aren't shedding tears over it."

"Is there any chance the first officers on the scene, Dunham and Rossi, knew the vehicle belonged to Hollis?"

"Hard to say, but from what I could tell, it looked random."

"Tell me about the wallet," Beau Lee said. "You suggested Dunham removed it before the ambulance and field supervisors arrived?"

"That's right. Dunham had told us to start securing the scene, and as I was walking away, I think I saw him take it off Hollis."

Finn looked like he wanted to slug Rory. Beau Lee could sense it and knew that if Finn's temper got the better of him, they could lose a critical witness. "I know it's hard coming forward like this," Beau Lee said. "It takes courage."

"Courage my ass," Finn said, glaring at Rory. "You were there at the scene. Why didn't you stop it?"

"Everything happened so fast. I was trusting my partner," Rory said.

Finn scoffed. "Trusting him to go along with the cover-up."

"Look, man, I have two years on the job. It was the first time I'd ever pulled my firearm with intent to use it, but had I known what we were stumbling into—"

"Let's stay on topic, Officer Caruthers," Beau Lee said. "All I want to know is if you're willing to go on record."

"It'll be the end of my career."

"A guy like you, I'm sure you'd land on your feet," Finn said.

"I've given up so much to wear this badge."

"There are other agencies you can work for," Finn said. "Plenty of departments need good, honest cops. If you think you still are after all this—"

"Let's keep Hollis in mind here," Beau Lee said. "Caruthers, you could do some good in helping us get justice for Hollis."

"I want to help. You have to know, this isn't what I set out to become," Rory said. "My parents warned me about joining the CPD. They told me I didn't know what I was getting myself into. They wanted me to get my MBA. Can you believe that? Go into finance and take over the family business one day."

"Doesn't sound too bad, kid," Finn said. "I know cops who didn't have a pot to piss in before the department."

"You don't understand. It's never been about a paycheck for me."

"Take it from me. This job takes more than it gives. So if it's not the paycheck, what the hell is it?"

"I know it sounds cliché, but I wanted to help people. Before I applied for CPD, I thought I was going to be a firefighter, but I washed out of training."

"What happened?" Beau Lee asked.

"Couldn't handle the damn ladder," Rory said. "Weak shoulders. So I hit the gym, took up boxing, and joined the CPD. For a while, it was great, but lately—"

"Enough," Finn said, tired of Rory's sob story.

Rory glanced at Finn and continued: "The job's still great, but it's filled with too many of the wrong kind of people."

"We need to determine the logical move," Beau Lee said. "We can go into the prosecutors' office. You can tell them exactly what you told us—"

"What if they don't believe me?" Rory asked.

Beau Lee rubbed his chin as he pondered. It was a rookie's word against seasoned veterans. Not ideal. In a trial, it would come down to Rory's credibility. Would a jury believe him? A guy with a couple of years of experience versus three hard-nosed veteran street cops? Then Beau Lee remembered: "Hollis's wallet," he said. "It was missing from the scene. Any chance it may be in Jack's possession?"

"Jack says he planted the wallet back in the vehicle," Rory said.

"Are you sure about that?"

"Yeah, that was the last thing he said during our argument before his partner took a swing at me."

"I've known men like Jack," Finn said. "Psychos with badges.

They get off on the power dynamics. Hurting people and getting away with it. I'd say there's an eighty percent chance Jack has Hollis's wallet."

"Peculiar question, friend?" Beau Lee asked.

"Because he'd be proud of it. Imagine the ego trip he'd be on if he shot a Black cop and got away with it. He'd want to keep a memento, something to remind himself of what he did."

"And be stupid enough to keep evidence around?"

Finn and Rory looked at each other and nodded. Not since they'd met had they felt as though they shared common ground, until now. They both knew Jack's type: arrogant and sloppy.

"Jack thinks he's sharper than everyone else, but he's far from it. I bet he's gotten away with doing this kind of shit for so long. I can tell he's comfortable," Rory said.

"A guy like Dunham is more criminal than a cop," Finn said.

"Then I'm afraid that's what we're dealing with," Beau Lee said. "A criminal with a badge. But we have to dot every i. Finn, we need you and Capes to go to the impound lot and see if the wallet's in the SUV."

"Not sure how we'll pull this off, but we'll figure it out," Finn responded.

"I get the sense that Jack's arrogance is his weakness," Rory added. "But there's more you should know."

"Okay," Beau Lee said.

"Jack said the ballistics report will show that Hollis fired his gun, but I know now that he didn't. I couldn't find any casings at the scene from his weapon the night of the incident."

"Does he have an in with ballistics?"

"I'm not sure. All I know is that I fucked up. The adrenaline was pumping, and I was trusting my partner. I saw Hollis's hand move, so I shot my gun, too. But that video made it clear to me—Hollis never had that gun in his hand. He may have been reaching for it, but he never got a hand on it."

"You're *sure*?"

"Yeah."

"So the ballistics report is bullshit," said Beau Lee. "Will you testify that Hollis didn't fire?"

"Yes," declared Rory.

"That's fodder for our case, but we'll need more," Beau Lee said, nodding with confidence.

"I'm going to try to help, but I can't go to prison. I have a family."

Beau Lee tried to be sympathetic, but remorse doesn't undo what was done, and justice must be served. "You'll need to work out a deal with the prosecutor. Immunity in exchange for cooperating against your fellow officers," Beau Lee said. "That's your best way to stay out of prison."

"It's time to lawyer up," Finn said. "I hope you've squirreled away a small fortune, 'cause you're going to need it."

Beau Lee rolled his eyes, annoyed by Finn's flippancy. "I know some good attorneys in the area who are well-versed in handling predicaments like yours. You may want to start putting things in place now."

Rory rubbed the nape of his neck. "My God, could things get any worse?"

Finn sneered. "You could be lying in a hospital bed with multiple gunshot wounds."

"Right . . . sorry," Rory said. "Didn't mean for it to come off that way."

"We just need you to keep getting information from Dunham and Rossi," Beau Lee said. "We don't have any time to waste."

"I can try."

"Once we confirm whether the wallet's in Hollis's SUV, we'll notify you immediately."

Rocky entered the chapel unable to contain her excitement. "Sorry to interrupt," she said, "but it's Hollis. His eyes are open. He's awake!"

"What?" Beau Lee asked.

"He's conscious, Mr. Cooper. It's a miracle!"

"Thank God he pulled through," Beau Lee said.

"The nurses are still checking his vitals, but they said he's alert and responsive." Rocky looked at Rory. "I'm sorry. I didn't catch your name earlier."

Beau Lee feared that telling the truth about Rory would send Rocky into a tailspin.

"Just an officer from my division," Finn said, the lie rolling off his tongue—he clearly sensed the same thing. "He came by to check on things."

"Oh, really? That's so sweet of you," Rocky said to Rory. "I'm glad someone else from Metra decided to show up. Hollis has been an exemplary officer, and more officers should remember that." She headed toward the door, then looked back as the men stood, unmoving. "Well, what are you waiting for? Let's go see him!"

"We'll be there in a second, Rocky," Finn said. "We're just finishing something up."

"Okay," she said, "but don't wait too long. I know he'll want to see your faces." She quickly walked out.

"He's alive," Rory said. "I mean, that's great—that's great news!"

"It took everything in me not to tell her you were one of the assholes that shot him," Finn said. "Rocky is a good woman who loves her husband dearly, and you nearly took that away from her."

"It's time for you to go, Rory," Beau Lee said. "Get us the information we need, and maybe we can help you."

Rory tucked his head. "Understood. I'll get you what you need. But please know: I really am sorry," he said before leaving the chapel.

"Can you believe that damn kid?" Finn asked. "The nerve of him showing up here."

"He's trying to help."

"Please, he's trying to save his own ass, that's what."

"Forgiveness is hard," Beau Lee said. "But worth it in the end."

Finn looked at the large cross on the wall. "I'm Catholic. We know all about forgiveness, but I don't think I've got it in me."

"I know where you're coming from. You'll get no judgment from me, but I've seen what hate and anger can do to a person. I promise you that the cost is too high."

"I'm envious you can turn the other cheek. Maybe I'll see things differently one day, but today ain't it."

"I have faith that that may change in time." Beau Lee pulled out his phone and dialed Capes.

"Rise and shine, Capes. There's been some developments. Meet me at the courthouse. We need to get the lawsuit filed as soon as possible."

23

BEAU LEE FILED THE FIFTY-MILLION-DOLLAR LAWSUIT AT ELEVEN A.M. AND managed to organize the press conference by one.

He held the conference on the steps of City Hall, where he stood with Attorney Alvarez, Capes, Brother Harpo, Rocky, and Jamillah and her husband, Tyrone. The wind and bits of snow barely smaller than rice grains pricked their faces, but Beau Lee saw it as a minor annoyance. His mind was on the task at hand.

Capes scanned the crowd for any potential dangers. Beau Lee was sure he'd made the right call allowing Capes to sleep in. The additional rest had made him sharper. He'd even gotten to a department store to purchase a cable-knit turtleneck sweater, slacks, and a proper coat—charcoal-gray wool, thermal lined, and quarter length.

Capes knew that if he showed up to a press conference in his hoodie and motorcycle jacket, not only would he freeze, but his attire could also delegitimize Beau Lee's agenda. Capes was an easygoing man, and he liked to conduct himself freely, but he owed his life to Beau Lee, who understood his history, saw who he was as a person, and helped him up when he fell down hard. Beau Lee always stressed the importance of "looking the part," so Capes would follow his lead. Black people, no matter the number of degrees and accolades, carried a stigma. A bigoted belief was that their success was not earned.

Rather, it was due to affirmative action and government handouts. Beau Lee aimed to counter that narrative, and Capes was proud to work for him.

Six news vans had arrived, and the crews were preparing to broadcast to millions of viewers across the world. Now, the world would finally hear the truth.

Beau Lee stood behind a podium. The news crews mounted their video cameras on tripods and jockeyed for the best angles.

It wasn't long before bystanders joined, and the crowd grew larger, chanting, "Justice for Hollis!" and "End police terror!" Beau Lee welcomed Hollis's supporters and protesters. They were acting on their First Amendment rights—it was democracy in action. People had to feel it in their guts, in their spirits, that the CPD's accounting of events was deceptive, and the more questions people asked, the more everyone would see the truth: that the CPD cops had lied and the police department was complicit in trying to conceal those lies.

He tapped the microphone, ensuring it was on, and began to speak. "My name is Beau Lee Cooper, and I am here today to announce that I, and the lawyers at our firm, along with our co-counsel Attorney Princess Alvarez, have been retained to represent Hollis Montrose and his family. Mr. Hollis Montrose, an off-duty Metra police officer, who, as you undoubtedly now have seen from the video uploaded on YouTube, was shot ten times by four Chicago police officers during a traffic stop. If the video didn't do enough to dispel allegations that this was a justified shooting, we're here to set the record straight." Beau Lee adjusted his hat as the frigid air coiled around his neck and ears. He cleared his throat and continued: "Hollis Montrose was a victim of racial profiling, and when those officers realized they had stopped one of their own, they didn't address their errors. Instead, they sought to silence Officer Montrose for good with ten bullets in his back, even though he was lying prostrate on the ground."

A reporter quickly interjected: "Mr. Cooper, what proof do you have that the traffic stop was motivated by race or that Mr. Montrose identified himself as a police officer?"

"These officers have already shown their lack of integrity. We've all seen the video, and the police report that I have right here illustrates their deception." Beau Lee reached into his coat pocket, pulled out Dunham's police report, and waved it for the crowd. "This report says that Officer Montrose's license plate was defaced, which, along with not signaling a lane change, was the reason for the traffic stop. However, I urge you to watch the video closely and tell me, do you see anywhere in that video where the license plate is not legible?"

The crowd roared, nearly drowning out the reporter. Was it anger? Disbelief? The opening of old wounds? Beau Lee was speaking to people's mistrust of a police department with a sordid and unscrupulous past. The department had done little to make the Chicagoans forget about its history of corruption. Misdeeds that were still fresh in people's minds, like the Summerdale District robberies that saw cops joining with known criminal Richard Morrison to rob businesses. Or the Midnight Crew, a group of cops who'd tortured innocent people, mostly Black men, into false confessions for thirty years before facing an investigation that brought their terror to an end.

"So I ask you, why, in a field like law enforcement, where Black people are scrutinized, harassed, ridiculed, and bullied far more than any other group, would Hollis Montrose undergo such abuse, emerge an exemplary officer, and serve his community to the fullest for decades, only to suddenly become maniacal and attack four policemen during a traffic stop? It lacks all logic and reason, and the Chicago Police Department and the City must know that we will not accept any attempt at a cover-up. What happened to Officer Hollis Montrose was an attempted murder of a good man!"

People resumed chanting: "Justice for Hollis! Free Hollis!"

The camera lights flashed, and reporters' hands reached high.

Beau Lee took Rocky and Jamillah by the hands and drew them closer. It's never easy for family members to face the cameras and reporters in the wake of a tragedy. Having to listen to what happened to Hollis was like reliving the night they learned he'd been shot. And while Beau Lee was not a fan of the theatrics, he understood that in his line of work, it took more than facts to shake people out of apathy—it took the delivery of a fire-and-brimstone preacher convinced that doomsday was near.

"Attorney Cooper!" a hefty reporter wearing a bubble vest with his news station insignia and galoshes shouted from the front. "There's been speculation that Hollis Montrose might've been targeted."

"If people are speculating, it's for good reason."

"Our understanding is that Officer Montrose has an ongoing lawsuit against the Chicago Police Department over harassment and discrimination. Is that true?"

Beau Lee remarked, "I think it would be best if my co-counsel Attorney Alvarez responds to that question."

Alvarez stepped forward and took a deep breath and then began to speak. "It's true that Officer Montrose is pursuing civil action against the CPD due to discriminatory treatment he received on the job as a hardworking African American police officer. Therefore, I can report that we're looking into all possible motives for the traffic stop and subsequent shooting," Alvarez concluded as she retreated and Beau Lee stepped back up.

A female reporter standing by the camera in the middle of the growing number of press yelled, "Attorney Cooper, do you think that with the release of the video the DA should charge the officers with attempted murder?"

"My legal team, along with Hollis Montrose's family, join people across Chicago, and all across America, in demanding that they charge these police officers for this unjustified shooting of Hollis Montrose. However, we know based on the history of fighting for justice in America, we cannot predict whether the district attorney will bring charges against these officers for the shooting of a Black man. But what we do know is what actions we can take, based on the Seventh Amendment of the United States Constitution, to get justice for Hollis Montrose. That is why today, we announce that we have filed a fifty-million-dollar lawsuit against the City of Chicago and its police department for this unjustified, unconstitutional, and unnecessary use of deadly force that has left Hollis Montrose cuffed to a hospital bed facing the possibility of paralysis."

Beau Lee looked at Mrs. Montrose and Alvarez, and then turned back to face the cameras. "Thank you. We will keep you updated as we continue to fight for justice. If you'd excuse us, Mrs. Montrose would like to return to the hospital to see her husband."

Beau Lee, Capes, and Brother Harpo escorted Rocky, Jamillah, and Tyrone from behind the podium to where a professional driver waited in an SUV. It wasn't safe for them to be seen getting into their personal vehicles. What Hollis had been accused of had inspired plenty of people to protest—and the ones who sided with the police wouldn't think twice before causing the Montrose family more harm. The men walked alongside Jamillah and Rocky, blocking aggressive reporters intent on asking more questions.

"How'd they know about the lawsuit?" Rocky asked Beau Lee.

"The CPD complaint and lawsuit are public record. They're attainable under the Freedom of Information Act. All it means is the reporters are doing their homework, which is encouraging. The more information we have out there about Hollis and the circumstances leading up to the shooting, the better."

He opened the rear door of the Expedition, ushered Rocky inside, and then helped Jamillah in. Before he shut the door, Rocky asked, "Are you coming by the hospital?"

"Right after I wrap up here."

"Good," she said. "Since Hollis is awake, he's starting to get his wits back. He'll be his old self in no time."

"I believe he will, Mrs. Montrose . . ."

"Call me Rocky," she said. "We're family now."

Beau Lee smiled. "All right," he said, then shut the door.

The SUV pulled away, and news crews clambered to snap more photos.

24

LATER THAT EVENING, BEAU LEE ARRIVED AT THE HOSPITAL. WHEN HE entered the waiting room, Rocky, Jamillah, and the other members of the Montrose family were gathered in front of the TV, which was airing a news broadcast. On the screen, a dark-haired white man in a gray suit, red-striped tie, and overcoat stood behind a podium next to a petite Black woman dressed in a beige overcoat. He introduced himself as Illinois State Attorney Peter DaSilva and the woman as Assistant District Attorney Miranda Dillard. He wasted no time reading the felony charges against Hollis.

> Four counts of brandishing a firearm.
> Four counts of aggravated battery with a firearm.
> Four counts of battery on a police officer.
> Four counts of attempted first-degree murder of a police officer.

It was what Beau Lee had expected, and it was made all the more terrible by the presence of two uniformed CPD cops stationed like sentries near the nurses' station. He knew there'd be other officers outside Hollis's hospital room now that formal charges had been filed, and despite Hollis's condition, they had surely shackled him to the hospital bed, which was police procedure.

Rocky shouted at the TV. "My God, they're really going for it! They're trying to turn my husband into a criminal. He didn't do this!"

Damn, Beau Lee thought. Before the clerk could even assign their civil rights excessive force lawsuit to the judge, DaSilva had filed the criminal charges. The prosecutors weren't wasting any time. But, neither was Beau Lee. The city had to be held responsible for the violent, near-deadly arrest of Hollis Montrose.

Next would come Hollis's bail hearing, and based on DaSilva's harsh language, Beau Lee feared it could be a fight to get Hollis a reasonable bail amount. Still, a more hopeful part of him believed that once his lawsuit was filed, a judge with enough reverence for the law would throw out the case altogether, citing the inaccuracies of the arresting officers' report and Darian's video. Yet, a judge who was impartial and didn't hold a favorable view of law enforcement would be a dream scenario, and Beau Lee had no time for dreaming.

Time was against him and his team. DaSilva and Dillard had a coalition that included the Chicago Police Department and the Fraternal Order of Police, a powerful union. Together, they had perpetuated a damaging narrative: that Hollis Montrose wasn't the police officer people thought he was. He was troubled and rageful, and during a traffic stop, he took that rage out on four unsuspecting police officers. It was a weak motive at best, but one that could be easily sold. There didn't need to be an explanation for Black violence, because enough people had been spoon-fed the idea that Black people had a propensity to cause harm and had attitudes and a disdain for authority. They were aggressive and showed no respect for legality. And as part of Hollis's demonization, they said he thought he was above the law.

The lies of four cops were far more powerful than the truth of any Black voice. The arresting officers said Hollis attacked them with his weapon, and their account of the incident would be presented as infallible, considering none of the officers were shot. It would be up to Beau Lee to prove otherwise. It had been years since he'd practiced as a criminal defense attorney, but he knew he and Alvarez stood as good a chance as any legal team if they could work effectively together.

Beau Lee hadn't noticed Finn standing with Rocky amid the many family members.

"Counselor," Finn said, making eye contact with Beau Lee. "Can you believe these charges?"

Beau Lee approached him. "It's an expected chess move," he said. "Our lawsuit put pressure on them."

"Mr. Cooper," Rocky said, standing with Jamillah. "This is awful. It's like we're living some kinda nightmare."

Jamillah rubbed her mother's shoulders. "It's going to be okay, Mama."

"It's nuts, is what it is," Finn said. "From what I hear, the CPD's roundtable only took thirty-five minutes to determine Hollis's charges. Prosecutors are out for blood."

"What about Joey Henderson and his girlfriend?" Rocky asked. "Are they willing to take the stand? They're the best chance we've got."

"They might be persuaded," Beau Lee said. "In the meantime, we'll need to craft a defense that's consistent with our lawsuit."

"It's time to play hardball," Finn said. "Dig into these cops' backgrounds."

"Capes can assist you," Beau Lee said. "I'll subpoena the officers' employee records, and then you two can start talking to people who know them."

"Might be tough, but I'll see if anyone close to them will talk. Ex-girlfriends or disgruntled wives, past partners willing to go on record about their conduct. There has to be someone who'd testify to the fact they hated—"

"Hated what?" Rocky asked, looking thrown by Finn's assertion.

Finn considered what he was going to say. "It could've been over one thing, and I think we all know what it is."

"What Finn's trying to say, Rocky, is that Hollis might've been racially profiled," Beau Lee said. "Meaning, there was no reason for them to pull him over in the first place. If we can prove the officers lied and the entire traffic stop was because they saw a Black man driving at night, we might be able to get the charges against him dismissed."

"Sounds like a long shot, but if you get a sympathetic judge, it could work," Finn said.

"Not sympathetic," Rocky said. "Just someone who's honest."

"Finn's right, it is a long shot," Beau Lee said. "But we'd be foolish not to try. I'll need to get an audience with the prosecutors. If they know their case hinges on the testimony of questionable cops with poor credibility, they could consider dropping this entire matter rather than risking losing at trial."

"Fair warning, DaSilva and Dillard are real ballbusters." And then, embarrassed by his crudeness, Finn covered his mouth. "Sorry, Rocky . . . Sometimes I forget I'm not joshing in the precinct."

"It's fine, Finn."

"I already left my information with the prosecutors," Beau Lee said. "I expect to hear something from DaSilva and Dillard soon. In a case like this, there's no way to know how receptive they may be to speaking to the defense."

"Why's that?" Rocky asked.

"If they're anything like the prosecutors I've encountered over the years, they'll want to go to trial if they think their case is strong. A case like the one against Hollis turns people into household names, gives 'em careers."

"And the video? What about that?" Jamillah asked. "People all over the world have seen what happened to Daddy."

"Prosecutors will absolutely try to discredit it. The fact that we can't see their faces or much of Hollis after the additional officers arrive won't help our cause."

Finn's cellphone rang. He pulled it from his pocket, glanced at the caller ID, and silenced it.

"Everything all right?" Beau Lee asked.

"It's Metra," Finn said. "I've been ducking the calls since yesterday."

"What's going on?" Rocky asked.

"I think they want to discuss Hollis's situation. Maybe assign me a new partner."

Rocky demurred. "They don't waste any time, do they?"

"It's the nature of the job, Rocky. I'm not proud of it."

"You sure you're up to go back to work?" Beau Lee asked. "Especially since we're in the middle of this mess?"

"Two sick days is usually my max."

"Beau Lee's right," Rocky said. "Maybe you should take some time off."

"Doing that would be like admitting something's wrong. I need to show my face and let brass and every officer in that precinct know that nothing's changed. Hollis is a good cop. I stand by him, and he will be vindicated."

Rocky embraced Finn. For a moment, it looked as if he was on the verge of breaking down. Beau Lee wondered if he'd given himself any time to grieve, to process what had happened to his friend and partner.

"Maybe some distance from this is good for you," Beau Lee said. "You've already put your neck out locating Joey and Darian."

"Yes, we appreciate you helping us, but you've got a family, too," Rocky said.

"My family knows where I stand on this. They have my back," Finn said. "They love their Uncle Hollis, and I know he'd do the same for me if the situation were reversed. It's why I can't let up. Not for a second."

Rocky stepped away from Finn, allowing him to collect himself. He pulled a handkerchief from his pocket and dabbed his eyes.

"Yes, Finn, but Hollis wouldn't want you ending up in the unemployment line," she said lightheartedly, the way Hollis would if he had been there to joke with them. "We're going to be okay," she added. "God is with us. He's on our side."

"I sure hope that's true," Finn said. "I've never been much for praying, but I've prayed hard for Hollis—harder than I thought I could, pleading with God to bring him through this."

"And did God answer?" Rocky asked.

"Yes, but He's not finished yet."

Rocky took Finn's hand. "Keep trying," she said. "He speaks softly, so listen hardest in the quietest moments."

"Yes, ma'am."

"Ooh," Jamillah said, rubbing her belly. "This baby's been kicking all day."

"How about we go find you a nice place to rest," Rocky said. "Somewhere you could put your feet up."

"Okay, Mama."

The two women left Beau Lee and Finn to further strategize. Though Beau Lee didn't want to admit it, the pressure was mounting. With the charges Hollis was facing, bail could be astronomical—if the court was willing to entertain bail at all.

25

NOW THAT HIS PARTNER AND GOOD FRIEND HOLLIS MONTROSE HAD BEEN indicted with four counts of attempted murder, Finn felt even more pressure to crack this case.

Capes followed him into the office, toward the front desk at the impound lot.

"Tell me again how those idiots managed to get into the impound lot?" Capes asked. "Doesn't that take a warrant or court order?"

"Not everyone with a badge is righteous," Finn said. "Some people can be bribed, bullied, or outright bought."

"I can't say I'm surprised."

Finn rolled his eyes. "They're people. As you know, people aren't infallible."

"Ain't that the truth."

"I'll do the talking," Finn said. "Just follow my lead."

The pair quickly learned that Finn was best suited to manage other cops, while Capes did better with civilians. The latter had an easy ability—some might call it charisma—to speak with people from all backgrounds. They were a bit like improvisational jazz players, each person knowing when to let the other have a solo.

"Officer . . ." Finn struggled to read the name tag. "Santiago."

"Something I can do for you?"

"We need access to the impound lot."

"Who's asking?"

"Officer Finn Doyle."

"Don't know any Doyle," he said. "What department are you from?"

"Metra."

Santiago's expression read of skepticism. Finn was losing ground. "And you need access to the vehicle impound lot?"

"That's right. Part of a special assignment."

"You have documentation?"

"Must've misplaced it, but you can call my supervisor," Finn said. "They'll vouch for me."

Santiago studied Capes, whose lack of a suit and tie made him seem out of place. "And who's he?"

"Don't worry about him. He's undercover."

"Nice try, pal," Santiago said. "Not sure what you're trying to pull here, but get lost and take your friend with you."

"Is that what you told Dunham and Rossi?"

"How'd you—"

"My understanding is you gave them access to the lot, and all it took was a smile," Finn said. "Did you give them the third degree, too?"

"Shit," Santiago said. "Wait, wait . . . Is this an integrity check? Are you with IA?"

Finn said, "You're smarter than you look, Sherlock. Now let us in before your day gets worse."

"Hold on a sec. I'm not getting written up over fucking Dunham and Rossi."

"It's out of my hands."

Finn started to turn away as Santiago grew more desperate.

"Just hear me out, please? I'll tell you what you want to know."

"What did they want?" Finn asked. "Give me details. Otherwise, I go to my supervisors, and you can sort it out with IA."

"Nothing major. It didn't seem critical. They just wanted access to the lot. Said something about a lost cellphone. I think it might've been Rossi's. I can't remember, but they wanted to check a vehicle they had impounded to see if the phone was there."

"Which vehicle?" Finn asked. "I need a description."

"I got it right here . . ." Santiago flipped the blocker until he located the vehicle. "I'll write the location down for you. It's no problem." Santiago wrote the information on an index card and handed it to Finn. "It's a gray Ford Expedition."

Hollis's car. Finn looked at the lot number and put the card in his pocket. "You make it a habit to give cops unauthorized access to the impound lot?"

"No, sir. It was a one-time thing, I swear."

Finn made an unconvinced noise.

"Are you going to report me?"

"My colleague here will need to take your information: Full name and badge number."

"Damn it," Santiago said. "I'm never going to get off desk detail."

Capes took out his notepad and pen. "Please spell your full name," he said, trying to emulate Finn's mannerisms and tone. He'd had enough interactions with police to know there was commonality in how they moved and spoke, and Finn was no different.

Santiago sighed and slapped his forehead. "I can't believe this shit."

"And speak clearly, please," Capes added.

Santiago provided his information between mumbled curses. Once Capes had it, Santiago opened the door leading to the impound lot.

Finn and Capes entered the short hallway leading outside. They walked down the aisle toward Hollis's vehicle. Capes pulled his cap's brim lower to shield his eyes from the blustery wind.

"So you went the integrity check route. I can respect that," Capes said.

"That idiot assumed that's what we were doing here, so I went with it," Finn said, squinting from the wind.

"I'm thinking such checks must've passed Dunham and Rossi by."

"Well, unless it's absolutely egregious, most officers get a slap on the wrist. Hollis's SUV should be right up here." Finn pointed to a dark-colored Expedition in the distance.

When they arrived, the door to the vehicle was unlocked. They immediately began searching the floorboards. After fifteen minutes, Finn banged the hood in defeat. "I don't think it's here," he said. "Either it never was, or someone got it before we could."

"And they removed the license plate," Capes said.

"Damn it. They must have the plate in evidence," Finn said.

"You think Caruthers lied?" Capes asked. "Beau Lee said he seemed confident."

"Maybe Dunham and Rossi lied to him."

"The stool-pigeon test?"

"You know about that?" Finn asked.

"Who doesn't? On the streets, it's the easiest way to tell a friend from a foe. Tell a man a lie and see where it spreads."

"Exactly! Dunham and Rossi were testing his loyalty by giving the information about the vehicle," said Finn.

"Then you know what that means," Finn said. "We might've walked right into something. Dunham and Rossi could be watching us right now."

"We need to go."

They walked quickly back to the office. Inside, they breezed past Santiago, who looked desperate for Finn not to report him, and exited.

"This is bad," Capes said. "Dunham and Rossi might know Caruthers is helping us. We need to warn him."

"The kid brought this on himself."

"These guys are dangerous."

"Of course they're dangerous. They're cops, and the worst kind at that."

Capes noticed a Plymouth Duster parked across the street. Two men with unfamiliar faces were inside watching them. "We got eyes on us," he said. "Older yellow two-door across the street."

"Don't make it obvious."

Finn and Capes casually got in the Crown Vic.

"You think that's Dunham and Rossi?" Capes asked, staying low in his seat.

"Odds are good that we just verified Caruthers is a rat."

Capes took out his phone. "We need to tell Beau Lee." He dialed over the speaker and waited. "Boss, we've got a problem."

"What's going on?"

"It was a setup. There was no wallet. Dunham and Rossi had eyes on us the whole time. They must know Caruthers has been talking to us."

"I'll try to reach Caruthers now," Beau Lee said.

"Be good if we knew where he lived," Capes said.

"Is that something you could help with, Officer Doyle?" Beau Lee asked. "I don't want you to overextend yourself on our account."

"My hands might be tied on this one," said Finn. "The best thing is to keep calling him and hope he picks up. If not, I'll figure out how to get his address, discreetly, by this evening."

The Duster revved loudly and took off, disappearing down the street and leaving behind a plume of smoke.

"We believe the other officers just took off," Capes said. "It's not looking good, boss. They could be going after Caruthers."

"Stand by," Beau Lee said. "I'll see if I can reach him."

Beau Lee ended the call.

"Can't believe we got played, and so did Caruthers," Capes said.

"Believe it. Those officers got plenty of tricks up their sleeves. Besides, Caruthers brought this on himself."

Capes knew he was right. Caruthers had participated in Hollis's unjustified shooting, and now he was reaping what he sowed. But it didn't make him feel any better knowing that Dunham and Rossi were out there potentially looking to get even. They had callously shot Hollis, and there was no telling what they were prepared to do to Caruthers.

LATER THAT EVENING BEAU LEE and Finn caught up with Rory at a café near their hotel. When Beau Lee was on the phone with him, he'd seemed ready to share his side of the story, insistent he hadn't double-crossed them. Beau Lee thought it was best they all meet in person and chat. Rory's jaw was tight as he stared out the window, sitting across from Beau Lee and Finn. The weight of his decision was heavy in the silence. "I'm not old enough to retire. I don't even have the years in," he said in a low voice. "But I'm done. I'm putting in for a medical leave and walking away. Call it stress, call it what you want—they've given me no choice."

Beau Lee narrowed his eyes. "The union?"

"They've made it clear," Rory said, turning to face them. "I broke the code. I talked to y'all and somehow they found out. Now I'm getting threats, unmarked cars parked outside my house, silence from people I used to eat lunch with every damn day. My parents and my fiancée are scared to open their doors. My siblings have asked me if I did something wrong." He paused, hands clenched. "I did the right thing—and it's ruining my life."

He pulled a folded affidavit from his jacket and slid it across the table like it burned in his hands. "I signed this because it's the truth. Hollis never touched his gun. Never fired. I'll testify to that. But you'll have to subpoena me. I'm leaving the city. I'm not saying where."

Rory pushed back from the table and stood. His movements showing apprehension as he stated, "I've said my piece. You don't have to agree with me, but please understand—I'm just trying to keep me and my loved ones safe."

He glanced at both Beau Lee and Finn, eyes clouded somewhere between guilt and defiance. "You want justice? Then get it. But don't expect me to die for it."

Without waiting for a response, he turned and walked out, the door closing behind him.

Outside the café, Rory leaned against the cool concrete wall, his breathing shallow. His fingers trembled as he pulled out his phone and dialed. When his father answered, he didn't say much—just, "It's done. I'm coming home." His voice cracked on the last word.

And for the first time in a long time, Rory didn't feel like a cop. He just felt like a man trying to survive.

Finn exploded in frustration. "What the hell was that? He's just gonna walk out like that? These new guys—no backbone, no resilience. Just bail when it gets hard."

Beau Lee tapped in with a calm but sharp voice. "Rory didn't run. He fired his gun with the rest of them. He's just as culpable, and he has a lot to lose. But when it came time to tell the truth, he stood alone. That kind of courage doesn't always wear a badge. Sometimes it walks away from one."

26

THE MORNING OF HOLLIS'S ARRAIGNMENT, BEAU LEE WOKE AT FIVE AND got dressed in his expertly pressed suit, then took a cab from the hotel to the courthouse. It was a big day. And though he had plenty of big days in his rearview, this one felt monumental. His mind raced the entire ride over. It would be his first appearance before a judge in the state of Illinois, and the only thing he heard in his head was Nellie cautioning him to be prepared for anything.

Rain poured. It wasn't cold enough to snow, but the temperature was dropping. Meteorologists forecasted an incoming storm, which was to begin in four hours. It seemed like there was always a storm brewing . . .

He stood on the courthouse steps under the awning as Alvarez approached in a wool coat, scarf, and leather knee-high boots. She held a large umbrella, and a briefcase hung off her shoulder. The stark look on her face suggested she'd had a restless night or had received bad news . . . or just hadn't had her coffee.

"Good morning," Beau Lee said. "How are you?"

"Been better," she said. "Terrible night. Couldn't sleep. Dreamed about my mother mostly."

"Your mother?"

"She always visits me when I've got a lot on my mind."

Beau Lee held the door to the courthouse lobby open for Alvarez and entered behind her. The heat was blasting. It felt like a sauna compared to outside. Beau Lee began removing his coat.

His hands were shaking.

"You got the jitters?" Alvarez asked.

"Could be too much coffee or anticipating the hearing."

"Didn't take you for the nervous type."

"If you don't get nervous before these things, then you probably shouldn't be practicing law."

"Nervous or not, we better be on point."

"Precisely."

"So, do you know much about the judge?" Beau Lee asked. "Any pointers you can share?"

"I wish," she said. "Just say a prayer that whoever it is will be the epitome of fair and impartial."

"A fair and impartial judge doesn't seem so elusive."

"In this city, you'd be surprised. On second thought, maybe you wouldn't."

"Nothing surprises me, but I will do my research once the judge is appointed."

"Well, I haven't had breakfast yet. I was thinking I'd grab a pastry from the café. Want to join?"

"You go on without me," he said. "I'll meet you inside."

Alvarez headed upstairs to the café while Beau Lee sat on a bench outside the courtroom. He took the opportunity to go over his notes in preparation for the arraignment. His phone rang—it was a number he didn't recognize.

"Hello?"

"Mr. Cooper . . . hello?"

"Tyler, is that you?"

"Yes, sir."

Tyler, Nellie's seventeen-year-old son, whom he had been raising as a single father since he was eight years old, was on the verge of graduating high school. Tyler was a phenom when it came to academics and on the lacrosse field. Beau Lee hadn't spoken to him in a few weeks. Not since the firm held its annual community cookout. It was rare for Tyler to call him. Something must be wrong.

"Shouldn't you be in school? A little odd to be hearing from you. What's going on?"

"It's Dad. He didn't want me to call you, but—"

"Nellie—is he all right?"

"That's why I'm calling. I took him to urgent care last night. His blood pressure was the highest we've ever seen it. Off the charts. Scared the mess out of us."

"Please tell me he's all right."

"He's fine for now, but that's the thing. The doctor seemed to think he was on the verge of a stroke. Had I not convinced him to get seen, who knows what might've happened."

"What do they think caused the spike?"

"They seem to think stress and lack of sleep were factors. Dad's been going nonstop with running things here in Houston, and I know I shouldn't have been snooping, but I overheard him talking to one of the legal assistants, and he seemed upset."

"About what?"

"Something about Chicago PD countersuing the firm."

"I didn't know anything about this."

"Well, it had Dad in a fit. I'm worried about him. I haven't seen him like this in a long time, Mr. Cooper. I'm not sure what to do."

"Take a breath."

"I'm sorry to unload all this on you."

"No, it's fine. You did the right thing calling me."

"Okay."

Beau Lee had assumed Nellie was managing well without him, but if Tyler was right and the CPD intended to countersue, it could be enough to overload Nellie. "Is he there now?" Beau Lee asked.

"He's in his office."

"Can you hand him the phone so we can talk?"

"Thank you, Mr. Cooper. I know he'll listen to you."

Beau Lee remained on the line while Tyler sought out his father. After a short time Nellie got on the line. "Hello?"

"What's going on, Frat?"

"I was just about to ask you the same," Nellie said. "Case updates?"

"We'll get to that, but what's this I hear about a trip to urgent care?"

"Oh, it was nothing. Tyler worries too much."

"Does he have reason to worry?"

"Isn't there always?"

"Be straight with me."

"I didn't want to drop this on you, but since it seems you already know, CPD is threatening to countersue us."

"For how much?"

"Fifty million. The exact figure you're suing them for."

"Talk about tit for tat," Beau Lee said. "What's their claim?"

"Defamation. Stems from the allegations you made during the press conference," Nellie said, starting to get worked up. "I wanted to keep this from you as long as I could. I knew you had enough to deal with, but I don't need to tell you how bad this is."

"Keep it from me? Since when do we keep things from each other?"

"I know. I'm sorry . . . I thought I was looking out for you, but I realized this might be the end of us."

"What are you saying, Nellie?"

"It's the police union in conjunction with the department. If their lawsuit's successful, they'll tank our firm. We don't have fifty million to pony up."

"Frat, you know I don't scare easily. There's no way they can sustain a defamation case, because they'd have to prove that we were knowingly saying something that was false. And based on everything that we know, we're simply alleging that they shot an innocent police officer who was Black. But please don't worry about all that right now. Just tell me . . . you going to see a doctor?"

"Got an appointment coming up this week."

"Good," Beau Lee said. "I'll check back with you when I get some time and update you on things. We're about to go into court."

"All right, Frat."

"Love you, man."

27

HARPO WALKED UP JUST AFTER BEAU LEE ENDED THE CALL.

"Good morning, Brother Harpo," Beau Lee said.

"Good morning to you."

The two men shook hands.

"How you feeling?" Harpo asked.

"Like Daniel in the lion's den."

"Never would have guessed that was your vibe this morning. I mean, you're upright, standing firm, with your chin up."

"Well, you know, brothers like us have mastered that art of cool confidence. Remember how we walked into that Louisiana courtroom? The whole lot of us looking like we owned the place."

Harpo laughed, reflecting on the fond memory. "Yeah, newspapers started calling us the Justice League."

"More like the *Just-Us League.*"

More laughter ensued. Harpo was so tickled he marched in place and slapped his thigh.

After he straightened up, he cleared his throat. "But it's not going to be like it was in Louisiana. In this city, people take to the streets. Once enough people hear about what happened to Hollis, the city will be battening down the hatches, 'cause the storm that'll roll through here will be unlike anything they've ever seen."

"But we need more ways to spread the word. Any ideas?"

"Glad you asked, my astute brother. I've got a few appearances lined up—radio, mostly. But I could use your help if you can spare the time. We gotta get your mug on the TV screens giving the people the rundown. Otherwise, it'll just be me hitting at least twenty radio and TV stations in the next five days."

"You make that sound easy . . ."

"Far from it, but what choice do I have?" Harpo asked. "Those cops tried to kill Hollis, and we have to get the world's attention."

"My gut tells me it wasn't random. There's something more going on here."

"I've been fighting CPD for most of my life, and I can tell you this: nothing, and I mean nothing, is coincidental with them."

Beau Lee had come to trust Brother Harpo's insights and observations. He'd been on the front lines of civil rights for decades, long before Beau Lee had passed the bar exam. He was the second-highest-ranking figure in the Nation of Islam, having risen to prominence when he participated in the Southern Christian Leadership Conference's Operation Breadbasket alongside Reverend Jesse Jackson.

The movement sought to improve the economic status of Black people by boycotting white-owned-and-operated businesses that refused to serve Blacks.

Harpo was a walking encyclopedia of U.S. history, especially the Civil Rights Movement, because he had lived it. He told of the turmoil brought about by the 1968 assassination of Dr. Martin Luther King, Jr. Riots erupted on Chicago's West Side. Countless arrests were made, and Harpo was on the front lines ensuring that those peaceful protesters received a proper legal defense. He was a hero of the people—a true proletariat—and an ally.

Alvarez approached them from the end of the hall holding a large paper cup. "Good morning, Brother Harpo."

"Good morning, Princess. You doing all right?"

"Ask me again after this arraignment." She looked at her watch and then at the courtroom's entrance. "We better go in."

"Yes, lead the way," Beau Lee said, then turned to Harpo. "I'll give you a call once the session's adjourned so we can strategize on those media appearances."

Harpo nodded. "Good luck in there."

Beau Lee and Alvarez entered the hall of justice. It was nearly empty, save for Jamillah and Tyrone. Rocky had remained with Hollis at the hospital.

The two attorneys stood behind the defense table across from Peter DaSilva and Miranda Dillard. Finn had advised Beau Lee that the prosecutors were as smart as they were relentless, especially DaSilva. When Beau Lee searched DaSilva's history online and learned he'd never lost a case, it gave him pause. Perfect records didn't always mean a prosecutor was a skilled litigator but could suggest their unwillingness to put justice before all else, even when the evidence pointed to police corruption and misconduct.

The judge entered the chambers and took her seat.

"All rise," the bailiff said. "The Honorable Judge Kathleen Lambert presiding."

The judge took the bench. She was an older woman with graying hair, though it was blond in the photo Beau Lee had seen of her online, and in it she had fewer wrinkles. He surmised it had likely been taken close to a decade ago, but there was no doubt the image of her now, in person, was far more commanding than a photo—even a good one.

"Please be seated," Judge Lambert said. "This hearing is for the *State of Illinois v. Hollis Montrose.*"

"Here we go," Beau Lee whispered to Alvarez, who looked fired up.

"In the case of Hollis Montrose . . ." She then rattled off Hollis's charges as if she were ordering food at a drive-thru: "The defendant has been charged with four counts of brandishing a firearm. Four counts of aggravated battery with a firearm. Four counts of battery on a peace officer. Four counts of attempted first-degree murder of a peace officer. Are the attorneys representing Mr. Montrose present?"

"Present, Your Honor," Beau Lee said.

"Please identify yourselves for the record."

"Attorneys Beau Lee Cooper and Princess Alvarez representing Mr. Hollis Montrose," he said.

"And where is your client?"

Alvarez took this one. "Officer Montrose is recovering from his very serious injuries in the hospital, Your Honor. We are entering a plea of not guilty on his behalf."

"Am I to understand that he's undergoing intensive care?"

"Yes, Your Honor," she said.

"I see," she said. "Considering Mr. Montrose's current condition and future recovery, when do you foresee his being well enough to appear in court?"

"Well, I'm not a physician, Your Honor, but Mr. Montrose's road to recovery will be long and demanding," Alvarez said.

"Naturally, but has either of you seen Mr. Montrose?"

"Yes," Beau Lee said.

"And have you spoken to his doctors?"

"Not directly, but I am privy to his condition," Beau Lee said.

"Then I take it you have some understanding of his current situation?"

"Yes, Your Honor."

"Good," she said. "Given that we cannot determine when Mr. Montrose will be able to appear, I see no reason to discuss bail at this time. The defendant will remain in police custody while recovering. We will set the bail hearing for next month, granted Mr. Montrose's condition doesn't worsen. Does the prosecution have anything to add?"

"Actually, Your Honor, we'd like to have bail set today if possible."

"And why is that?"

"As we noted in our filing, Mr. Montrose is accused of a heinous crime. While we understand that he is currently in no position to be moved to an inmate facility, that could change from now to the hearing date. We therefore prefer to have bail set at this time rather than at a later date."

"I see. Mr. Cooper and Ms. Alvarez, do you wish to say anything else on your client's behalf?"

"Yes, Your Honor," Alvarez said. "If Mr. Montrose improves, his family would like him to come home, where he could be cared for."

"Are you suggesting he can't receive proper care while incarcerated?"

"Mr. Montrose is not a criminal," Beau Lee said. "I shouldn't have to remind the court that he has the presumption of innocence and, given that he's still a law enforcement officer, has access to a much higher quality of care as an employed citizen than what he would receive as an inmate."

"You raise a good point, Mr. Cooper. However, as the prosecution suggested in their filing, this case is sensitive, to put it mildly. The longer it takes to adjudicate, the more volatile things could become within the communities that make up our city. In addition to that, Mr. Montrose's training as a law enforcement officer presents its own risk. Therefore, in the interest of time and public safety, I'd like to hold the bond hearing today. Are you prepared to move forward?"

Beau Lee looked at Alvarez, who shrugged. "Yes, Your Honor. We are prepared."

"Taking into consideration the gravity of the crimes levied against Mr. Montrose and his access to firearms, I am denying bail."

"Denied? On what grounds?" Beau Lee balked. "Hollis Montrose isn't a flight risk and poses absolutely no danger to society, especially in his current state. You're talking about a man who has never fired his weapon on or off duty at anyone."

"Allegedly," Judge Lambert said. "Don't forget why we're here."

"Your Honor, this veers into preposterous territory," he said.

"Like I said, Mr. Montrose's experience as a law enforcement officer poses significant risk. If allowed bail, his knowledge of police procedure could aid him in evading law enforcement."

"You think he'd flee?"

"I wouldn't presume to know what Mr. Montrose would or wouldn't do if given the opportunity. I can only consider the risk."

"But the man can't even walk, and if he is to survive, he may never walk again. He will surely need round-the-clock care. I must reiterate that he is a longstanding member of his community and a respectable policeman. He's highly decorated and is a pillar in his community. I have here a statement from his partner, Officer Finnegan Doyle, and numerous officers who attest to my client's integrity. By not allowing Hollis Montrose bond, you are violating his constitutional rights—"

"Excuse me, Mr. Cooper. I hope you don't think you can come into my courtroom and lecture me about constitutionality. You need to tread lightly."

"Easy, Beau Lee," Alvarez said in his ear. "She's about to see red."

Beau Lee tempered his voice and composed himself. "I mean no disrespect, Your Honor, but this is beyond rational."

"Much like the crimes Mr. Montrose has been accused of."

"Yes, *accused*, Your Honor. Not found guilty. It is unconstitutional to punish a man before he can stand trial. Especially a sworn peace officer with no criminal history."

"I beg your pardon," Judge Lambert said, leaning over the bench. "My decisions are not punitive, and I reject the implication."

Beau Lee turned to Alvarez. "What the hell is going on? We're getting railroaded."

"Welcome to Chicago," she said. "Judges and prosecutors tend to be in cahoots."

"Your Honor, please? I implore you," Beau Lee said. "My client has roots in this community—his family, his job—he has no intention of going anywhere and looks forward to his day in court. There are no grounds to deny Hollis Montrose bond, and doing so could put his life in jeopardy."

"Jeopardy?"

"Police officers face unprecedented threats when incarcerated, and Mr. Montrose's health conditions put him in unnecessary peril. Why deny him the opportunity to be with his family, where he can be cared for and protected until he can actually stand trial and defend himself? At least consider house arrest."

Judge Lambert was unmoved. "The decision stands. Bail is denied," she said without further reconsideration. "If Mr. Montrose is to survive and becomes well enough to stand trial, he will be remanded in the Cook County Jail."

Beau Lee looked at DaSilva and Dillard, who seemed beyond pleased. The hearing had been a farce. Lambert had chosen to deny Hollis's bond before stepping foot in the courtroom, and her partial stance reeked of prejudice and malfeasance.

"That will be all," the judge said. "As for the trial date, I will make a determination based on Mr. Montrose's health status, and you'll be informed when the date is set." The judge slammed the gavel with finality. "Adjourned."

28

BEAU LEE AND ALVAREZ GATHERED THEIR THINGS AND PREPARED TO leave.

"Not how I imagined this going," Beau Lee said. "We were skating uphill the entire time."

"I knew there was a chance we'd get shot down, but I was completely wrong about the odds."

DaSilva and Dillard were already walking down the aisle, headed toward the exit. It was clear they wanted to avoid Beau Lee and Alvarez, and that meant they weren't looking to discuss Hollis's charges or make a deal. Not that Beau Lee would entertain any form of plea bargain. He believed wholeheartedly in Hollis's innocence and was dead set on getting him acquitted of all charges.

Once outside, Jamillah and Tyrone came up to Beau Lee. He'd already anticipated what she'd ask, and he was prepared for the difficult conversation.

"How can the judge just deny Daddy's bail like that?" Jamillah asked. "It doesn't make sense. His record is clean. He's a cop, for goodness' sake."

"Not in the judge's eyes, I'm afraid."

"We're very sorry, Jamillah," Alvarez said. "We weren't expecting the judge to take such a hard line."

"It just isn't right what they're doing to him."

"No, it isn't, but your father is fighting for his life in that hospital right now, which means we have to fight for him out here."

Jamillah and Tyrone held hands. Jamillah's free hand rested on her belly. "So what happens next?"

"We'll appeal the bond denial, which could take some time, but we likely won't convene for trial until seven or eight months out. During that time, we'll undergo discovery—collect as much evidence as we can and get our witnesses in order. Our goal will be to make our case so compelling that the prosecution will drop the charges and pivot their efforts toward the real criminals: the cops who shot your father."

"So we have a few months to prove Daddy's innocent?"

"Yes, in a way, but during that time, the prosecution will also be building its case."

"Mr. Cooper, Mama said you've found the girl who recorded the video, right? That alone should be enough to get them to drop the charges. It's all on tape. Who can argue with that?"

"I'm afraid it's not as cut and dry," Beau Lee said. "Video footage helps, but it's not enough on its own. We'll need witness testimonies. Not just the young lady who recorded the video, but also"—he lowered his voice—"we've identified a police officer who was there at the time of the shooting, and he may be willing to cooperate."

"Wait . . . you have an officer who's willing to talk?" She sounded as if someone had told her pigs could fly.

"It's not a guarantee and I don't want to be presumptuous, but if what he says checks out and he accepts the subpoena, it might be enough to get Hollis's charges thrown out."

"You're saying this cop is actually willing to get on the stand and testify against other cops?"

"I believe so, but I've been having trouble getting ahold of him. He hasn't answered his phone for a few days. Capes has been looking for him, but so far, he's come up empty and I'm getting worried."

"Well, you've got to find him," Jamillah said. "He might be Daddy's only shot at getting free."

"My hope is that he's laying low, given what he's up against."

Jamillah squeezed Tyrone's hand and took a deep breath.

"Everything all right?" Beau Lee asked, glancing at her belly with concern.

"It's fine. All this excitement has the little one doing somersaults," she said. "I know it's not much, but it makes me a little hopeful knowing a cop might be willing to testify. It means they aren't all rotten, you know?"

"Hope is a good thing," he said. "We've all got to hold on to that."

"Yes, Mr. Cooper, we do."

Beau Lee looked over at the prosecutors, who were gathered near the elevator. He caught DaSilva's eyes, which were ice cold and peered like daggers.

"If you'll excuse me for a moment," he said, leaving Jamillah and Tyrone with Alvarez. He walked in DaSilva and Dillard's direction.

"It's Cooper, right?" DaSilva asked with a slimy grin.

"That's right, Attorney Beau Lee Cooper."

"Thought you had a setup in Houston?"

"I go where I'm needed."

"I had no clue you practiced criminal defense."

"Well, I've had what you might call a storied career. Worn lots of hats."

"And now you're here in a Chicago courtroom. What are the odds?"

"Sadly, pretty high, from what I've seen. So high that maybe I should open a branch of our firm right here in the city."

"Chicago's got enough lawyers looking to make a buck."

"Well, I tend to set up in places that are in desperate need of justice and equality."

Dillard scoffed; she held what looked to be a Von Baer briefcase. Beau Lee had seen a few. It was a luxury item in the legal profession that some saw as a statement of success—a subtle way of announcing they'd made it. He couldn't help but wonder how many wrongfully convicted people Dillard had locked up to afford such an indulgence.

"A little hyperbolic, don't you think?" she asked, tightening her grip on the case's leather handle.

"I wish it were, but Hollis Montrose's case is just one of the many injustices dating back decades."

"With all due respect, Mr. Cooper, our state has locked up a significant number of people who have shown their contempt for society through murder, narcotics, sex trafficking, and rape. Should I go on?"

"Chicago's reputation isn't lost on me," Beau Lee said. "However, not recognizing that there's a criminal element, not only on the streets but in the police departments, is one-sided."

Dillard looked as if she were about to combust. "Can I ask you something?"

"Go ahead."

"Do you ever grieve fallen officers?" she asked. "I mean, when it's a clear-cut case of murder, do you take the time to pray for the officer's family? Or are your prayers only reserved for those who are, as you say, victims of injustice?"

"I don't want to see anyone lose their lives, and I cast my prayers far and wide, Ms. Dillard. But one dead officer doesn't excuse the killing of an unarmed person. Let's not forget about Hollis Montrose. He's a police officer, too, or did you forget? Does the notion of *Back the Blue* not apply to Mr. Montrose?"

"I'm only interested in justice."

"That makes two of us," Beau Lee said. "But when faced with insurmountable evidence, will you be courageous enough to do the right thing? Or are you blinded by your desire to see another Black man locked away, cop or not?"

Beau Lee had known since the day he was old enough to understand his place in the world that police across America existed in a protected and rarefied space that made them, for the most part, untouchable. Harming one was met with severe repercussions. Murdering or attempting to murder a cop, in the eyes of those in law enforcement, meant crossing a Rubicon of criminality from which there was no escape or redemption.

In Illinois, killing a police officer was considered a capital crime that was punishable by the death penalty or life without parole, and there was no telling which the prosecutors would pursue.

DaSilva said, "It looks like we have differing opinions about the 'right thing,' Attorney Cooper, but I will say this: From where I'm standing, a cop killer is no longer on the streets, and that's a win for the entire city."

"Cop killer? Do you really believe a veteran police officer would attempt to open fire on fellow officers?"

"Most officers wouldn't, but Hollis Montrose isn't most officers, is he?"

"That's ludicrous."

"How well do you know your client?" DaSilva asked. "Before you start questioning our case's validity, you might want to look at his history. And I mean take a long, hard look, because Hollis Montrose might be a police officer, but I'd submit to you: What type of police officer is he?"

"You don't know what you're talking about."

"If your client decides to come clean about what happened that night, give me a call. If Hollis changes his plea to no contest, it'll save us all a lot of time and paperwork. Might even save him some years."

"He's innocent, and I'm going to prove it."

"There's no need to litigate this in the hallway, Mr. Cooper," Dillard said. "We'll have plenty of time for that in court."

Alvarez slowly approached, probing everyone's body language—Dillard's defensive posture was evident from across the hall. "Attorney Cooper. Everything all right?"

"Yes. I was just introducing myself to prosecutors DaSilva and Dillard. Since we'll be seeing a lot of them, I thought it best for us to be on speaking terms."

"And we didn't properly meet?" Dillard said, giving Alvarez the once-over.

Alvarez had done her homework. Maybe her suit and shoes didn't carry the same price tag as Miranda Dillard's, who'd seen her share of success over the years, but Alvarez still had her conscience. She could sleep at night knowing she was fighting to make a difference.

She didn't doubt that Dillard thought she was working for the *people*. Having emerged as an outspoken advocate for harsher mandated sentencing, it was clear that she wasn't content with being a prosecutor. She had political aspirations and, in time, would surely take the hard-red path of ultra-conservatism to achieve them.

"I'm Princess Alvarez. Co-counsel."

"Princess? That's your legal name?"

"Since day one."

"Cute."

DaSilva looked at his watch. "We better go," he said. "We've got that meeting." He gave Dillard a slight nod before directing his attention to Beau Lee. "Nice hat, by the way. Very retro."

The elevator doors opened, and DaSilva and Dillard entered. They stood silently as the doors shut. Beau Lee stewed. He was a civil man, not one to raise a fist or throw stones. Instead, he used the law as his weapon. But it was time to go on the attack—get in front of the cameras like Brother Harpo had suggested and tell the story Hollis couldn't tell.

"Aren't they a charming duo," Alvarez said disdainfully. "Can't believe that woman said *cute*. I never imagined that word could sound so demeaning."

"Sorry you were on the receiving end of that, but remember, it's all part of the game. They want to get in our heads. Make us doubt our case."

"Well, that's not happening."

"Good," Beau Lee said, taking out his phone. "Give me a moment. I need to make a call."

"All right."

He stepped away and dialed Capes. "It's me," he said. "You got a minute?"

"Sure, boss. What's up?"

"The judge denied bail. The moment Hollis is deemed well

enough, he's going to be locked up. We can't let that happen, so I need you to do whatever you can to find Rory Caruthers so we can subpoena him like he asked, and maybe we can spare the Montroses more pain."

"I'm doing my best, but he's probably staying at an address that's not in the database if he means to get away from Dunham and Rossi."

"Give Finn a call and see what you two can figure out."

"He said it was risky, boss. Didn't sound like he wanted to assist with this particular mission."

"Give it another shot," Beau Lee said. "Let him know about Hollis's bail denial. It might light a fire under him."

"Okay. I'll see what I can do."

"Thank you, Capes."

29

JACK QUICKLY FELT THE FOLLY OF NOT HAVING WORN A THICKER COAT. HE was sure it was ten degrees colder than when he'd first entered the bar, or maybe it was the cold beers that had chilled him.

After two hours of drinking, he'd successfully offended the bartender with his comments about Obama's election and had been booted from his neighborhood drinking hole—a lifetime ban. It was like the entire country had become pussies overnight. Card-carrying members of the PC Brigade.

Whatever happened to free speech?

He leaned against the bar's brick wall, which had been tagged with graffiti. Nothing gang related. It was the type of markings produced by aimless youth with too much time on their hands. Jack was one of those kids once, smashing mailboxes with his father's old golf club and toilet-papering his math teacher's house at two in the morning.

He pushed himself off the wall with his heel and flagged an oncoming taxi. A yellow cab pulled up to the curb. Jack approached, trying to hide his intoxication.

The driver unlocked the doors and Jack got in the back.

The driver was wearing a head covering and had a thick Chicagoan accent. Jack figured he was from Bridgeview or Chicago Lawn, where most Muslims lived.

"Good afternoon," the driver said. "Do you have an address?"

Jack stomached his disgust. He couldn't remember the last time he'd had a white cab driver, especially an Irish one. It had to have been in the early nineties, he thought.

"I don't know where to take you," the driver said. "I'll need an address."

"It's Rosehill."

"You talking about the cemetery?"

"You know it, then?"

"Sure, but don't the gates lock at five o'clock? It's already four."

"Then you need to get moving."

"It'll take some time with traffic . . ."

Jack reached into his pocket and pulled out his billfold. He opened it and took out a crisp bill, then dangled it for the driver to see. "An extra twenty if you drive like you've got a pair."

"Look, man, I can't afford a ticket right now."

"Don't worry about it," Jack said. "You'll be fine."

"What do you mean? I'm the one who'll have to pay."

"You get pulled over, and I'll deal with it, all right?"

"Really? And what the hell are you going to do?"

Jack flashed his badge. "I'm a cop, asshole. CPD."

"Oh, shit. I'm sorry, Officer. I didn't—"

"Yeah, yeah, just fucking get me there and we're square."

The driver shifted into drive, checked his side-view mirror, and gassed it. The engine made a grinding noise, and Jack thought the transmission had slipped out of gear. Most cabs in the city were shit boxes, filthy and poorly maintained, and this cab was no exception.

Jack closed his eyes and tried to ignore the musty odor and foreign driver who'd irked him. He mused, "What happened to America?" It had gone from a glorious country to a garbage dump right before his eyes, before the country's eyes, and no one seemed to notice.

Were people under some spell? Why couldn't they see what was happening under their noses? America was being lost to a foreign invasion.

WHEN HE ARRIVED AT THE cemetery, the driver parked near the entrance, where there was a wrought-iron gate and an information booth that looked empty. Jack paid the driver the fare of thirty-two dollars.

"What about the extra twenty?" the driver asked. "I got you here before it closed."

"Oh yeah," Jack said, balling up the twenty-dollar bill and tossing it in the man's face. "A deal's a deal."

The driver glared, straightened out the money, and smoothed it against the dashboard until it was flat again. "Asshole," he said under his breath.

Jack slammed the door and began walking toward an opening in the fence. He listened as the cab sped away; he hadn't given any thought as to how he'd get home. The cemetery was minutes from closing, and there weren't any cabs waiting around. If he had been marginally sober, he might've planned things out better.

He cut across the lawn as it began to snow, and walked toward a black headstone in the distance. No matter how drunk he got, he'd always know the way. When he reached the grave, he sat down quietly for a moment. The ground was frozen; he felt as if he were sitting on a block of ice. The headstone's façade was caked in snow. Jack brushed it away, revealing an inscription etched into the marble.

> HERE LIES THEODORE BRISCOE.
> HUSBAND.
> FATHER.
> LOYAL FRIEND.

"God, I miss you, brother," Jack said, and his mind faded back to when Briscoe first took him under his wing, and the times they spent together as mentor and mentee.

* * *

THEODORE BRISCOE WAS THE KIND of officer who thought he was the department. With more than twenty-five years on the force, he spoke with authority, swaggered through roll calls like a general, and never missed an opportunity to remind rookies who built the foundation they walked on. He took Jack Dunham under his wing like he was passing on a bloodline.

"This job's not for the weak," Briscoe had told him on his first day. "And it damn sure isn't for people who think they can change it."

To Jack, Briscoe was a legend. Rough around the edges, sure—but loyal, smart, seasoned. The kind of man who kept score and made sure the right people got what was coming to them. But everything shifted the day the city announced its new chief of police.

The new chief was Black. A younger man who'd climbed the ranks, had a clean record and a graduate degree. Teddy Briscoe was furious. He'd already ordered a fresh navy suit and had rehearsed his speech in front of the mirror—he thought the job was his.

"They gave it to a goddamn affirmative action hire," Briscoe sat in the break room, slamming his badge down. "You work your whole life, and they pass you over for a monkey with a college degree."

Jack didn't say anything. He just nodded, watching the man he admired unravel.

From that day forward, Briscoe's mentorship took on a different meaning. Every patrol ride, every briefing, every training session came with sharp reminders of whom the city "belonged" to.

"We gotta take back our city," Briscoe said one night as they drove through the South Side, lights off, windows cracked. "We can't let these affirmative action monkeys have control."

Jack looked out the window with a blank face.

Briscoe wasn't just venting. He believed it. He believed that the department—and the city—were slipping through white fingers, and it was their duty to get it back. He filled Jack's head with stories from the eighties and nineties—times when "cops had real power," and "respect meant fear." He trained Jack in technique, in discipline—but also in resentment.

Months later, it all exploded.

A standoff erupted after a Black man, reportedly armed, refused to exit his vehicle during a high-risk stop. Briscoe took command, ignoring backup procedures and escalating the situation. The gunfire lasted less than two minutes. When it was over, Briscoe was on the pavement, bleeding out. The suspect—who'd been shot five times—was barely alive.

Jack arrived moments after Briscoe went down. He ran past other officers, slipping in blood. The man who taught him everything lay dying on the cold concrete, his badge still pinned to his chest as he took his last breath.

Jack didn't cry at the funeral. He stood like stone, arms locked, jaw clenched. The old guard turned out in full dress blues. The new chief gave a eulogy about "service and sacrifice," but Jack barely listened. He heard only Briscoe's voice in his head—angry, proud, unfiltered.

A week after the burial, Jack received a letter from Briscoe's estate attorney. Briscoe had left him something: a small black lockbox, the kind you keep under your bed or in the back of a closet. Jack took it home, placed it on his kitchen table, and sat in silence for a long time before finally opening it.

Inside were dozens of yellowed papers: handwritten notes, arrest reports, printed photos, and clippings from internal complaints. Each one detailed a moment in Briscoe's career involving Black citizens—arrests, interrogations, "use of force" reports. Tucked beneath the last folder was a small envelope labeled FOR JACK.

He opened it.

This is how to keep those monkeys in check in our city that we run.
 I want you to study these reports, learn from them. Use what fits.
Adapt the rest. Figure out which tactics work best in which situations.
 You've got what it takes. You're not like the soft ones coming through now.

> *Remember, we have to make sure we have control of our city. Make sure you train the young ones like I did for you.*
>
> *One day you'll have your own lockbox of mementos. Keep running the city.*

Jack stared at the note, the words bleeding through the paper like oil. The hatred wasn't hidden anymore. It was laid bare—recorded, memorialized, passed down like a family heirloom. He ran his fingers over the edge of one of the police photos: a young Black man with a busted eye and busted lip, and an autopsy report of death by excited delirium. Also clipped to the photo and the autopsy was a Georgetown Hoyas headband that showed this punk was a top lieutenant in the Gangster Disciples street gang. In the report, Briscoe had written, "Noncompliant. Resisting arrest. Put officers' safety in danger. I wanted to make sure that every officer got to go home safely."

There were seven more descriptions left in the locker for Jack to study and learn from.

Jack closed and locked the box. He placed it in his bedroom closet behind his winter gear and shut the door.

He didn't tell anyone about it. Not the department. Not the chief. Not even the other officers who'd quietly revered Briscoe.

But something in him had shifted.

At night, he sometimes replayed Briscoe's voice in his mind. The jokes. The insults. The warnings. He heard them in the quiet between dispatch calls, in the long shadows at traffic stops. The lessons weren't just methodical. They were generational.

Briscoe may have been buried, but his ideas were not.

And Jack had inherited more than just a lockbox.

30

IT WAS 8:19 P.M. WHEN THE CPD CRUISER ARRIVED AT JACK'S HOUSE WITH him in the back seat, wrapped in a foil blanket and smelling of vomit. An older Black officer, with a veteran's demeanor and a salt-and-pepper beard, had driven Jack home from the cemetery after the groundskeepers found him passed out in the snow.

The officer got out, walked around the car, and opened the rear passenger door. "You're home, Dunham," the officer said. "Looks like you've got company." Jack swung his foot down onto the pavement and climbed out. He couldn't feel his fingers and toes, and he smelled of wet garbage with a hint of piss. He was certain that he'd soiled himself but wasn't sure if the pissing had occurred while he was in the cemetery or the cruiser.

"Ah, fuck. What are they doing here?" Jack said, noticing his wife, Corrine, on the porch talking to the prosecutors, DaSilva and Dillard. "This day keeps getting better and better."

"Yeah, well, you owe me."

"Sure, sure, I'll take care of you," Jack said. "You just keep this little episode between us, got it?"

"You get me those Bulls tickets and I won't say shit. Make sure they're courtside, too."

"Don't worry, you'll be so close you'll smell what Derrick Rose had for dinner."

The officer left Jack standing on his walkway and got back into the cruiser.

Jack approached the steps leading to the porch but didn't attempt to climb them. He was still drunk from the bottle of whiskey he drank at the cemetery, and his joints were so cold that he worried his toes would succumb to frostbite.

"What the hell is going on?" Jack asked. "Didn't know you two suits made house visits."

"They're here to see you," Corrine said. "But I'm sure that's no surprise." She was petite with auburn hair and a weathered face, and she was draped in an oversize turtleneck sweater. Jack thought Corrine dressed only slightly better than the bag lady who lived in an alley on his patrol route. His wife's usual daily attire was a massively big shirt and soiled UGG boots. After almost fifteen years of marriage, he'd forgotten what she'd looked like in her prime. Seeing what she'd become after two kids and no job was enough to make him want to give up on women altogether.

Thank God for Heaven, he thought. She breathed new life into him and gave him an outlet from his wretched marriage.

"Where are the kids?" he asked.

"Inside, where else?"

"Then go see about them. I'll deal with whatever the hell *this* is."

"Where the hell have you been, anyway?" she asked. "The kids were worried about you."

"Did you hear what I said? Go the fuck inside, will you?"

Corrine sucked her teeth and flipped Jack the bird. Her middle finger was crooked. Jack had drunkenly broken it five years ago when things got physical during an argument.

"You're such a dick," Corrine said before going inside and slamming the door.

DaSilva and Dillard stepped off the porch and met Jack on the walkway.

"Officer Dunham, you're a hard man to get ahold of," DaSilva said.

"Well, you found me, didn't you?"

"We've been waiting around for a few hours. Do you usually disappear like that and not tell your wife?"

"You come here to give me marital advice?"

"We need to talk about the Hollis Montrose shooting."

"Do I have a choice?"

DaSilva sniffed the air. "We could always have you come down to our office in the morning, maybe after you've sobered up, if you'd prefer. Just curious, though, how much have you had tonight?"

"I'm Irish. I can't get drunk," Jack said proudly. "Not that it's any of your business what I do off the clock."

"You really think being publicly intoxicated is wise, given the spotlight that's on you right now?"

"Are you talking about that little press conference Montrose's lawyer gave where he spewed conspiracy theories about Chicago PD? The nerve of him to question the integrity of our department," Jack said, then hawked a loogie onto the frozen lawn. "I'll have you know that my fellow officers and I, who, mind you, have received numerous honors, didn't do a damn thing wrong. We followed procedure and did our fucking jobs. End of story."

"Glad to know you watched the press conference," DaSilva said. "I won't have to fill you in."

"I saw everything I needed to see. Read my report. It's all in there. What more do you need?"

"We have read it," Dillard said. "That's why we're here to clear a few things up. You stated that Hollis Montrose didn't have identification on him at the time of the traffic stop—no driver's license and no police ID. Is that correct?"

"That's what the report says . . ."

"You also stated that you were unable to read the license plate because it was illegible. Are you suggesting the license plate had been manipulated in some way that prevented you from reading it?"

"Look, lady, it was dark, and the guy was swerving, and—"

"It's A.D.A. Dillard," she said sternly. "Not lady."

"Apologies," Jack said, smirking. "Look, A.D.A., we tried to run the plate but couldn't get a good read on it. It happens."

"We had the impound lot take photos of the tag." Dillard opened her briefcase. She removed an 8x10 picture of Hollis's license plate. "It looks like it's been tampered with—bent here," she said, pointing to the creases in the metal.

"Yup, looks that way."

"However, that video that's circulating doesn't seem to show this kind of damage. Are you saying this is the plate you saw on Hollis Montrose's vehicle when you initiated the stop?"

"I don't know, maybe," Jack said. "Like I said, it was dark."

"And you'll testify to that in court? That you aren't sure of the condition of the plate because it was dark?" Dillard asked.

"Yeah, that's what I said."

"Had you ever seen or met Hollis Montrose before that night?" DaSilva asked.

"No, why?"

"But you are aware he was formerly an officer with the Chicago Police Department?"

"News to me."

"You're telling us that you didn't know that?" Dillard asked. "You expect us to believe that?"

"Believe whatever the hell you want, but I'm telling you that I had no clue who the guy was when we pulled him over. Now, can I go inside? I'm wet. I'm freezing my balls off. And I'd like to avoid pneumonia."

"One more thing," DaSilva said. "Montrose filed an official complaint against the CPD and a lawsuit before leaving the department years ago, after which he took a position with Metra."

"So?"

"In both the complaint and lawsuit, he names officers who verbally harassed him during his tenure and states that he was passed over for numerous promotions."

"All that, and the guy still got on with Metra? They must've been desperate."

"Montrose cites off-duty incidents in which he was called racial slurs and was threatened with physical violence if he told anyone."

"Off-duty incidents?"

"That's correct," DaSilva said. "One of the incidents occurred when a group of officers was at the bar celebrating an officer's promotion and another during an officer's retirement party. He said four or more officers singled him out and assailed him with racial slurs."

Jack rubbed his hands together and blew his hot, foul breath to warm them. "Will you get to the point?" he said. "What the hell does that have to do with me?"

"According to our records, you were employed by CPD at the same time."

"You know how many cops are on the force? I'm telling you I don't know the guy."

"You're positive you never had a run-in or interacted with Montrose in any capacity? Not even during one of these off-duty events?"

"Read my fucking lips: I. Don't. Know. Montrose. The first time I laid eyes on him was during the traffic stop."

"Dunham, you need to be aware that your entire record is going to be called into question. Do you understand that?" Dillard asked. "Anything you keep from us will only hurt our case, and you don't want that, because it would cost you whatever career you have left."

"Save the threats, lady."

"A.D.A. Dillard."

"Wow, your husband must love you," Jack said. "Or maybe you don't swing that way, huh?"

"You better watch your mouth," Dillard said. "I can make your life a living hell."

"Can't get any worse. Now, if you'll excuse me, I'm freezing, and I need to take a leak."

"We'll be in touch, Officer Dunham," DaSilva said. "And I shouldn't have to tell you this, but don't leave town."

"Next time you want to have a little chat, I'll be sure to have my union rep present," Jack said, and made his way upstairs and onto the porch. He fumbled with the door, unable to get a firm grip on the handle, and finally staggered inside.

His sons were running around with lightsabers. They were only two years apart, and after drinking, he could barely tell one from the other.

"Stop running in the house!" he shouted. "And your room had better be clean."

The boys stopped and gauged their father's surly mood, then raced upstairs to their room.

Corrine came up from the basement holding a laundry basket. "Those two looked pretty serious," she said. "What'd they want?"

"It's nothing."

"Definitely looked like something to me."

"They just wanted to ask me some questions. Don't bust my balls about it."

"What kinds of questions?"

"Routine stuff about a case."

"Just any case? Or do you mean the one you got suspended over?"

"I'm not suspended," he said. "I'm on paid leave. There's a big fucking difference."

"Can you not curse while the kids are around, please?"

"They're upstairs, they can't hear shit."

"Can you just do as I ask for once?"

"Whatever," he said, nearly falling as he struggled to take off his boots.

"Seems like whatever got you put on leave was just the excuse you needed to get wasted."

"Sue me, I had a beer."

"Just one?"

"Yes, I had a beer or two, so what? I risk my life day in and day out. I put food on the table and keep a roof over our heads. I deal with the worst people this city has to offer and get shit pay in return. Then I come home to you, and well, you're no peach, are you? So yeah, I fucking drink."

"What did I say about the language?"

"Give me a break—"

"You can save the pity party because I've heard it all before."

"What the hell do you know? Why do I even bother explaining anything to you? You haven't worked a real job in fifteen years."

"I got eyes, Jack. I see what's going on. You can lie to DaSilva and Dillard, but you can't lie to me."

"Save it, will you? I've had to listen to enough assholes today who think they know best. Like they've got it all figured out."

"You'd better hear me, Jack." Corrine set the basket on the floor and squared up to her husband. "Whatever you did, I'm not going to let you take our family down with you."

Jack grabbed her by the shoulders and shook her viciously. "Don't you threaten me," he said. "You better remember, everything you've got came from me. Without me, you'd have nothing."

"You're hurting me," Corrine said, trying to wrench out of his grip. "Let go."

"Threaten me again and see what happens to you."

Jack's fingers dug into her flesh and she cried out, "Let me go!"

The boys appeared at the top of the stairs. The oldest, Aidan, said, "Dad?"

"Mind your business. Your mom and I are just talking."

"Why's mom crying?" their other son, Martin, asked. Though Jack never vocalized it, Martin was a mistake. He always thought things might've been different between him and Corrine if it had only been Aidan. They might've managed better with one kid, but two had brought about more stress and more sleepless nights, pushing their marriage to the brink.

"Don't do this in front of the boys," Corrine said.

Jack looked at his sons' faces. Their expressions reminded him of Hollis's face the night they shot him. Fear was present, but helplessness, too, like there was nothing Hollis could do to stop the inevitable.

He let Corrine go and stepped away from her. She quickly rushed upstairs to the boys and ushered them to their room.

31

BEAU LEE HAD TAKEN THE ELEVATOR FROM THE LOBBY OF ALVAREZ'S building to her office. He entered the room with a large box. "It's here," he said, setting it on Alvarez's desk as Capes looked on. "The courier just dropped it off."

Alvarez popped up from her seat, eager to dig into the records. Beau Lee couldn't hide his exuberance, either. He was like a child on Christmas morning, hoping to have received the ultimate gift—evidence that would suggest Hollis's shooting was anything but by the book. If he could demonstrate that the officers had participated in racial profiling in the past or had a record of biased policing, it could be the leverage they needed.

"Man, that's a big box," Capes said. "Those records must go back decades."

"Even with the three of us, it'll take some time to go through all this," Alvarez said, pulling out files. "Some of these look to be fifty pages thick."

"That's a good sign," Beau Lee said. "It means these guys have long histories with lots of contact with the public."

"Let's just hope these records haven't been tampered with," Alvarez said. "CPD likes to cover for their own."

Beau Lee's phone rang; he pulled it from his pocket, glanced at the screen, and answered: "Officer Doyle. Please tell me you've got good news."

"That's Doyle?" Capes abandoned his task and listened in on Beau Lee's phone call. "Please tell me he's got something on Caruthers."

"Counselor," Finn said, "I've got Caruthers's address, but I'm not sure if he still lives there. He mentioned bouncing after we spoke to him at the café. The listed address, which might be old now, is in Wicker Park. I'm ready to head over there to cover our bases. Just say the word."

"Well, thank the Lord. How about you pick up me and Capes in an hour so we can head over to Caruthers's place together?"

"Not a problem," Finn said. "I'm just finishing some things up here at the precinct."

"Should I ask how you got Caruthers's information?"

"Nothing nefarious," he said. "Turns out he'd put in for a transfer to Metra five months ago and was waiting for an interview. I just had personnel send over his application."

"He did say he wanted to leave CPD," Capes said.

"It could speak to issues in the department's culture. Might even help show that what happened to Hollis was more than an isolated incident. Anyway, I'll see you soon."

Beau Lee ended the call.

TWENTY MINUTES LATER, HE SHOUTED, "Bingo!" and pulled Jack's file from the box. "Let's see what we have here." It was, as anticipated, chock-full of citizen complaints. Two of which were incidents involving improper use of force. Jack had been required to attend anger management classes and undergo a psychological evaluation, the results of which were not included in the file. His supervisor described him as an "exceptional officer who is an asset to the city and important in the department's mission to reduce incidents of crime."

Over the years, Beau Lee had read numerous police files like Jack's and knew how to separate the fluff from the smoking gun. The citizen complaints painted a far more authentic picture than the commendations or a supervisor's assessment. Despite that, he also knew that the citizen complaints could be easily dismissed as retribution from disgruntled citizens who were upset over their arrests.

Next, he read Chaz Rossi's file. As a new officer, he had little experience. There were no commendations, and one citizen complained that he had aided Jack in pinning an elderly woman to the ground. The woman had been suspected of shoplifting, and the arrest led to abrasions to her arms and legs. However, an even more damning complaint stood out in which both Jack and Chaz were cited. A man alleged he was arrested without cause and that Jack had stolen his wallet.

Beau Lee set the complaints aside to scrutinize later and continued sifting through the box. He located four more complaints. Two for Rory Caruthers and two for Leonard Johnson. Both stemmed from incidents in which individuals were being arrested while intoxicated. One individual suffered a dislocated thumb while being arrested outside a bar he'd been thrown out of. The other individual was an unhoused man who'd been arrested for public intoxication after urinating on the window of an upscale restaurant in West Loop. It was noted that the urination occurred in full view of diners, including two city council members. The man claimed that during the arrest he was struck multiple times by Johnson, resulting in injuries to his face and neck.

Beau Lee continued to dissect the files, taking detailed notes. He was already drafting Hollis's defense in his head, thinking of how best to present the blemished officers to the jury. It wouldn't be advantageous to demonize them all, as he was certain that Rossi and Johnson had arrived on the scene and entered a situation they didn't fully understand. Still, they weren't without responsibility and needed to be held accountable. But the ringleader, the man who had instigated the entire ordeal, was Jack Dunham, and there was something Beau Lee still wasn't seeing . . . something that seemed to exist just below the surface but had not yet been revealed, and he was convinced it would turn the case upside down.

32

JACK SHOWERED, ALLOWING THE STEAMING WATER TO CASCADE DOWN HIS face until he was sober enough to think straight. Afterward, he dried off and wrapped the towel around his waist. He opened the bathroom door that led to his and Corrine's bedroom and sat on the edge of the king-size bed, which he rarely shared with Corrine. When he wasn't in Heaven's arms, he usually slept on the couch or in his La-Z-Boy.

Corrine was still up in the boys' room. She was probably telling them how horrible Jack was and scheming to leave him. He would almost respect her if she did.

With the haze of the alcohol starting to lift, clarity crept back in.

Jack did most of his thinking at the bar he'd now been banned from, and without the neighborhood watering hole, he'd need to steal away to consider the mess he'd found himself in. The visit from the prosecutors meant they were evaluating him and his credibility. He knew his record would be called into question, specifically his share of citizen complaints. There'd been minor disciplinary action, but also commendations, such as the Medal of Valor for his courage and heroism, granted by the 100 Club of Cook County. They would certainly vouch for him; Jack was a good cop. Maybe he slipped up now and again, but no more than anyone else with a badge who actually did their job. It was impossible to be a perfect cop—invested and actively working to reduce crime and not get into some shit now and again. And if put on the stand, he'd tell an entire courtroom exactly how hard he worked for the citizens of Chicago, no matter their race, gender, or station in life. Then, he'd argue for his reinstatement—no, he'd *demand* it—and explain how one good cop is better than ten bad ones, that without him patrolling, citizens were less safe.

It all sounded valiant in Jack's head. He imagined the headline in the police union's newsletter: "Hero Cop Defends His Career, Name, and Reputation." The conservative news media would eat it up. There wouldn't be a chance in hell of his being railroaded by the rainbow coalition and kumbaya crowd, who loved demonizing hardworking cops and hated traditional American policing, which meant taking a hard stand against all crimes, no matter how small.

Chicago was a dangerous cesspool no matter who was in the White House, and the country needed to be reminded of the hell that cops went through having to police places like it, Detroit, New York, Los Angeles . . .

He stood up, walked to the closet, and reached for a shoebox on a high shelf. Inside, wrapped in an old rag, was Hollis Montrose's wallet. "What are you doing?" Corrine asked, standing in the doorway.

Jack scrambled with the wallet and box and shoved it all back on the shelf. "Didn't think you'd come back down."

"Maybe I shouldn't have," she said, suspiciously eyeing the shoebox.

"So, what do you want?"

"I never wanted the boys to grow up in a broken home like I did. I don't know what happened to you. Maybe you've always been this way and I was too blind to see it."

"I smelled meatloaf. Is it ready?"

"I'll leave it on the stove for you, but it's better if you eat it in here, away from us."

Jack shut the closet door. "Just let the boys know I do love them." Corrine ignored the request. "Are you going out later? The forecast is calling for heavy snow."

"What's it matter?"

"It doesn't. I only want to be able to tell the boys where you are in case they ask." She was silent for a moment, then approached her husband. Looking him in the eyes, she said, "I'm tired of hurting. Aren't you?"

"It's all I've ever known."

"Then let this be it. Plenty of Catholics get divorced nowadays."

"Yeah right, and have you take half my pension? Not in a million fucking years."

Corrine sighed. She looked as if she were on the verge of tears again. "Sometimes I wish I knew what happened to the man I married."

"That makes two of us."

33

WHEN THEY ARRIVED AT RORY'S APARTMENT BUILDING, THEY FOLLOWED A female resident inside. Beau Lee knew that if it hadn't been for Finn's making small talk and flashing his badge and a smile, they wouldn't have gained entry. Finn had violated numerous policies as a sworn officer, which conflicted with Beau Lee's moral code. Here he was, fighting police corruption, particularly officers who, under the color of authority, had broken laws, violated policies, and violated people's civil rights. Yet, he stood by as Finn did the same. Should it have mattered that Finn was working to get justice for Hollis? How could Beau Lee justify violations when it was the same behavior that might've led to Hollis's being pulled over and shot?

He wasn't sure he wanted to explore the answer, fearing he wouldn't like the direction it would take. Self-evaluation could be messy, and while Beau Lee never shied from it, he knew it would require Gigi to serve as a sounding board.

God, he missed his wife . . .

"You guys stand clear," Finn said before knocking on Rory's door. "Officer Caruthers, open up! If you're in there, we need to talk."

Capes used his foot to nudge three boxes stacked next to Rory's door. "Guy's got a lot of packages out here," he said. "He hasn't been out in a minute."

More knocks, harder this time. "Caruthers, it's Doyle. Hey man open up, will you? We only want to talk and make sure you're all right."

"You think he made good on his word and left town? Could account for the packages," Beau Lee said.

"I thought he meant after the trial. An open shooting investigation means you keep your ass local."

Capes looked unconvinced. "Still, dude might've bounced . . ."

"Nah, not Caruthers. Doesn't seem like the type," Finn said. "He put in for a transfer to Metra—I don't think he'd just tuck tail and run."

"Unless someone gave him a good enough reason," Beau Lee said. "I suppose everyone can be incentivized."

"You ain't never lied, boss," Capes said. "But I don't think he's here. Should we call it?"

"Damn it," Beau Lee said. "We have his affidavit, but I was hoping he'd see right and agree to be our star witness. It would mean so much more to the judge and jury. I worry the affidavit's going to be disqualified as hearsay."

"Hold on," Finn said, ready to knock again. "I think I hear someone inside."

"I don't hear anything," Capes said.

"You sure? Thought I heard someone call for help."

Beau Lee instantly grew worried. "I know what you're doing, Finn. It's a bad idea."

Finn smiled. "Yeah, maybe," he said, just before kicking the door open. "No point in arguing now."

Inside, the curtains were drawn and the place stunk of stale pizza. Clothes were strewn about on the couch and floor, and dishes were piled in the sink.

"You in here, Caruthers?" Finn shouted, but there was no answer.

"I'll check the bedrooms," Capes said, heading toward what looked like a large suite.

Beau Lee stayed in the living room surveying the mess. It was clear that Rory hadn't been home for days. He looked for signs of foul play—evidence of a struggle, like broken items or blood, but there was none.

Capes returned from his search. "Nada," he said. "Guy's gone."

"Yeah, looks like he left in a rush," Finn said.

Beau Lee sucked his teeth. "The question is, did he leave on his own accord or by force?"

"So, what are we going to do about his door?" Capes asked.

"I'll leave my card," Finn said, placing it on the entry table. "If he shows up, he'll know to call me."

"Let's get out of here," Capes said. "I don't think we want to have to explain this to the superintendent or the cops."

"Agreed," Beau Lee said, leading them out.

34

HOLLIS HAD BECOME FRAIL. THE NIGHT HE WAS SHOT, HE WEIGHED 192 pounds. After a month in the hospital, his weight had plummeted to 138 pounds.

He lacked the strength to do much, but by the grace of God, he appeared to be making progress every day. The feeding tube had been removed, and he was consuming liquids through a metal straw. The doctors and medical staff were amazed by his progress. Even the cops stationed outside his door seemed to marvel at his recovery. When Hollis attempted to speak, producing a few syllables at a time, Rocky basked in God's miracle and thanked the Lord every day.

"We're here, Hollis," she said to her husband as Jamillah stood beside her. "You will overcome this, my love. God isn't finished with you yet. And neither are we." Rocky began to pray: "Our Father, who art in heaven, hallowed be thy name. Thy kingdom come. Thy will be done . . ."

She knew that if the family stood on the solid rock of faith, they would get through the greatest tribulation they had ever faced. In the end, Hollis's triumph would change the world. It would be his testimony, and when people spoke his name and learned about his story, they would know that God was real.

Beau Lee entered the hospital room with Capes.

"We just got word," Beau Lee said. "The appellate court gave us a hearing date so we can argue Hollis's bail denial."

"Thank goodness," Rocky said. "It's been wrecking my nerves."

"It gives us one more shot in front of new judges."

"So no more Lambert?"

"Not at this hearing. We'll have three new judges to argue why Hollis should be given a reasonable bail. And if we win, we'll go back to Judge Lambert to set the bail amount," Beau Lee said. "And hopefully these judges will be more impartial."

It had become clear that Lambert was making an example out of Hollis, and her decision ignored his standing in the community and the fact that he had no prior charges of any kind. It was rooted in bias and spite.

"Finn and Capes will discuss the matter with our video experts. We believe we can show that the license plate was legible based on the video. Finally, we've got some good news."

Beau Lee turned to Finn and asked, "Is it possible that the police department still has possession of the damaged license plate in case it's to be entered into evidence during the trial?"

IN DOWNTOWN CHICAGO, THE *North City Weekly Press* was a bipartisan newspaper and one of the last independent publications still in print. After Rocky had spoken to a reporter at length, they'd published an exposé on the front page. The series continued for several weeks, with more information about Hollis's case added in each subsequent issue.

Rocky had the fourth installment tucked under her arm when the nurses placed Hollis in a wheelchair for the first time. She couldn't keep herself from crying as they wheeled him, arms shackled, through a secure wing of the hospital. They were accompanied by two CPD officers and a member of the Nation of Islam whom Harpo had tasked with keeping Hollis safe from crazies and the officers standing guard.

Rocky knew that not all the police could be trusted, and a few on

Hollis's rotation couldn't hide their derision for her husband and their family, so she was thankful for the security of Harpo's friend.

The fact that Hollis had even survived was a miracle, but Rocky feared what would happen if he wasn't able to walk and function well enough for Cook County Department of Corrections medical staff to be able to properly care for him. The doctors couldn't forecast his full recovery, and he still required round-the-clock support. He was unable to urinate without the aid of a catheter, and his bowel movements were few and far between. Ultimately, she knew Hollis feared he would not be able to walk again. However, he was trying his hardest to communicate, and Beau Lee and Alvarez took full advantage of the moment. They spent a considerable amount of time with Hollis each day, collecting information and trying to jar his memory from the night he was shot.

"Did you recognize any of the officers who stopped you?" Beau Lee asked. "An identifying feature or distinctive way they spoke?"

"No, I don't remember much," Hollis said. "Everything's coming up blank."

"Do you remember if you had your wallet in your pocket at the time the police pulled you over?" Beau Lee asked.

Hollis replied, "I can't remember."

Rocky interjected, "You always have your identification when you drive. That night wouldn't have been any different. You've been driving all your life and never got a traffic citation. There's no reason you wouldn't have had your wallet."

"Thanks for that, Mrs. Montrose," Beau Lee said. "We need Hollis to try to remember on his own. Hollis, can you remember anything having to do with your wallet that would have kept you from identifying yourself?"

Rocky looked on, hoping her husband would recall something that could help. She'd been told he was experiencing what doctors referred to as "missing time": When a person experiences something traumatic, their mind works to remove the event to protect them from pain, thus resulting in memory loss. While the memories often return, it's impossible to know when. It could be weeks, months, or years before Hollis might piece together exactly what happened that night.

Beau Lee reached into his briefcase, removed Hollis's laptop, and placed it near Hollis's free hand. "Thought I'd return this to you," he said. "We analyzed it and probed the hard drive for several days, but I'm afraid we weren't able to access your data cloud."

Hollis huffed as he tossed the laptop aside and said, "I just wish I could remember more."

"The tide will turn in our favor," Alvarez said. "Something will break, I'm sure of it."

"You've got a good number of photos on your laptop," Beau Lee said. "Plenty of your grandkids. If you can go through them, it might help bring your memories back. Sometimes flooding the brain with positive images helps provide clarity."

Tears streamed down Hollis's cheeks as he began to look through photos of his grandkids. Rocky hugged her husband, and he wept on her shoulder.

"I saw photos of the playroom you were designing," Beau Lee said. "I guess you were documenting your progress?"

"All that HGTV I was watching," Hollis said with a smile. "It had me thinking I was a big-time contractor."

The men laughed, and the mood lifted.

"You'll get your chance to finish the room soon enough," Rocky said, wiping her and her husband's tears. "And you know the grandkids will love it."

Rocky moved a chair next to his bed. They were silent as Hollis clicked through the images—snippets of his life before the shooting. It seemed to brighten his spirit.

Finn entered the room holding a large, colorful tin of Garrett Popcorn, a Chicago staple and Hollis's favorite snack.

"What's that you got there, Doyle?" Hollis asked. "Is that what I think it is?"

"Your favorite," he said, holding up the tin. "A few of us pooled our money together and ordered you the biggest one we could find."

"Well, what are you waiting for?" Hollis asked, rubbing his palms together and nearly salivating. "Get that thing open."

Rocky was grateful there was still enough of the old Hollis left. The shooting hadn't completely destroyed him, and despite the uphill legal battles they were facing and the reality that he'd never walk again, he still managed to joke and smile, and that meant the world to her.

35

BEAU LEE AND ALVAREZ WALKED INTO THE STATELY DISTRICT COURT OF Appeals courtroom prepared to argue as if Hollis's life depended on it—because it did. If Hollis were released from the hospital and transferred to Cook County Jail, it was unlikely he'd survive due to the inadequate medical care provided by jail officials and the ever-present threat from other inmates.

Once settled at the defense table, Beau Lee observed the district attorneys' side of the courtroom, where DaSilva and Dillard sat with a self-righteous air. As co-counsels, their synergy was undeniable—two distinct yet complementary forces. They wore dark clothing, attire suited for a funeral—sharp black suits and American flag pins fastened to their lapels.

"It's like seeing Vader and the Emperor conspiring to build the Death Star," Alvarez said.

"Didn't take you for a *Star Wars* fan."

"I'm not a fan of the prequels, but the originals can't be beaten. You?"

"I'm more of a Trekkie."

"Why does that not surprise me."

"Tell me how you're feeling, Alvarez."

"Like my stomach is doing somersaults."

He smiled at her. "Good. You got this."

Alvarez nodded. "One thing's for sure: I know they didn't prepare as hard as I did, and preparation counts for a lot. Still, there's no way to predict the outcome of these things."

"You're ready for whatever they come at us with."

"Thank you, Beau Lee, but a couple of prayers won't hurt."

"That I can do."

"All rise," the bailiff shouted. "Hear ye, hear ye. All who have business before this honorable court, let them come forward, and they shall be heard."

Three appellate judges walked out in their robes and took their seats on the bench. The clerk of the court announced the first case on the docket: "*State v. Hollis Montrose*, the Defendant Appeals Denial of Bail."

Unlike the first bail hearing, the courtroom was filled with people, including Hollis's family, friends, and fellow officers; media outlets; and protesters Beau Lee recognized from outside the hospital.

Tensions were running high.

The chief judge looked out into the courtroom and announced, "Will counsel for the defense make their presence known before the court?"

Beau Lee stood up and said, "Beau Lee Cooper, along with Princess Alvarez, on behalf of the defendant Hollis Montrose."

"Very well. And for the State?"

DaSilva and Dillard stood. "Prosecutors DaSilva and Dillard, representing the State," DaSilva said.

"Is the plaintiff's counsel ready to proceed?" the chief judge asked.

Alvarez walked to the podium in the middle of the room and began, "May it please the court?"

"You may proceed, Ms. Alvarez."

"Your Honor, we are here today to appeal the district court's denial of my client, Mr. Hollis Montrose. He was denied bail for charges associated with an officer-involved shooting. This incident left Mr. Hollis critically injured, and as a result of his extensive injuries, he now faces permanent paralysis from the waist down. It's important to note that while the State frames this incident as four officers reacting to a dangerous man who was allegedly reaching for his gun and discharged it, there is no evidence to support this claim." Alvarez shot a glance at Dillard and DaSilva, hoping to gauge their reactions. She wanted to see them uneasy, if only slightly, but they both looked apathetic to her plea. She continued: "What we do know is that Mr. Montrose repeatedly identified himself as a police officer before he was shot in the back ten times. Mr. Montrose, like anyone charged with an offense, is presumed to be innocent until proven guilty in a court of law. The Supreme Court is clear that 'liberty is the norm, and detention prior to trial or without trial is the carefully limited exception.' *United States v. Salerno*, 481 U.S. 739, 755 (1987). Therefore, by denying him bail, his civil rights are being violated. Mr. Montrose is an upstanding family man and a police officer and has no criminal history. He deserves to be treated justly, as any other defendant would with his favorable history—"

The chief judge raised his hand, interrupting Alvarez, and said, "Thank you, Ms. Alvarez. Ms. Dillard, what is the State's position?"

"May it please the court," Ms. Dillard began. "The weight of the evidence against Hollis Montrose is significant, and the danger posed by him against his fellow law enforcement officers was quite serious. Mr. Montrose committed a violent and egregious act. We have concerns that he poses a danger to the community. As a police officer, the crime for which he is accused constitutes a betrayal of public trust. If the violation of that oath wasn't enough, the severity of the allegations alone justified the court's decision to deny bail. This court must consider that prior to this incident, Mr. Montrose was an officer at Metra, which gives the State concerns about his flight. Access to these connections at Metra could potentially facilitate evasion of law enforcement."

Another judge interjected, "That's a stretch, Ms. Dillard. Isn't Mr. Montrose in intensive care and paralyzed?"

"Your Honor, in my and Attorney DaSilva's careers, we have seen every evasion tactic in the book. Nothing, and I mean nothing, is unfathomable when we're considering a desperate criminal. No one is above the law, including and especially law enforcement officers. Hollis Montrose should be subject to a higher standard as he was in a position of public trust, which he has violated. If all of this wasn't persuasive enough, we were notified this morning by forensics that Mr. Montrose tested positive for gunshot residue."

Alvarez was rattled to her core but did her best to maintain her stony composure. She gave Beau Lee a hard look, as if to express her confusion.

Blindsided again.

Dillard continued. "Your Honor, the evidence is clear. Send a message to Mr. Montrose and other would-be offenders by upholding the lower court's decision to deny bail."

"Ms. Alvarez, would you like to respond?" the judge asked.

"We were unaware of this alleged new finding," she said. "It's the first we've heard of any gunshot residue being found on our client."

"Do you have any additional arguments for the court to consider?"

Alvarez continued: "In addition to this unprecedented surprise, the arguments proffered by Ms. Dillard are beyond the realm of understanding and completely illogical. Mr. Montrose is in no condition to flee and has no intention of evading legal proceedings. There is no reason for the court to believe that he should not be allowed pretrial release. As a reminder, the court can impose various conditions, with respect to 'the least restrictive condition, or combination of conditions, that will reasonably assure the appearance of the person as required and the safety of the community,' 18 U.S.C. section 3142(c)(1)(B)."

"We are familiar with the statute, Ms. Alvarez."

"Of course, Your Honor. As for the pretrial conditions the court can choose to impose, they will ensure public safety without undermining public confidence." Alvarez took a beat to catch her breath. Her adrenaline and rage were drying out her mouth. "It's for these reasons we respectfully ask that the court overturn the lower court ruling and grant Mr. Montrose bail with any conditions the court sees fit."

The judges turned off their microphones and mumbled among themselves. Then, the chief judge said, "We will take this matter under advisement and issue our ruling. For now, this court is adjourned."

It was back to the waiting game, with Hollis's freedom once again left in limbo.

36

JACK'S UNION REP HAD CALLED HIM THAT AFTERNOON TO INFORM HIM that Internal Affairs had closed the investigation and had deemed the shooting to be within policy. The police union began the process of getting him and his fellow officers fully reinstated. At the same time the news emerged that they were cleared of any wrongdoing, Hollis Montrose was fired from his job at Metra. Jack thought it was a good indicator that the buzz around the case would soon die down, and knowing Hollis would lose his health insurance and pension was like the cherry on top of his ten bullet wounds. Jack hoped the loss would crush him enough that Hollis would plead guilty and the entire ordeal would end. Then, life could go back to normal, with him and Chaz on patrol and Hollis's meddling attorney, Beau Lee Cooper, returning to whatever rock he'd climbed out from under.

Jack arrived at Heaven's apartment shortly after two A.M. She'd told him earlier that day her roommate was out of town, visiting her parents in Florida, and they'd have the place to themselves. It was the first time Heaven had invited him inside, and it felt like a relationship milestone.

She lived in a brownstone on Cleveland Avenue in Lincoln Park. It was a nice neighborhood—quiet and safe. He felt tense as he walked the stairs and rang the doorbell. Going to Heaven's home felt more like they were dating and less like hooking up. He'd been treating women as playthings for so long that he wasn't sure how to treat Heaven as something more, but he liked her enough, and he was willing to try.

Heaven answered the door in a silk robe, having just showered after her shift at the bar. She smelled like vanilla and lavender.

"Hi, handsome," she said, leaning in to kiss him. The moment their lips touched, he felt like the world had stopped spinning. "Your lips are so cold. Hurry, come in and get warm."

"You smell great," he said, touching her bare stomach. "Soft, too."

"Hurry, Jack. It's freezing out there."

Heaven led him into the living room, which was lit by flickering candles. Soft music was playing; she had set the mood. The place was well furnished on a grad student's budget: a cream-colored couch, a bookshelf crammed with books, and a dining room table that looked to be fashioned from reclaimed wood. There was wall art and floral tapestries. The first word that came to Jack's mind was *trendy*, a term he seldom used, if ever. It felt reserved for people with money and college degrees who shopped at the luxury retail stores on Oak Street that sold brand names he couldn't pronounce.

"Nice place."

"Thank you."

"You've got a lot of books."

"Yeah, mostly stuff for school. What do you like to read?"

"Oh," he said, taking a seat on her couch, "between the job and everything else, I don't have much time for reading."

"I get that . . ."

"Have you decided what you're going to do after graduation?"

Heaven paused and said, "Oh, I don't know yet. The job market is shit, so I'm not getting my hopes up. Why do you ask?"

Jack wasn't sure why he'd asked. After all, it went against his rule of knowing very little about his mistresses because ignorance was bliss, but Heaven was different, and they'd come to a mutual understanding that their relationship would be transparent. The more Jack told the truth, the more Heaven seemed invested in him.

"You're inquisitive tonight," she said, sidling up next to him. "Something on your mind?"

"It was just a question."

"No, it's fine. I like the curious you. Kinda turns me on."

Jack grinned, leaning back against the cushions. "Well, you always turn me on," Jack said.

"You seem very happy today."

"There's a lot of reasons to have hope. Today was a good day."

"Then let's make the night even better."

"When you put it that way, I'd love a drink."

Heaven met his eyes, a slow smile tugging at her lips, before finally rising to pour him a shot of Jack Daniel's. "You sure you don't want any nachos?"

"All I want is you wrapped up in my arms. But I need to talk to you for a few minutes about something serious."

"What is it?"

"The shooting of that Black cop is all over the news, and I want you to know the truth. Me and my fellow officers, we're trained to protect each other. When we saw him grabbing his gun, we all lived up to our oath. And that is to make sure that our fellow officers get home safely when the shift is over. Understand?"

"Yes, I do understand."

Jack rose and joined Heaven at the drink cart. He embraced her from behind, his mouth against the back of her head; the smell of her shampoo comforted him. "But this so-called civil rights lawyer is trying to turn the city against us. Even though all I've ever done is to try and protect the city by keeping law and order. And putting the crazy animals in check. You know what I mean?"

Heaven turned around and looked at Jack as if she really understood. "Of course. I've always seen you as my protector."

"During this trial, these lawyers are going to say some pretty bad things about me. I just want to know when the smoke clears and when all this is over, you'll still be by my side for the long run," Jack said, looking deep into her eyes.

"I'll be here for you, by your side, forever and ever. I love you, baby, and there's nothing anybody can say to make me stop loving you. I just want to be with you all the time."

"After all this is over, we're going to be together. I promise you. You make me so happy."

37

THE COLD HIT THEM LIKE A SLAP IN THE FACE—CHICAGO'S WINTER showed no mercy. Finn and Capes had been going around taking testimonies from folks who had submitted complaints about Jack Dunham. They were collecting affidavits to be extra prepared for the trial, but they were confident their findings only confirmed what the team already knew. But Finn and Capes weren't done. They had one more name. One more door. That door belonged to Jack Dunham.

"We need to do a stakeout at Jack's house and watch for his wife, Corrine, to come out," said Capes firmly.

Finn nodded. "If anyone knows the truth about Jack, it's his wife."

They hopped in their car and headed toward the Dunham household. They pulled up to a modest but well-kept two-story home nestled on the edge of a quiet neighborhood. After an hour or so of waiting, a small white SUV pulled into the driveway driven by a middle-aged woman who seemed to be wearing life's struggles on her shoulder.

Finn and Capes approached her before she got to the front door.

"Mrs. Dunham, I'm Officer Finn Doyle, and this is Investigator Brent Capers. We just have a few questions—it won't take long."

Corrine hesitated, then turned to face them. As she did, she told the children to go on into the house. Then she waited on the porch as Finn and Capes joined her.

The conversation that followed was layered with hesitation, grief, and hints of buried truth. Corrine was careful—too careful—like someone who'd spent years learning how to speak without really saying anything.

Finn began, "We know that officer-involved shootings can be traumatic for everybody. This one is impacting my fellow police officers and law enforcement agencies throughout the region. As you may have seen on the news, Hollis Montrose was also a police officer." He paused here to see if she would have any kind of response or reaction. When she remained quiet, he continued. "We're speaking with Officer Montrose's family, along with the families of the other officers involved. That's why we've come to speak with you today. Have you noticed whether your husband may be experiencing any mental health issues?"

"Jack is the same always, every day," Corrine replied.

Capes chimed in, "What about any heightened emotional responses or more aggressive behavior in his day-to-day life?"

"No. Like I said, Jack's the same Jack as he always is, every day."

Finn said, "Are you aware of whether he's taken advantage of any of the mental health services that the department offers?"

"I am not aware. We don't talk about his work much. We try to leave his work at work and not let it affect our family life."

Finn nodded his head. "I see. Thank you very much for your time, ma'am."

Before they left, Capes reached into his coat pocket and pulled out a card. He handed it to her slowly, holding her gaze.

"If anything else comes to mind, anything at all," he said, "please don't hesitate to call me day or night. Doesn't matter what time it is. We're only trying to get to the truth of what happened here for the benefit of all involved."

Corrine took the card but didn't say a word. She just nodded, her fingers curling tightly around the edges.

Back in the car, Finn audibly exhaled. "She's hiding something."

Capes stared out the window. "Yeah. And I think whatever it is, it's big."

38

AT FIVE A.M., THREE MEN FROM THE DEPARTMENT OF CORRECTIONS ENtered Hollis's hospital room, along with nursing staff. It had been a night of broken sleep for Rocky, who had worry on her mind. She'd just dozed off in a vinyl recliner when she was startled awake by a well-built bald man in cargo pants and a tactical jacket. He brushed past her and began unshackling Hollis's wrist from the bed rail.

"What's going on here?" Rocky asked. "Are you taking my husband somewhere?"

The bald man was cavalier. "We're with the Prisoner Transport Security Division, ma'am. We've been ordered to take your husband to the Cook County Department of Corrections."

"Ordered by whom?"

The man pulled an envelope from his pocket. "The judge's office, ma'am. If you have issues, you'll need to take it up with the judge presiding over his case."

Rocky opened the envelope and read the document. It was a transportation order signed by Judge Kathleen Lambert.

"I don't know the particulars. My job is to transport people who've been remanded to custody. I suggest you contact your attorney, if you have one."

Hollis was under the influence of pain medication, and he didn't make a fuss. "Something wrong, Rocky?" he asked. "Are they taking me for more X-rays?"

"No, sweetheart. Just do as they say. I'm going to fix this." Rocky reached into her purse, took out her phone, and dialed Beau Lee.

"Men are here, and they're taking Hollis away," she said. "They say they're with the Department of Corrections."

"The judge must've issued the transportation order," Beau Lee said.

"But he isn't well enough to go to jail, and the doctor told me his paralysis isn't improving. There has to be something we can do," she said, her voice unsteady, as though fighting to hold back panic and tears at once.

"Let me call Alvarez," he said. "The appellate court is dragging its feet on the appeal, and we'll need to apply more pressure."

"They won't give him the proper care in jail, you know that," she said. "This can't be happening. Hollis needs to stay in the hospital."

"I understand, and I'm going to get working on this right now."

"All right," she said. "Thank you."

The nurses secured Hollis to the wheelchair and were prepared to wheel him out of the room when the bald man took hold of the handles. "We'll take it from here," he said, motioning for the nurses to step back.

Rocky attempted to follow them but was stopped just shy of the elevator.

"Everything's going to be okay, Hollis. Don't worry. We're going to fix this." The elevator doors opened, and the bald man ordered his fellow officers to remove all the visitors and personnel who were on it, forcing them to disembark on an unintended floor. Once the elevator was empty, he pushed Hollis inside.

Rocky felt helpless as she watched the doors close.

And she did the only thing she could think of: She prayed for her husband, her children, and everyone who loved Hollis. She prayed for moments of peace in the midst of her family's torn-up state, and most of all, she prayed for deliverance.

39

TWO WEEKS HAD PASSED, AND HOLLIS WAS STILL IN THE COOK COUNTY Jail. Rocky was at Alvarez's firm discussing the case with Jamillah, Beau Lee, and Alvarez. Harpo came in and embraced her. He tried to reassure her that even though Hollis was in jail, there were people on the inside who guaranteed they'd look out for him.

"It's not about protecting him from the other inmates, it's about making sure he's receiving adequate healthcare. And there's nobody you have on the inside that can guarantee that," said Rocky.

"Please calm down, Mama," Jamillah begged. "Your blood pressure will rise again. Then you'll need healthcare, too. I'm getting too close to my due date and cannot handle the stress of both of my parents being hospitalized."

"I just hate the thought of him in there and all the things that could be happening to him," Rocky said as she located a plush leather club chair and nearly collapsed into it.

"I'm so sorry, ladies," Beau Lee said. "It's an awful thing that's happening here. A travesty of justice if I've ever seen one. Unfortunately, Judge Lambert has all of the discretion to make these decisions. Based on the state attorney's petition and the political pressure of the police union, she chose to order Hollis be confined to Cook County

Jail as he awaits trial. We knew that once his condition improved, the judge could order him to jail. Regrettably, that day has come."

"There must be something we can do to get him out of there," declared Rocky. "I'm telling you they're not equipped to give a person who is paralyzed the proper medical care. They keep trying to give my husband a death sentence to cover up their crimes!"

We've filed an additional petition with the appellate court to review Hollis's bail denial on the grounds that he isn't a flight risk. He doesn't own a passport, and he requires ongoing medical attention. The petition cites other cases in which suspects were charged with violent crimes against law enforcement and had been granted bail. I hope it'll speed up their ruling."

"I pray it will," Rocky managed.

"He won't be there for long, Mama," Jamillah said. "God has ordained it. Daddy's going to get out."

"We need to see him," Rocky said. "I need to know he's all right in there."

"I don't know if it gives you much comfort," Alvarez said, "but from what we've been told, he's spending most of his time in the medical wing receiving care."

"You mean he isn't with the other prisoners?"

"He's likely had minimal contact with anyone outside the infirmary. In this case, his condition would require him to be kept isolated."

"But I know how they treat ex-police officers in jail, and who's going to protect him when he's no longer in the infirmary?"

"It's not something we advertise, but the Nation of Islam has significant membership in the correctional system," Brother Harpo said. "Many of our brothers have found enlightenment during their darkest hours. I've informed our members to look out for Hollis and to protect him at all costs."

Beau Lee's phone rang. He quickly patted his pockets and came up empty. "Now, where'd I put that thing?" He dug in his briefcase, which was in the chair next to him, found the phone, and answered it before it went to voicemail. "Hello?" He nodded as he listened. "Thank you," he said, then ended the call.

"Who was that?" Alvarez asked.

"The court clerk. We've got a trial date."

"Already?"

"December nineteenth."

"DaSilva and Dillard must be cooking with butter," Brother Harpo said. "Not to mention, it's an election year, and DaSilva'll want to tout Hollis's case as his crowning achievement."

Capes entered the room with two pizza boxes, a salad, and a liter of cola. It was going to be another long night of trial preparation. "I got dinner," he said. "One extra cheese and one veggie pie. Chicago style, of course."

40

ALVAREZ'S OFFICE HAD BECOME GROUND ZERO FOR THE JUSTICE FOR Hollis Montrose Trial Team. Beau Lee and Alvarez were updating Nellie by conference call since he was still assisting from Houston.

"Tomorrow marks the one-month anniversary since Hollis was shot," Alvarez said. "And it's been two weeks since we made the appeal, and they're taking their time while Hollis sits in jail. We should push the issue again with the trial judge at the case management hearing tomorrow."

"We can try to bring it up again, but I don't think Judge Lambert is going to change her ruling unless the appellate court overturns her decision," explained Beau Lee. "And who knows how long it will be before they make their decision. We've got to come up with another plan."

"Well, partner, we're all ears," Nellie said.

"Let's call a press conference tomorrow after the hearing. The public needs to know what's going on," Alvarez said.

"What would we announce, other than it being one month since the incident? The public knows how long it's been," Nellie said.

Before Alvarez could respond, Beau Lee said, "You know what? It's been a long day. I'll sleep on it. Let's discuss this more after the case management conference. By then, Lord willing, I'll have a plan."

* * *

THE NEXT MORNING, BEAU LEE, Alvarez, and Capes made their way down the icy sidewalk toward the courthouse. The holiday season was in full bloom and decorations hung from every light post on West Washington Street. A bitter wind howled through the towering skyscrapers, carrying with it a biting chill. The unforgiving weather offered a brutal and somber backdrop for the battle Beau Lee and his team were waging against the city's corruption, which felt as endless as its winter. The news trucks were already lining up in anticipation of the press conference, which was to come after the case management hearing. With so much on the line, Beau Lee couldn't anticipate what he'd have to say post-hearing. His only desire was to ensure that Hollis was free to see Christmas and the New Year. Reporters and camera crews approached Beau Lee and his team, shoving microphones in their faces.

"Attorney Cooper, can you share any news with us before you go into court?" one reporter asked. Beau Lee said nothing.

"Did the appellate court make a ruling on your appeal?" another reporter asked.

"Are you going to ask Judge Lambert to reconsider bail for Mr. Hollis Montrose?"

Beau Lee continued to ignore them, likening their pestering to that of buzzing gnats.

Beau Lee saw Brother Harpo's car parked down the block and Harpo escorting Rocky, Jamillah, and Tyrone. Behind them were a group of young activists chanting, "We gon' do the most! To get justice for Mr. Montrose! We gon' do the most! To get justice for Mr. Montrose! We gon' do the most! To get justice for Mr. Montrose!"

They met at the top of the courthouse steps. Beau Lee smiled as he greeted Rocky with a hug and took her by the hand. Together with Alvarez, they entered the courthouse with Beau Lee feeling exuberant as he heard the chants, battle cries for justice.

* * *

"ALL RISE!" DECLARED THE BAILIFF as Judge Lambert walked in.

The courtroom was animated with rank-in-file police officers on one side of the courtroom and community activists from Chicago's South Side on the other.

The press was present in the back corner, with one press pool camera in the back simulcasting to the other news stations. Judge Lambert was matter-of-fact in her questions.

"Mr. DaSilva? Does the State have anything new to report at this case management conference?"

DaSilva stood up and sifted through some papers. "Your Honor, may I approach to give this report to the clerk for the file?"

Judge Lambert nodded her head and said, "You may. What are you presenting to the court, and have you given a copy to the defense counsel?"

"Your Honor, we notified the court of appeals that the gunshot residue test on Hollis Montrose was completed. Those reports are to be entered into the clerk's file. In addition, we presented Mr. Cooper and Ms. Alvarez with the report at the appellate court. Outside of those actions on our behalf, we continue to wait for the internal affairs investigation to be fully completed and final reports issued," he said before retreating and taking his seat.

Judge Lambert looked at the defense counsel's table and asked them the same question.

Beau looked back at Rocky and Jamillah holding hands as they listened intently. Then he stood. "Your Honor, as the defendant continues to wait for the appellate court to render its decision on his right to bail, and as the defendant continues to wait for the State Bureau of Law Enforcement and the Internal Affairs reports to be released, and despite a month having passed since the shooting that left him paralyzed, and the fact that there is a video where you can clearly see everything that happened in the shooting, the defense is compelled, at this time, to invoke Hollis Montrose's constitutional right to a speedy trial," proclaimed Beau Lee.

DaSilva shot up. "Objection, Your Honor! As the defense counsel said, we don't have any of the investigative reports completed at this time. Neither the State nor the defendant has the culmination of evidence to review in this case."

"Your Honor, the State of Illinois, based on whatever evidence they've gathered, concluded that there was probable cause to arrest and charge Hollis Montrose with very serious capital offenses. Therefore, it is elementary criminal procedure, based on the constitution of the United States of America, that when a citizen's liberty is put at stake by the government, he has the absolute right to demand a speedy trial, so that his liberty will not be paralyzed for an indefinite amount of time," Beau Lee retorted.

Judge Lambert shook her head. "Mr. Cooper, do you understand that your moving for a speedy trial gives everyone involved in this proceeding little time to prepare?"

"Yes, I do, Your Honor."

"Madam Clerk," Judge Lambert summoned, "when were Mr. Hollis Montrose's charges filed?"

The clerk immediately started typing on her computer in search of the answer to the judge's question. "The record shows that the charges were filed by the state attorney on November 8, 2008," the clerk said. "Your Honor, that was thirty days ago."

"Under the State Constitution, we would have 120 days from that date to bring this matter to trial. Mr. Cooper, that would give you only ninety days. That would give the State only ninety days. And that would give this court only ninety days to take this capital felony criminal case to trial."

The judge clenched her jaw; her nostrils flared and her face went beet red. Her glasses slipped beyond her nose as she tapped lightly against the wooden desk, and when she looked up, her visage had twisted into a scowl. It cast a shadow of disdain across her otherwise composed demeanor.

There were rumblings in the courtroom. Alvarez leaned over and whispered in Beau Lee's ear, "Are you sure you want to do this? How are we going to be ready for a trial in three months?"

Beau Lee looked at her and said, "Hollis Montrose's survival depends on our being ready."

"Attorney Cooper, are you going to maintain this demand for a speedy trial, knowing the enormous stress that you'd be placing on this court?" Judge Lambert asked, clearly irritated.

"Your Honor, I answer that question very earnestly. Is the court going to maintain the denial of bail for Hollis Montrose, knowing the enormity of stress that it places on his liberty, his life, and his family?" Beau Lee said, matching the judge's vigor.

Judge Lambert removed her glasses as she began to speak. "Until we hear from the appellate court, my ruling stands, Mr. Cooper." Then, louder, "Is there anything further from either party in this case management? If not, this court is now adjourned." Without waiting for replies, she slammed the gavel.

Beau Lee felt his phone buzzing, and upon retrieving it, saw three messages from Nellie.

90 days?! What are you doing, Frat? was the first.

There's no way we can provide an adequate defense against those charges in that amount of time! read the second.

Are you trying to get an ineffective assistance of counsel bar complaint filed against you?! read the last text.

Beau Lee put his phone away and stood up along with everyone else. As the bailiff said, "All rise," Judge Lambert left the courtroom.

"Beau Lee Cooper, you sure are bold, I give you that. I knew we'd get along," Alvarez said.

"I can't take all the credit. When I first decided to take this case, I asked God to help us," Beau Lee said.

Just as he turned to leave, Beau Lee met eyes with DaSilva. DaSilva shook his head as if disgusted. "Is that how it works down in Houston? Do your best to annoy the judge and then request that she reconsider her previous ruling against you?"

"Well, down in Houston, I don't have to fight the Chicago machine, and I mean the whole trifecta: the police department, the state attorney's office, and the judge," Beau Lee said coolly. "But it doesn't matter, DaSilva. The truth is on our side. You're just grasping for straws."

"Your bail motion failed. Your appellate case is likely to fail. Your civil suit will almost definitely go down the drain. *That* would be my truth," DaSilva said, and he made his departure.

Rocky came up to Beau Lee and gave him a big hug. "Thank God for you, Beau Lee Cooper."

Before he could respond, Harpo chimed in. "Attorney Cooper, you sho' know how to bring the funk! You knocked all the Chicago powers that be on their heels after what you pulled today," he said with infectious jest. "Man, people are blowing up my phone from all across America. What did I tell you, Miss Rocky, we needed Beau Lee Cooper on this case."

"I thank the Lord for him every day," Rocky said, and turned to Alvarez. "And you, too, Princess. You make a great team."

"Okay, okay. Now let's get out of here. The media's waiting. The news has got to be breaking all over America." As they walked out, Beau Lee's phone buzzed again. This time the message was from Gigi, and it read: "Darling. Is three months enough time to adequately prepare?"

It would have to be.

41

IT HAD BEEN ANOTHER LONG NIGHT FOR ALVAREZ, BEAU LEE, AND CAPES, who'd been working in Alvarez's office. The initially pristine space was now littered with boxes, papers, takeout containers, and chairs at odd angles as the team shifted around, working in different areas.

"It's hard to believe that tomorrow marks thirty days since our last case management conference. Time is not our friend, Beau Lee. Time is not our friend," Alvarez said.

"I figure the DA's office is sweating just as much as we are. And all things considered, our case is stronger than theirs."

"Beau Lee Cooper, I don't know if that's your sincere belief or if you're just trying to put your game face on to keep the team inspired."

"I learned a long time ago as a young trial lawyer that if you don't believe in your case, you'll never be able to convince a jury to believe, either."

"I hear you," Alvarez said, and took a sip of her coffee. "Now, for the case management hearing tomorrow, I'm thinking we should check the docket to see what motions the state attorney has filed."

"Okay, good idea."

Alvarez opened her laptop and a moment later startled. "Oh my God! We finally got a ruling—the appellate court just issued its ruling!"

Beau Lee rose from his chair and looked over her shoulder. "What's it say?"

"It's seven pages long, so I'm scrolling down . . . to the end . . . Here it is . . ." she said, then began to read: "It is hereby ordered that the above styled matter is REVERSED and REMANDED to the lower court to issue a reasonable bail for the defendant, Hollis Montrose."

Beau Lee pumped his fist. "Yes!" he shouted. "I cannot wait to see DaSilva's face in the morning. This'll wipe that arrogant smirk right off it."

Alvarez gave a round of high fives. "Tomorrow can't come soon enough," she said.

"It's like my granddaddy said. Every now and then, the sun even shines on a dog's butt," Beau Lee said.

THE NEXT MORNING, THE ATMOSPHERE in the courtroom was charged. Rocky, Jamillah, and Harpo observed Beau Lee and Alvarez from their seats. Like Beau Lee, they were all cautiously optimistic that the appellate court's ruling would facilitate Hollis's release.

DaSilva and Dillard looked uneasy, and Beau Lee presumed it was because the appellate court's ruling had caused them a measure of angst.

Judge Lambert entered the courtroom from her chambers with haste.

"All rise," announced the bailiff as the judge took the bench.

"I don't want to waste any time this morning," Judge Lambert said, speaking quickly. "I've reviewed all the motions from the district attorney's office, and each one has been granted. And I understand that the appellate court issued their ruling as it relates to giving bail to Hollis Montrose. I'm ready to take up this matter at this time. Does the State have a position?"

DaSilva stood and cleared his throat. "Your Honor, we recognize the bail amount is to be set by the court, but we request that the amount reflect the violent nature of the crimes Mr. Montrose is accused of committing."

"Noted," the judge said. "Do you have a bail amount in mind?"

DaSilva spoke with the same righteous indignation that he'd displayed throughout the proceedings. "The State recommends that Mr. Montrose's bail justly reflect the attempted murder of the four brave police officers involved. Therefore, bail is to be set at two million dollars. Five hundred thousand for each man who nearly lost his life."

Beau Lee was flabbergasted at the number. He nearly had an out-of-body experience—he felt as if he were standing right in front of the judge, mouth agape and speechless. But he knew that wasn't how he appeared. The man the judge and prosecutors saw had a clenched jaw, and he was boiling with anger it took every ounce of his being to control.

"What is the position of the defense?" the judge asked.

"The State's demand for a two-million-dollar bail is outrageous considering all the extenuating facts and circumstances, Your Honor. Mr. Montrose is unable to pay a bail that high. It's the equivalent of setting no bail at all. Not to mention, the video shows that Mr. Montrose was pinned to the ground during his arrest and couldn't have fired his weapon," Beau Lee said.

"Objection!" bellowed DaSilva. "Judge, we clearly established in this court that gunshot residue was on Hollis Montrose's hand, which substantially supports the fact that he fired his weapon."

"Mr. DaSilva, your objection is noted. Please sit down. As for you, Mr. Cooper, the subject of gunshot residue leaves me to seriously consider Mr. DaSilva's request," the judge said.

Alvarez blurted out, "But Your Honor, it isn't conclusive."

"That remains to be seen," the judge said, visibly annoyed. "The court is ready to rule: In light of the court's findings, which are a part of the record, and taking into consideration the gunshot residue test, which indicates Hollis Montrose fired his weapon at officers the night of his arrest, the court orders that five-hundred-thousand-dollar bail be set for each count of attempted murder, totaling two million dollars."

Beau Lee stood up in a huff and declared, "Objection! This is preposterous."

"Attorney Cooper. Please sit down. I am not finished," Judge Lambert said. Her tone carried a sharp edge. She leaned slightly forward, her gavel poised in her hand as her eyes swept across the room. "The court also finds there is an additional five-hundred-thousand-dollar bail for the remaining charges of aggravated assault and the reckless display of a firearm, concluding that the entire bail amount for Hollis Montrose will be 2.5 million dollars."

"My God . . ." Beau Lee muttered.

"How can this be happening right now?" Alvarez said. "It's like we're in a nightmare."

Judge Lambert continued: "And Mr. Cooper, Ms. Alvarez, if you have a problem with the court's decision, you can file another appeal with the appellate court. But as for this court, the decision is final. Is there anything further from either party?"

DaSilva stood up, eyed Beau Lee, and seemed to gloat. His smirk had returned. "Your Honor, pursuant to your order, since we have already presented the State's witness list and all evidence we plan to present at trial to the defense, we ask the defense to do the same. We are requesting their witness list, evidence, and any other relevant information they plan to enter into the record. Considering we only have sixty days before trial, we need this done expeditiously, if we are to be in accordance with the speedy trial scheduling order."

"Attorneys Cooper and Alvarez, you would need to provide that information within the next five days," Judge Lambert said. "Will that be a problem?"

Alvarez gritted her teeth, fury locking her jaw, as Beau Lee stood up and swallowed. He heard Gigi's voice in his head say, "You better humble yourself for the sake of this case."

"Sometime today, Mr. Cooper."

"Apologies, Your Honor," he said, working to get his thoughts in order. "Now that our bail has been ordered by the court, the defense has reconsidered its position regarding its speedy trial motion and are open to a continuance by the court to make sure that the court and all parties have sufficient time to prosecute and defend this case."

"Oh no, Mr. Cooper," the judge said. It was a cold reminder of her authority, not just to Beau Lee but to the entire courtroom, which Beau Lee feared would erupt into protest. "Despite my cautioning you, it was your choice to move for a speedy trial, and a speedy trial is what you'll have. The trial date is set for March 8, 2009, which by my calendar is ninety days from today. I hope that will be speedy enough for you."

Beau Lee steadied his eyes at the judge, though on the inside he felt the weight of the enormity of the time restraint he was now under. "Yes, Your Honor," he said.

The judge banged her gavel and stood, signaling the end of the hearing. Her expression was as resolute as the mahogany wood columns behind her.

The bailiff shouted, "All rise!"

Beau Lee and Alvarez stood and watched Judge Lambert exit the courtroom as swiftly as she had come in.

42

WORD OF THE APPELLATE COURT'S RULING—THAT HOLLIS MONTROSE would receive bail—had spread like wildfire through newsrooms across America. The question everybody was asking, at least those who weren't present to hear it, was how much it would be. Outside the courthouse, over twenty cameras crowded the view. By the time Hollis's crew exited the building and reached the bottom steps, they'd been ambushed by a barrage of news crews, and they hadn't yet formulated their message.

A reporter yelled at at Rocky: "Since the appellate court granted your husband a reasonable bail, when will your family be getting him out of jail?"

She felt like a deer in headlights, because the truth of the matter was, she didn't really understand everything that had just transpired, but she did know they didn't have $2,500,000 lying around. Since time was of the essence, before they could create a narrative, Beau Lee stopped mid-stride, holding hands with Rocky on his left, and raised his right hand, causing the whole wave of commotion to come to a sudden stop. He knew that if he didn't speak up now, the narrative would be beyond their control. The Chicago Press, being well-versed in spontaneous press conferences, immediately propped up a podium out of nowhere in front of Beau Lee, Alvarez, Rocky, and the rest of the team. Within sixty seconds they all had their microphones mounted atop it.

"We just learned that despite the appellate court's issuing an order that Mr. Hollis Montrose, a law-abiding, nonviolent police officer with long-established ties to the community, was to be granted a reasonable bail because of the presumption of innocence until proven guilty, Mr. Montrose's exemplary life prior to this tragic incident is evidently irrelevant. The Chicago machine doesn't believe any negro in Chicago is presumed innocent until proven guilty. How else could it be said that a man who makes a police officer salary of fifty thousand dollars per year could be given a 2.5-million-dollar bail? A bail of that amount is tantamount to no bail at all. Even when we get close to the goal line, they move the goalpost on us." Beau Lee had been fighting a bigoted system for over ten years, but he would always be overcome with emotion at the discrimination Black people had to endure in such a blatant fashion. It was obvious he was wearing his emotions on his sleeve and wasn't behaving like the calm, collected crusader of justice that everyone had come to expect.

A reporter yelled out, "Attorney Cooper, does this mean you're going to appeal Judge Lambert's new bail order?"

"No, even though we strongly disagree with the ruling, we will not appeal. We believe that would take too long, as Hollis Montrose is in a jail that's not equipped to provide for medical needs. He is literally fighting for his life," Beau Lee said, pure adrenaline and emotion fueling his remarks. "We will make our appeal to the good people in Chicago and across America to raise this astronomical amount of money. At this moment, the Free Hollis Montrose bail campaign begins. The outcome for Mr. Montrose will be decided by the charity and the goodwill of the people of this country. The justice we are seeking will come from us. We will free Hollis Montrose despite the judge's ruling."

Beau Lee was filled with conviction. The activists started to chant until it reached a fever pitch: "Free Hollis Montrose! Free Hollis Montrose! Free Hollis Montrose!"

Beau Lee, Alvarez, and Capes escorted Rocky from behind the

podium and headed to where a professional driver was waiting in an SUV. Tyrone and Jamillah were in close proximity as he clutched his pregnant wife's hand.

As they entered the vehicle, Rocky asked Beau Lee, "Are you coming by the jail later?"

"I have a few things to see about, but yes, I certainly will."

"Good," she said. "I know Hollis might not show it yet, but he's listening. I've been telling him about you and all the work you've been doing to help us. I know he's smiling on the inside."

"I believe he is, Mrs. Montrose."

"I already told you, call me Rocky. And something tells me when he gets his wits back and properly meets you, you two are going to be fast friends."

Beau Lee smiled, then shut the door. The vehicle backed out of the parking space while news crews clamored to snap more photos. As they drove through the parking lot, a dark-green sedan sped up behind the SUV, then came around on the left side. The passenger window lowered. Beau Lee felt fear in the pit of his stomach, like he was watching the worst-case scenario unfold in slow motion. He began running toward the SUV, yelling, "Go! Drive!" fully expecting the barrel of a handgun or rifle to appear. "Capes! Check the green sedan—it's about to do something," he yelled. Capes and the press saw what was happening and started in that direction as well.

In an instant, arms extended out of the front passenger and back seat windows of the sedan. "Die, nigger cop killers, die!" They began throwing eggs against the side of the SUV, and the impact was startling enough to force the driver to make an abrupt right turn. He instinctively jerked the wheel, causing the vehicle to veer into the embankment. The tires screeched and there was a barrage of horns as the sedan sped through the parking lot in the opposite direction.

Before the journalists and photographers could turn their lenses, Beau Lee started running in the direction of the green sedan.

"Boss, hold up!" Capes shouted. "Stop, wait a minute!"

It was as if Beau Lee couldn't hear a thing as he continued sprinting after the green sedan. He didn't stop running, and with every step, he could feel the anger inside him boiling even more. His rage had returned, and this time, it had blinded him to danger as he continued sprinting across the parking lot. He ran another ten yards until he could no longer see the sedan. Then, he looked back and realized that Capes had been sprinting behind him, and the news crews with their cameras had recorded the entire ordeal.

"They're gone, boss," Capes said, breathing hard.

"You get the license plate?"

"Didn't have one."

"Damn it."

"They won't get away with it," Beau Lee said. "We will not be intimidated by these racist cowards. I refuse to let them. I won't let them bury Hollis Montrose."

The road to justice was fraught with moments like these, which were surreal and haunting and packed with pain. These were strange days, Beau Lee thought, where a Black man could ascend to the highest office in the land, yet unarmed Black people were still being gunned down in the streets by police, and the families had to suffer further indignities like being pelted with eggs—and sometimes worse.

"People are sick," Capes said. "No telling who or what might've been in that car."

"Sick and crazy," Beau Lee responded. "And it's only going to get worse now that we elected the first Black president."

"I hear you, boss," Capes said, pulling him away. "But I gotta get you away from danger. Boss, you gotta remember there are a lot of crazy people out on these streets. My job is to keep you safe. You gotta listen to me. Let's go!" He continued to pull him away as the news crews started to close in.

43

GIGI STARED AT THE TV, GRIPPING HER PHONE TIGHTLY AS SHE WATCHED footage of Beau Lee chasing a green sedan through a Chicago parking lot on the five P.M. news. The driver's vehicle swerved dangerously. Reporters were already throwing out assumptions about what had transpired, and Gigi's fear was making her sick to her stomach.

She hit Beau Lee's number and waited, tapping her foot anxiously. The phone rang twice before he picked up. "Gigi, I—" Beau Lee began, but she cut him off immediately.

"Don't you 'Gigi' me! What the hell were you thinking, chasing down that damn sedan? Are you trying to get yourself killed?" she snapped, her voice sharp with worry.

Beau Lee let out a deep sigh. "No choice, Gigi. They could have been connected to the case. I couldn't stand by and watch while they escaped."

"You're not a cop, Beau Lee! You're an attorney. You belong in the courtroom, fighting in *that* arena—not out here on the streets with Capes like Will Smith and Martin Lawrence!" Gigi said, her voice firm. "Bring your ass home. Now."

There was a long pause before Beau Lee responded, "I was planning to come home this weekend. I already had a flight booked for tomorrow evening, which would allow me to be there Friday night and all day Saturday before I fly out on Sunday. But I'll have Nellie change it to a seven o'clock flight tomorrow morning, because I love you, Gigi, and I know you're upset with me. I'll see you in the morning."

"Good," she replied, her voice softening but still resolute. "And when you get here, we'll finish this conversation. You need to understand that the most important job you have is being a father to your child—making sure her future is filled with love, hope, and you in it. Beau Lee Cooper, I love you, but you need to hear what I'm saying to you today."

Beau Lee didn't argue. The call ended, and Gigi took a controlled breath, trying to steady her nerves. She knew the case had Beau Lee stretched thin, but this was getting out of control. He was too close to the edge, and she had to pull him back in.

44

BEAU LEE WAS STARTLED OUT OF HIS SLEEP AS THE PLANE TOUCHED DOWN in Houston. His frequent flights were typically an opportunity for him to catch up on much-needed rest. But who was he kidding? Nothing compared to being in bed and actually getting a good night's rest. He yawned, gathered his briefcase, and exited the aircraft swiftly to make his way to baggage claim.

Beau Lee stood watching as the other passengers' luggage crept around the carousel. In addition to his fatigue, his mind was still on Hollis's bail predicament, but he was also eager to see Gigi. When he finally spotted his luggage coming down the conveyor belt, he snatched it and quickly headed toward the exit.

Outside, he spotted Nellie's black SUV idling in the passenger pickup area and made a beeline toward it.

Nellie was in the driver's seat, but he hopped out as Beau Lee approached. "How was your flight?" he asked. "Did you get some rest?"

"Not much," Beau Lee said.

Beau Lee knew he was going to have to explain what he was thinking during his attempt at a foot chase back in Chicago. While this was no laughing matter, Beau Lee chuckled about the fact that he'd almost caught those cowards. But he quickly snapped back to the reality of what had just occurred with them throwing eggs at him after the press conference. He understood all too well it could have been something much more dangerous than eggs. He took a few deep breaths. Beau Lee offered a silent prayer thanking God that it didn't end badly . . . and braced himself. He was sure Nellie had plenty to say, and despite knowing he'd probably be right, Beau Lee was in no mood to be chastised. There was just too much else at stake.

After helping Beau Lee put his luggage in the car, Nellie wasted no time. "Frat, what the hell made you think it was safe to run after that shitty sedan? That reminded me of O.J.'s Bronco," Nellie said, offering some levity at the situation. He and Beau Lee both laughed for a few moments.

"But, I think you're in too deep. Don't you realize how much you're putting at risk? It's not just your life on the line, it's also everyone else's around you," Nellie declared.

"Look, Nellie. I know what I'm do—" Beau Lee tried to assert before Nellie interrupted.

"I don't think you do," he said. "Frat, I know you're concerned with Hollis's freedom. But I'm concerned about *your* life. And just so you know, Gigi was almost inconsolable last night after she spoke with you. She called and gave me a mouthful. She thinks all of our firm members are okay with your attempt at playing Superman in Chicago. I told her that's not the case. I had your back and did my best to calm her down. But you have to know how worried she is."

Nellie continued. "I'm pretty sure she's waiting to plead her case for when you walk through that door. That woman loves you."

"And I love her," Beau Lee said instinctively. Feeling exasperated, he tried to rationalize. "Yeah, Nellie, I already know. She gave me an earful over the phone last night."

Nellie started, "But Beau—"

This time Beau Lee cut him off, saying, "Hold on, I let you say your piece, Frat. Now hear me out. If I let the enemies of equality win, then what does that say about me? Why did I become a civil rights attorney in the first place? Am I supposed to sit back and let injustice prevail? If I don't fight for Hollis Montrose, who will?"

Nellie took a deep breath and said, "Frat, I admire your conviction. We all do. But you need to be realistic. Have you considered what happens if you're not here to keep fighting? You're not Superman. You can be harmed . . . or worse."

"My fallibility is never far from my mind."

"Not only your fallibility, but the law firm's vitality."

"What do you mean?"

"The firm is now defending a defamation lawsuit filed by the Chicago police union, which is costing us money we don't have. And it doesn't matter how frivolous the lawsuit is, the cost of defending it is expensive."

"You think I don't understand that? I know what our firm is up against."

"Do you? Because we're having to spend a lot of the funds we just received from the bank settlement. I shouldn't have to remind you that that money was earmarked for the expansion."

"When we win the Montrose case, the settlement will be enough to replenish that account ten times over."

"Gunshot residue was found on Hollis's hands—you know what that means. Winning this case will be a long shot at best. But most importantly, Frat, the danger around you is clear and present. Do you want this to be the last case you fight?"

An airport cop appeared at Nellie's window and tapped on the glass. "Move it along," he said. "This is strictly a loading zone."

"Got it," Nellie said. "Sorry, Officer."

He shifted into drive, waited until traffic was clear, and then merged into the line of vehicles headed out of the airport.

"Nellie, do you think for one minute that I, Beau Lee Cooper, am going to throw in the towel?"

"Jesus, Beau Lee, I'm not telling you to give up, but you've gotta understand there's a price to be paid for all this, and you don't pay it alone: We all do. Gigi, me, Capes, Brother Harpo, and even Alvarez."

Beau Lee rebutted. "The fight for justice always comes with a price. It's what we all signed up for."

"I won't pretend I'm not worried," Nellie said. "I have an uneasy feeling that this isn't going to end well."

"I have those same feelings at times, too. But that worrying is what landed you in urgent care."

"I told you, it was nothing. Just a little high blood pressure."

"We all need to take care of ourselves," Beau Lee said. "If I promise not to take any unnecessary risks, you've got to promise to look after yourself."

Nellie rubbed his chest, as if to recall the pain he'd experienced a few weeks ago. "All right, Frat," he said. "I get your point."

"Likewise."

Beau Lee offered a fist bump. "We good?"

"Yeah, we're good," Nellie said, reciprocating the gesture as they pulled up to Beau Lee's house. "Not sure that'll be the case for Gigi, though. I'm sure she'll have a lot to say."

Beau Lee chuckled. "Yeah, I know. I'll holla at you later. Thanks for the ride, Frat."

"No problem, we will connect later, Frat."

As Beau Lee opened the front door, he heard Gigi call out, "Beau Lee Cooper, is that you walking through this door?"

"Yes, beautiful, it's me." He entered the living room, and Gigi was standing there with her arms crossed. He walked up to her and gave her a long hug and said, "Baby you don't know how much I missed you, as he kissed her on the cheek. He could hear the sound of Bianca's laughter and yells as she played Mario Kart. Beau Lee went to his daughter and gave her a long kiss on her head.

Bianca giggled and said, "Dad! I'm playing!"

Beau Lee just smiled, walked back to Gigi, and leaned in to hug her again. As Gigi took in the sight of her husband, she saw the simultaneous weariness and determination in his eyes.

Gigi said, "Beau Lee, I am so happy to see you, but baby, we have got to talk about what I saw on the news yesterday. I seriously can't believe you'd put your life at risk, knowing you have a daughter, wife, and family at home."

Beau Lee rubbed the back of his neck. "Gigi, baby, I just got here, and I don't want to have this conversation right now. I have a million and one things running through my mind right now, and I have to prepare these motions for the case by tomorrow."

"No, Beau Lee, we're not putting this conversation off." Her voice was sharp, but she walked behind him and helped massage the knotted area of his neck. "What the hell were you thinking? You're way too emotionally attached to this damn case, and it's eating you alive. Do you really think I'm going to stand by, watch you risk your life, and say nothing?"

"Gigi, do you understand this isn't just a case to me?"

"I know, but I should never have seen my man on TV putting his life in danger the way you did. You've lost your damn mind."

"This is a Black man's life—one who has been an upright citizen, who is well-respected in the community and the police academy, and he's lying in a jail bed fighting for his life. His family's counting on me. Hell, *he's* counting on me to fight for him, for justice. You can't possibly think I'm just gonna walk away from this case, him, and every Black person in America who's been falsely accused by the system of whiteness. Gigi, do you not understand what's at stake with this case?"

"I know exactly what is at stake. You ain't gotta remind me of that," she shot back. "But let me ask *you* a question. What good will you be if you're dead or seriously injured? The whole system is corrupt, and Chicago is dangerous, and them white folks play with a different set of rules. And baby, if you aren't careful they'll come for you and yours."

Beau Lee said, "Gigi, honey—"

Gigi interrupted and raised her voice slightly. "Beau Lee, you're a damn good attorney, and you know that what I'm saying is nothing but the truth. The problem is, you don't understand that you're not invincible, and these godforsaken streets don't care about you, your passions, or your principles. The streets are the streets, and they don't give anything about a Black man. I'll be damned if I sit here watching you lose yourself and not say anything about it. Baby, I need you to use wisdom and understanding as you navigate this case. For me. For Bianca."

Beau Lee really wanted to explain to Gigi, tell her she didn't understand, but in his soul he knew she was right. "Well, I can't recuse myself and let someone else handle this case. People are depending on me, and I just can't see another Black man lose to the system."

Gigi sighed, her expression softening. "I'm saying you need to think long and hard about what's most important. If your heart and head aren't in the right place, you're not gonna be able to give this case what it needs. I'm not saying you need to step back, but what I *am* saying is don't you dare keep moving forward without a solid plan and strategy. It also must be a plan that doesn't involve you chasing after cars like a man who ain't got no sense."

The room went silent for a moment, and Beau Lee stared at the ceiling while his mind replayed Gigi's words, his daughter's laughter, and Capes yelling at him to stop running. What Gigi said remained at the forefront of his mind and heart, and without the shadow of a doubt he knew she was right.

Beau Lee exhaled, and his eyes met with Gigi's. "You're right," he said. "I'll think about how to move forward and not put myself or anyone else at risk."

Gigi gave him an encouraging hug. "That's all I'm asking, Beau Lee. We're in this together, remember? Baby, you don't have to carry this weight by yourself. We got you!"

45

THE BASEMENT OF THE QUINN CHAPEL AME CHURCH HAD SEEN MANY gatherings, but never one quite as large as five hundred people as what Beau Lee and Harpo had organized to raise funds for Hollis's release. Fortunately, only 10 percent of the total amount was necessary to make bail, but they were still staring at a hefty quarter-million sum. The Hollis Montrose Bail Fund had been launched within days of his arrest, spearheaded by a coalition of activists, faith leaders, and community organizers. They had worked tirelessly to raise donations, organize fundraising efforts, and spread the word across the city, and despite their valiant efforts, they were far from reaching the sum for Hollis's bail.

Standing in the church's basement was like being in a cultural museum—it was holy ground. The church had a long, rich history. For over a century, it had been part of the Underground Railroad, offering a sanctuary for enslaved Africans fleeing bondage and persecution. They hid in the basement and slept on oak floors and in the pews before traveling farther north.

During the Great Migration, Black families escaping the Jim Crow South poured into the church's halls and built a thriving community around hope and resistance.

Decades later, the church would become a hub for civil rights leaders who strategized and laid the groundwork for boycotts and marches against red-lining, police brutality, and a litany of racist policies that forced many Black Chicagoans into poverty.

And tonight, the room was filled beyond capacity; voices wove together, taut with urgency and frustration. Folding chairs scraped against the floor as more people squeezed in and stood along the walls. Church bulletins fluttered in restless hands. At the back, elders exchanged knowing glances, their faces weighed down by the notion of having fought similar battles over the decades. Near the front of the room, Rocky sat with her hands clasped tightly in her lap. Her posture was stiff, as if she were bracing for the unknown.

At the podium, Reverend Cleaver raised his right hand.

The attendees immediately quieted.

He bowed his head, drawing in a slow, steady breath, then lifted his voice, deep and steady, and prayed: "Heavenly Father, we come before You tonight as a people who know struggle, as a people who have fought for every inch of freedom we've ever had. Our brother Hollis Montrose was left for dead by the same system he served. But Lord, we know you are a God of justice. And we will not wait idly. Tonight, we rally for Hollis. We stand for truth. We stand for justice. And we will not be moved or deterred. We have complete faith in you, God, that you will free Hollis Montrose from bondage. But as you teach us in your word, faith without works is dead. This great legal crusader has been putting in the work, and we stand with him. I give you Attorney Beau Lee Cooper."

The prayer was followed by a deep, resounding "Amen."

Reverend Cleaver turned to Beau Lee, who was standing in the wings, and gestured for him to come to the podium.

Beau Lee adjusted his suit jacket and stood behind the microphone. He cleared his throat as he angled the mic. "They tell us Hollis Montrose is guilty because they need him to be guilty. Because if he's innocent, that means someone else is responsible. And they don't want to ask those questions, because they fear the answers. See, those answers would be an indictment of the policies and culture that exist in the Chicago Police Department, and within the city." A murmur of agreement spread through the room.

"We didn't get to this place overnight," he added. "What happened to Hollis Montrose is a culmination of decades of poor, racially insensitive, and downright hateful policies, which is why Hollis Montrose was left bleeding in the street, then thrown in a cage. Now they're holding him for ransom. Two hundred and fifty thousand dollars. That's the cost of an innocent man's freedom."

People began to clap loudly, but Beau Lee wasn't finished. He raised his hand and silenced the crowd. "But we're not waiting for them to grow a conscience and do what's just and right. We intend to bring Hollis home ourselves."

Reverend Cleaver joined Beau Lee at the podium. "Church family, I know times are tough," he said. "We're facing a terrible recession, but if we can't depend on our community, who can we depend on? We'll be passing out envelopes so you may donate and collect donations for the Free Hollis Montrose bail campaign."

Beau Lee added, "We ask that you give whatever you can to help us fund Hollis's bail and share his story with everyone you can."

A deacon began passing out manila envelopes to the crowd. Many people were reaching into their billfolds and purses, pulling out five- and ten-dollar bills, giving what they could. It was a beautiful sight. The community was galvanized around one noble cause: Hollis Montrose's freedom.

46

LATER THAT DAY, THE SCENT OF FRYING CATFISH AND SMOKED TURKEY necks filled the air, mingling with the sounds of voices, laughter, and gospel music playing softly from a speaker near the food tables. They had migrated to a different church—St. Sabina—and the parking lot had been transformed into a full-fledged fundraiser, with folding tables draped in plastic cloths, aluminum trays of steaming food, and volunteers working at breakneck speed to keep up with demand.

Rocky Montrose moved through the organized chaos taking orders, checking on the kitchen, and managing the cash box. The steady rhythm of people handing over money and collecting plates should have reassured her, but instead, it only made her feel the weight of how much was left to do.

Her stomach was tight. Her body ached. But there was no time to stop.

She stepped behind a stack of supply crates for just a second, pressing her fingers to her temples, trying to will away the pounding headache creeping in.

The weight of everything—Hollis's suffering, the money they still needed, the never-ending battle against a system that had no mercy for them—threatened to buckle her.

She inhaled sharply, but it did nothing to calm the tightness in her chest.

She gripped the edge of the crate, her fingers digging into the plastic. She was so tired of being sick and tired.

A voice surprised her. "You all right, Mrs. Montrose?"

She turned to see an older woman with silver hair tucked beneath a cloth headwrap, her dark eyes kind but knowing.

Rocky forced a smile. "I'm okay."

The woman studied her for a moment, then shook her head. "Baby, it's all right to not be fine. It's all right to be tired."

Rocky swallowed the lump in her throat. "I can't afford to be tired."

The woman took her hand, squeezing it gently. "That man of yours needs you. But we as a community got your back. So, you don't have to hold this weight all on your own."

For the first time that evening, Rocky let herself breathe.

She nodded, blinking back the heat in her eyes, then straightened her spine. "Thank you." She turned back toward the food line, voice strong again.

"Plates! Fifteen dollars a plate!"

Just as Rocky was settling back into the rhythm of work, she heard a commotion near the entrance. Voices sharp and tense.

A city official, a white man in a stiff suit, stood at the edge of the parking lot, clipboard in hand, his badge gleaming under the streetlights.

"You got a permit for this?"

Rocky turned, her exhaustion instantly sharpening into frustration.

"It's a church fundraiser."

"You're selling food. Which means you need a temporary vendor license."

Capes, standing nearby, stepped in before Rocky could respond. "This is about Hollis Montrose, isn't it?"

The official shrugged, unreadable. "No license, no fundraiser."

The crowd turned toward them, a quiet energy shifting.

Rocky exhaled through her nose, stepping forward until she was eye to eye with the man.

"You shut this down, you explain to every person here why you don't want us raising money for an innocent man."

People began pulling out their phones. Murmurs spread. Someone in the back shouted, "Y'all really trying to stop this?"

The official hesitated and then backed off. He tucked his clipboard under his arm and returned to his vehicle.

"We're not stopping," Rocky said. "Everyone, keep serving. We still have a lot of bail money to raise."

47

DALEY PLAZA PULSED WITH LIFE AS THE COMMUNITY CELEBRATED THE Martin Luther King, Jr., holiday. Over the last few days, Beau Lee, Alvarez, and Rocky had been guests on a few high-profile radio shows secured by Nellie to make sure their voices and pleas were broadcast to a wider population—across all of Chicago and all of America. And they were excited to be here now, protesting for Hollis's freedom. Voices were rising and colliding like ocean waves, but instead of battering rocks and beaches, they crashed against the steel and glass of downtown Chicago's towering buildings.

Looming above it all was the Picasso sculpture—an enormous, abstract iron figure that had stood watch over the plaza since 1967. A gift from the artist himself, it was both mysterious and familiar, depending on whom you asked. Tonight, it seemed to lean in, tilted ever so slightly toward the crowd below. Banners waved beneath its shadow, catching the harsh white glare of the streetlights.

But on this particular King holiday, protesters were chanting "Justice for Hollis!" "The Badge Didn't Save Him—Now We Have To!" "Who Do You Call When the Police Are the Criminals?"

Children clutched the edges of signs with their small hands, their eyes bright with energy, even if they didn't fully grasp the weight of the words they carried.

At the center of the crowd, a makeshift stage had been set up. Reverend Cleaver took his place at the microphone.

His voice boomed through the speakers.

"Who keeps us safe?"

"WE DO!"

"Who locked up Hollis?"

"THE POLICE!"

"Who's gonna bring him home?"

"WE ARE!"

The chants rolled through the crowd like a wave, stronger with each call, fueled by urgency and rage.

Then came another voice, Sharonda Jenkins, a local activist. She stepped up and gripped the mic.

"Hollis is not the first, and he won't be the last if we don't fight back." She turned, looking out over the faces in the crowd. "But this city underestimates us. They think we'll accept this. They think we'll go home and move on. But tell me, Chicago—are we moving on?"

"NO!"

Then came Beau Lee. "They say justice is blind, but we know that's not true. Justice sees just fine. She just doesn't see us."

The crowd roared.

"But if the system won't see Hollis, then we will make them see him. We will make them see every dollar we raise. Every voice we lift. Every step we take toward his freedom."

The voices swelled again, fists raised, signs lifted higher.

AS ROCKY LEFT, SHE CARRIED with her a sense of hope sparked by the support of the community. Their hugs, prayers, and presence had wrapped around her like armor. Rocky felt their help in her spirit; she knew that the fight was bigger than her, but she had an army of soldiers to fight with her for the freedom of her husband. It gave her strength, and that was just what she needed as she made her way to see Hollis at that godforsaken jail. Hollis needed to know that there was a village outside those concrete walls that was rising up on his behalf.

48

THE SOUTH SIDE COMMUNITY ART CENTER HAD BECOME THE BASE OF OPerations for the Hollis Montrose Bail Fund, its organizers, the fund's leadership, and volunteers. Many nights were spent there counting all the donations.

After two weeks of consistent efforts by Rocky, Beau Lee's legal team, and the community, the final donation numbers were calculated just before midnight inside the center, where a small group of Hollis's supporters had gathered. Beau Lee, Rocky, Capes, and Harpo were all present, awaiting the final tabulation.

At the center of the room, DeShawn Perry, the lead organizer of the bail fund, was hunched over a laptop tallying the last of the donations. He muttered calculations under his breath, the clicking of the keyboard the only sound in the space.

Harpo paced near the edge of a table with his arms crossed. Rocky stood near the door, her hands clenched at her sides.

Beau Lee had been patient for the last few hours, but he couldn't wait any longer. "What's the number?" he asked.

DeShawn exhaled and turned the laptop screen toward them. "$28,672."

The room went still.

Rocky massaged her temples and took a sharp breath.

Capes let out a low whistle. "Man. We worked our asses off."

Nellie muttered, "Not even close."

Harpo shook his head, voice tight. "Not enough. Not even close to enough."

Rocky sat down on a folding chair and stared at the floor.

DeShawn leaned forward, running a hand down his face. "We made a dent. But a dent ain't bail."

Silence.

Rocky finally lifted her head, her voice quiet but unshakable. "Lord, you gotta help us. We're doing all we can."

Beau Lee nodded, but the words sat heavy in his chest.

Outside, the city moved on—cars honking, neon lights flickering, laughter spilling from restaurants and bars.

Inside the community center, in a cramped room filled with the weight of despair, the team sat in silence.

They had worked. Fought. Sweat. Pushed.

And it still wasn't enough.

Hollis wasn't just waiting for bail anymore—he was running out of time.

And the number on the spreadsheet was more than just short—it was a death sentence.

Suddenly, Jamillah stood up, breaking the silence. Almost hysterical, she screamed, "This can't be happening. This can't be happening right now!" Tyrone jumped to his feet and said, "J, what is it?"

Rocky saw the puddle at Jamillah's feet and said, "Oh my God, her water broke!"

DeShawn said, "I'm calling 911. She's going into labor!"

49

JAMILLAH'S HOSPITAL ROOM SMELLED OF BABY LOTION AND ANTISEPTIC. The excitement of witnessing the miracle of life renewed their hope in the world. The newest addition to the Montrose clan was a beautiful baby girl named Hope, weighing five pounds and eight ounces, with all ten fingers and toes. She wailed at the top of her lungs when the doctor smacked her little tush, revealing that she had a strong set of windpipes.

Beau Lee, Alvarez, Capes, Finn, and Harpo were in the hospital room celebrating with Tyrone, Jamillah, and Rocky. They were elated, and it was the first time in a long time that everyone wore some semblance of a smile. But then Rocky and Jamillah looked at each other, both knowing whose absence loomed. Hollis had been counting the days until his next grandbaby would enter the world.

The next day, the team met at Alvarez's office to game-plan Hollis's bail situation. Harpo sat scrolling through his phone. He'd been compulsively checking the bail fund account in case there'd been an uptick in donations, but the money wasn't there. They had done everything possible to raise the funds—town halls, radio interviews, rallies, church fundraisers—but there was no turning $28,672 into $250,000.

"Man, by my calculation we still have to come up with $221,328 to get Hollis out of jail," Harpo announced for everybody to understand the calculations.

"I just know we are gonna figure out a way to get the money to get my daddy out of jail," Jamillah responded. "I refuse to lose hope."

"Jamillah, baby girl, I wasn't in any way suggesting that we lose hope. I was just letting you all know where we stand. When you've seen the things I've seen, you never lose hope." Harpo gave Jamillah a hug.

"Hope and faith are required of everybody in this room," Rocky interjected. "That's what I keep reiterating to Hollis—hope and faith. We have to believe in the scripture. Faith is the substance of things hoped for, the evidence of things not seen."

Harpo then hugged Rocky. "And that's just what I will reiterate to Hollis when I go see him for my three P.M. visit today," he said.

Across the room, Capes leaned against the wall with his arms crossed, silent but watchful. He turned to Finn, who was standing beside him, and whispered, "Man, we need a break in this case. When do you think we should go trail Jack again?"

"We should do surveillance on him for the rest of the day up until the midnight hour to see if that will give us any new leads," Finn answered. "We have to do something to give Hollis some hope."

As they all left the office their souls were weary, but their faith was resolute and unrelenting.

LATER AT THE JAIL, HARPO was hit with the smell of something deeply familiar and unpleasant—a sharp mix of bleach, sweat, and something older like metal rusting under too many years of fluorescent light. It was the same smell that had clung to his clothes all those nights he'd counted cinderblock walls instead of stars. His stomach tightened. For a split second, it was like no time had passed, like he was twenty-four again, shackled at the wrists, waiting on a judge who barely looked at him. He hated how familiar it felt. The echo of footsteps down the corridor, the buzz of the heavy doors locking behind him, even the low murmur of voices talking to the families through a glass window, it all pulled him back to the weight of lost years.

But then he reminded himself: He wasn't staying, and he was there to remind Hollis that he wasn't staying, either. As he had made countless visits to remind other brothers who were locked in the cage to never lose hope.

He exhaled slowly, steadying himself. Gratitude swelled in his chest. He wasn't perfect, but he wasn't lost anymore. Life had given him a second chance, and he'd taken it.

That's why Hollis mattered. Why this fight mattered. Because Harpo knew what it felt like to be forgotten behind those walls. And he refused to let Hollis sit there believing this was all his story would ever be.

So, as he picked up the phone, staring through the glass at his friend, he thought *I made it out. And I'll make sure Hollis does, too.*

HOLLIS SHIFTED SLIGHTLY, WINCING AS he adjusted his position. He could barely move his lower body. He'd tried, over and over, but the doctors had been clear: The bullets had severed his spinal cord, and he wasn't going to be walking anywhere ever again. Hollis was paralyzed for life.

"What now?" Hollis rasped.

None of the men answered.

"I know what's next," Hollis muttered. "Straight to prison from Cook County Jail."

Harpo sighed. "We're still trying, man. Every day we're getting a little closer. Two weeks ago, there was an order for you to be in custody with no bail. Now we can get you out, as long as we raise the money. So just keep the faith. We're getting close."

"The problem is how long it'll take to get a ringer, Finn. How long will it take?" asked Hollis. Finn has no response. Silence once again filled the room.

After a few moments, Harpo's phone began to buzz.

The vibration cut through the silence. He almost didn't answer. What was the point? He already knew what the bondsman was going to say—they didn't have the money.

But something in his gut told him to pick up.

"Harpo," came the familiar voice. His tone was even, but there was something different this time. "I got miraculous news for you," he said. "Comes with a bit of mystery, though."

Harpo sat up. Capes straightened, watching closely.

"What?"

"Someone just paid the full $250,000 bail."

Silence. Shock swallowed the room.

Harpo's heart nearly stopped. "Wait—what?"

"You heard me," the bondsman said. "Some prominent person's lawyer contacted me and informed me that their client was making a donation and sent payment to cover the entire bail amount. The lawyer made clear that his client wished to remain anonymous."

Harpo was on his feet now. Capes narrowed his eyes, reading the shift in his posture.

"No name?" Harpo asked.

"Nothing. And the attorney was very clear—if anyone tries to figure out his client's identity, the bail will be forfeited."

"Are you serious?"

"As a heart attack." Harpo couldn't believe what he'd just heard. Freedom had a price, and somehow it had been paid, and Harpo knew he'd never forget this moment. It was the day mercy came wrapped in $250,000.

Harpo turned toward Hollis, who was watching him carefully. Harpo looked back, then lifted his phone and called Rocky.

"Rocky, we just got a ringer. The bondsman said we received an anonymous donation covering Hollis's entire bail amount," Harpo said.

There was a long pause, filled with the sound of her catching her breath. Then she let out a slow, teared-soaked laugh. "Ain't that somethin'."

* * *

BEAU LEE COOPER STOOD NEAR the conference table, his hands resting on its surface, taking in the news.

"Wow," he said, shaking his head. "I wasn't expecting that."

Harpo looked like he was still processing it. "None of us were."

Nellie leaned back in his chair, arms crossed. "That's a hell of a donation."

Capes smirked. "Okay, so who are we thinking? Oprah?"

"Michael Jordan?" Alvarez threw in.

"Barack Obama?" Nellie mused.

"Could've been the Pope for all we know," Harpo said. "But whoever it was, I'm just grateful. I thank God for 'em."

Beau Lee nodded. "Yeah. Whoever they are, they did something good."

Nellie tapped his pen against the table. "This is going to become one of those great urban legends, like who killed Jimmy Hoffa? Now people will be asking for years to come who bailed out Hollis Montrose."

Harpo said, "I don't care who it was, all I care is that Hollis Montrose is coming home."

To which Nellie heartily agreed, "Amen."

And that was it. No overthinking, no tension. Hollis Montrose was coming home.

THAT AFTERNOON, ROCKY STOOD OUTSIDE the jail, arms wrapped around herself in the cold.

When the doors slid open, it took everything in her not to burst into tears.

Hollis was in the wheelchair, his hands resting on the arms, his legs still. His clothes were looser on him now, his body thinner, his movements slower. But he was here. He was free and Rocky was taking him home.

She moved before she could think, closing the distance and kneeling in front of him, gripping his hands tight. "I thought I'd lost you," she whispered.

Hollis let out a weak chuckle. "By God's grace, I'm still here."

Behind them, the team stood in quiet relief.

Capes muttered, "Are we really just gonna pretend this ain't crazy?"

Beau Lee didn't look away. "No need to overthink a blessing."

Capes exhaled. "Man, a quarter million anonymously! That's some kind of divine intervention. I want some divine intervention for me, too!"

Harpo laughed and said, "Capes, you crazy, man. Now we just need some more divine intervention to happen in sixty days, when this trial begins."

Nellie nodded. "You're right, Harpo. But seriously, time is of the essence. We really need to get to work if we're going to have any chance of success in this trial."

Beau Lee knew Nellie was right. The gift of the donation had cracked open a door, but money alone wouldn't win Hollis his freedom. What lay ahead was long nights, relentless preparation, and a courtroom where every word would be weighed like gold. As grateful as he was for the miracle that had arrived, Beau Lee understood that this was a blessing, but freedom wasn't guaranteed until the truth rang louder than the lies that had put Hollis in chains.

50

A MONTH HAD PASSED SINCE HOLLIS HAD COME HOME. HE WAS MAKING modest progress but remained paralyzed from the waist down. Jury selection had occurred, and it had been exhausting. After five long days, the prosecution for the State of Illinois and the defense team for Hollis Montrose had finally decided on twelve citizens to make up the jury. Even though the jurors came from all walks of life, it was baffling to Beau Lee that the ultimate twelve-person pool included only two African Americans. He thought to himself, *For God's sake, this is Chicago! There are Black people everywhere in Chicago.* The four extras were alternate jurors, all of whom were Caucasian. There were potential African American jurors who'd been struck from the panel based on Judge Lambert's rulings that the State had given sufficient nonracial reasons for doing so. But in Beau Lee's mind, it was just the Chicago machine doing what the Chicago machine did. But it didn't matter, because he knew he had a winning case based on a mountain of reasonable doubt that not even a conspiracy between the judge and the prosecutor could suppress. Or so he thought.

Rocky, Jamillah, and Tyrone, along with Harpo and Capes, were all sitting in the front row behind the defense counsel's table observing Beau Lee and trying to understand what just happened on how jury selection was completed. They were confused at best, and disturbed at worst by the makeup of the jury. They'd counted at least six African Americans who'd been dismissed.

Beau Lee was seated with Alvarez and Nellie as they scoured the jury charts.

Nellie leaned over and whispered to Beau Lee, "Are you going to renew your objections that six out of eight African American jurors were excused from the jury for pretextual reasons?"

Beau Lee shook his head and said, "No." He counted the number of potential Black jurors on his chart. "Alvarez, you know all the names and the reasons for each appeal, right?"

"I sure do, Beau Lee," she said.

"All rise," the bailiff said as the judge walked back into the courtroom.

"Now that we've selected the jury, we'll go through the pretrial motions so you all will know what evidence will be allowed when we start on Monday morning and you can prepare sufficiently through the weekend," Judge Lambert explained. "I'll begin with the recorded video of Mr. Montrose's arrest. Mr. DaSilva, I will hear from you first."

DaSilva stood up. "Your Honor, Attorney Dillard will argue this motion for the prosecution."

The judge nodded her head. "Very well."

Prosecutor Dillard walked up to the podium. She had changed her hair color since the last court appearance. It was lighter. "Your Honor, the State's position is that this videotape should be ruled inadmissible because the prejudicial value outweighs its probative value. It is irrelevant based on the more reliable evidence, like the gunshot residue on the defendant's hands," she said. "Furthermore, the video's poor quality should be deemed unreliable in aiding the jury as fact finders. And finally, Your Honor, the State would object to the video being admitted as evidence because of the exorbitant amount of pretrial publicity that it has garnered. We have officers with impeccable records of professionalism who would offer eyewitness testimony that is corroborated by all of the physical evidence, including again the gunshot residue, the illegible license plate on the defendant's vehicle, and the fact that the video was taken one hundred yards away and therefore you can't hear what the officers are saying to the defendant. The State will argue that the jury would be prejudiced by the video and the assumptions made by the defense lawyers since the jury cannot hear the legal verbal commands that were given by the police to the defendant before they opened fire. Therefore, Your Honor, based on these arguments and all the ones that were briefed and submitted to the court earlier, we respectfully request that you deny the video's admissibility as evidence," she said with conviction.

"Does the defense have arguments to present?" Judge Lambert asked.

Beau Lee stood up and said, "Attorney Alvarez will present the arguments for the defendant."

Alvarez walked up to the podium. "May it please the court?"

Judge Lambert responded, "You may proceed."

"Your Honor, the defense contends that the video is very important and gives the jury a first-hand unbiased account of what happened in the shooting and paralysis of Hollis Montrose. Not only does the video show that Mr. Montrose's license plate was legible, but it also shows that Mr. Montrose was already on the ground when the police officers started firing. It offers incontrovertible evidence that Mr. Montrose never touched his gun or fired it."

"Objection," Attorney Dillard yelled out. "The State and our experts contend that that cellphone video could not capture what Hollis Montrose was doing with his right hand since the left side of his body was the predominant vantage point."

"Your Honor, it is clear that the officers started discharging their firearms before Mr. Montrose's hands were near his hip," Alvarez said with a tinge of pugnacity. She was gearing up for a sparring match with Dillard.

"I will note the objection, but this is a hearing where I will hear arguments from both parties and then make my decision on the video's admissibility. Ms. Alvarez, you can continue."

Dillard's objection had disrupted Alvarez's momentum. She took a moment to find her footing again. "Your Honor, it is important to note that even though the State makes the argument that the cellphone video doesn't capture what is being said during the altercation, the number of gunshots being fired can be heard from the cellphone video recording. We contend that those gunshots are factually important for the jury. The video's free of bias, and its probative value outweighs any prejudicial value."

"Thank you. I will issue my rulings as follows: In the matter of the video, it can be admitted. However, only selected portions will be shown to the jury. As for the license plate, that video cannot be admissible in accordance with the best evidence rule, which would be to present the tangible license plate before the jury that we have here as part of the evidence in this trial. I will give an instruction to the jury that the police officers had sufficient probable cause to stop the defendant's vehicle based on the condition of the license plate."

Alvarez looked to Beau Lee, who was taking notes as the judge spoke.

"As it relates to the audio, the defense counsel is not allowed to speculate about what is being said based on the video," the judge said, looking harshly at Beau Lee, as if to anticipate his antics. "However, the defense will be allowed to play what audio there is on the recording so that the jury can hear the gunshots captured on the video. I rule the vantage point of the video was limited to the left side of the defendant's body with his firearm being on his right side. The police officers on the scene had the superior vantage point, and therefore the defense counsel will not be able to argue inferences pertaining to what Hollis Montrose might've been doing with his right hand."

Alvarez had joined Beau Lee in taking notes and both were writing furiously across their legal pads.

"And finally, with the poor visibility of the video, there is no degree of certainty an inference can be drawn as to whether Officer Jackson Dunham's hands actually touched Hollis Montrose's hand when he handcuffed Mr. Montrose. This concludes my rulings as to admissibility of the video into evidence. So govern yourselves accordingly," Judge Lambert said.

Beau Lee stood and said, "Your Honor, since you are only allowing very few parts of the video to be admitted into evidence, I would like to put the defense's objections to your ruling on the record."

"Continue," the judge said.

"With all due respect, by allowing the video to be admissible, the prosecutors can argue that the jury should not believe what they see on the video," Beau Lee said. "But why can't the video be allowed to speak for itself? Neither party should be limited in what arguments they can make regarding the video. We reiterate that the entire video should be admitted for the jury to view in its entirety."

"Your objection is noted," the judge said, barely acknowledging Beau Lee's point.

"If I may continue, Judge . . ." Beau Lee wasn't going to relent, despite Lambert's annoyed glare. "Limiting what arguments we are allowed to make only serves to mislead the jury, despite what they are able to see with their own eyes."

"Are you finished, Mr. Cooper?"

Beau Lee exhaled slowly to calm the fire that was building in his chest and nodded.

"Good," the judge said. "Let me be clear: My rulings are final. I'd suggest you focus on your client's defense and prepare for the trial's start on Monday rather than waste the court's time and mine. Good day." She slammed her gavel without giving Beau Lee a second look.

Alvarez shook her head in disbelief. "Unreal. How can someone who's supposedly impartial continue to rule in favor of the prosecution on nearly every motion?"

Nellie joined them and began to pack up boxes with Capes. "Frat, this is gon' be tough, but I got faith."

Jamillah was shaking her head and tears ran down her face. "Attorney Cooper, it's so obvious they're lying on my father. They're going to send him to prison all based on a big lie that he shot at the police when it's clear from the video that he did no such thing!"

Beau Lee turned toward the family. "It's worse than a lie," he avowed as he handed her his handkerchief.

She took it and dabbed her eyes. "Attorney Cooper, what can be worse than a lie?"

Beau Lee put his hands on his hips and looked back at the empty judge's bench.

"When you're reminded that racism is as American as apple pie. And the words on the court wall, like *liberty* and *justice,* to you they don't apply. That's worse than a lie."

51

IT WAS LATE AFTERNOON WHEN THEY ARRIVED AT THE BROWNSTONE ON Cleveland Avenue in the picturesque neighborhood that was worthy of a postcard.

"Vic was right. The neighborhood looks *mighty swell*," Finn said as if he were auditioning for an episode of *Leave It to Beaver*. The street was lined with trees and historic homes. "How much do you think these places go for? I'm betting eight hundred thousand or more."

"Probably," Capes said, looking at the address in his notepad. "I think this is the place." He pointed at the speckled brick home with large windows.

They walked up the short flight of stairs to the front door, and Finn rang the bell. "Yeah, I could get used to living in a place like this," he said. "It's got charm, you know?"

"Not me. After living in Texas, I can't imagine being back in a brick city. It's too congested. I need space to roam."

"Who is it?" a woman's voice called from an upstairs open window. "Whatever you're selling, I'm not interested."

Finn left the porch and stood on the steps looking up at the woman. "Sorry to bother you, miss. Is this your home?"

"I live here," the woman said. "Why?"

"Well, it's a stunning home."

"Look, if you want to buy it or something, call the owners. I'm renting."

"Actually, if you don't mind, we'd like to ask you a few questions."

She looked perplexed. "About the house?"

"No, no," Finn said with a smile. "It's about an acquaintance of yours. Officer Jack Dunham."

The woman became silent and appeared hesitant.

"Did you hear me, miss?"

"Are you cops? Because you look like cops."

"I'm Officer Finn Doyle with Metra, and this is my associate, Mr. Capes."

"He a cop, too?"

"No, more like a community liaison. We just have a few questions for you, if you don't mind."

"What do you want to know about Jack?"

"Oh, so you do know Officer Dunham?"

"Yeah, I know him, but I don't see how I can help."

"Like I said, it's just a few questions. No pressure," Finn said. "How about you come down and chat with us? We'll stay right here on the stoop."

"Um, all right," she said, "I'll be down."

"We appreciate it."

She left the window and opened the door a few seconds later, stopping in the frame as if uncertain. She was wearing fitted jeans and a slouchy pink sweater, which was sliding carelessly off one shoulder. Her silence toward Finn was deliberate. Finn's jaw tightened, and he cleared his throat with impatience. "What's your name?"

She tilted her head, and unmoved asked, "So, what do you want to know?"

"Let's start with your name," Finn said, flashing his badge. "And then we'll work down a list of questions."

"Heaven."

"Say again?"

"My name is Heaven Willoughby."

"Quite the name you've got there. Very uplifting," Finn remarked.

"Most people think it's biblical, but my parents were hippies and just liked the way it sounded. How'd you get my address, anyway?"

"That's confidential, Ms. Willoughby, but what I can tell you is that we're here to help."

"Just tell me, is Jack in some kind of trouble?"

"I'll let my colleague fill you in . . . Mr. Capes?"

"Officer Dunham was recently involved in a shooting while on duty. We'd like to know how he's doing."

"And you came here?" she asked. "Are you surveilling him?"

"Like we said, that's confidential."

"Um, okay, but why am I talking to you guys and not the CPD?" She looked at Finn suspiciously. "Didn't you say you worked with Metra?"

"It's kind of a joint effort with the community and departments," Capes said. "Think of it as a special task force."

"Maybe I should call Jack."

"How well do you know Officer Dunham?" Finn asked.

"Excuse me?"

"I mean, are you involved with him?"

"That's personal, and I don't see how that pertains to a shooting."

"We're just trying to get a sense of how he's doing. Consider this a welfare check. No matter what you tell us, it won't negatively impact Officer Dunham in any way. It's just to help us be sure he's getting the support he needs."

"All we're trying to do is look after Jack, Ms. Willoughby," Capes said. "You understand, don't you? It's important to make sure he's good." He tapped his temple. "You know, mentally, post-shooting."

"What shooting?"

"You weren't aware?" Finn asked. "Officer Dunham was recently involved in a shooting while on duty."

"This is the first I've heard about it."

"Does the name Hollis Montrose mean anything to you?"

"Wait . . . isn't that the man who's been all over the news? He's in the hospital, right?"

"Well, no. Not anymore."

"So, let me get this straight," Capes said. "You had no idea that Jack was involved in a shooting?"

"No, he didn't tell me anything about it. I mean, he was a little upset when the press conference came on, but he never said he was involved."

"I see."

"And you're here because the department's worried about Jack's mental health?" Heaven asked. "No offense, but I didn't think that was a huge concern for cops. Isn't that what booze and strip clubs are for? I lived with this all my life; my dad was a cop."

"Consider our coming here the first step in police departments' taking mental health more seriously."

"Okay," she said. "That's great, I guess. It really is, and I'm all for accountability. But I really don't know about all this, and I don't see how I could help."

"Can you tell us about Jack's demeanor lately? You said he was upset at the press conference regarding the Hollis Montrose shooting."

"Well, uh, now that you mentioned it. He has been acting a little differently lately."

"Different? How so?"

"I don't know. He's been edgy more than usual, I guess."

"Has there been any violence?"

Heaven stammered, "No . . . that's not—I mean, that's not Jack. He's a good man."

"You still haven't told us how it is you know Officer Dunham."

"He's a friend."

"A friend?"

"Yes, a good friend."

Capes could always tell when someone was lying, and Heaven

wasn't very good at it. He thought that maybe they were pushing her too hard, but he worried they wouldn't get another chance to talk to her. "So, he hasn't talked to you at all about anything going on at work?" he asked. "Maybe how he's been feeling lately?"

"Feelings. Are we even talking about the same man? Look, this whole thing is making me uncomfortable."

"We're just working through a backlog," Finn said. "Checking off boxes, that's all."

"I think we can conclude this," Capes said. "Just so we're clear, in your opinion Jack's fine?"

"That's right," she said. "Maybe he was dealing with some stress, but he's a cop, and that goes with the job, right?"

"Ms. Willoughby, you've been very helpful," Capes said. "And if you need anything, just give me a call." He handed Heaven his business card, but not the one with Beau Lee Cooper Law Firm emblazoned on it. Rather, it was a card with very little identifying information—MR. BRENT CAPERS with PRIVATE INVESTIGATOR below his name was printed on one side, and his phone number was on the other. He reserved the cards for situations in which less was more and didn't want to drag the firm into a potential legal conundrum.

The men turned to leave while Heaven toyed with the card. "They say Hollis Montrose was shot in the back," she said. "Is that right?"

Capes faced her. "Yes. Ten times."

"That's horrible," she said. "Is he going to be okay?"

"He's pretty far from okay. In fact, he'll never be able to walk again."

She sighed. "There was something Jack said . . ."

"Yes?"

"Does the name Teddy Briscoe mean anything to either of you?"

Capes and Finn glanced at each other, but the name didn't ring any bells. "Can't say it does," Finn acknowledged. "Is that one of the officers he works with?" he asked.

"It's just that when he was watching the press conference, he remarked how ridiculous all of this was. He said something about that his mentor Teddy Briscoe would have already had this case all buttoned up," Heaven said.

"Did he say this Teddy Briscoe works with him at CPD," asked Finn.

"I don't know," Heaven answered.

Then her cellphone rang. "You all should talk to Jack. I gotta go."

As she shut the door, they headed toward the end of the block, where the Crown Vic was parked.

"She's definitely sleeping with him," Finn said. "And she's covering for him, too."

"She was acting funny, that's for sure. What do you make of the whole Teddy Briscoe thing?"

"No clue," Finn said. "But one thing for sure, we need to find out who Teddy Briscoe is."

52

Jack walked in and slammed the door so hard that Corrine almost spilled her coffee. She didn't flinch, though. She just kept stirring, slow and steady, as Jack stomped into the house, bringing the cold air and his foul mood right along with him.

He didn't take off his work shoes and didn't even shake off the snow clinging to his jacket. He moved straight to the kitchen, shoulders tight, face twisted, full of anger.

"You cook?" he snapped.

She nodded toward the stove. "Kept it warm for you."

Jack grabbed a bowl and filled it, slamming the ladle against the pot. He dropped into the chair across from her and ate as if the food had done something personal to him.

"Fucking Beau Lee Cooper," he muttered between bites. "That asshole was out there stirring shit in the news again today. Press everywhere. He's trying to fix the trial even before it starts. He's got people chanting Montrose's name like he's some kind of hero and trying to make us out to be the bad guys. Meanwhile, the department wants us out there protecting the protesters. What a joke. What has this country come to?"

He stabbed at his food, barely tasting it.

He was talking erratically, the rage pulsing through his body. "It's the same damn cycle. Same people, same protests, same bullshit. And that bastard Cooper—he loves it. Loves making us look like the villains. Loves putting a damn camera in his face and pretending he gives a shit."

Corrine listened quietly, hoping that Jack wouldn't be too loud and wake up the boys who were upstairs sleeping. She had learned long ago that Jack didn't need responses—he needed a place to put his anger. But today, his frustration ran deeper than the job.

Jack was pissed about something else, more than just this Cooper figure. She could tell. He was agitated. Wound tight. Like a man who'd been denied something he expected to have.

Corrine could hear his phone vibrating in his pocket. He took it out and pushed some buttons, but she knew not to ask about why he was mad and why he was ignoring the calls.

Jack sat there biting his fingernails, stewing in something Corrine couldn't quite name.

As she finished up the dishes and cleaned the kitchen, Jack's phone continued to buzz, and he finally stepped outside to take the call.

Corrine kept running the water in the sink but moved closer to the front door to try to listen. She took a wet rag with her and was prepared to look as though she'd been polishing something off.

"What are you doing?" Jack said.

Even though Jack was whispering, Corrine could hear every word.

"Why are you calling me incessantly? You know you can't call me back to back."

A beat.

"Babe, I told you I'd call you when I could," Jack responded.

Babe?

"Was it the investigators from internal affairs or that traitorous white cop who's Hollis's partner? They came to my house, too. It's like they're trying to watch my every move, but we got something in store for all of them."

It sounded like the investigators who'd tried to question Corrine last time also found the person currently on the phone with Jack.

"Goddamn it. I knew it was those fucking guys. With this trial about to start, they're getting desperate. Everybody's on edge. What were they asking, baby?"

Hearing her husband call another woman an affectionate nickname should have pained her. But Corrine had long known the reality of her relationship with Jack—it was all about the boys. She just needed to keep them safe. There was no love between her and Jack.

"I know you will, Heaven, and I'll go through fire for you, too. You did good, and after this trial everything'll be back to normal, but it'll be better than normal, 'cause I made up my mind." He moved a bit farther from the door but was still within earshot. "After this is over, I'm leaving Corrine and filing for divorce so we can be together all the time. This whole case has made me see what the important things are and just how much you love me. You never doubted me once throughout this whole thing. So just hang in there until we can put it all behind us, and then we'll be together forever. Will you hold on and wait for me? Just until we can sort things out and get this trial behind us."

Corrine could see Jack just a little through the window. He was smiling at whatever Heaven was saying.

"And we'll have the best life together. I promise you."

Corrine hurriedly returned to the sink and continued with cleaning the kitchen. While her arms made small circles on the counter, so too did her mind turn.

A divorce. *He said he would divorce me.* She couldn't believe that he would just throw away their family just like that. Then she thought about the custody battle they would have over the boys and suddenly felt a sharp pang of fear. What about her boys? Jack would want to take them, if for nothing but his pride.

When he came back inside, she tried to appear nonchalant. "You want a beer?"

"Yeah," he grunted.

She grabbed a Budweiser from the fridge and set it down in front of him next to his half-eaten dinner.

Jack glanced at the bottle before looking up at Corrine. She could see the storm clouds reentering his eyes. Whatever levity he was afforded outside on that phone call no longer staved off the anger from before.

"You're out of Miller Lite," she said, by way of explanation.

He stared at her. "You didn't buy more?"

His voice was deceptively calm, but she knew him well enough to hear the edge under it.

"Maybe your new wife will get you the right beer," she said.

Jack scoffed, and shook his head. "You were eavesdropping on me, huh, Corrine?"

He stood up and grabbed the beer, but he didn't open it. "So the cat's out of the bag. I'm leaving you, Corrine, because you don't believe in me and you don't make me happy anymore," he concluded.

"So you would just throw away your family just like that?"

"I am not throwing away my family. I am just throwing you away. I think the boys will be better off with their father."

Corrine cried out at that. "You son of a bitch. I'll never let you take my boys from me."

Jack whipped his arm forward, cracking her across her face. Corrine reared back and when she turned around to glare at him, he saw that he'd busted her lip open. "You know not to test me, Corrine."

Jack started to walk toward the door, but she grabbed his arm. "Did you hear me? I said, you are not taking my boys from me."

Jack tried to shake her off but Corrine held on. "Get away from me, Corrine. I told you not to test me."

"If you try to divorce me, I will make your life a living hell. I will take your pension, this house, and I'm not gonna let you get custody of my boys. You and your hussy will have to languish on the streets after I'm done with you."

Jack turned swiftly around and backhanded her, knocking her off-balance and sending her crashing into a small glass coffee table. She dropped face-first into the table, and he could tell her eye immediately started to swell. As Corrine began to lose consciousness, she thought she could hear Jack saying something to her.

Jack knelt down next to her and whispered harshly, "What did I say, Corrine? You brought this on yourself. I work all day. I don't want to come home and have to deal with your drama anymore. Now, I gotta deal with this trial tomorrow and I don't need your shit right now. We will deal with our situation once this trial is over. You hear me. This is not the end of this." He grabbed his coat and walked out.

Corrine lay there holding her left eye. There was a cut underneath from the broken glass, and it had started to bleed. As she lay there battered and bruised, she said to herself, "I won't let you take my children."

53

THE COURTROOM WAS PACKED. REPORTERS AND SKETCH ARTISTS WERE present. It was a high-profile trial and Beau Lee had a sense that his sketch would make it onto the evening news.

The room could accommodate around a hundred people. Family, friends, and supporters of Hollis and Rocky had made a point to be there. Hollis's supporters were professionally dressed; many were senior citizens who'd been activists over the years, but there was also a good share of young activists who'd been fired up after attending the rallies Beau Lee had held for Hollis over the past four months.

Rocky, Finn, Jamillah, Tyrone, Capes, and Harpo were in their usual seats in the row behind the lawyer's table where Beau Lee, Nellie, and Alvarez were sitting. Capes was right behind Beau Lee, and Nellie was within earshot of them. Baby Hope lay in her car seat between Jamillah and Tyrone and was sound asleep.

DaSilva was eager. Beau Lee knew he'd come out swinging, as there was no way he'd allow the bloviating Beau Lee Cooper—the name the right-wing media, especially radio jockeys, had given him—to best him.

DaSilva's task was simple. He represented the City of Chicago, and in doing so, he'd have to put the uppity Beau Lee in his place. The city was an unscalable wall, and Beau Lee wouldn't get a chance to put his feet on so much as one brick of it, let alone climb it.

On the State's side of the courtroom were uniformed officers from the Chicago Police Department. Their presence was a powerful display of force that was not lost on those from across the aisle, many of whom were from the African American community.

"All rise," the bailiff said.

The judge walked in. "Good morning, ladies and gentlemen. We will begin with opening statements made by both parties. The State will go first. Mr. DaSilva, you may proceed."

DaSilva stood up and walked to the podium. "Good morning, ladies and gentlemen. On behalf of the State of Illinois, I present the case that the defendant, Hollis Montrose, is to be held accountable for his criminal actions that put four good, hardworking police officers' lives in jeopardy." He walked the length of the jury box, making full eye contact with each member, a tactic used to help build rapport. "Members of the jury, I want to make clear to you all that it was Hollis Montrose's conduct alone that led to these officers fearing for their lives, resulting in their having to fire multiple shots to subdue him, a violent suspect. Now, the defense is going to suggest that you should have sympathy for the defendant because he suffered these life-changing injuries, but the evidence will show that Hollis Montrose fired his weapon at police officers, and these valiant men did what they were trained to do by neutralizing the threat and defending their lives."

DaSilva spent the next ten minutes victim blaming and asserting that Hollis failed to identify himself as a police officer, became aggressive, and ultimately fired his pistol at officers before they miraculously took him into custody. It was his attempt at spreading "copaganda," the notion that police officers were inherently good and justified in all their actions, no matter the outcome. He added, just before concluding, "If Hollis Montrose had been obeying the law and the officers' commands, he would've gone home to his wife that fateful night. Instead, he did the opposite, and today, he's wheelchair-bound." DaSilva paused for dramatic effect, and then concluded, "And we will prove beyond a reasonable doubt that it's no one's fault but his own."

"And for the defense, Mr. Cooper, you may proceed," the judge said.

Beau Lee walked to the podium. "This case is a tragedy. Mr. Montrose was shot and paralyzed, and the government actors, be it the police or the prosecutors, continue to try to prevent you from knowing the truth." Beau Lee left the podium and stood before the jury box, gesticulating as he calmly spoke. "The reason I'm so confident in our defense is because we have the truth, the whole truth, and nothing but the truth on our side. We intend to tell you the full story. While the State seeks to obscure the facts that would make you question why Mr. Hollis Montrose was even charged with these alleged crimes, we ask that you look beyond the false picture Mr. DaSilva will try to paint of Hollis Montrose and see that he is not only a law-abiding citizen who has never had a criminal record, but also that he is a police officer who has served this city—one he loves—for decades, first as a Chicago Police Department officer, and then as a Metra police officer. So, there is only one thing I ask you to do during this case, and that's to constantly ask yourselves: Why would a veteran policeman and law-abiding citizen suddenly engage in a heinous criminal act like the ones he's been accused of? What I hope you'll realize is, it doesn't add up."

54

Judge Lambert looked at the prosecution's table and said, "Mr. DaSilva, you may call your first witness."

"Your Honor, at this time the State will call Police Captain Brady O'Keefe, who supervised the police officers and detectives involved."

Captain O'Keefe walked before the court and was sworn in and seated in the witness box.

"Captain O'Keefe, state and spell your name and position and years of experience for the records."

O'Keefe responded with the spelling of his name, his title as police captain, and that he'd been with the Chicago Police Department for twenty-four years.

DaSilva paced slowly in front of his desk, taking his time. "Captain O'Keefe, am I correct that the police chief has assigned you the role of training, retention, and discipline of police officers within the department?"

"That is correct."

"As it relates to the incident involving Hollis Montrose, you would have headed up the investigation into the matter for the department?"

"That is correct. But our internal investigation is separate from Internal Affairs and the State Police Commission."

"Thank you for explaining that, Captain O'Keefe. And is it correct that all of your investigations arrived at the same conclusion?"

Alvarez leaned over to Beau Lee and whispered, "We should object." Beau Lee shook his head.

"We more or less all arrived at the same conclusion."

"It would be inappropriate for you to talk about their conclusion. I want you to focus specifically on your conclusion."

"Yes, sir, Mr. DaSilva," answered O'Keefe.

"I want to first call your attention to the evidence collected at the scene of the shooting." DaSilva asked a few quick questions that were all easy affirmatives for O'Keefe—whether they impounded Hollis's SUV that night, preserved the evidence in the normal chain of custody, preserved the license plate.

"I want to show you what has been pre-marked as State exhibit number one. Please identify it and explain to the court that this is how this evidence was collected at the scene of the incident," DaSilva said, then asked for the exhibit from the clerk, who handed him the license plate, which had been sealed in a plastic bag.

"Thank you," he said. He removed the bent metal plate from the bag.

"Captain O'Keefe, is this the license plate that was taken from Hollis Montrose's vehicle and the condition in which it was on the night in question?"

"Yes, this is the license plate, and the condition it was in."

"And as you sit here in this courtroom today, can you tell the jury whether you arrived at any conclusions based on the condition of this license plate, and what those conclusions were?"

"First, we concluded that because of how the plate had been damaged, it would make it difficult for an officer to correctly identify what the letters and numbers on the plate were," he said, pointing at the damage. "You can see how the bent areas make it unreadable. Therefore, we concluded that the arresting officers would not have been able to accurately relay the plate over the radio and that no information would've been provided by dispatch, such as the registered owner."

"Thank you, Captain O'Keefe," DaSilva said. He had an easygoing demeanor that the jurors seemed to favor. "During the gunshot residue exam, were Mr. Montrose's hands properly secured in plastic to allow for the responding officers to perform the examination?"

"Yes, it is indicated in the gunshot residue report."

"And what did that report conclude?"

"Due to the residue on his hands, the state crime lab concluded that Hollis Montrose had fired his weapon."

"I want to call your attention to the third piece of evidence that I believe you reviewed in your investigation. Did the responding officers recover the casings from the discharged weapons?"

"Yes, we did. According to our report," explained Captain O'Keefe, "there were ten casings located on the scene. The casings recovered matched Jack Dunham's weapon. The same was the case for Chaz Rossi, Leonard Johnson, and Rory Caruthers."

"Thank you, Captain O'Keefe. Based on your objective findings, and the officers' incident reports, did your department arrive at a conclusion regarding the incident involving Mr. Hollis Montrose?"

"Yes, we did. We determined that based on the officers' testimonies, which corroborated the evidence collected at the scene, it was justifiable homicide and appropriate use of force that adhered to department training, policies, and the laws of the State of Illinois."

"Thank you, Captain O'Keefe, for the in-depth analysis of your investigation. I have no further questions at this time, Your Honor. I will pass the witness."

55

BEAU LEE WALKED UP TO THE PODIUM AND GREETED THE MAN. HE WAS trying to keep his breathing in check and reminded himself that it would be a marathon, not a sprint.

"Would it be safe to say that the Internal Affairs division and state investigators all reviewed and incorporated statements taken during your initial investigation?"

"I think they have what we provided them."

Beau Lee stood with his hands relaxed by his sides. He knew that composure would serve him well, especially as a Black attorney facing a majority white jury. "Can you confirm whether or not the state investigators relied solely on your department's cursory investigation, or did they seek any findings on their own?"

"I can't tell you what they did in their investigation."

"Can one presume that if your investigation yielded errors, then the State's would've had the same errors in their reporting?"

DaSilva stood up and exclaimed, "Objection! Argumentative!"

The judge looked at Beau Lee. "The objection is sustained," she said in an irritated tone.

Without being fazed, Beau Lee moved on to his next question. "Captain O'Keefe, it was not lost on me, and I'm sure not on anybody else in this courtroom, that your report makes no mention of the video that recorded the incident. Is that because it contradicts your conclusions?"

"Objection!" DaSilva shouted. "The statement of the facts. The video was referenced in the report as unreliable."

"Your Honor, I believe the defendant has the right to inquire as to why Captain O'Keefe did not explain his findings as it relates to the video that recorded the incidents leading up to the shooting."

"Mr. Cooper, I will allow you a very limited examination on this issue."

"Thank you, Your Honor. Captain O'Keefe, what were your findings as it relates to the video that showed the defendant, Hollis Montrose, face down on the ground with his hands above him, being shot in his back by the Chicago police officers?"

"As the district attorney said, we found the video unreliable because it was dark and it was very distant," O'Keefe said. "A person with reasonable vision could not see that far and definitely could not hear what was being said from a hundred yards away. Based on our training and policy, we collected as much objective evidence and firsthand witness accounts to determine whether a video would help us arrive at any different conclusions. We found that all of the eyewitnesses and the objective evidence were consistent with what we saw on the video."

"Then why didn't you lead with the video that shows us what happened in the shooting?"

"Objection!" DaSilva shouted again. "Mr. Cooper continues to badger the witness when he doesn't get the answer he wants, Your Honor."

Beau Lee fired back. "Your Honor, I'm just pointing out to the court that if the video showed that Mr. Montrose had done anything criminal, this police captain would have led with it. The defense believes that this is further evidence of the relevance of the video."

"Mr. Cooper, I have issued my rules on the video, and the jury will be able to evaluate the testimony from this witness and all other witnesses. If the police captain believes that the video is irrelevant, then the jury can accept his testimony or not. It's that simple. But I will not allow you to argue with a witness. The objection is sustained."

Beau Lee looked back at Alvarez, who just shook her head, then he continued. "Captain O'Keefe, a few moments ago you stated that you collected firsthand witness accounts from everybody on the scene, correct?"

"Yes, we did. That is our policy."

"So in fact, you are saying that the only firsthand witnesses were your police officers. Correct?"

"Those are the only eyewitnesses that we were able to ascertain," answered Captain O'Keefe.

"You didn't collect a statement from Hollis Montrose, did you?"

"Objection," DaSilva said. "Mr. Cooper knows his client has a Fifth Amendment right against self-incrimination."

"I am perfectly aware of my client's constitutional rights. The fact of the matter is that the police did not even attempt to take a statement from Hollis Montrose to see if he agreed that the video showed that he never fired his weapon. They only sought to validate evidence that helped them get to the conclusion that exonerated their officers."

"Mr. Cooper, your client may waive his Fifth Amendment privileges if he wishes to testify during this trial," Lambert said. "But I won't allow you to badger witnesses. The objection is sustained. Now, do you have any other questions for this witness?"

"One last question. Captain O'Keefe, would it make sense that a law-abiding citizen like Hollis Montrose, a police officer with no criminal history, would be driving without his wallet and identification on his person or anywhere in his car?"

"Objection, calls for speculation."

Beau Lee retorted, "I'm not asking whether they arrived at a conclusion. I am asking whether they even raised the question during the investigation, or if they simply took the police officers' word—that Mr. Montrose didn't have his wallet on him on the night in question—as the truth."

"It's straightforward, Mr. Cooper. If we'd recovered a wallet from

Mr. Montrose's person, it would have been placed in the police inventory. I don't see why this question is relevant at all."

"We believe it would be very relevant if Mr. Montrose were to take the stand."

There were rumblings throughout the courtroom as people reacted to Beau Lee's floating the idea of Hollis telling his story. It would be welcomed by Hollis and his family, but Nellie had advised against it. Hollis wasn't fully healed, and his memory of the night was still blurry.

The judge banged her gavel. "Order in the court! As for you, Mr. Cooper, it will be up to you and your client whether he'll take the stand, but let's avoid theatrical speculation. Do you have any more questions for this witness?"

"I do not." Beau Lee returned to his seat.

56

DASILVA CALLED SANTIAGO GARCIA, THE IMPOUND CLERK, AS HIS NEXT witness, but was quick with his line of questioning, mainly addressing whether Garcia had followed standard protocol. So Beau Lee was quick to follow up when it was his turn to cross-examine.

"Officer Garcia, you attest that you followed standard protocol, correct?"

"Yes, sir."

"So you recorded the suspect's vehicle when it entered the impound lot? There was no deviation?"

"I was not working when the vehicle came in, but I would suspect the procedure was carried out the same way as when any vehicle is impounded as part of a police investigation."

"Well, you certainly could've had access to the footage of the video that showed when it came into the impound lot?"

Officer Garcia leafed through his folder and scanned several pages of photographs. "No, for some reason, there were no video footage or photographs showing the intake of that vehicle."

"Isn't that convenient? Because if we had that video or at least photos, the members of the jury would be able to see whether the license plate was damaged when it arrived at the lot."

"Objection," DaSilva said.

"Sustained," answered the judge. "Move on, Mr. Cooper."

"Understood, Judge," Beau Lee said. "Officer Garcia, we don't have the video footage of the vehicle arriving at the lot, but we do have the video footage of Officer Jackson Dunham and Officer Chaz Rossi arriving at the lot a few days later. You are aware that these officers visited the lot, correct?"

"Yes, sir," Garcia said reluctantly.

"Your Honor, at this time, the defense moves to enter the video footage from the impound lot from November 13, 2008, which was eight days after Mr. Montrose was shot during a traffic stop."

The judge permitted the video with a nod and Beau Lee handed the video tape to the clerk.

"You were working the day Officers Dunham and Rossi arrived at the lot, correct?"

Garcia nodded and said, "Yes. Officer Rossi said they needed to search the vehicle."

"Were they accompanied by detectives, or did they have a warrant?"

"No, they came alone and didn't have a warrant."

"Yet you allowed them to search the vehicle?"

"Yes."

"I see," Beau Lee said. "And you weren't with them while they searched the vehicle?"

"No, I'm not allowed to leave the entrance of the impound lot when I'm on duty," he explained.

"Could you not have found another officer to accompany them?"

"No other officer was available at the time."

"How long did they stay on the lot?"

"About twenty minutes."

Beau Lee gathered that Garcia had nothing to hide. This wasn't about him. For the most part, he seemed practiced and ready for every question Beau Lee had asked thus far.

"That would leave plenty of time for them to have tampered with evidence without anyone knowing."

DaSilva screamed, "Objection!" He looked genuinely shocked at Beau Lee's audacity.

Beau Lee responded, "Your Honor, I'm merely asking the witness, since he wasn't there, if he knows what these two officers did while they were unsupervised with this crucial piece of evidence, which could show that they were lying about not being able to read this tag."

"Mr. Cooper, you will wait for my ruling, and you will not give speaking objections in my courtroom," the judge said, exhibiting little restraint. Her patience was wearing thin. "The objection is sustained, based on its call for speculation that is unfounded. The jury will disregard those questions."

"I have but one final question, Officer Garcia," Beau Lee said, knowing it was best to move on. "Isn't it peculiar that out of all the vehicles that are videotaped and photographed when they're impounded, that this would be the one vehicle that mysteriously has no record of being admitted?"

There were some questions Beau Lee just had to ask. A jury can disregard on paper, but it would color their assessment of the rest of the trial and the other information they'd be provided.

"Objection! Speculation!" DaSilva said.

"I will withdraw the question," Beau Lee said, knowing it would happen. "But I'm curious, what happened to the vehicle? My understanding is that it was sent to dismantling."

"Yes," Garcia said. "It was dismantled in error."

"How could a thing like that happen?"

"It was incorrectly tagged," Garcia said. "It was given a pink tag, which indicates vehicles that have reached the maximum amount of time they could be on the lot. They're either sent to auction or, if they're deemed salvage, they're sent to a dismantler."

"And Mr. Montrose's SUV was tagged as a salvage vehicle?"

"Correct."

"Who would have been responsible for tagging these vehicles?"

"Multiple people in our department have the authority, but usually it's the lot superintendent."

"Is that who tagged Mr. Montrose's SUV?"

"No," Garcia said.

"Who did?"

"I did, sir."

"And why you?"

"The superintendent wasn't available, and I was told to update the vehicles. Somehow the suspect's vehicle was logged incorrectly and received the pink tag."

"Yes . . . somehow," Beau Lee said. "No further questions."

57

DASILVA ROSE TO CALL THE STATE'S NEXT WITNESS. "STATE CALLS TO THE stand Detective Roger Fowler."

After the witness introduced himself and spelled his name for the record, DaSilva began his direct examination.

"Detective Fowler, where are you currently employed?" asked DaSilva.

"I'm currently employed at Illinois State Police Division of Criminal Investigation, specifically the Division of Forensic Sciences Unit. I'm an analyst and I work in our crime lab analyzing trace evidence. DNA, gunshot residue, fingerprints, and bloodstain pattern analysis."

Fowler spent five minutes explaining his experience and other elements of his résumé to the members of the jury, then DaSilva turned to the judge. "Have you been qualified to testify regarding gunshot residue and trace evidence in this investigation?"

"Yes."

"At this time, I would like to tender this witness as an expert in gunshot primer residue analysis," DaSilva said.

"Any objections?" Lambert asked very matter-of-factly.

"Yes, Your Honor," said Beau Lee, rising from the defense table. "Permission to voir dire the witness?"

The judge cut a look at Beau Lee. She made no attempt to hide her annoyance as Beau Lee walked to the podium.

"Not so fast, Mr. Cooper, you will have an opportunity to cross-examine the witness. There is no need for a voir dire at this time. This witness shall be tendered as an expert. You may continue, Mr. DaSilva."

Beau Lee stood flat-footed, debating with himself whether to argue with the judge, but ultimately decided against it.

DaSilva seemed to rejoice as Beau Lee took his seat.

"What is gunshot residue, Detective Fowler?" asked DaSilva, directing his attention back to the witness.

Fowler cleared his throat and adopted a professorial tone. "In layman's terms, gunshot residue is a collection of particles that are released from a gun when it is fired. But, the more academic definition that is generally accepted in our profession is gunshot primer residue, which are the microscopic particles that are released from a firearm when it is discharged. Primarily, we're looking for burned or molten particles that contain the big three chemical components commonly found in gunshot residue: lead, barium, and antimony."

"How do you test for gunshot primer residue?" DaSilva asked, shifting his weight at the podium and angling his body toward the jury to ensure they were paying attention.

"To test for gunshot primer residue, we would start by using a GSR, a gunshot residue collection kit," Fowler said. "That kit would include gloves, labels, and vials of adhesive lifts. We use the adhesive lifts and dab random areas of the surface we're assessing: clothes; nearby objects; and body parts, like a person's hands. The adhesive will pick up particulate matter. We then use our scanning electron microscope to see what particulate matter is on the adhesive."

"When those adhesives are analyzed under the microscope, what can you learn?" asked DaSilva.

"If large quantities of residue particles are shown from our testing, we can conclude that the person or object tested was in the vicinity of a firearm when it was discharged," he said.

"What surfaces did you examine in this case?"

"We were tasked with evaluating several articles of Mr. Montrose's clothing, including the shirt he was wearing, his pants, and his hands," the detective responded.

"And when you placed those adhesive lifts from Mr. Montrose's hands under the electron microscope scanner, what did they reveal?"

"We found that Mr. Montrose's hands tested positive for gunshot primer residue."

"And what did you conclude after completing your testing, Detective?"

"We concluded that Mr. Montrose had fired a gun, which is consistent with what we see on the video."

"Objection! There is nothing in the video or any evidence that showed Mr. Montrose touching a gun!" Beau Lee shouted as he sprung from his seat.

"Overruled. The jury will have an opportunity to evaluate the video evidence, and I am sure you will cross-examine him on this issue," said Lambert.

"Your Honor, I am opposed to his being allowed to make any misstatements of the evidence at any point of the trial."

"I've made my ruling, Mr. Cooper. Mr. DaSilva, you may continue."

Beau Lee could sense Alvarez stewing beside him.

"Detective Fowler, based on your years of experience and your qualifications as a forensic scientist and all of the evidence that you reviewed in this case, can you tell the jury what your expert scientific opinion is?" asked DaSilva.

"Based on the gunshot residue test that revealed a significant quantity of primer residue particles on his hands, it is evident that these particles are the result of the defendant's firing his gun."

"Thank you, Detective Fowler. I have no further questions at this time," DaSilva concluded.

58

BEAU LEE CUT TO THE CHASE. "DETECTIVE FOWLER, THAT LAST STATEment that you made before the jury as to what your opinion was is actually different from the previous answer you gave."

DaSilva squirmed in his chair and appeared confused.

"No, I recall that the statements were the same."

"Are you sure about that?" asked Beau Lee.

Detective Fowler looked at the prosecution with apprehension. "The statements were the same," he repeated.

Beau Lee picked up his notes and dictated the questions and answers from DaSilva's cross-examination of Fowler. "If need be, I can have the court reporter read them back. Would you like me to do that?"

"Yes, I would like that, because I don't think I said what you're saying."

The court reporter read the statements exactly as Beau Lee had stated them. "Thank you, Madame Court Reporter," Beau Lee said, watching as Fowler grew flush. "Detective Fowler, do you understand the huge difference between the two statements you made in front of this jury this morning?"

"No, I don't," Fowler said.

Beau Lee took a deep breath and faced the jury. "You said in your previous statement that we concluded that Mr. Montrose had fired a gun, which is consistent with what we see in the video. To which I objected because the video does not show Hollis touching a gun. Then, the prosecutor asked you for your opinion again. That time, you didn't mention him touching the gun in the video. Was that just an oversight, or was that intentional, because you know that nowhere in that video shows Mr. Montrose touching a gun?"

Detective Fowler shook his head. "That's not accurate. I said based on the evidence, which would include the video, that's how I arrived at my conclusion."

"So, you're going to stand by your notion that in that video, you see Mr. Montrose touching a gun?"

"I just know what was reported to me in the officers' reports."

"Alas, Detective Fowler, you are changing your testimony again. Now you're saying your opinion is based on the officers' reports and not the video."

DaSilva stood yet again and said, "Objection, Your Honor, defense counsel is badgering another witness."

"Your Honor, I am not badgering the witness," Beau Lee said. "I'm just trying to get clarity on how he arrived at his opinions."

"The objection is sustained. As I am reminding you again that the jury will be able to evaluate all of the evidence that has been admitted in the trial at the appropriate time. Now move on, Mr. Cooper."

"Detective, how long have you been working in the Illinois State Police Division of the Criminal Investigation Crime Lab?"

"Thirteen years."

"You are employed by the State of Illinois, which also employs Mr. DaSilva?"

"Correct."

"How many cases have you and the state attorney, Mr. DaSilva, worked on in those thirteen years?"

"At least a hundred."

"Detective Fowler, in those hundred cases, have you ever found that the gunshot residue in question did not come from the defendant firing a gun?"

DaSilva interjected, "This is outside the scope of the direct examination, Your Honor, and it is irrelevant."

The judge gave an exhausted sigh as if she were nearing the last straw. "Mr. Cooper, I agree with the prosecutor. This is completely irrelevant. We are not entertaining other cases."

"Detective Fowler, you are familiar with the limitations of gunshot residue analysis?" Beau Lee asked.

Detective Fowler steadied himself. "All scientific testing has its limitations, but it can be concluded with a reasonable degree of scientific certainty that Mr. Montrose tested positive for gunshot primer residue."

"I appreciate your answer, sir, but wouldn't you agree that a main limitation to a gunshot residue test is that it cannot conclude where those particles that were deposited on the subject came from?"

"That is correct. However, as I have said multiple times, based on the totality of the evidence in this case, I have concluded it came from the defendant shooting the weapon."

Beau Lee paused for a moment and smiled. "Mr. Fowler, that is not what I asked you. Please answer my question. Can you do that?"

"Objection, Your Honor. Counsel is deliberately antagonizing the witness."

"Sustained. Mr. Cooper, you are treading on thin ice," said the judge.

"Your Honor, I just want him to answer my question, which is, Detective Fowler, yes or no, can a gunshot residue test conclude how the particles got on an individual's person?"

After sucking his teeth, Fowler conceded, "No, the gunshot residue test itself cannot conclude where the particles came from."

"Finally, we agree on something," Beau Lee said. "Now, Detective, you would agree with me that gunshot residue particles can readily be transferred to other objects and surfaces, or from one person to another?"

"It can," the detective answered.

Beau Lee continued. "A gunshot residue kit cannot tell you if the particles found on an individual were transferred from the individual shooting the gun or the individual making contact with someone who fired a gun?"

"No, it cannot."

"Thank you, Detective Fowler, I have just a few additional questions," Beau Lee said very solemnly. "I have had a chance to review your report, and I noticed that it was only Mr. Montrose's hands that tested positive for gunshot residue. Not his shirt, nor his coat, nor his scarf tested positive for gunshot residue. Is that correct?"

"Yes. My report is my report. We indicated everything that showed a positive test for gunshot residue."

"And it was only on his hands?"

"Yes, only his hands."

"Your team also collected the bullet casings that were supposedly discarded after my client's gun was fired, correct?"

"Yes."

"What about the bullet's trajectory?" Beau Lee said. "Did you analyze that?"

"Yes," Fowler said. "We evaluated the ballistic report."

"And what did you find?"

"Mr. Montrose's weapon was fired in the direction of the officers from a relatively prone position, resulting in the bullet striking a concrete wall approximately ten yards away."

"Can you explain what it means when a gun is fired from the prone position?"

"When a shooter fires from the prone position—lying flat on the ground—the firearm is typically stabilized against the earth," Fowler said, working to regain his sense of authority. "From a trajectory standpoint, this position naturally results in a lower muzzle height relative to the ground. Meaning, a bullet would travel upward due to an upward cant, or angling, which is likely why the trajectory indicated that a bullet was fired over the officers' heads, because their bodies were lower to the ground as they attempted to subdue the suspect."

"Do you claim that it was a near miss?" Beau Lee asked. "That one bullet fired from my client's gun somehow missed all four officers and was perfectly lodged in a wall?"

"That's what the evidence supports."

"How is it physically possible for my client to have fired a gun from the prone position, as you say, and not get any residue on his clothing or body besides his hands?"

"I don't know, but it's possible."

"I'd like to show an exhibit that depicts an illustration of a shooter in a prone position based on Detective Fowler's report." Beau Lee removed a covered easel to reveal a large rendering of a shooter lying on his side, holding a gun with his arm extended. "As you can see, based on this illustration, in order for my client to have fired a shot, his body would need to have been slightly rolled, with significant weight on his arm and shoulder, and his arm couldn't have been fully extended. Meaning, the firearm would have been closer to his face and body."

Fowler straightened up and studied the illustration.

"Firing a weapon from this position would've been insanely difficult given the angle," Beau Lee said as he shined a laser pointer against the rendered figure. "There is no way the weapon could've been stabilized against the ground, so the bullet would not have traveled over the officers' heads, but rather low and wide, potentially striking at least one of them. That's if the shooter had the necessary dexterity to even fire at all. What are your thoughts now, Detective?"

"A difficult shot, but not impossible," Fowler said. "As you said, with enough dexterity, the weapon could've been fired."

"I have here my client's most recent physician's report." Beau Lee handed a copy to Fowler. "Take a look, Detective. What do you see?"

"It says Hollis Montrose suffers from arthritis."

"Yes. Mild rheumatoid arthritis. Common with officers his age," Beau Lee said, taking the report back. "After years of report writing, it isn't surprising that he developed arthritis. However, the condition causes joint and muscle stiffness. While my client is able to fire his firearm from a traditional stance, such as Isosceles or Weaver, to fire a gun from such an odd position would mean he'd need to be a contortionist. Not only that, but he couldn't fire from any position that would limit his mobility."

Fowler was silent.

"So, I ask you again, can you definitively say that the particles on the defendant's hands likely came from the gun's blowback? Or is it possible that someone who fired the weapon transferred the particles to my client's hands?"

DaSilva said, "Objection, Your Honor! Calls for speculation!"

Before the judge could rule, Beau Lee interjected with, "I withdraw the question. I think that as you said, the evidence will speak for itself. No further questions."

59

THE NEXT WITNESS WAS SARGEANT LEONARD JOHNSON, WHO HAD BEEN with the Chicago Police Department for eighteen years. Johnson was a slight man, and the gap between his teeth was noticeable, something Beau Lee was sure had exposed him to some ridicule in his early years. But as Johnson sat in the witness box, he exuded a distinct air of confidence. DaSilva asked him to explain what he'd seen and how he responded to the call the night of Hollis's shooting, but the questioning and direct examination revealed nothing that Beau Lee didn't already know from Captain O'Keefe's testimony.

Next up was Sargeant Chaz Rossi, who had been with CPD for four years. Beau Lee was buzzing. DaSilva had been pitching softballs to each of the police officers so far, and Rossi started like the others had by explaining the events of the night.

"It was a little after midnight when we observed a Ford Expedition swerving like it was a drunk driver or something. Officer Dunham activated the sirens and we tried to read the license plate, but it was defaced, so we couldn't get a clear vision of it."

"Then what did you do?" DaSilva prompted.

"We had to chase it for a few minutes, but when the SUV finally came to a stop, we got out of the cruiser and approached Mr. Montrose's vehicle with our hands on our waists on our service weapons.

Given that he was evading us when we first asked him to pull over, we weren't sure what to expect. The suspect seemed annoyed and began yelling at Officer Dunham. Officer Dunham extracted Mr. Montrose from the vehicle and ordered him to the ground. Shortly after, backup arrived. That's when we saw he had a gun on his side. We told him to keep his hands stretched out above, with his palms face down toward the ground. The suspect continued yelling, asking for our badge numbers and calling us racists. And then he moved his right hand down and retrieved his gun and fired two shots at me. That's when we all fired."

"Officer Rossi, was there anything obstructing the defendant from taking a direct shot at you?"

"No, sir."

"When the defendant fired his gun, what went through your mind?"

"I saw my life pass before my eyes. I thought he was going to kill me." Rossi said this dramatically, putting a hand to his chest for effect. Alvarez couldn't help but roll her eyes.

"And Officer Rossi, in that life-or-death moment, you fired your weapon along with your fellow officers as you were trained to do, correct?"

"Yes, we did."

"Based on where you were positioned, did you have the best vantage point to see that Mr. Montrose did shoot his gun at you?"

Beau Lee and Alvarez didn't even try to object that one. They let it roll, knowing it would only further aggravate the judge, and they wanted to save their objections for the truly dire ones.

"Yes, I did. My partner, Officer Dunham, confirmed that the suspect's weapon had been fired when he retrieved it from him."

DaSilva brushed his hands together and passed off the witness to Beau Lee, who walked up like a cobra readying to strike. He calmly approached the podium. "Officer Rossi, did you state that one of the reasons you pulled over Officer Montrose was because you claim his license plate was defaced?"

"That and he was driving like he was drunk."

"I will take that as a yes—that one of the reasons you and Officer Dunham pulled him over was because his license plate was defaced. Then, is it policy that once evidence like a vehicle is inventoried and impounded, it is not to be tampered with from that point forward?"

"Objection. Defense counsel is trying to create a false narrative. There is no evidence of anybody tampering with anyone's vehicle in this case."

Beau Lee said, "Your Honor, I am asking whether it is Chicago Police Department policy that once a vehicle is inventoried and impounded that it is not to be tampered with in any way without documentation."

"I will allow him to answer the question as to what he knows the Chicago Police Department's policy on this matter to be." The judge finally gave him one, and Beau Lee felt a spike of adrenaline at the minute victory.

"Thank you, Your Honor. Officer Rossi, you can answer the question."

"No, you're not supposed to tamper with evidence once it's been impounded."

"Can you tell me, why is there video of you and your partner, Officer Jack Dunham, going to the impound yard and fiddling with Mr. Montrose's vehicle?"

Rossi looked unusually stony. "We didn't do anything to his SUV. We went to find out if he'd left his wallet inside it with his identification, since everybody was making such a big deal about him not identifying himself."

"Then what you did in the impound yard that day was innocent? Neither you nor Officer Dunham defaced Mr. Montrose's license plate to fit your narrative?"

"Objection," DaSilva said. "There is no evidence to suggest that these officers did anything inappropriate."

Beau Lee responded, "If they didn't do anything inappropriate, Officer Rossi should be able to give his answer in this courtroom."

DaSilva fired back, "The question is calculated to mislead the jury, and that's why I put my objection on the record."

"I note your objection on the record. Officer Rossi can answer the question."

Officer Rossi looked at the judge and DaSilva and asked, "Do I answer?"

"Yes, you can," Judge Lambert said.

"Yeah, it was innocent. We didn't do nothing to that tag."

"If it was so innocent, then why didn't you all document it in your police reports, per policy, that you made a visit to the impound yard to go inside Mr. Montrose's vehicle, knowing that it was the subject of a very important case?"

"We were just trying to see one way or the other if he really had his wallet and identification in his SUV since we couldn't find any on him that night."

"I understand your answer, Officer Rossi, but that still doesn't explain why you didn't document it."

Rossi shrugged. "We were just moving so fast that it slipped our minds."

Beau Lee was successfully backing Rossi into a corner. "You all were moving so fast, but based on video surveillance of the entrance and the exit of the impound yard, you guys were there for over twenty minutes. Why did it take so long?"

"Objection!"

"No need to rule, Your Honor. I will withdraw the question." Beau Lee was keeping something far more important in his back pocket. He did what he'd set out to do with Rossi on the impounded car.

"Okay, Mr. Cooper, move on, but with a little less commentary," the judge said.

"Officer Rossi, are you aware that there was a cellphone video that captured the entire incident between you and the other Chicago police officers?"

"Yes."

"Are you also aware that the video does not show Mr. Montrose firing his gun?"

"Objection! Judge, you've previously ruled on this matter," DaSilva said.

Beau Lee responded, "Your Honor, I am asking what he observed on the video."

"The objection is sustained with my previous ruling, counselor."

Beau Lee decided to try another tack. "Officer Rossi, are you aware that when guns are fired, sparks of light can be seen?"

"I don't know. That depends on the person's eyesight."

Beau Lee shook his head subtly. "You mean to tell me that you couldn't see the sparks of light when you fired your gun?"

"Objection, argumentative," DaSilva cried out.

The judge announced the objection sustained.

"Officer Rossi, after the shooting stopped, did you observe Mr. Montrose making any movements?"

"No, not after the shooting stopped."

"Were you aware that the two bullets that you fired entered into Mr. Montrose's body?"

"Yes, I suspected that they did because of the close proximity."

"Officer Rossi, it's paradoxical that you acknowledge the close proximity between you and Mr. Montrose at the time of the shooting. If you all were so close to one another and you shot two rounds and they both went into Mr. Montrose, then how come neither of the two shots you claim Mr. Montrose took struck you?"

"Objection. Calls for speculation."

Sustained again.

"Officer Rossi, since you had such close proximity to everything, did you observe your partner retrieving Mr. Montrose's gun and his wallet after he handcuffed Mr. Montrose?"

"I know he retrieved his gun. We never found a wallet on the suspect."

Beau Lee knew his next line of questioning wouldn't fly, but it was worth saying out loud. "Let me get this straight: Mr. Montrose, who has never been arrested in his life, who has never gotten a traffic citation, was driving his vehicle recklessly and did not have his driver's license or his identification on his person when you all stopped him? Does that make any sense to you?"

"Objection, argumentative."

"I withdraw. No more questions, Your Honor."

60

WHEN JACK DUNHAM WAS CALLED TO THE STAND AND SWORN IN, DASILVA asked the same question he'd asked both the previous officers and it was curious that Dunham's response about the events of the night were nearly verbatim of that of his partner, Rossi's. Shortly after Dunham's recounting, Capes received a flurry of phone calls. Beau Lee looked over to see what the fuss was about, but Capes only moved to dismiss himself and take the calls outside. Beau Lee knew that he had put all his irons in the fire and not all of them proved worthy. He wouldn't be able to use all of them during this trial, but that was how it always was. A good attorney must be prepared beyond what was necessary.

Shortly after Capes stepped out, DaSilva moved to the witness box.

"Based on your experience in training, was everything you did by the book, Officer Dunham?"

"Absolutely. One hundred percent," Jack said a little too quickly.

"Now that some time has passed and you've been able to review every circumstance in your mind of the traffic stop that night, would you change anything that you did in any way?"

"Attorney DaSilva, as I sit here today, I wouldn't change one single thing that I did that night," Jack said. "I mean, if this guy would have been able to shoot Officer Rossi, then he could have got a round off on me, too. I took it as my responsibility to make sure that me and all my fellow officers got home to our families. I know too many good cops who didn't survive a stop."

"I have no further questions. Thank you, Officer Dunham. I am glad that you and all your officers made it home safe."

Beau Lee began his cross-exam as he walked up to the podium. "Mr. Montrose swore that he had his wallet in his back pocket. Do you know who took it, since he was unconscious due to the shooting?"

"No, I do not, Mr. Cooper. You are assuming that he had a wallet on him that night."

"Now, that is something that doesn't add up to me." Beau Lee put his hands on his hips, the way his mother used to when she was stumped. "Why would a law-abiding citizen who always obeys the law and has never gotten so much as a traffic ticket be driving without a license? Do you have any idea?"

"Law-abiding citizens don't shoot at police officers," Jack said.

"We will get to that in just a minute, Officer Dunham. But for now, I want to ask you a direct question. Did you or the officers on the scene take Hollis Montrose's wallet, which contained his driver's license and badge?"

"Now, why would any of us do that, Mr. Cooper?" Jack leaned forward, a near smile on his face.

Beau Lee staved off the fury in his chest. Jack's display of arrogance was why this case was so important: to get justice for Hollis. Jack would be an obstacle in that effort, and Beau Lee reminded himself of how important it was to keep cool in the court of law. "Is your answer yes or no?"

Jack took a breath and sat back. "Of course not, Mr. Cooper."

"You didn't answer my question, Officer Dunham."

"Objection. He's badgering the witness, Your Honor," DaSilva said.

"I will sustain the objection. I believe the witness has answered the questions sufficiently. Now move on, Mr. Cooper," Judge Lambert said.

"Your Honor, I want to note for the record that the witness never answered yes or no to my direct question."

"Attorney Cooper, I acknowledge that I heard Officer Dunham respond by saying of course they didn't take his wallet. Now ask your next question."

Beau Lee took a deep breath and proceeded. "Officer Dunham, how much time passed before you went to handcuff Mr. Montrose after the shooting stopped?"

"I don't know. I wanted to make sure that all the officers were safe, and I wanted to make sure that he wasn't going to put any of my fellow officers in jeopardy."

"So how long did it take, Officer Dunham? You were there."

"I'm not sure. I just know I was more concerned with my officers' safety."

"You can't give me an estimate, Officer Dunham?"

"Objection, asked and answered."

And sustained.

"Officer Dunham, would it help if you reviewed the cellphone video that was taken of the shooting incident by a bystander as to how much time passed after you shot your weapon and then handcuffed Mr. Montrose?"

"Objection, Your Honor, this goes outside of your prior ruling regarding the video."

Beau Lee interjected with, "Your Honor, I know that you allowed only parts of the video to be presented to aid the jury as fact finders. The witness said he doesn't know how much time has passed, but the time clearly can be seen on the video because there is a time stamp. And this will show how much time passed before the shooting stopped and when Officer Dunham put his heel in the back of Mr. Montrose and handcuffed him. It is very factual and beyond debate."

"Mr. Cooper, you have been trying to get around my ruling on the video throughout the trial," Judge Lambert said. "I am not going to allow you to get things that are inadmissible in through the back door. The objection is sustained."

Beau Lee took the hit. He was always ready with the next comeback, because when you grow up in the hood, you have to know how to play the dozens.

"Officer Dunham, do you have any reason to dispute that in less than forty-seven seconds after the last shot was fired, you were on top of Mr. Montrose putting your hands over his hands and handcuffing him?"

"Objection, Judge, he is still trying to go around your ruling."

"Sustained," the judge said, snapping. "As I have ruled, the jury will get to watch the video and glean whatever evidence they feel is important from it without your commentary, Mr. Cooper."

"Yes, ma'am, Your Honor, absolutely," said Beau Lee with the slightest hint of cynicism. He turned his attention back to Dunham. "Would you agree that when you fired your gun, there was gunshot residue on your hand?"

"I suppose."

"Following that, would you agree that your hand with the gunshot residue would have touched Mr. Montrose's hand when you put the handcuffs on him?"

"I don't know," Jack answered nonchalantly. "As I said before, I was concerned about me and my fellow officers' safety."

"Sir, are you trying to tell this jury that you can't remember that your hand made contact with a man who you were putting in handcuffs?"

"Objection, argumentative."

"Sustained."

Beau Lee paid them no mind and tried again. "Would you have any reason to believe that your hand would not have touched his hand when you put the handcuffs on Mr. Montrose?"

"No," Jack said reluctantly, eyeing his attorneys.

"Then you would agree that the gunshot residue on your hand would have made contact with Mr. Montrose's hand?"

"The gunshot residue on his hand would have made contact with my hand, too."

"And that is presuming that Mr. Montrose shot his gun, correct?"

"He did shoot his gun. He almost killed my partner, and I would have been next," Jack said, getting heated.

Beau Lee smiled. He was a seasoned trial lawyer, but this moment never got old. Jack's last statement got Beau Lee exactly where he wanted to take this cross-examination.

"Officer Dunham, this is a presumption that you have made during your entire testimony: that Mr. Montrose fired his gun at your partner, Officer Rossi. In fact, Rossi said he fired at him twice."

Jack elaborated in animated fashion and put two fingers in the air. "That's right, he shot at us twice."

"Thank you for that confirmation of your sworn testimony, Officer Dunham. Your Honor, at this time I would like to play the video based on your pretrial ruling. I believe that the record will reflect that the government stipulated to that part of your ruling."

"Mr. Cooper, where are you trying to go now?" the judge said.

"Your Honor, we would simply like to play the video and let the jury listen to the shots that were fired."

"You may proceed in accordance with my pretrial ruling."

As the clerk played the video, the jurors watched intently, some even cringing while others looked away. At its conclusion, Beau Lee stared directly at Jack and then asked, "Did you hear ten shots fired?" Jack didn't answer—he just looked at DaSilva.

Beau Lee waited for what seemed like an entire minute and then broke the silence in the courtroom. "Officer Dunham, did you count ten shots?"

"No, I didn't. It was hard to tell because there were fireworks going off all night because of the election," Jack said through gritted teeth. He was doing his best not to concede anything to Beau Lee.

"Would you have any reason to disagree with your police captain, who said he heard ten shots from the video?"

"If that's what he said, then I guess that's what he heard. Like I said, I can't tell how many shots were fired when I listen to that video."

"Would it surprise you if not only your captain said that there were ten shots fired, but also the ballistics report showed they only found ten casings from gun shots that were fired on the scene?"

"Objection, Your Honor," DaSilva announced as he stood up. "The witness testified that he can't tell how many shots were fired from the video, so these questions become argumentative. Additionally, the prior question has been asked and answered."

The judge nodded. "I am overruling the objection for now, but Mr. Cooper, I am not going to give you much more leeway."

"Thank you, Your Honor. We've deduced that the officers fired ten shots, which can be confirmed by the audio on the video and the casings identified by ballistics. And the records show two casings originating from Officer Rossi's gun, two from Officer Johnson's, one from Officer Caruthers, and five from your gun, Officer Dunham. I think we can all agree. You claimed Mr. Montrose also shot his gun twice. Officer Dunham, what I want to know is if you are testifying that Officer Montrose fired two shots from his gun, then where are the casings from his gun?"

Alvarez was smirking. Beau Lee could feel his heart pounding as he waited for the response, which came quickly.

"Objection, speculation," DaSilva said. "How is Officer Dunham supposed to know what they did or did not do at the scene?"

Alvarez stood up for this one. She had agreed to let Beau Lee handle the cross-examinations and statements, but she was particularly fired up. "Your Honor, they want to ratify conclusions of the homicide investigation when it is beneficial to their argument, but they want to object when it shows that Hollis Montrose never fired his gun."

"I object again, Your Honor. Now Ms. Alvarez is trying to testify using misinformation and innuendos," DaSilva said, and gave Alvarez a pointed look.

"I sustain the objection. Mr. Cooper, do you have another question?"

"Yes, I do, Your Honor. Officer Dunham, isn't it true that Mr. Montrose never fired his gun at the scene? And the only reason he had gunshot residue on his hand is because you touched his hand?"

DaSilva slammed his fist on the table and screamed, "Don't answer that question, Officer Dunham. We object, Your Honor. Mr. Cooper continues to try and dance around the rules by arguing conclusions that are supposed to be decided by the jury."

"Sustained. I am shutting this down. These are conclusory statements and inappropriate questions for the witness. Now, Mr. Cooper, I am going to ask you again: Do you have any appropriate questions for the witness?"

Jack bore a shit-eating grin, the smile of someone who'd always gotten their way and was getting it again.

"Yes, Your Honor. Officer Dunham, does the Chicago Police Department do thorough investigations based on your experience with the department?"

"Yes, I will say we do."

"Do they take their jobs seriously when they do investigations?"

"Of course they do."

"Would you say that when doing a thorough investigation where it was alleged that a suspect had fired two shots at police officers, it would be important to find his shell casings?"

"Objection," DaSilva said, this time with far less conviction. Beau Lee watched as the smile fell from Jack's face.

"There is no need for him to answer. I withdraw the question."

"Then ask your next question," admonished the judge.

"Officer Dunham, who was Theodore Briscoe?"

"He was my first partner, my mentor, and one of the finest police officers to ever wear a CPD uniform," Jack said with pride. "Tragically he lost his life in the line of duty two years ago when he was shot by some thug from the South Side of Chicago."

"Would you be surprised to know that Teddy Briscoe was named in a discrimination lawsuit along with other officers from CPD that was filed by Officer Montrose?"

"Objection," barked DaSilva. "Relevance."

"Sustained," agreed the judge. "Attorney Cooper, what is the relevance of this line of questioning?"

"Your honor, Officer Dunham just lamented that Officer Briscoe was his hero. I would like to explore whether or not that fact of him being named in a discrimination lawsuit filed by Hollis Montrose that led to several officers being reprimanded had anything to do with Officer Dunham shooting Mr. Montrose," explained Beau Lee.

"I am not going to allow this fishing expedition. Like I said, the objection is sustained," Judge Lambert repeated.

"Do you have any further questions, Attorney Cooper?"

"Not at this time, but I want it on the record that the defendant believes this issue of his discrimination lawsuit involving Officer Theodore Briscoe and other CPD officers is relevant to his case."

"So noted," said Judge Lambert. "Any redirect, Attorney DaSilva?"

"None, your honor."

"Then, Officer Dunham, you can step down from the witness stand," said Judge Lambert. "The court will be in recess for twenty mintues."

Beau Lee looked over at the counsel table at Nellie to glean his thoughts on the cross-examination. Nellie gave him a subtle nod. The bait was set.

61

SHORTLY AFTER RETURNING FROM RECESS, BEAU LEE CALLED AN EXPERT witness to the stand to clarify the validity of the video, which he did well. What was surprising was that the State did not take the opportunity to cross-examine, as Alvarez was sure they would do, but she gathered it could be because DaSilva was just that confident. The judge had been heavily favoring the State, which left Alvarez and Beau Lee at a disadvantage. However, Beau Lee looked completely at ease, perhaps even as confident as DaSilva by the end of what seemed to be a perfect line of questioning regarding the contents of the video.

Alvarez kept the same confidence of Beau Lee in the back of her mind after recess when she called Darian to the stand. She and Joey had arrived the night before the trial. They were exhausted from the long drive in from Philly, and Beau Lee was worried that Darian would have trouble handling DaSilva's aggressive line of questioning.

"Ms. King," Alvarez said, "can you please explain to the court what you saw the night Hollis Montrose was shot."

"I was studying for my exam when I heard what sounded like shouting over a loudspeaker. Then I saw blue lights, so I went to the window and looked. That's when I saw a dark-gray SUV and a police car behind it."

"At what point did you start recording on your phone?"

"One of the officers went over to the SUV and pulled the driver out. That's when I started recording."

"Do you recognize the driver in the courtroom today?"

"Yes."

"Can you point him out?"

Darian pointed to Hollis, who sat with his back straight in his wheelchair. "He's right there," she said. "Hollis Montrose."

"And the officer who pulled him out of the vehicle, do you recognize him?" Alvarez asked. "Is he present in the courtroom today?"

Darian pointed to Jack, who was sitting next to Chaz and Leonard on the bench behind the prosecution's table. All three men were in uniform, military pressed with crisp, starched lines.

"Please note, Ms. King has identified CPD Officer Jackson Dunham."

Jack looked perturbed and muttered to Chaz, who sneered at the girl.

Alvarez continued. "What happened after Officer Dunham pulled Officer Montrose out of the vehicle?"

"I could hear through the open window, Mr. Montrose saying something to the officers, but I wasn't sure what."

"At any time did you hear Mr. Montrose say he was a police officer?"

"No. I was too far away to hear anything he said."

"What happened next?"

"Then, another police car pulled up. When the officers got out, they surrounded Hollis . . . I mean, Mr. Montrose."

"And . . ."

"I couldn't see what was happening to Mr. Montrose," she said. "The officers blocked my view."

"At this time, I'd like to inform the jury that the video that has been heavily circulated in the media has not been entered into evidence," Judge Lambert said. "Please rely only on Ms. King's testimony. You may proceed, Attorney Alvarez."

Alvarez glanced at the jury, some of whom seemed surprised by the judge's announcement. She had fought to present the video recording as evidence, but after people around the world had seen it, Judge Lambert ruled that portions of the video were not admissible into evidence.

"Ms. King, please tell the court what happened next."

"I heard lots of yelling," she said, "and then gunshots."

"Before the shooting, what were the police yelling?" Alvarez asked. "Could you understand what was being said?"

"Only some words," she said. "One of the officers yelled 'gun' and 'drop the gun.'"

"Did you see Mr. Montrose holding a firearm at the time he was shot?"

"No," she said. "When the officers moved, I could see Mr. Montrose lying still on his stomach, and his hands were empty."

"He wasn't moving at all?"

"No, he wasn't moving."

"Then what happened?" Alvarez asked.

"One of the officers took something from Mr. Montrose's waist and put it on the hood of the police car."

"Any idea what the item was?"

"It looked like a gun."

"And this came from Mr. Montrose's waist? Not his hand?"

"That's right," she said. "Then the officers were talking to each other. They seemed upset, too. Like they were arguing—"

"Objection," DaSilva shouted. "Conjecture. There's no way Ms. King would know what the officers were discussing, or the context."

"Sustained," Judge Lambert said. "Ms. Alvarez, please instruct your client to keep to the facts."

"Certainly, Your Honor." Alvarez addressed Darian, saying, "Just tell me exactly what you saw, Ms. King."

"Okay. I'm sorry . . . The police were talking to each other. Then, I saw an officer take something else from Mr. Montrose."

"Something in addition to the firearm?"

"Yes."

"Could you see what it was?"

"Not really, but the officer took it from Mr. Montrose's pants pocket."

"Would this be the front or the back pocket?"

"Back."

"Do you see the officer who removed this object in the courtroom today?"

"Yes," she said, pointing to Jack. "He's right there."

Alvarez looked at the court reporter, who was typing vigorously. "For the record, Ms. King has identified Officer Jackson Dunham," she said. "Please continue, Ms. King. What happened next?"

"An ambulance came, and more police cars."

"Ms. King, at any time during the event, did you see Mr. Montrose point his firearm in question at the officers?"

"No," she said.

"Did you hear Mr. Montrose threaten to shoot or harm the officers?"

"No."

"At any time, did you see Mr. Montrose attempt to get up from the ground?"

"No."

"Thank you. That will be all from the defense."

DaSilva turned to Dillard to see if she was ready to proceed. She'd been feverishly taking notes and waiting for her opportunity to step up. Being second chair felt like a support role, and it was a very important support role. Dillard had to pay close attention to witness testimony and keep track of evidence. It could be overwhelming, but she wouldn't let DaSilva see her sweat. Because of her efforts, DaSilva assigned her to do the cross-examination of Darian King just yesterday. She stayed up all night getting ready. And, ready she was. Dillard grabbed her notes and nodded at DaSilva. It was go time.

Dillard stood and moved from behind the prosecution's table. She walked hard, her high heels clicking and echoing off the courtroom walls. "Ms. King," she said, "you stated that you began recording out of concern."

"Yes."

"Concern for whom?"

"I don't know. I guess the driver of the SUV. Mr. Montrose."

"And what made you so concerned?"

Darian seemed unsure of herself. "The way he looked," she said.

"The way he looked? Can you elaborate?"

"He looked afraid."

"Afraid?" Dillard repeated. "Joey Henderson's bedroom window is approximately twenty-two feet from where Hollis Montrose's vehicle was parked at the time of the incident. Are you suggesting that you were able to see Mr. Montrose's face through the driver's side window at that distance?"

"Yes, I could see him."

"Oh, I don't doubt you could see him, but being able to determine his facial expression? Well, that's quite a gift."

"Objection," Alvarez said. "The witness already stated she could see Mr. Montrose. This is badgering."

"Sustained," Judge Lambert said. "Ms. Dillard, shall we get on with it?"

"Yes, Your Honor. Ms. King, at what point could you determine Mr. Montrose's skin color?"

"What?"

"Let me rephrase. Since you claim you were able to see facial details from that distance, I presume you were able to see that Hollis Montrose was Black?"

"Um . . . yes," Darian said. "I could see he was brown or dark-complected."

"Is that why you decided to record?"

"His skin color had nothing to do with it."

"Would you have recorded if the driver was of another ethnicity? For example, Asian or white?"

"I don't know . . . probably."

"Probably? Is it possible that your motive for recording the video had more to do with Mr. Montrose being Black and the officers in question being white?" Dillard asked. "Maybe you were hoping to catch some kind of impropriety, knowing the racial politics that could potentially play out?"

"No," Darian said, "it had nothing to do with race."

"Then why did you upload the video to YouTube? Why not turn it over to the police so it could be properly investigated?"

"I was worried—"

"About what?"

". . . that the police wouldn't do anything."

"Really? And why is that?"

"I mean, you see it in the news all the time," Darian said. "People get pulled over, and the police do something terrible to them, and no one learns about it until months or even years later. I didn't want that to happen to Mr. Montrose. I wanted people to know the truth."

"How many views has the video garnered?"

"I don't know."

"Well, I can tell you," Dillard said. "It's had over eight million views. That's a lot, wouldn't you say?"

"Yes."

"Do you know what happens when a video goes viral, Ms. King?"

"A lot of people watch it, and it gets likes."

"Sure, sure, and that translates into dollars. So, tell me, how much money have you made from the video?"

"Money? I haven't made any money."

"Is that so, Ms. King? Do you know how much money that video has generated in advertising?"

"How would I know that?"

"Because that's how it works. You post the video. It gets lots of views, and you pocket a share of the advertising revenue."

"I don't know what you're talking about," Darian said. "I haven't collected any sort of revenue from the video."

"I'm afraid that isn't true," Dillard said. "According to YouTube's analytics, the video has made over thirty thousand dollars since it was uploaded."

"You've got it all wrong. We haven't collected a cent, and if we did, we would've given the money to the Montrose family."

"*We?*"

"Yes, me and my boyfriend, Joey."

"Joey Henderson?"

"Yes."

"Tell the court, Ms. King. Did you or Joey upload the video to YouTube?"

"Joey uploaded it," Darian said. "It was just easier since he already had an account."

"Which means any revenue the video generated would go to the person whose account was used. So, to be clear, are you telling me that Joey Henderson uploaded the video you shot to his account and distributed the link?"

Darian looked at Joey as he sat in the rear of the courtroom. "Yes," she said. "Joey uploaded the video."

"I see," Dillard said. "Well, it's a shame that Mr. Henderson has profited from such an unfortunate incident."

Darian looked at the defense table with shame in her eyes. "It was never about money. Never. I'm so sorry, Mr. Montrose."

"That is all from the prosecution," Dillard said, returning to her seat.

Alvarez leaned over to Beau Lee and whispered, "How the hell did we miss that?"

"I don't know," he said. "Didn't consider the video's monetary value."

"We better hope there's no more surprises."

The two attorneys watched as Darian left the stand in tears and exited the courtroom, pursued by a flustered Joey.

62

RORY CARUTHERS HAD BEEN MIA FOR MONTHS. AFTER BEAU LEE AND Alvarez were unsuccessful subpoenaing him, as Caruthers himself had requested, they decided to log him as a witness in case he was still making up his mind, knowing how reluctant he'd been at the café months back. But when Capes returned to the courtroom from answering his rapid-fire phone calls and told them Caruthers had been killed in a motorcycle accident just last night, not too far from his father's house, where Caruthers grew up, Beau Lee and the team were shocked. It was tragic on many levels, but the timing was clearly suspicious. Beau Lee had felt certain that even though Caruthers had gone into hiding because of the pressure he faced for standing up against the blue wall, Caruthers would show up and testify in the trial that Mr. Montrose had never pulled his gun. But he never imagined that the guy would be found dead only months after they'd visited his apartment.

The accident had occurred at six-thirty P.M. when Rory went through a busy intersection and failed to stop for the red light. He had supposedly lost control due to faulty brakes. Beau Lee notified the court as soon as he found out. Beau Lee acknowledged in his mind that this was a devasting blow to their case. Because Caruthers was the only person on the scene that night besides Mr. Montrose who was going to testify that he did not shoot his gun.

After the judge was advised of the news, she placed the court in recess for the rest of the afternoon. Beau Lee and Alvarez were devastated to say the least. An honest man was dead, and even more, this was a blow to Hollis's case. Rory knew what happened and had been willing to testify that he never saw Mr. Montrose discharge his firearm.

"You think his accident was legit?" Capes asked during the recess. "I wouldn't be surprised if Jack and Chaz messed with his bike."

"Me neither," Beau Lee said. "Not that we could prove it."

Alvarez tried to remain calm and looked at Beau Lee for any sign of what he was thinking. He'd suddenly grown quiet and seemed to be deep in thought. She knew he was disturbed about the way the trial had been unfolding. But this? An important witness being tragically killed in a motorcycle accident? She felt as though she were in an episode of *Law & Order* and no one had informed her. The trial was starting to feel unreal. But as being the consummate professional and advocate he was, Beau Lee had not let the judge or her rulings, DaSilva and his antics, the crazy egg-throwing white supremacists, or anything else get him off his game thus far. He was fighting like she knew he would. But the death of a witness?

Alvarez wiped sweat from her brow and thought to herself that being a litigator was not for the weak. As confident as she was in her career as an attorney, she wasn't fully prepared for the Hollis Montrose trial. They were both at the top of their games, but they just couldn't catch a break. Watching Beau Lee and trying this case with him had been an experience like no other, and she was grateful they'd been able to put their differences aside to fight for Hollis. But now it was time to put her Ivy League education to work. There was no way she would let the news about Rory Caruthers sink this case. Beau Lee was fiercely advocating despite all the setbacks, and she knew he needed her more than ever.

She pulled out her trial notebook and began combing through her notes for what felt like the millionth time. She was looking for something, anything to get them back on track. And then, just like that, there it was. With all the craziness, she'd almost forgotten about Officer Caruthers's affidavit. But then she considered that there was probably no way the judge would admit it. She knew the hearsay rules better than most law professors. Nevertheless, she turned to Beau Lee and said, "We still have Rory's affidavit. I know it's a long shot, but we have to try to find a way to get it entered into evidence."

Beau Lee took a deep breath. "We don't have any other alternatives. So do your best to see if we can find some theory to get over the hearsay rule. But I would be shocked if this judge did us any favors."

Alvarez told Beau Lee she was going to return to the office and start researching exceptions to the hearsay rules. She would do her part, and legal research was one of her strengths. In fact, she was basically a research queen, and she had declared in her mind that she would not sleep tonight until she came with an argument as to why this affidavit should be admitted into evidence. Although she was emotionally and physically drained, this new challenge gave her a burst of energy. She grabbed her rolling briefcase and Beau Lee gathered his things so they could depart together. Capes led the way out a side exit to avoid the media. The case had garnered so much attention that the media was always waiting outside, ready to bombard Beau Lee with questions.

It wasn't that Beau Lee didn't have anything to say about the tragic turn of events, but out of respect for Rory's family, he decided against making a statement on his untimely death. As soon as he opened the side exit door, Capes saw the driver waiting as he'd requested. They got in and headed to Alvarez's office to regroup.

63

THE NEXT DAY, BEAU LEE AND ALVAREZ ENTERED THE COURTROOM FEELing somewhat confident. Alvarez's research was spot-on, and she helped craft compelling arguments that would get the judge to rule in their favor. Beau Lee provided a copy of the affidavit to the State and was ready to ask the judge to enter it into evidence. DaSilva chuckled and wished him luck when Beau Lee handed him the affidavit, going so far as to say, "You'll need it. It's hearsay and the judge will never let it in." He was absolutely right.

Judge Lambert, seemingly less rigid today, entered the courtroom. She asked the attorneys whether any business needed to come before the court in light of yesterday's news before the jury was brought in. Attorney Dillard said that the State was ready to proceed, then turned to Beau Lee with a slight grin.

Beau Lee began. "Yes, Judge, due to the untimely death of Officer Rory Caruthers, we would ask the court to admit an affidavit that was prepared and signed by Officer Caruthers into evidence. He was prepared to testify to the facts herein."

Before he could finish, DaSilva interrupted and said, "Objection, Your Honor, the affidavit is hearsay."

"If I may, Your Honor," Beau Lee said.

The judge used a tone that Beau Lee didn't recognize. "You may. Go ahead, Mr. Cooper."

"This affidavit by Officer Rory Caruthers was signed and properly notarized. We promptly filed it in accordance with the court's pretrial deadlines as it was intended to be used with Officer Caruthers's testimony. The affidavit addresses facts that are relevant to Mr. Montrose's defense. In Officer Caruthers's absence, the affidavit provides direct evidence that contradicts testimony proffered by the State. As a former police officer, his testimony would have been credible as he was present at the scene of the incident in question."

"Mr. DaSilva? Ms. Dillard?" The judge turned to hear the State's argument.

Dillard spoke up. "Thank you, Judge. This is Rules of Evidence 101, and Mr. Cooper knows it. Officer Caruthers's affidavit is an out-of-court statement being offered to prove the truth of the matter asserted, which we all know to be textbook hearsay. Further, there is no exception that applies. For that reason, we ask that the court deny Mr. Cooper's request."

"Attorney Alvarez, do you have case law to present to the court?" Lambert said.

Alvarez stepped forward and presented additional arguments. "Judge, actually, we believe the affidavit would qualify as a dying declaration and opposing party admission, and that it should be substituted for Officer Caruthers's live testimony because of his untimely death and curious circumstances surrounding it."

"Objection, Judge! What are they insinuating?" DaSilva said.

In a surprising move, the judge told DaSilva to take his seat and allow Beau Lee and Alvarez to finish making their argument. Lambert began reviewing the case law as Alvarez returned to counsel's table.

Beau Lee continued. "Judge, we believe Officer Caruthers was afraid for his life. He decided to split from his fellow police officers on what happened that night. We know this to be true because he left town and was initially unwilling to meet with us. While this may be only circumstantial evidence, it indicated his fear about coming forward. However, his conscience wouldn't allow him to continue living in hiding. He had to tell the truth. So, he reached out to us and set up the meeting. Further, the affidavit is directly related to what happened during Hollis Montrose's arrest. Officer Caruthers was under extreme emotional distress, and he made his statement voluntarily, even though he knew he'd be contradicting the stories of his fellow officers. Finally, as Officer Caruthers is conveniently no longer alive to testify for the defense, we feel even more strongly in the validity of his testimony through this affidavit."

DaSilva stood up in anticipation of arguing against every one of Beau Lee's points. There was no way he could allow the affidavit in. Beau Lee could tell he was sweating this morning. For the first time since the trial began, Judge Lambert was engaged with him, and her tone seemed more amenable.

"Thank you, Mr. Cooper. That's enough, Mr. DaSilva. Please sit down. I'm ready to make my ruling. Mr. Cooper, you are absolutely right that the untimely death of Officer Rory Caruthers is suspicious. I look forward to learning about the facts uncovered in the investigation of his death. These are situations that are troubling to the court and cast doubt upon the testimony of his fellow officers."

Beau Lee tried not to break eye contact with the judge while thinking to himself that she might actually rule in his favor. He didn't look at DaSilva but could feel him seething.

"With that said," the judge continued, "Officer Rory's affidavit is textbook hearsay, plain and simple. There's no way I can allow the affidavit into evidence. Bailiff, we are ready for the jury."

Stunned by the judge's words, Beau Lee returned to counsel's table with Alvarez. He knew Lambert was going to rule in the State's favor. The case couldn't be going any worse. But he needed to shake himself out of his pity party. When he heard the bailiff once again call for all to rise, Beau Lee knew he now had to do the one thing he'd hoped he wouldn't have to.

64

BEAU LEE STOOD UP AND TOOK A DEEP BREATH. "AT THIS TIME, THE DEfense will call Mr. Hollis Montrose."

Every criminal defense lawyer knows that in a criminal trial, the last thing you want to do is put your client on the witness stand. It doesn't matter how much you try to prepare them. Once they're on the stand, it is open season from the prosecutor, and there's very little you can do to stop it. Every question that either DaSilva or Dilliard would ask Mr. Montrose would be deemed relevant, and there was no end to the line of questioning once the decision was made for him to take the stand in his own defense. As they say in wrestling, it's no-holds-barred. But Beau Lee deemed it the only card left to play. Even though he was trying to work on something to save Mr. Montrose, at this moment he had no other witnesses to call.

Finn came into the well of the courtroom and pushed Hollis's wheelchair to the front of the witness stand. "Thank you very much, Office Doyle," said Beau Lee deliberately. "Your Honor, will you have the clerk swear in the witness?" The judge nodded.

The clerk came forward and asked Mr. Montrose to raise his right hand. "Do you swear to tell the whole truth, and nothing but the truth, so help you God?"

"Yes, ma'am. I promise with my whole heart that I will," Hollis said.

"Mr. Montrose, let's start with a bit of your background," Beau Lee said. "What is your birth date, and where were you born?"

"I was born right here in Chicago on March 17, 1953."

"You also attended school here in Chicago, correct? Where did you graduate from high school?"

"Yes, I did. I graduated from Wendell Phillips Academy High School, class of 1971."

"Mr. Montrose, you were a police officer, weren't you? Tell me about the length of your career in the department."

"Yes, sir. I became a police officer at the Chicago Police Department in 1983, and I stayed with the department for sixteen years. From there, I joined Metra. I've been there going on a little more than nine years."

"So, Mr. Montrose, you've been serving your community as a police officer for twenty-five years?"

"Yes, sir. I am very proud of being a police officer and my lifelong work."

"Mr. Montrose, we thank you for your service protecting the community," Beau Lee said, making sure the jury fully understood that Hollis Montrose was also a police officer. The only difference between him and the cops who shot him was that they were white.

DaSilva debated objecting but decided against it, reasoning that it could backfire and bring even more attention to Mr. Montrose's police career. He'd get his turn soon enough to set the record straight on who he considered Hollis Montrose to be.

"Mr. Montrose, have you ever been convicted of a crime in your life?"

"No, sir."

"Have you ever even been arrested before in your life?"

"No, sir."

"Have you ever had any brushes with the law before in your life?"

"No, sir. Never. Up until the early-morning hours of November fifth," he said.

"And that's what we're here to talk about, Mr. Montrose. Can you tell the members of the jury what you remember about that night?"

"Yes, sir. It still seems like a nightmare. It was the worst day of my life—I thought I was going to die," he recalled as tears started to form in his eyes. "The hospital psychologist said that I may have some mental blocks trying to remember every detail. But I remember leaving my part-time job for Gunderson Security after my shift had ended at midnight. I was going to stop by Officer Finn Doyle's house before I went home to my wife, Rocky. Well, that's her nickname. Her name is Raquel, but everyone calls her Rocky. She's sitting over there behind my lawyers' table. Thank God for that woman, because without her love, I wouldn't be here today."

DaSilva stood up slowly. "Objection, Your Honor, respectfully."

"Sustained."

Beau Lee walked back to his table, found a box of Kleenex, and handed it to his client. "Mr. Montrose, if you would, continue telling us about that night when you were shot by the Chicago police officers."

Mr. Montrose took a tissue. "Yes, sir," he answered, wiping his tears. "I had just exited the 58-B off-ramp. I merged onto South Yale Avenue and turned left on Sixty-third. I drove for about two miles and then turned right on South Woodlawn Avenue. Flashing blue lights appeared in my rearview mirror, but there were no sirens. I remember thinking they were going to go around me to pursue someone else, because I hadn't done anything. I remember looking at the time—it was around 12:17 A.M. At that point, I realized they were trying to pull me over. I reached into my pocket, where my wallet was, so I could be ready to show the officers my police ID."

Beau Lee held up his hands in front of him. "Hold on. You had your wallet with your police identification on you in your pocket that night?"

"Oh yes, sir. And I told the officer that I was a police officer. And

I had both of my hands where he could see them. I offered to show him my badge and ID."

"So did you show the officer your badge and ID?"

"No, sir. Because when I offered them to him, he responded by yelling at me to shut my mouth. Then he opened up my car door and yanked me out. I said again, 'Man, I'm a police officer!' His partner came around from the passenger's side of my car with his gun pointed at me. They were yelling at me to shut my mouth and get down on the ground. They were telling me to put my hands flat on the ground above my head. And I had them there the whole time, telling them I'm a police officer. And one officer said something about, 'I don't care if your Black President Obama is in the White House, you need to shut up, because you all are still not in charge. We are still in charge. And you do what we say.'"

"You remember the officer making a reference to President Obama the night you were shot?"

"Yes, sir. He said something to the effect that it doesn't matter if he is the president and that we're still in charge."

"What did you take that to mean, Mr. Montrose?"

"I didn't know what it meant. All I know is they were yelling with guns pointed at me from multiple directions. Then other officers arrived and started pointing their weapons at me, too. I was afraid for my life."

"And what happened next from what you can remember?"

"I was yelling that this is just a misunderstanding. I heard one of the officers who arrived on the scene say, 'What do we have here?' The officer that yanked me out of the car said that I was weaving like I was drunk or like I was on something, and I interrupted him and said I wasn't weaving. Then the officer who yanked me out of the car kicked me in my side. I could tell he'd cracked my ribs. It was extremely painful. The pain overtook my whole body. I remember recoiling and reaching up to protect my ribs. Then I heard somebody yell, 'Gun, gun!' I tried to say no, that it was a misunderstanding, but all of a sudden, I started to feel hot burning sensations in my back, in my buttocks, my leg, and my shoulder. Afterwards, I felt nothing. I thought it was the end of my life."

Hollis was sobbing by the end. The courtroom was still, but you could hear quiet sniffles from the crowd, and one juror took her napkin to wipe her eyes, while another juror desperately tried to keep his lips from quivering. The weight of Hollis's pain hung heavy in the courtroom.

"Mr. Montrose, I'm so sorry you have to relive this."

"It's okay, Mr. Cooper. I relive it every day when I wake up and try to get out of bed thinking I can still walk."

"Is it true that as a result of the police officers shooting you, that you are now paralyzed from the waist down?"

"Yes, sir. I will never be able to walk again. I'll never be able to control my bowels again, either. And I'll never be able to make love to my wife again. And that is very hard to deal with. I was an independent person. Now I have to have people change my diaper like I'm a helpless infant. But I think of my wife, Rocky, because she and my family and my friends have been there by my side."

DaSilva stood up again. "Your Honor. Respectfully, I must object based on relevance."

"I understand, Mr. DaSilva. The objection is sustained. Mr. Cooper, please move on," she said softly.

"Mr. Montrose, do you ever remember taking your wallet out of your pocket?"

"No, sir."

"Do you remember having handcuffs put on you?"

"No, sir. I was completely unconscious. I only knew they put handcuffs on me from the video."

"Objection," DaSilva shouted more aggressively. "Hearsay, and I will ask that his answer be stricken from the record."

"Sustained. The jury will disregard the defendant's reference to the video."

"Mr. Montrose, you didn't put handcuffs on yourself, did you?"

Mr. Montrose smiled faintly. "No, sir. I did not."

"Were you made aware that one of the officers on the scene put handcuffs on you?"

"Objection!"

"Sustained."

"Mr. Montrose. Did you ever fire your gun that night during this traffic stop?"

"No, sir. I did not, Mr. Cooper."

"Mr. Montrose, did you even retrieve your gun on the night of the traffic stop?"

"No, sir, Mr. Cooper."

"Mr. Montrose, did you comply with all of the officers' commands during the traffic stop?"

"Yes, I did, Mr. Cooper."

"And yet they still shot and paralyzed you."

"Objection. Improper question."

Sustained again, but it didn't matter. Beau Lee was cooking with gas now and not letting up on the momentum. He knew he'd get a few objections, but he felt good about driving his point home.

"Mr. Montrose, can you think of any reason why these police officers shot you that night during this traffic stop?"

Objected for improper questioning—sustained.

He kept going. "Mr. Montrose, do you feel that there's anything you could have done to prevent these police officers from shooting you?"

Objected for relevance—allowed, in a shocking move. Beau Lee nearly turned to look at Lambert but stayed focused.

"No, sir, Mr. Cooper. I can't think of anything I could have done to prevent them from shooting me like they did, because I can't change my skin color."

Beau Lee stood there for a moment in complete silence, letting what Mr. Montrose said sink in for the whole court. "Thank you, Mr.

Montrose. I have no further questions, Your Honor. I pass the witness."

"I think this is a good time to take our lunch recess for today. The court will be in recess for one hour. Then at that time, we will begin with the cross-examination of this witness by the district attorney." Then the judge struck her gavel.

65

WHILE COURT WAS IN RECESS, ROCKY SIGNALED TO HOLLIS BY TOUCHING her heart, reassuring him that faith and hope were still in the room. Beau Lee and Alvarez approached the family to provide words of encouragement while regathering their courage to finish this battle. After recess, Attorney DaSilva began his questioning. "Mr. Montrose, you have a lot riding on this case, don't you?"

"I know that if the jury finds me guilty of these charges, I'll have to go to prison."

"But you have more than that at stake, don't you, Mr. Montrose?"

"I don't know what you mean, sir."

"Are you aware that you, through your lawyer here, filed a fifty-million-dollar excessive force lawsuit against the Chicago Police Department?"

Beau Lee tried to object for relevance but was shot down.

"I know my family and I filed a lawsuit for what they did to me."

"Mr. Montrose, you have been humble. This isn't just any other run-of-the-mill lawsuit. To quote your lawyer, Mr. Beau Lee Cooper, 'We filed this fifty-million-dollar lawsuit, the largest police brutality lawsuit in city history, to send a message, to make a point.' So, I ask you again, Mr. Montrose. You have a lot riding on this trial, don't you?"

"If you say so," Hollis answered, feeling angry and frustrated that he would even be asked such a question.

Beau Lee was uncomfortable knowing there was nothing he could do to save his client from this assault.

"Mr. Montrose, it's not what I say. It's what you and your lawyers have said. But now that we've made that point, I will further explore your motivations today. You like filing lawsuits, don't you?"

"No, sir. I don't."

"Didn't you file a lawsuit against the Chicago Police Department for employment discrimination, filed by your other lawyer, Attorney Alvarez?"

"Objection, Your Honor. Relevance," Beau Lee shouted, agitated.

"Overruled, Mr. Cooper. You opened the door when you asked him about how long he worked at the Chicago Police Department."

DaSilva repeated the question and Montrose responded affirmatively.

"And that lawsuit is still pending, correct?"

"Yes, sir."

"So, you've got two lawsuits pending against the City of Chicago?"

"Yes, sir."

"And apparently Mr. Cooper and Ms. Alvarez have a great financial interest pending on this case."

"Objection. Improper. Argumentative. And relevance," Beau Lee said.

"Sustained. Move on, Mr. DaSilva," the judge said.

"Mr. Montrose, in your discrimination lawsuit, you said that the white police officers at the Chicago PD had a racist culture, and within that racist culture, you experienced discrimination on a systematic basis, correct?"

"Yes, sir."

"And in that lawsuit you said you'd suffered PTSD, didn't you?"

"Yes, sir."

"And you also plead in the lawsuit that the discrimination created a hostile work environment. And that you had to leave the Chicago Police Department because you felt that if they didn't do anything about it, you feared that you would retaliate against these white police officers. Isn't that correct?"

"Yes, sir. That's how I felt."

"Mr. Montrose, isn't the truth that when these officers pulled you over, it triggered your PTSD and you gave in to your emotions and you shot at these police officers, namely Chaz Rossi, who was there on your right side?"

Beau Lee stood. "Objection, Your Honor. Improper question and misstatement of the facts!"

"Overruled, Mr. Cooper. You opened the door and you argued your case. Now Mr. DaSilva gets to argue his."

"Thank you, Your Honor," DaSilva said. "Mr. Montrose, did the traffic stop in this shooting trigger your PTSD?"

"No, sir."

DaSilva scratched his head for a second. "It didn't? You mean to tell me that this wasn't a traumatic enough experience to trigger your PTSD?"

"Not at first. I just thought it was all a misunderstanding—"

Before he could finish his answer, DaSilva fired off another question: "But at some point during the traffic encounter, your PTSD was triggered, wasn't it?"

"No, you're trying to put words in my mouth."

"I'm just trying to see when your PTSD was triggered. Because you understand that when your PTSD is triggered, the science says you don't really know what happens during those episodes, correct?"

Beau Lee stood up, flabbergasted. "Objection. Your Honor, really? He's now the prosecutor and the psychological expert?"

"Judge, this is straight from the pleadings in his employment discrimination lawsuit. The lawsuit discusses when his post-traumatic stress disorder is triggered and his reactions from it."

"Overruled, Mr. Cooper."

Beau Lee shook his head in disbelief.

"Thank you, Your Honor. Mr. Montrose, have you ever heard anybody else say anything about President Obama, and that they had the power in this traffic stop, except you? Because that's the first time I've heard anything like that in this case. It's not in any of the police reports."

"I know what I heard, sir."

"Are you sure you heard this and it wasn't just your PTSD?"

Hollis nearly shook with anger; it was clear that he was having a hard time controlling the timbre of his voice. "Sir, you're trying to make it sound like I'm lying. Like I'm crazy. That these officers were justified. You all think us Black people are crazy when we try to explain our lived experiences during our encounters with the police all the time. Even when they shoot and kill us, you all try to justify it. What they did to me was not justified!"

"Your Honor, the defense asks for a brief recess to allow Mr. Montrose a moment to confer with counsel," Alvarez said.

DaSilva decided to add on. "Mr. Cooper and Ms. Alvarez can confer with their client after I conclude my cross-examination."

"Your Honor. I object to this continuous badgering and improper questioning of Mr. Montrose," Beau Lee said.

"I understand your objection, Mr. Cooper. It is not proper grounds for me to interrupt a cross-examination just because your client is upset with the questions. Do you have much longer to go, Mr. DaSilva?"

"Not much longer, Your Honor. I think I'm making it clear to the jury what really happened here."

Beau Lee stood up, but before he could say a word, the judge intercepted. "Sit down, Mr. Cooper. I'm going to watch for any badgering of Mr. Montrose in the next few minutes since this examination is almost over."

"Thank you, Your Honor," DaSilva said, and returned his attention to the witness stand. "Mr. Montrose. You were trained as a police officer, correct?"

"Yes, sir." Mr. Montrose answered in a more contained manner.

"So you were trained as to when an officer is justified in using reasonable force, even and up to the use of deadly force?"

"Yes, sir. But I never had to shoot anyone in my twenty-five years as a police officer."

"Thank you for that, Mr. Montrose. But my question was, simply, you were trained as to when an officer is justified in using reasonable force, even and up to the use of deadly force?"

"Yes, sir."

"Let's ignore for a moment what the officers have testified of you shooting at them during the traffic stop and assume your version of the narrative, Mr. Montrose. Let's assume that you're a police officer and conducting a traffic stop and the suspect is lying on the ground with his hands above his head, and you notice that he has a gun at his waist. And all of a sudden, despite your verbal commands for him to keep his hands outstretched with his palms touching the ground, he starts to move his hands down toward the gun. Wouldn't it be justified for you to shoot at the suspect before he gets to his gun and could shoot your fellow police officers?"

"But I wasn't reaching for my gun, sir," Mr. Montrose affirmed.

"But Mr. Montrose, how were these officers to know what you were reaching for?"

"If he hadn't kicked me, I wouldn't have reached for my rib cage. It was a natural reaction to protect myself, as I thought he was going to kick me again."

"See, you're making statements that no one has made in the case prior to your testimony. There is nothing in any police records that mentions someone kicking you in your side. But here's my question: Is an officer justified in shooting to stop the quickly evolving threat of a suspect having a gun and ignoring verbal commands, and reaching towards the gun? Yes or no?"

"Well, like I told you, sir. I never shot anybody in the line of duty. And now that you mention it, no officer or investigator took my statement."

"Judge, I would ask for that to be stricken as nonresponsive."

Beau Lee: "Argumentative."

"How is that argumentative, Your Honor? I simply asked him a yes-or-no question based on his training as a police officer for twenty-five years."

"Objection is overruled. The witness will answer the question based on his training and experience."

"Thank you, Your Honor," DaSilva said, eyeing Beau Lee with derision. "Mr. Montrose. Yes or no?"

"Sir, I can't answer that question, because like I said, I never shot anybody in the line of duty."

"Is the real reason you can't answer the question because if you acknowledge it was justified, then it prevents you from being able to go forward with your fifty-million-dollar lawsuit against the City of Chicago?"

Beau Lee objected, but before the judge was able to decide, DaSilva withdrew. "Even Mr. Cooper would agree that a blind bat can see what's happening here. I have no further questions."

Beau Lee, Alvarez, and Nellie looked at one another for a moment as Officer Doyle pushed Hollis's wheelchair back over to the defense counsel's table. Beau Lee couldn't help but notice Rocky sobbing during the assault and battery that DaSilva had projected onto her husband. Beau Lee knew that DaSilva would score points when he decided to put Hollis on the witness stand, but this was far worse than what he could have imagined. Beau Lee prayed to God for a Hail Mary to save Mr. Montrose from being found guilty, from being incarcerated for a lengthy period of time, but most of all, from dying in prison.

Beau Lee had one last move, but it was the riskiest one he'd ever had to entertain. If it backfired, it wouldn't just be Hollis Montrose not getting justice, but it could mean Beau Lee's facing a major defamation lawsuit and a possible disbarment. At that moment, looking at Hollis and his family—physically battered and spiritually bruised—Beau Lee was a little boy again, taking a vow to defeat racism and discrimination no matter the risk.

66

"MR. COOPER, DO YOU HAVE ANY MORE WITNESSES TO CALL?" JUDGE LAMbert asked.

There was a moment of silence. Beau Lee looked over at Nellie, then at Alvarez, and finally over at Hollis Montrose, whose head was bowed in despair.

"Mr. Cooper. Do you have any more witnesses to call," she repeated.

"Your Honor, I would like to call a rebuttal witness."

There were rumblings in the courtroom. "Is this a new witness or have they testified in this trial previously?" the judge asked.

"Your Honor," Beau Lee started. "This is a new witness who has offered not only to rebut what was said during this trial by the police officers, but also to rebut the statements that were made in all the criminal investigations, including the Internal Affairs investigation, the Chicago Police Department investigation, and the State of Illinois Department of Law Enforcement investigation."

Nellie was thrown. He checked his notes and nervously tapped his feet as he contemplated what was at stake. What on earth was Beau Lee doing? He scribbled out a big question mark and gestured for Alvarez to look.

Alvarez just mouthed at him, "I don't know."

"That's a big statement," Judge Lambert said. "Who is this rebuttal witness?"

Beau Lee took a deep breath. "Corrine Dunham," Beau Lee announced. "The wife of Officer Jackson Dunham, who testified during this trial."

The courtroom exploded with chatter. Capes and Finn then slipped out of their seats and exited the courtroom.

"Objection, Your Honor." DaSilva and Dillard were up out of their chairs. "What does she have to offer?"

"Everything," Beau Lee said. "Her testimony will contradict what her husband and these other officers testified to during this trial. And it will exonerate Hollis Montrose."

The sketch artist was drawing like a fiend. Reporters were typing in live updates on news sites and on social media at the unexpected turn.

Harpo leaned back and stole a glance at Jack, who appeared agitated. Chaz and Leonard were whispering something to him. Jack brushed them away.

Nellie shot Beau Lee a questioning expression. They met eyes, then Beau Lee looked away, his face unreadable.

"Your Honor," DaSilva said. "I object based on spousal immunity. A wife's testimony against her husband is not—"

"Your Honor," Beau Lee interrupted. "Under the Federal Rules, the spouse who is called to testify can either invoke spousal privilege or choose to waive it and testify. Corrine Dunham has been married to Officer Jack Dunham for eighteen years. I tell you today, with everything I stand for, that she has some important testimony that is relevant in every way to this case."

Judge Lambert gazed out at DaSilva, Jack, and all the other police officers packing that side of the courtroom. She then regarded Beau Lee. For a fleeting moment, her eyes met Rocky Montrose's. Then she looked at Hollis, whose look of dejection persisted.

The judge cleared her throat. "This better not be theater, Attorney Cooper," she said sternly.

"On my word, it's not."

"All right, I'll allow the rebuttal witness."

"Thank you, Your Honor. The defense calls Mrs. Corrine Dunham to the stand."

Capes and Finn opened the courtroom doors and walked on either side of Corrine. She had on dark sunglasses and was dressed in a rust-colored suit over an ivory blouse. She wore conservative low black heels. A few whispers spread through the courtroom as she took the stand. She turned to face the courtroom and the judge had the bailiff swear her in before she sat down.

"Ma'am, can you please state and spell your name for the record," Beau Lee asked.

Corrine complied and the judge made a request. "Mrs. Dunham, would you kindly please remove your sunglasses?"

"Yes, ma'am," she said softly. She then removed her sunglasses. The gasps were audible and plenty.

Judge Lambert's breath caught at what she was seeing. She banged her gavel. "Order! Order in the court!"

Corrine's face was a mosaic of black and blue. Her left eye was bruised and bright red. It was evident that her lip had been busted. And the right side of her chin was badly bruised.

My God, Rocky said to herself.

Nellie and Alvarez couldn't take their eyes off of her. None of them could. The sketch artists were on overdrive.

Harpo was speechless. After a moment, he composed himself, leaned over to Capes, and whispered, "What kind of monster did that to her?"

Capes gave him a look that seemed to say it was obvious.

Judge Lambert was on the brink of being emotional. She struggled to contain herself. "Mrs. Dunham, are you sure you're okay to give testimony in this courtroom today?"

"I'm fine, Judge," Corrine said.

"Okay then, Attorney Cooper, you can proceed."

67

THE DIN OF THE COURTROOM WAS A LOUD HUSH. THOSE IN SEATS WERE clearly titillated by what was happening, and the judge had to repeatedly ask for decorum. Beau Lee took his time approaching the witness stand. He was wary of the risk he was taking, but it felt good to play an ace.

"Good afternoon, Mrs. Dunham. Can you please tell the members of the jury how you came into contact with our office?"

"Sure, I originally spoke with Mr. Hollis Montrose's partner, Finn Doyle, and your chief investigator, Brent Capers."

"When was the first time you spoke with them?"

"They approached as I parked my car and was about to walk into my house one day."

"What did they say to you?"

"They asked me if my husband ever mentioned anything to me about the shooting of the Black police officer that was all over the news."

"And what did you tell them?"

DaSilva stood up. "Objection, relevance! And hearsay!"

"Overruled," said Judge Lambert, her tone strangely sharper toward DaSilva than it had been all trial.

"Thank you, Your Honor," Beau Lee said. "You may answer the question, Mrs. Dunham."

"I told them that no, he did not. They gave me their business card and said if I ever wanted to tell them something, or if I wanted to help get the truth out for whatever reason, then to call them."

"When you told them that you had not talked to your husband about the case, was that true?"

"No, it wasn't."

"What conversation did you have with your husband about this shooting?"

DaSilva objected loudly. "This is hearsay."

"Overruled!" said the judge again sternly. "After she finishes her testimony, if you want to recall your client to the stand, then I will allow it. Mrs. Dunham, you may answer the question."

"When it first started breaking on the news, I asked him if he was involved in the shooting. And he barked at me about why I would think he was involved. I just said, 'Well, I remember you were working that night, that's all.' He cussed at me and said that I should have more faith in him. And then he stormed out of the house."

"Did you tell your husband that Officer Doyle and Investigator Capes had approached you at the house?"

"Yes, I did."

"And what did he say?"

"He mainly cursed about you after he asked me what they wanted to know and how I responded."

"Was that the end of it?"

"Yes it was," Corrine said. "But he kept talking about you, Mr. Cooper, as if you were the worst person that could ever have come to Chicago."

"Now, for some reason that doesn't surprise me," Beau Lee said. "But Mrs. Dunham, the question I want to ask you, and what everybody wants to know, is what made you change your mind and call back my investigator?"

"On Monday morning, Jack came home in a foul mood. He'd been out the entire night before."

"Was that normal for him?"

"Sometimes he does that. Always said he was collecting OT."

"Was that his excuse this time?"

"Yes. I noticed his phone kept vibrating, but he ignored it. Figured it was something he wasn't telling me."

Another bout of objections by DaSilva based on speculation, but they were overruled.

"Please continue, Mrs. Dunham," Beau Lee said.

"Jack stepped outside to take the call, but I managed to overhear it was someone he was calling 'Babe,' so I gathered it was another woman. From the snippets of conversation, it sounded like maybe they were talking about an investigator questioning her, the same as happened to me. When he came back in, we argued and it led to a struggle where he hit me with the back of his hand. I fell and hit my face on the corner of the table causing me to bleed badly."

"The bruises and abrasions on your face are the result of your recent interaction with your husband, Jack Dunham?"

"Objection, Your Honor. I have to object to relevance. This is all hearsay."

"Mr. DaSilva, please sit down. The court will hear this woman's testimony." The judge was clearly sensitive to Corrine's horrific ordeal. "You may answer the question, Mrs. Dunham."

"Yes they are," she said softly. "One of many times he's hit me."

"When was the last time he hit you?"

"A few weeks ago," she said. "But during this last fight, he told me he would divorce me and that we would have the court decide who was more fit to raise our two sons, me or him and his new woman. I said to myself I am not going to let him get away with this, I don't care if he leaves me but I was not going to let him take my boys. They are all I have in this world," she said, tears now streaming down her face.

"What did you do," Beau Lee asked softly.

"I found what he was hiding in the garage."

Beau Lee couldn't help but be pleased. Typically he liked to pay devoted attention to his witness, but out of the corner of his eyes, he saw DaSilva looking as though he might shit a squirrel. He allowed himself a glance back at Jack Dunham, who had already apparently shit one. And it felt good. But there was even more to come.

68

UNLIKE AT THE START OF MRS. DUNHAM'S TESTIMONY, THE COURTROOM now was entirely silent. Beau Lee thought for a moment about something he heard his mother say when he was a little boy: It was so quiet you could hear a rat piss on cotton. Everyone was hanging on Corrine's every word.

"I had gone into the garage to gather the holiday decorations because I wanted to give my two sons the best Christmas that I could even if I had to do so by myself," Corrine said. "That's when I saw he'd taken out an old safe we bought when we first got married. I used to keep money in it when I was working. When we had the boys, Jack forbade me from working. He said there was no reason for his woman to work since he was the provider and had a good job."

"Tell me about the safe," Beau Lee said. "What did you find?"

"I figured out what the combination was and opened it thinking I'd find evidence that he'd been cheating on me. Maybe gifts he planned to give his new woman—"

"Objection! Your Honor, this is all hearsay," DaSilva said, making one last plea to prevent whatever grenade Mrs. Dunham was about to drop. "Clearly Mrs. Dunham is a woman scorned. While I understand, that is still no reason for her to be able to sit here in this courtroom and cast aspersions on the entire Chicago Police Department.

Her qualms with Officer Dunham are a private matter. For Christ's sake your honor, what could she possibly offer to show that the other officers and their reports were false?"

Beau Lee interjected, "Judge, I think Mrs. Dunham can answer Mr. DaSilva's question. Please let her proceed for just one more minute to answer that question."

"The objection is overruled. You may answer his question, Mrs. Dunham."

Corrine took a deep breath and looked straight up at Beau Lee. "If they were telling the truth that Mr. Montrose did not have his wallet on him the night that he was shot, then how did it end up in my husband's safe in our garage," she concluded as she paused to open her purse and retrieved a ziplock bag that had a wallet and papers in it.

The courtroom erupted. Rocky raised her hands up to the heavens and whispered, "The truth will set us free."

The judge struck her gavel. "Order in the courtroom."

"Mrs. Dunham, what is in this ziplock bag?" Beau Lee asked.

"Mr. Montrose's wallet and a letter from Teddy Briscoe to Jack telling him how to protect the blue wall from those people."

The courtroom was buzzing. Reporters were posting every word that Corrine uttered in real time.

Alvarez took a picture of that moment in her mind of Mrs. Dunham handing the wallet to Beau Lee Cooper from the witness box with the judge looking down and the words above the courtroom awning reading "WE WHO LABOR HERE SEEK ONLY TRUTH." Alvarez realized at that very moment that they were making history.

Judge Lambert struck her gavel and said, "Order in the court! Order in court."

Word of what was happening in the courtroom was making it around the city, the country, and the world. News teams were gathering out in front of the courthouse; cameras were being set up. Banks of microphones. Beau Lee Cooper was no longer scaling Chicago's unclimbable wall. He was dismantling that wall brick by brick.

Jack chose then to take his leave.

"Your Honor," Beau Lee said, calling out. "I don't think Officer Dunham should be allowed to leave the courtroom."

The judge looked up and asked the bailiff to apprehend Jack.

"If anything, Jack Dunham should be arrested for domestic violence," Beau Lee said, and then pointed toward Corrine. "We heard the evidence in this courtroom today along with ocular proof."

A bailiff took custody of Jack and put him in handcuffs.

Beau Lee made eye contact with Capes, who had received the call from Corrine earlier in the trial. "As a critical member of my team likes to point out, ocular proof will always be the thing. I tip my hat to him."

Jack cried out, wrestling against the bailiff. "Corrine! How could you do this to me? Corrine?" While the bailiff pulled him away, he screamed louder. "How could you do this to me to help these people? How could you do this to our family?"

Corrine responded calmly. This was something she had thought about for a long time. "No, Jack, *you* did this to *our* family."

"These people," Harpo said, echoing Jack, and shook his head. "We are nothing to him."

"I hope he has a long time to choke on his words 'these people,'" Jamillah said, as she shook her head in disgust about how nefarious people could be.

Corrine was devoid of emotion as she watched her husband being taken away in handcuffs.

Beau Lee said to the judge, "I have no further questions for Mrs. Dunham. I pass the witness."

The judge looked at DaSilva and Dillard, who sat at their table looking startled and spent. "Mr. DaSilva, Ms. Dillard, do either of you have any questions for Mrs. Dunham?"

DaSilva shook his head. "We have no questions."

Beau Lee walked to the witness stand and took Corrine's hand to help her down. "You don't have to suffer any more abuse from him. Neither physical nor mental."

Judge Lambert looked out at the chaotic courtroom. She banged her gavel and demanded, "I need quiet in this courtroom!"

When the frenzy finally cooled, the judge made an announcement. "Based on the evidence presented by Mrs. Dunham, I am inclined to grant a directed verdict in favor of defendant, Hollis Montrose. Does the State have any objections to the court's ruling?"

DaSilva looked at Dillard, who gave a barely perceptible shake of her head. "The State has no objections," he said.

"Then this case is dismissed. Mr. Montrose, you are a free man and this court is adjourned."

There were adulations and hallelujahs throughout the courtroom with hugs of congratulations.

Beau Lee walked over to DaSilva and Dillard and shook their hands.

"Right is right," Beau Lee said. "Mr. Montrose is an innocent man. Now the city of Chicago needs to do the right thing."

DaSilva nodded in agreement. Beau Lee felt it symbolic that the two of them had acquired a mutual respect for each other. Beau Lee appreciated that DaSilva wasn't a sore loser and recognized the merit of the court. It seemed as if there was hope for the healing to begin.

EPILOGUE

Three Months Later

THE SMELL OF MESQUITE AND CHARCOAL DANCED THROUGH THE AIR, TANgled with the soulful sounds of Frankie Beverly and Maze blasting from the speaker. Kids were chasing bubbles, grown folks were slapping dominoes on folding tables like they were laying bricks, and somewhere in the mix, a cousin's cousin was frying fish in the back of a pickup truck. The Montrose backyard was alive with laughter, hugs that lingered too long, and plates piled too high.

This was what freedom looked like.

This was what victory tasted like.

This was *Black joy*—unapologetic, loud, and earned.

Hollis Montrose sat under a tent in the shade, stronger than he had been in weeks. While holding a plate of ribs, he was gently rocking the bassinet that his beautiful three-month-old granddaughter was comfortably resting in. Rocky stood beside him in a beautiful colorful sundress and summer straw hat with a wide brim, and her arm draped protectively over his shoulder.

"Hollis, you know you can't eat all of that barbecue. It'll have your blood pressure sky high," she warned, wagging her finger in the air.

"Woman, if I survived ten bullets, then I know I ain't gon' let a little high blood pressure kill me," he said with a grin.

Rocky gave him side-eye, then kissed his temple. "Sweetheart, I didn't lose you to the shooting, and I'm not going to lose you to hypertension. Now put that rib down like I said," she scolded.

Beau Lee Cooper sat across from Gigi, both of them balancing paper plates on their laps and trying to avoid barbecue sauce on their clothes. Beau Lee had already lost that battle—baked bean stain and all.

Also attending the celebration was the entire trial team: Capes, Alvarez, Nellie, Harpo, Finn, and his wife. Finn was really happy to be at the cookout. It was a new experience for him and his wife, but Beau Lee, Hollis, and Rocky knew it wouldn't be a victory celebration without Finn. And victory celebration it was, because it had just been announced the day before that the city of Chicago had agreed to a record forty-five-million-dollar settlement lawsuit that was filed on behalf of Hollis Montrose.

Gigi said, "Be careful, Beau Lee, you gon' end up getting barbeque sauce all over that beautiful linen suit I picked out for you."

Capes then said, "Well, Gigi, with this settlement, I think he'll be able to buy another one."

"Capes, don't go spending the money before we get the check," Nellie chimed in. "We got to make sure that a big check like that won't bounce and that it clears the trust account."

"One thing I can say is that I've lived in Chicago all my life. I think the city check will clear," Finn said in jest.

"I still can't believe we pulled it off," Alvarez said, sipping from a red Solo cup. "I know it's been three months since the last day in court, but I'm still in awe of how you did it, Beau Lee. I mean, the tension was thicker than Auntie Debra's banana pudding," she said, laughing. "My heart was racing, but I got to tell you, Beau Lee Cooper, it seems like you were calm, cool, and collected no matter what."

"I knew my brother was going to do his thang," Harpo said, looking over at her. "Both of y'all did y'all's thang."

"It was a team effort," Beau Lee nodded as he reflected about that last day of trial. "We made 'em tell the truth. On the record. Under oath. And Hollis, we didn't let them twist your story into something that fit their comfort level."

"They tried, though," Rocky cut in. "Whewww—every time I watched the news, I'd get so mad. The way they tried to criminalize my king. They wanted to bury him before he even got out of that hospital and had a chance to prove his innocence."

"They didn't count on my wife being louder than their lies," Hollis said, squeezing her hand. "And they *damn sure* didn't count on Beau Lee Cooper and Princess Alvarez being willing to burn the whole courtroom down for the truth."

"Now, hold on—" Alvarez lifted her eyebrow and grinned. "I wasn't trying to burn anything. I was just lighting the match and letting *Beau Lee do what he do.*"

Beau Lee chuckled and leaned back in his chair. "Ms. Rocky, it was just God using me to fulfill his promise to you. You remember when we first met, you said that God told you that your husband would not die in prison. So with His help, we brought him home to you."

"Amen. Amen," Gigi affirmed.

"You sure did bring him home to me," Rocky said with joy. "Even though we got a lot of rehab to do, I declare my husband is gonna walk again one day."

"From your mouth to God's ears, baby," Hollis said softly.

Gigi, Harpo, and Finn said amen in unison.

Beau Lee's phone started buzzing. He glanced at it to see who it was. A private number. Probably another case. Another emergency. Another Black life in the crosshairs of corruption.

He let it ring.

Twice.

Three times.

"Go on," Rocky said gently. "We know what you do."

"You gonna get that?" Alvarez asked.

"No, he's not," Gigi answered, giving him one of those looks.

He dropped the phone back into the cupholder on the lawn chair. "Not today. Gigi's right. Justice is always the priority. But *so is this*. This moment. This win. This breath."

He reached for his sweet tea, lifted it in a quiet toast.

"To survival," Alvarez said.

"To fighting and winning," added Rocky.

"To the truth," said Beau Lee.

Hollis raised his rib bone. "To the Beau Lee Cooper Law Firm, good barbecue, and still having my damn life to live."

Laughter erupted around the table. Someone shouted for spades players. Somebody's uncle hollered, "Don't act like you wasn't reneging last week!" The playlist shifted to "Before I Let Go," and line dances kicked off in the grass like clockwork.

"Come on, Mama, Mr. and Mrs. Doyle, Mr. Beau Lee and Mrs. Gigi, I'm about to teach you how to line dance like us young people," Jamillah yelled.

Justice had been served, but the real victory was this:

Black folks gathered under the sun, fed and free.

They had survived. They had told the truth.

And nobody—*nobody*—was turning down a plate.

The fight would continue tomorrow.

But today, they laughed and enjoyed the moment.

ACKNOWLEDGMENTS

Every book has its own story, but *Worse than a Lie* is a work of fiction born out of a deeper truth. This work emerged from years spent standing in courtrooms, walking through communities devastated by injustice, and carrying the weight of stories that America too often tries to erase. It was born out of the collective cry for justice, the determination of families, and the steadfast belief that truth, no matter how uncomfortable, can never be silenced forever.

My career has taken me to the intersection where power meets the people where law collides with lived experience. I've stood beside grieving families, faced down powerful institutions, and refused to allow injustice to become the final word. But this book is different. Here, the page becomes the witness stand. The testimony is our lived reality. And the verdict belongs to all of us.

A project of this magnitude doesn't come to life through one voice alone. It takes a community of brilliant, committed, and passionate individuals who lend their gifts to make something enduring.

I want to begin by acknowledging my beautiful family and my village, especially my wife, GC; my daughter, BC; my mother, HC; and all my family members and loved ones. You all are my foundation, my heartbeat, and my why. Every fight for justice, every case, every long night is anchored in my love for you all. GC, your unwavering strength and grace hold me steady when the storms of this work rage. BC, you are the light that keeps me focused on the future we're building. Your laughter, your spirit, and your dreams remind me why the fight must continue not just for today, but for generations to come. Thank you all again, for your patience, your love, and your faith in me. I love you more than words can ever fully express.

To my extended family both far and near, thank you for being my bedrock. Your prayers, encouragement, and belief in this mission have carried me farther than you may ever know.

To the families who have allowed me to stand with you in moments of unimaginable pain, you are the soul of this book. Your courage gives this work purpose. Your trust humbles me. Each page is etched with your resilience and your refusal to let injustice have the last word. This novel belongs to you as much as it does to me.

To my colleagues, co-counsel, movement partners, and fellow soldiers for justice, thank you. This fight is not for the faint of heart. It requires brilliance, endurance, courage, and faith. Together, we have turned pain into power and tragedy into testimony.

I would like to extend my sincere gratitude to Lolita Files, whose creative partnership has been instrumental to me bringing my vision to life. From the earliest conversations, she understood that this novel had to be more than an argument; it had to breathe. So, Lolita, thank you for your brilliance and dedication to helping me breathe life into this narrative.

To my brother, Cameron S. Mitchell, thank you for being more than just my manager. You are a steady force, a trusted voice, and a true partner in every sense of the word. Your strategic insight and belief in my vision burns eternally.

A special thank you to Attorneys Brooke Cluse, Kamillah Moore, Gabrielle Higgins, Chris O'Neal, Natalie Jackson, Sue Ann Robinson, Liza Park, Steve Rabinovici, and Dr. Asha Jones as well as Jaret Prussin, Kareem Ali, Cliff Jones, Uzoma Obasai, Jamarcus Crump, Renae Brown, and Arthur Reed: Your brilliance, tactical vision, and unwavering commitment have been invaluable in shaping this journey. Each of you brings a unique strength to the table whether through sharp legal analysis, visionary leadership, or behind-the-scenes strategy. Together you represent the excellence, dedication, and heart required to move this work forward. I am profoundly grateful for your support, your leadership, and your belief in this mission.

To Meredith, Christy, Andrew, Darnell, Keya, Alyssa, and Shelby, otherwise known as my UTA team, thank you.

To Jenny Chen and the publishing team, and everyone who worked tirelessly behind the scenes, thank you for understanding the urgency and sacredness of these stories. Your professionalism, patience, and precision helped ensure that this book stands as both a record and a rallying cry.

To the readers, thank you for picking up this novel, for opening your hearts and minds, and going on this thrilling ride with me. My hope is that this book stirs something inside you. That challenges you. That pushes you to stand boldly in your own sphere, to speak truth in the face of silence, and to act where others might turn away.

This is more than a novel. This is a declaration. A testimony. A living document that bears witness to our struggle and our strength. The lie may seem compelling, but the truth endures above all. And when we speak that truth together, we can fortify the foundation for justice over injustice.

—Attorney Ben Crump

ABOUT THE AUTHOR

Attorney BEN CRUMP is listed among the Most Influential People of 2021 by Time100; he is one of *Ebony* Magazine's Power 100 Most Influential African Americans and one of The National Trial Lawyers Top 100. Crump was the 2014 NNPA Newsmaker of the Year, and he is referred to as Black America's attorney general. Through a steadfast dedication to justice and service, renowned civil rights and personal injury attorney Crump has established himself as one of the nation's foremost lawyers and advocates for social justice. His legal acumen has ensured that those marginalized in American society are protected by their nation's contract with its constituency. He is the founder and principal owner of Ben Crump Law.

bencrump.com
Instagram: @attorneycrump
X: @attorneycrump
Facebook.com/attorneycrump
TikTok: @attorneycrump

ABOUT THE TYPE

This book was set in Baskerville, a typeface designed by John Baskerville (1706–75), an amateur printer and typefounder, and cut for him by John Handy in 1750. The type became popular again when the Lanston Monotype Corporation of London revived the classic roman face in 1923. The Mergenthaler Linotype Company in England and the United States cut a version of Baskerville in 1931, making it one of the most widely used typefaces today.